What a Girl Wants

ALSO BY LINDSEY KELK
FROM CLIPPER LARGE PRINT

About a Girl

This large print edition published in 2014 by
W F Howes Ltd
Unit 4, Rearsby Business Park, Gaddesby Lane,
Rearsby, Leicester LE7 4YH

1 3 5 7 9 10 8 6 4 2

First published in the United Kingdom in 2014
by HarperCollins*Publishers*

Copyright © Lindsey Kelk, 2014

The right of Lindsey Kelk to be identified as
the author of this work has been asserted by her
in accordance with the Copyright, Designs and
Patents Act, 1988.

A CIP catalogue record for this book is available
from the British Library

ISBN 978 1 47127 164 9

Typeset by Palimpsest Book Production Limited,
Falkirk, Stirlingshire
Printed and bound by
www.printondemand-worldwide.com of Peterborough, England

FSC Mixed Sources
Product group from well-managed
forests, and other controlled sources
www.fsc.org Cert no. TT-COC-002641
© 1996 Forest Stewardship Council

PEFC Certified
This product is
from sustainably
managed forests
and controlled
sources
www.pefc.org
PEFC PEFC/16-33-415

This book is made entirely of chain-of-custody materials

What a Girl Wants

Lindsey Kelk

W F HOWES LTD

For Audrey Hardware.

We never did come running to you when we'd broken both our legs but we did turn up with just about every other ailment on earth and you were always there. If I can find half the love, strength and resilience you had, I'll be OK.

PROLOGUE

On the one hand, you might have said my day wasn't going terribly well.

But on the other, I *had* told Amy that I wanted to make big changes in my life and there weren't many lifestyle changes more significant than swapping a luxury Italian palazzo for a prison cell.

And my second prison cell in two weeks, at that. Clearly I was going for some sort of record. It was one thing to say you wanted to start over, it was another thing to start over as someone on the 'no fly' list because you were considered an international flight risk. I was almost certain the generally accepted way of society was to go the other way.

I took a deep breath, blew it out hard and examined my bitten-down fingernails while trying to remain calm and wait for someone to appear and make this entire mess go away. Ideally someone I knew, accompanied by someone with a working knowledge of the Italian legal system, but at this point, as long as they didn't have a gun, a pair of handcuffs or a pointy stick, I'd be happy. And if they did have a gun, a pair of handcuffs or a pointy stick, but also came bearing biscuits, I'd probably be just as happy. Did everyone get this hungry in prison? Had I missed dinnertime?

'This is what happens when you're too busy working to watch telly, like normal people,' I admonished myself. 'If I'd watched *Bad Girls* or *Cell Block H* like Amy, instead of doing my homework, I would know these things.'

I traced a shallow line in the cement floor with the bare big toe on my good foot and wondered how it got there in the first place. I'd been thoroughly searched on my way in and anything that might have hacked a seven-inch gash in a concrete floor had been removed from my person. Hairgrips, the belt from my dress, even my bra. I had nothing left on me but my knickers and my beautiful bright pink dress. At least, most of it was still bright pink – there was quite a lot of muck and a few well-placed splotches of blood around the hem. But still, I *had* told Kekipi not to give me a dress with a train, so this was entirely his fault. Well, apart from all the bits that were my fault. Which was most of them.

Making a noise that sounded a little bit like a frustrated walrus, I rolled myself onto my side, the rough concrete of the bench scratching against my skin. At least they had been consistent in their decorating, I thought. Very clear message: minimalist, spare, modern. And it really only smelled very faintly of piss. However, my hair had not fared well in the evening's adventures and since

2

no one in the police station had considered serum a basic human right, it was an unmanageable, knotted mess. I attempted to run my fingers through the dark copper curls, working them out slowly. If nothing else, it would pass the time until my fairy godlawyer appeared and made everything OK. I lasted about seventy-four seconds before I got bored and gave up. Plus, I really was hungry.

'Excuse me,' I called in a weak but terribly polite voice. 'Excuse me? Is anyone there?'

Everything had been such a loud, Italiano, excitable mess on my way in that I couldn't quite recall *exactly* what had happened. I remembered being pulled out of the car by the overenthusiastic police officer but with my hands cuffed behind my back and my hair flouncing around in my eyes, I had focused all my energy on not falling over, given that I was basically lame on one foot and wearing a full-length ballgown. After that there had been some shouting and some crying, both by me, then a woman police officer had come over, tutted a lot, then taken away my aforementioned stabbier items. At some point, a phone had been thrust into my hands but the only numbers I knew by heart were Amy's and Charlie's and there was no way on God's green earth that Charlie was going to speak to me – which only left me with one option. And of course, Amy's number went straight to voicemail. The next thing I knew, I was shoved back here with an antiseptic wipe for my foot and two plasters. Apparently you couldn't kill yourself with two plasters.

I could hear the distant sounds of a busy police station beyond the reinforced walls, lots of doors slamming and distant sirens, but apparently no one could hear me. Or if they did, they didn't care.

I was starting to lose my English temper.

'Is anybody even *there*?' I shouted from my concrete block. 'Helloooo?'

Of course. When you wanted some privacy, there was an entire wedding's worth of people around to witness your felonious behaviour, but when you were wondering whether or not it was possible to get a cup of tea and a biscuit, nothing but crickets.

No one was coming. No one cared. Nick didn't care, Charlie didn't care, Amy was otherwise engaged, and who on earth knew where she would be by now?

Just as I was considering fashioning a *Blue Peter*-style pillow out of my frock, there was a loud kerfuffle along the corridor: raised voices, jangling keys and a lot of scuffling. Ooh, maybe I was getting a cellmate.

I sat up straight, my heart pounding.

Shit! Maybe I *was* getting a cellmate.

Gathering my skirts up around my waist, I stood up and held my breath. I wasn't quite sure what I was going to achieve with my ready-to-pounce pose – I was still in a ten by ten cement cell with iron bars where a door should be – but whatever was coming my way, I was ready for it. Unless she or he was bigger than me, in which case they would be wearing me like a glove puppet by dawn. I was not cut out for life on the inside. I would make a terrible prison wife, I had no discernible crafting talents, and the time Amy tried to give me an amateur tattoo with her compass and a pot of Indian ink she nicked from the art room, I passed out behind the humanities block and missed the first ten minutes of my mock French GCSE.

Before I could work out the appropriate way to greet a fellow criminal in a language I couldn't speak (not an easy task without my iPhone), two navy-clad officers burst through the door to the cell block, shouting at each other and the blur of arms and legs they held between them. I stepped back into the corner, trying to tie the skirts of my dress into a manageable knot in case I needed my legs free for kicking but there was no time. While I was faffing with the fabric, a third police officer was sliding open the bars so his mates could chuck my new best friend in beside me.

Only it wasn't my new best friend.

It was very much my old best friend.

'Police brutality!' Amy shouted, scrambling to her feet and grabbing at the cell bars as the *polizia* scarpered as fast as possible. 'I'm totally writing to my MP about this! As soon as I find out who my MP is.'

'Amy?' My skirts slipped out of my hand and fell to the floor with a damp slap.

'Tess!' She turned towards me, all wide eyes and filthy face, and flew over, wrapping her arms tightly around my cold shoulders. 'You're OK!'

'I think we're both pretty far from OK,' I pointed out, glancing around at our less than salubrious

5

surroundings. 'What's going on? Is Kekipi with you? They let me call someone and I called you but I got your voicemail.'

'Oh, no way!' She let go of my arms and laughed, before collapsing happily on my concrete block. 'I called you! How funny is that?'

'So funny that I might throw up,' I replied, awkwardly folding myself up on the floor. My knees had decided that standing up was overrated. 'Where's Kekipi?'

'Don't know; I didn't see him after they locked me up.' Amy placed her hands behind her head and closed her eyes, her own floor-length gown having actually fared quite well. At least, hers didn't have any blood on it. 'I'm sure he's coming. I've got to hand it to you – you don't do things by halves these days. No one could accuse you of being boring any more, could they?'

I crawled forward a couple of feet and wrapped my hands around the bars, pushing my nose out as far as it would go and trying not to cry. I thought of Nick and the look on his face. I thought of Al and how disappointed he would be in me when he found out about all of this. And I thought of Charlie and how I could possibly ever make things up to him. Sniffing at the empty corridor and staring up at the full moon through a tiny window across the way, I sighed.

'No,' I said to a half-asleep Amy. 'No one could accuse me of being boring.'

CHAPTER 1

I stood on the street outside my flat for five full minutes before braving the four concrete steps up to the door.

For five long years I had wrestled with the knackered lock, shoulder-barged the warped wooden door open, and called this place home, but after three short days away I was petrified of stepping over the threshold. Admittedly, it was fair to say I hadn't been on terribly good terms with my flatmate, Vanessa, when I left. For some reason, she hadn't taken kindly to me borrowing her life for a week, though I'd done a pretty good job with it, even if I did say so myself. Of course, she had chosen not to focus on the elements of our 'falling out' that she was at least somewhat responsible for – like how she'd been passing *my* photos off as hers for years on end, and how she'd been shagging Charlie, my Charlie, behind my back. That all seemed to slip her mind when she stood screaming in the street that I was the crazy one and if I ever stepped foot in the flat again, she'd have me arrested.

Fingering the key ring in my pocket, I forced myself

up another step. She couldn't actually have me arrested for going into my own flat, I reminded myself, and besides, it was half past eleven on a Thursday morning: she wouldn't be at home anyway. Given that Vanessa was absolutely shit at her job, her dad had been paying the mortgage on our flat since we moved in and she had a standing Thursday lunch date with him to justify her existence whenever she was in the country. I'd only met Vanessa's father once, but I had to assume no matter how good he was at making Scrooge McDuck quantities of money, he couldn't really be that bright because Vanessa had him wrapped around her little finger, even though he was pretty much the only man on earth she couldn't sleep with to get what she wanted. The whole daddy– daughter thing was a mystery to me. Maybe if I batted eyelash extensions and tossed a long blonde mane at my dad, he would pay all my bills too. Unlikely, given that we hadn't spoken in almost a decade, but you never know.

One more deep breath in and I was at the top of the stairs, face to face with my knackered red front door. Keys in hand, I rested one palm against the glass pane and pressed my ear against the wood, just to make sure. Hmm. Could I hear something? I should have brought Amy with me. Yes, my best friend was small in stature but she was very big on violence and I did not relish the thought of opening this door to a furious former flatmate without her by my side. Why was I here?

Maybe I should just turn tail and run back to Amy's house, get back under the covers, watch the rest of *Step Up 3* and pretend I didn't need any of my old things. And then I looked down at the T-shirt I had borrowed from Amy that morning. A five-foot-ten woman should never borrow clothes from a five-foot-nothing girl. I loved unicorns as much as the next girl but neon pink unicorns on a cropped black T-shirt? The world wasn't ready to see my belly button and neither was I. I needed my things.

That was, provided Vanessa hadn't burnt all my clothes, chucked them in the street or used them as tea towels and toilet paper. I let out a quiet laugh and shook my head: what a silly thought. She hadn't used a tea towel in the five years I'd known her, so that was hardly about to change. But without me there to buy bog roll, *that* was a definite possibility.

'You're being stupid,' I whispered to myself as I pulled my sad phone with its broken screen out of my pocket and forced it to shuffle through my contacts until I found the number for our landline. This was a telephone no one but my mother and the world's finest telemarketers had attempted to call since 2007 and yet, every time it rang, Vanessa had the receiver in her hand within three seconds, 'just in case'. I had to assume she had once given Brad Pitt that number in a bar and was still waiting for his call.

I listened as the line connected, the two long

9

bleats on my phone translating into two short rings inside. It was fair to say I felt something of a twat, stood on my own doorstep, dialling my own land-line from my own mobile, but I figured it was better to feel like a bit of a bell-end than to get into another public slanging match with a psycho. But when the phone inside stopped ringing and I heard the lovely lady from BT invite me to leave myself a message, I hung up and forced my key into the lock and merrily kicked the door wide open.

'Home sweet home,' I said with a sigh.

Even though it had only been three days since I'd left, the flat felt strange. The last time I'd left it, I'd been freaked out by the fact that nothing at all had changed in my absence. I wished I could say the same this time around. My keys always lived in the empty bowl by the door and I dropped them gently, listening to the familiar clatter before I stepped into the living room. Fuck. Me. Either Vanessa had started shagging the Tasmanian Devil or we'd been visited by seven very angry burglars. It was difficult to say which was more likely. The floor was covered in broken plates, broken glass and assorted empty bottles; picture frames had been pulled off the wall and dashed on the floor, which I figured explained the glass; and, most heartbreaking of all, my beloved *Buffy the Vampire Slayer* DVDs had been hurled around the room like mini Frisbees. She really knew how to hit a girl where it hurt. Picking my way through the debris, I grabbed handfuls of copper locks and tethered my hair back into a ponytail before I braved my bedroom, preparing myself for the inevitable devastation.

Pausing, I closed my eyes, pushed the door open and stepped inside.

'Oh. Wow!'

If I'd walked in on a family of baby elephants having a tea party with Julia Roberts and the Queen, I couldn't have been more surprised. My room was exactly as I had left it.

Closing my bedroom door behind me, I did a quick visual check. My suitcase was still sitting by the door, the bed sheets still rumpled from mine and Amy's sleepover on Sunday night, the mug full of tea still on the nightstand, albeit a bit scummier than I had last seen it. My clothes were still in the wardrobe, unhung pictures still propped against the wall. Whatever madness had possessed Vanessa while she trashed the rest of the flat, she must have run out of steam before she could take my room apart.

Or she booby-trapped it . . . I froze for a second, taking another look around and searching specifically for anything explosive-looking.

Once I was satisfied there were no landmines hidden under my Ikea rug, I got down to business. Whatever had gone on while I'd been camped out in Shepherd's Bush at Casa del Amy, all I wanted to do was get my things and go. Unzipping the still-full suitcase by the door and dumping the contents

11

on my bed, I swapped out the dirty clothes for clean ones, mentally shaking my head at my wardrobe choices. To the left of my case, a sea of colourful silk lay on the bed – the clothes I'd borrowed from my friend Paige – and to the right, a regimented tumble of black trousers, white shirts and the odd navy jumper – my everyday outfits. I didn't half love a V-neck. The wildest item of clothing in the right-hand pile was a houndstooth-check pencil skirt, and while I could try to pass that off as *Mad Men* chic, in reality it was something my mum had bought from the M&S outlet in Doncaster that didn't fit her when she got home and she couldn't be arsed to take it back. Surely there had to be some middle ground between a cropped neon unicorn T-shirt and the adult equivalent of a particularly crappy school uniform?

Once my suitcase was full of my depressingly few essentials, I sat myself down on the bed beside it and stared at my room for a moment. *Now* what was I supposed to do? Leave the rest of it and never return? I couldn't stay with Amy much longer. Six people to one toilet was already madness and adding a seventh really seemed to have pushed a couple of her flatmates past their tentative grip on sanity, but moving into a new flat would mean finding the money for a deposit, furniture, toilet paper, washing-up liquid and Sky Plus, and I was completely broke.

I stared at the small rubber duck I had rescued from the bathroom and waited for a response.

He usually had a lot to say for an inanimate object but in this instance he was uncharacteristically quiet.

'Suppose I don't have any choice,' I said out loud, to break the eerie silence of the abandoned room. 'Back to Amy's it is.'

'Or you could go to Milan,' the duck pointed out. 'That's an option.'

'Shut up, duck,' I said, unzipping the suitcase and shoving him deep inside. That would teach me to look to a bathroom accessory for advice. 'What do you know?'

Milan.

Sitting on the edge of my bed, swinging my legs back and forth, I pulled on the end of my ponytail. Milan, Milan, Milan.

And that was when I heard someone kicking the door open.

'Shit bollocks bastard!' I leapt to my feet, panicking at the sound of Vanessa's voice right outside my bedroom. I looked left. A shoddily constructed wardrobe that would not hold an elf, let alone me. I looked right. Wall.

'Yes, Daddy, I said I know.'

The front door slammed behind her and her keys clattered in the bowl beside the door: the bowl that I had dropped my keys into ten minutes earlier.

'But I'm having a shitty week and I'm not in the mood for lunch,' Vanessa whinged. 'Why can't you take me out for dinner instead?'

Without a better a solution, I dropped to my knees and rolled underneath my bed, pulling my spare winter duvet over my head. Trying my best to splutter silently through many months of dust, single socks and poorly disposed of chocolate-bar wrappers, I shuffled backwards until my feet hit the wall. As I swiped loose strands of hair and dust bunnies away from my face, I felt something sharpish scratching against my skin. I grabbed at it, hoping that whatever it was, it had the power to grant wishes, only to discover it was, in fact, a condom – an out-of-date Durex condom, still in its shiny, promising wrapper.

And there we had it: I was twenty-eight years old, with my freezing cold tummy bared to my filthy bedroom floor in a two-sizes-too-small T-shirt, with a duvet over my head, being physically attacked by expired prophylactics.

There was no way to sink any further.

'Somewhere nice . . .' I listened while Vanessa continued to barter with her father, wondering whether or not I could pull the condom over my head like a stocking and charge out the front door without being recognized. 'Nobu?'

I wanted to go to Nobu. Cow.

'No, Daddy,' she whined from the living room. It seemed the shithole she had created didn't bother her nearly as much as it did me. 'I have a headache. I need to stay home and rest this afternoon. I know, I'm probably working too hard.'

Well, that wasn't brilliant news, was it? How was

I supposed to get my case of clean knickers out of the flat if she wasn't going to sod off back out for lunch? For the sake of my sanity, I forced myself to ignore the 'working too hard' comment.

'OK, make it for eight. I'll see you there.'

On the upside, it seemed as though she hadn't seen my keys in the bowl by the door and so there was a chance I could get away with this if I stayed very quiet and didn't attempt to move for the next seven hours. As unlikely as it sounded, that option did actually seem preferable to trying to get out of the flat while Vanessa was still in it, despite the fact I was suddenly desperate for a wee. My bladder had a terrible sense of humour. I imagined this was exactly how Anne Frank felt. Only worse.

I hated not being able to see what was going on. I hated lying underneath my filthy bed, clutching a broken phone in one hand and a condom that had gone off in 2012 in the other. I hated that this was how I found out that I was apparently claustrophobic. Hyperventilating ever so slightly and trying to ignore my as-yet-undiscovered claustrophobia, I concentrated on the sounds outside of my bedroom. A dustbin lorry in the street, high-heeled pacing in the other room, some muffled swearing. Then, after what felt like forever, I heard the shower running.

When you lived with someone for five years, you got pretty used to their bathroom habits and no matter how much of a rush Vanessa might be in, she was incapable of taking anything even

15

approximating a quick shower. This was my chance. Scrambling out from under the bed, I tried to forget how badly I needed the toilet, grabbed my suitcase from the bed, and headed for the front door. Mere microseconds from freedom, my sweaty palm was on the door handle when a blurry silhouette appeared behind the pebbled glass and a sharp rap on the wood frightened me out of my skin.

'Miss Kittler? It's the police. Can you come to the door?'

The fucking police? Why were the police here? Although my curiosity had been well and truly piqued, I knew all too well what had happened to the curious cat and I didn't have eight lives to spare.

I scuttled back into my bedroom as fast as my feet could carry me. As far as I could see, I had two choices. Either I went back under the bed with five years' of filth and the saddest condom in existence, or I could climb out of my bedroom window. Which would be worse, having London's finest find you hiding underneath your own bed or climbing out of a window and dropping twelve feet onto potentially spine-shattering concrete? Either way, I was very likely to wet myself. As a second knock rattled the door frame and the water stopped running in the bathroom, I made my decision. Spine-shattering concrete it was.

Pushing the window open, I pulled up the handle on my suitcase and dangled it down as far as it would go. When it was just a couple of feet off the floor, I let it drop, biting my lip to stop myself from

16

screaming when it busted open in a silent explosion of M&S cotton pants, followed by a softened, but still sickening crack, as my camera made a mad dash for freedom across the courtyard.

'Hold on, officers, I'm coming!' Vanessa called out to the third rap on the door.

'On the upside,' I told myself as I hoisted myself up onto the windowsill and perched my bum right on the edge, 'this isn't even the second stupidest thing I've done this month.'

Peering down at the Rorschach test of underwear beneath me, I inched forwards, questioning more or less every choice I had ever made in my life. Well, at least if I fell and broke both my legs, that would answer the Milan question for me. There weren't many fashion photographers jetting around the world in full-body casts. Peeping up at me from underneath next-door's unbearably pretentious potted herb garden, the rubber duck raised a nonexistent eyebrow and waited, expectantly.

'Oh God, I'm being so stupid.' I no longer cared about being heard. I cared about not dying. 'What I am *doing*? I'm not jumping out of my own bloody window!'

White knuckles wrapped around the window frame, I twisted around, ready to cock my leg over and in. Unfortunately, I seemed to have forgotten that unless a certain Nick Miller was the one positioning my legs over my head, I was one of the least flexible women on the face of the earth. Getting back inside the flat was going to be a damn sight harder than getting out of it. Somehow, I had managed to get my back up against the UPVC frame and my bum half on and half off the ledge when I realized the belt loop of my jeans was stuck somewhere on the lock. And it was while wriggling around in this impossibly ridiculous position, one leg in and one leg out, doing the hokey cokey twelve feet above the floor, that my door flew open and two uniformed policemen and one towel-clad former flatmate burst into the room.

'Don't move!' shouted policeman number one.

'Come back inside the house!' yelled policeman number two.

'Without wanting to be rude . . .' My voice was awfully high. 'Can you pick one? I can probably do the don't move one but I'm not sure I can get back inside the house.'

'Stay where you are, Ms Kittler,' said policeman number one, who seemed far more interested in what Vanessa was barely covering with her towel than whatever crime they imagined I had committed, 'we've got this.'

'Thank you,' she said, a whimper escaping her throat as she cowered behind policeman number two. 'I was so scared. She must have broken in while was in the shower.'

'What?' I squeaked as policeman number one began to move slowly towards me. 'I didn't break in. I used my keys – I live here!'

'We'll sort all this out down at the station.'

Policeman number two approached with his hands held out towards me. And in one of those hands was a pair of handcuffs. 'Now just get down off the ledge.'

'I'm not going down to the station,' I said, one hand up in a surrender-friendly position, the other still clinging to the window frame for dear life. 'I didn't break in.'

I stared at the scene in front of me with utter disbelief. Vanessa, safe behind the boys in blue, gave me a wicked grin while wrapping her towel a little tighter.

'I want her arrested,' she said. 'Please take her away.'

'I am so going to kill you!' I let go of the window frame fully to try to unhook my jeans from the arm of the lock. 'This is ridiculous.'

'You heard that!' Vanessa shrieked. 'She threatened to kill me!'

Everything that happened after that was a blur. I wasn't sure if it was self-preservation or a rage-induced blackout, but without warning, I felt my mind leave my body and float up into a cobwebby corner of my bedroom, watching as the scene unfolded. The policeman that wasn't copping a feel of my treacherous flatmate rushed over to me as soon as I let go of the window frame and reached behind my back. As he came towards me, my belt loop decided it didn't need to be caught on the window lock after all and that's when I realized the only thing that was keeping me balanced in the first place was said belt loop hooked around said window lock.

The fall from the window didn't seem too bad. I did manage to land on top of my great big pile of pants, and at best I was a little bit dazed while at worst I was completely concussed. But looking on the bright side, it was probably better not to be entirely conscious when you were being read your rights and then carted off to the police station in handcuffs, wasn't it?

CHAPTER 2

'I've told you,' I said, pressing my palm against the throbbing pain in my shoulder, 'a thousand times. It's *my* flat, *my* home. Yes, Vanessa owns the flat but I pay rent. My keys are in the bowl by the door. I didn't break in.'

'Then remind me why you were climbing out the window with a suitcase full of Miss Kittler's belongings instead of using the front door?'

Once the officers had established none of my bones had been broken, it was off to the police station for questioning, despite my loud and varied protestations. So far, so *The Bill*. I had suffered assorted indignities, including being fingerprinted at the same time as a very large skinhead I was sure that I recognized, and then I was left in a small interview room with a female detective who looked about as happy to be there as I did, although she was considerably less bruised and considerably better dressed. Or at least her clothes seemed to a) fit her and b) actually belong to her.

I glanced around the interview room while I tried to work out what to say. It wasn't as bad as I had thought it might be. More Jobcentre waiting room than terrifying cell – and when you had a friend like Amy, you became very familiar with the inside of the Jobcentre waiting room.

'We live together, we've had a bit of a domestic,' I explained, wondering how likely a couple of Nurofen and a cup of tea were if I asked very nicely. 'I didn't want to talk to her so, you know, I jumped out of a window.'

Made perfect sense to me.

'So you two are a couple?' the detective asked, her eyebrow raising for a second and then dropping back into its standard position very quickly. Clearly someone had already had her sensitivity training.

'We are so not a couple!' I winced at both the idea of going out with Vanessa and the pain in my shoulder. 'She's horrible. She threw a cat at me once. I'd rather go out with you.'

'Excuse me?'

'The cat was fine,' I backtracked quickly. 'Vanessa is my flatmate. Or I'm her flatmate. Or I was her flatmate. I'm moving out, clearly, but I have paid rent for this month so I wasn't breaking in.'

'Just breaking out,' she said, incapable of keeping her eyebrow in its rightful place. 'And why did you have Miss Kittler's camera in your suitcase?'

This was the only part I was going to struggle with. 'It used to be my camera,' I said. 'I gave it to her one month when I couldn't pay my rent but then I borrowed it back for something. That's all it was, I wasn't stealing it.'

'You were borrowing it?'

'Yes.'

'Without asking?'

'Yes.'

'Which is commonly known as stealing.'

I had been brought up to be very respectful of the police. Even now, I couldn't walk past them in the street without feeling improbably guilty or mentally humming the tune to 'If you want to know the time, ask a policeman' but this was getting silly.

'I really haven't done anything wrong,' I said, attempting to remain as calm as humanly possible. 'She's just trying to cause trouble for me.'

'It just sounds very unlikely, doesn't it?' The detective leaned back in her chair, crossed her legs at the knee and tapped a biro against the pad in front of her. 'I mean, what would you think if you were me?'

'I'd think I had better things to do than get involved in a petty squabble between two flatmates. Aren't there proper criminals out there who need catching?' I asked before snapping my mouth shut.

I really had to get a handle on my temper. This was just like the time I lost my shit at work and knocked that girl's mug off her desk. Kind of . . .

'Oh, yes, hundreds,' the detective said, sitting up and brushing her dark blonde bob behind her ears. 'Although I am really enjoying wasting hours of my time and thousands of pounds of taxpayers' money on your petty squabble.'

Thoroughly chastened, I sank into my uncomfortable plastic chair and looked at the floor.

'I'm sorry,' I said, working on my most humble expression. 'Really, I am. Obviously I didn't wake up this morning and plan on falling out of a window but the whole Vanessa thing really is a ridiculously long story and you wouldn't believe me if I told you.'

'Why don't you try me?' she said. 'I do like a good story and I've already heard most of them.'

'Fine.' I folded my arms carefully underneath my boobs. I didn't like showing midriff to a police officer, especially a dirty midriff that had been sweeping my bedroom floor an hour ago. 'But you really won't believe it.'

'I'm so sorry to have caused you so much trouble.' Tracy the detective gave me a very gentle hug and carefully slid the strap of my handbag over my undamaged shoulder. 'Are you sure you don't want to go to the hospital? I'd be much happier if you'd let them check you out.'

'I'm OK, really,' I assured her. 'All I need is a stiff drink.'

'And somewhere to live,' she added. 'I'll text you later about that friend of mine – she might still be looking for someone.'

'Thanks. That would be awesome.' I pulled the strap of my bag over my head. 'I really appreciate it.'

It turned out Tracy could believe my story although

she hadn't heard one quite so dramatic in a good while. It also turned out she did not care for women who took advantage of other women or women who effed their friend's would-be boyfriends behind their back. And while there was very little she could do about the fact that Vanessa had demanded her camera back, she could let me off with a warning and give me a nice cup of tea while I told my story. I even got my Nurofen in the end, but only after I had retold my story to every woman in the police station.

'I can't believe there are really women like that out there,' Tracy said, shaking her head as she walked me out of the interview room, signalling for someone to bring me my battered suitcase. 'I'm so sorry for the mix-up. I could have someone drive you to the flat and wait while you collect the rest of your stuff if you want?'

'No, it's fine,' I said, really just wanting to leave. 'Don't worry about it.'

'OK, but you have to promise to let me know what you decide about Milan.'

There it was again. Milan.

I solemnly promised, and with one last round of hugs from every woman who happened to be in the general vicinity of Shoreditch police station, I gave them an awkward wave goodbye and padded outside into the sunshine. It had turned into a beautiful day. I hadn't really noticed the weather when I was falling out my bedroom window and being bundled into a police car.

'Of everyone we know, you are the last person I ever expected to be picking up from the cop shop.'

I squinted into the sunshine and my face relaxed into a smile. Leaning against the blue metal railings, phone in one hand, Tesco's carrier bag in the other, was Charlie Wilder, all six wonderful feet and three beautiful inches of him.

'Stagnate and die,' I said, smiling at the sight of him, relieved, safe, awkward, a little bit giddy. 'I'm mixing things up a bit.'

'I had noticed,' he said with a single nod.

We stood an uncomfortable three feet apart, neither of us moving in for our customary hug. I hadn't seen Charlie since I started my self-imposed exile in Amy's bedroom three days ago, and before that I hadn't seen him since we got drunk, got naked, and got it on, so it was understandable that things might be a touch awkward.

'Do you want to tell me how you managed to get arrested?'

I thought about it for a second. 'Not really.'

'Fair enough.' Charlie held out the Tesco bag and took my suitcase without a word. Such a gent. 'I got you these. I hear they're not big on snacks in there. Not that I'd know first-hand, of course, never having actually been arrested myself.'

'Actually they were very nice,' I said, taking it and delving inside. Ooh, Galaxy. 'Once I explained everything.'

'Sure you don't want to explain it to me?' he

asked, eyeing my T-shirt as I tore off the wrapper. 'Are they making you wear that as part of your punishment?'

'No and no.' I gave him the side eye and rummaged around the rest of his offerings. Diet Coke, Skittles, a bag of those fresh-baked giant chocolate chip cookies – he'd made an effort, all my favourite unhealthy things.

'Whatever, I'm glad you called me.' He took a single step closer and I could smell his aftershave and see the almost black rings around his dark brown irises and his thick, curly copper hair and – oh bloody hell, I was about to fall over.

'Woah!' Charlie reached out and grabbed me before I could go down, pulling me in close and holding me upright. There were no two ways about it, being held by Charlie felt really, really good. 'Let's get you home. And then you can bloody well tell me what's going on, whether you like it or not.'

Feeling equal parts faint and confused, with just an edge of lady horn, I let him wrap his arm around my shoulders and bundle me into a waiting Addison Lee taxi, leaving my new friends, Vanessa's camera and any remaining shred of dignity with Shoreditch's finest.

Charlie's flat was a typical man flat. The walls were white, the curtains were blue, and all of the furniture orbited an obscenely large television in the corner of the living room. Its satellite PlayStations

27

and Xboxes blinked their welcomes as I dropped my handbag on the leather recliner and let Charlie guide me over to the sofa. I'd sat on this settee a million times – God, I'd gone to DFS and helped him choose it – but today I felt strangely uncomfortable, as though I didn't know where I should look or what I could touch. The framed *Goodfellas* poster I had given him four Christmases ago stared down at me as I perched on the edge of the settee, pressed my thighs tightly together, and smiled gratefully when Charlie reappeared from the kitchen with a glass of water and the codeine I remembered feeding him when he knackered his knee the year before.

'How many more years until you've actually paid for this?' I asked, patting the settee as he sat down beside me, at a respectful distance. Which wasn't that easy when he was six three and I was five ten. Charlie and I had a tendency to make most furniture look Lilliputian.

'Three, I think.' He pushed his coppery brown hair off his face, one or two strands refusing to comply and sticking to his forehead. 'I'm assuming it'll completely fall apart or something. That's how I'll know it's officially mine.'

'Right,' I nodded in agreement and sipped my water. Water was good. A shower would be better, but I still felt a bit weird and I couldn't see what good would come of him holding me up in there. 'Yeah.'

I'd known Charlie Wilder for ten years. I knew

28

his height and his date of birth and his blood type. Our hair and our eyes were exactly the same colour. I knew when he had lost his virginity, I knew he lied about having a trial for Newcastle when he was fifteen, but things had never, ever been weird between us until I knew what his penis looked like.

'Right, yeah,' Charlie echoed. 'You all right?'

'I'm fine,' I said, attempting to sit more upright, look more composed. While wearing a cropped neon unicorn T-shirt? 'Apart from falling out of a window and spending all afternoon in a police station, I, sir, am right as rain.'

'I'm glad you called me,' he said, taking the empty glass out of my hand and placing it on the floor. Our fingers didn't touch once. 'Been waiting to hear from you.'

What I wouldn't have given to be having this conversation in any other outfit.

'I know.' I felt the edge of my thumbnail between my teeth and concentrated my attention on the blinking clock on his Blu-ray player. I was fairly certain it wasn't six fifteen in the morning and I quite badly wanted to go over and fix it. 'I'm sorry.'

'Don't be sorry.' I watched as Charlie pushed his Converses off with his feet, one at a time, then kicked them across the room to their home beside the door. 'I know I dropped a load of shit on you on Monday. It's not like I expected you to have an answer right away.'

I smiled and looked down the sofa at my best friend and saw someone I wasn't even sure I knew. 'I always have an answer right away though, don't I?'

'Well yeah, there is that,' he replied with a soft laugh. 'Got to admit, I wasn't expecting you to take this long to get back to me.'

I had been in love with Charlie from the very first day of university and every day since. He was The One. He was the man I imagined walking down the aisle with, the man I wanted to father my children. I wanted him to change my plugs and catch my spiders and know where we kept the paperwork for the car insurance and everything else that went along with a happy, long life together. Only, for ten long years, all I had been to Charlie was the one who reminded him about Mother's Day, the one who was always available for lunch or a pint after work. I was the girl who explained that petrol station carnations were never an appropriate apology, the one who went with him to weddings when he didn't have a girlfriend.

It turned out there were lots of different interpretations of The One.

And then, two weeks ago, under the most romantic of circumstances – drunk on cheap vodka on the bottom bunk of my childhood bed – we had finally done the deed. It had been wonderful and not just because I hadn't had sex in so long that there were expired condoms underneath my bed; it had been genuinely, toe-curlingly fantastic. Right up until Charlie threw me the 'I don't want to ruin our friendship' curveball the morning after and I found out he'd been secretly shagging Vanessa.

Of course, as soon as I told him to take his tainted peen as far away from me as humanly possible, he decided he wanted to make a go of it. And not only that, but he wanted us to start our own advertising agency together. Because going out with each other after everything that had happened wasn't potentially messy enough, clearly we needed to throw a professional relationship into the mix as well.

'There's been a lot of stuff going on . . .' I let out a tiny yawn, the pain in my shoulder ringing as I moved. Well, that was definitely the last time I jumped out of a window. 'I don't really know what else to say.'

'I had noticed you're not at your most chatty,' he said. 'You haven't really told me anything about Hawaii. You still don't want to talk about it?'

'Honestly, I sort of just want to go to sleep,' I admitted. 'And maybe have a bath and not be wearing Amy's clothes any more. Not necessarily in that order.'

What I really meant was, I'd rather go back to the police station than talk to Charlie about what had happened in Hawaii.

'In that case . . .' Charlie stood up and stretched. He was ever so tall. 'I'm going to pretend to go and have a wee when really I'm going to clean the bath, then I'm going to fuck off and leave you to

31

have a nap for a bit. Thank God that's not your top. I was about to stage an intervention.'

'I went to Hawaii,' I replied, 'I didn't go insane.'

'Understood.' He saluted, picked up my empty glass, and headed for the kitchen. I was already fully foetal on the settee and snuggled into the cushions I had made him buy in the Heal's sale when he returned.

'Drink this,' he ordered, holding out a fresh glass of water. 'And I'll run the bath.'

Lying on the settee, listening to the bath water run and watching dust dance around the living room in the late afternoon sunshine, I could easily imagine things working out with Charlie. It would be so nice to have someone to look after me and he knew me so well. It could be so wonderful. The job I'd always wanted, the man I'd always wanted. It was the life I'd dreamed of.

But I couldn't stop myself from wondering what would happen if I went to Milan. I couldn't stop myself from wondering what might happen with Nick . . . Hooking my foot through the handle of my handbag because I was too lazy to sit up and get it, I dragged it along the settee and dug around for my phone. The screen was so badly shattered I had to tilt it this way and that to get a clear view of my inbox but it was pointless. There was nothing to see. No new emails, no missed calls, no new text messages. Nothing from Nick; nothing at all. Three days of silence, otherwise known as an eternity.

'Do you want bubble bath?' Charlie called from the bathroom. 'I've got bubble bath. Why have I got bubble bath?'

'Because you're a woman?' I asked, sliding my phone under my back and refastening my ponytail on top of my head. Long, thick curly hair looked amazing on celebrities. In real life, it was nothing but a pain in the arse. 'Yes to bubble bath, please.'

'Right, it's running,' Charlie said, emerging with his sleeves rolled up and a slightly flushed face. At least I knew the bath had been properly scrubbed. Charlie was one of those blokes who believed that because you cleaned yourself in the bathroom, somehow that made the room itself self-cleaning. I really hoped I was catching the towels on a good day . . . 'You want a T-shirt or something? I don't think I've got any underwear to lend you.'

'I think that's probably a good thing!' I replied. 'Thank you. For coming to get me and everything.'

'It's not as if you haven't had to look after me before, is it?' He stood at the side of the settee, staring down as if he'd never seen me before.

'What?' I stared back up. 'What is it?'

'I have missed you,' he said.

I held my breath and felt my heartbeat skip a little faster than I might have liked.

'You daft cow,' he added.

My heartbeat slowed back down.

For a second, neither of us said anything and neither of us moved. I looked at Charlie, all tall and broad and floppy, brown hair. He looked at me, all tall and badly dressed and flat on my back.

'I've got to go out for a bit,' he said, breaking the silence and making for the door. 'You know where everything is. I'll be back for tea. See you in a bit,' he said, shutting the front door carefully behind him.

'See you in a bit,' I repeated and waited until I heard the outside door slam shut before retrieving my phone from under my bum and dialling Amy's number.

'Yo yo yo,' she answered immediately. 'I wondered where you'd got to.'

'Been a long day,' I replied. I wasn't nearly awake enough to fill her in on my adventures in house-breaking. 'I'm at Charlie's.'

'Oh really?'

'No need to sound so scandalized,' I said. 'It's just Charlie.'

'Charlie who has been calling me every day because you've been refusing to speak to him?'

'Yeah, that one.' I stretched my legs out in front of me, my shoulder singing out in protest at all movement. Padding into the bathroom, I checked the running water. Charlie's bath filled slowly – new information to add to my encyclopaedic knowledge of his existence.

'Shall I come over? Bring snacks?' Amy asked. 'We could make him watch *Notting Hill* again. That's always good for a laugh.'

'I think I probably ought to talk to him about

some stuff,' I said with a yawn. Between the pain-killers, the steamy promise of the tub and the general combined stress of the day, all I wanted to do was get in the bath and get into bed so I could pretend all of this was just a dream. 'Do you mind?'

'Yeah, you want to "talk" to Charlie,' she said. 'And I want to talk to Channing Tatum.'

'Well, if he calls, send me a text.' I yawned and dipped my hand into the water. 'See you tomorrow.'

'See you tomorrow,' she replied. 'Enjoy your "talk".'

Setting my phone safely on top of Charlie's bathroom cabinet, I stripped off and sat on the side of the bath. When I'd made my phone call, when I decided it was Charlie I wanted to see, I hadn't really had too much of a plan. I couldn't ask Amy to come and get me from the police station because then I'd have to explain how I got there in the first place and it would have been really hard for her to collect me if she was being arrested for killing Vanessa. Charlie was the easier option; he wouldn't give me a hard time and he would also bring snacks. But it did mean I was going to have to have a conversation that I had been putting off for the best part of a week. And in less than twenty-four hours, I had to have another conversation I'd been avoiding: a meeting with my agent, a meeting about Milan.

Sliding into the tub, I tried to get my shoulder under the water without soaking my hair. It would take forever to dry.

All I had to do was work out what I wanted. That was easy, wasn't it? Only I didn't know *what* I wanted, and the more I thought about it, the less certain I became. I didn't just look before I leapt, I had visited the jump site, called the insurance company and done a full risk analysis and yet I still couldn't come to a decision. I had never struggled like this before but ever since Hawaii, my compass was off. Instead of giving me a straight up yes or no, my brain had turned into a Magic 8 Ball. The outcome is unclear; ask again later; better not tell you now.

I opened the hot water tap with my big toe and watched as the mound of bubbles covering my body grew and grew and just as quickly, popped and vanished.

With a loud and obnoxious sigh, I slid deeper into the water. Sod my hair – it was already a mess.

Being a grown-up was rubbish.

The sun was fighting a losing battle when I woke up on the sofa. The room was pleasantly warm and you couldn't tell how badly it needed hoovering now the light had faded away. I wriggled my toes inside the pair of socks I had found, sniffed and deemed fit to wear, and yawned loudly.

'She wakes!' Charlie called from the kitchen. 'Better?'

'Sooo much better,' I said. The painkillers had reduced the shooting pains in my shoulder to a dull ache and my head felt altogether less stuffed with cotton wool after the nap. 'You should get injured more often, I like those tablets a lot.'

'Brilliant, you've been here for three hours and I've turned you into a junkie.' He leaned around the door, spatula in hand. 'What will Amy say?'

'Amy will want to know why you've got a spatula in your hand,' I suggested. 'What's going on in there?'

'I'm making dinner.' Charlie looked incredibly happy with himself. 'I'm making dinner for us.'

'I take it back, I'm not better,' I sat up, pulling my second borrowed T-shirt of the day over my knickers. Amy's was too small; Charlie's was too big. Maybe one day I'd find one that was just right. 'I must have hit my head as well as my arm because I think I'm hallucinating. You burn baked beans.'

'Losing his job does strange things to a man,' Charlie said, disappearing back into the kitchen. 'I've had to amuse myself for too long. There's only so many times you can play *Grand Theft Auto* and watch *Breaking Bad* before you start thinking a life of crime is a viable option.'

Until two weeks ago, Charlie and I had worked together at Donovan & Dunning, an advertising agency in Holborn. I ran the creative team and Charlie was an account manager, which mostly meant that I spent fourteen hours a day worrying over whether or not the target demographic would respond better to a happy squirrel selling them toilet paper or a friendly-looking bear, while he

37

took the people who owned the toilet paper company out for dinner and then asked them for more money. But, like lots of agencies run by men who liked to blow all their money up their nose rather than into their employees' pension fund, Donovan & Dunning was not prepared for the recession and had gone rather spectacularly bust, leaving me, Charlie, and about forty other people, out of a job.

'So you're going for *Come Dine with Me* instead?' I asked. 'This is a very interesting development.'

'I'm not very good,' he acknowledged, reappearing in the living room with two very full glasses of white wine. What went better with codeine than wine? 'But I'll get there. I'm making a chilli but I didn't have any kidney beans so I used Heinz. That's all right, isn't it?'

'No,' I said, sipping the wine and trying not to wince. Charlie had never been much of a wine drinker; clearly this had been bought in for my benefit. I couldn't help but wish it hadn't been. 'You can't put baked beans in a chilli, but I'm really impressed that you tried.'

'Then you'll be completely wowed by my ability to call for a pizza,' he said, sitting down next to me and pulling his phone out of his back pocket. 'Because I'm amazing at that.'

'A man's got to have a talent,' I replied.

His legs pressed against his too-big socks I was wearing and squished my toes in a way that made me feel warm all over. Or it could have been the wine, I wasn't sure. Whatever discomfort had been between us before my nap had dissolved and all I wanted to do was stare at him in silence while he faffed about with the Domino's app. But that could have been the wine too.

'Pizza will be here in forty-five minutes,' he said and turned to me with a grin. I quickly sipped my wine and hoped my face didn't look as red as it felt. 'So what should we do for the next forty-five minutes?'

'Stop it,' I shouted, swatting Charlie's arm away from my face. 'I hate this.'

'You're so bad,' he laughed, hammering the buttons on his control pad and beating my character into a bloody pulp on the screen in front of us. 'How can you possibly be so bad?'

'Because I've been drinking for the last hour on an empty stomach,' I said, adding a hiccup for emphasis and throwing my controller down onto the sofa in protest as he ripped the head off my character with unrestrained glee. 'And I don't have a penis.'

'Loads of girls are good at games,' Charlie argued as his phone lit up on the sofa between us. 'You're just shit. Thank God the pizza is here so I don't have to kill you again.'

Folding my legs up underneath me, I watched him run downstairs to pick up the pizza and smiled the smug smile of a woman who was spending the evening playing computer games and drinking wine with her crush. It was every girl's dream, wasn't it? Here I was, wearing his favourite Arsenal T-shirt and a pair of big floppy socks, looking adorable. Or at least I looked adorable in my imagination; I had no interest in checking out how true that assumption was in a mirror. This was everything I'd ever wanted. Well, maybe I hadn't pictured quite so many rounds of *Mortal Kombat* in our future, but the pizza was definitely a plus.

'Dinner is served!' Charlie pushed through the door with an enormous white pizza box, a matching plastic bag hanging from his wrist. 'Do you want some Coke?'

'Is it diet?'

'No, it isn't diet.' He placed the pizza carefully on the not-really-clean-enough floor and handed me a napkin.

'Then I'll stick with the wine.' I held out my glass for a refill.

'Wine and pizza . . .' He grabbed the almost empty bottle from the side table and poured. 'We're practically Italian.'

I flipped open the lid of the pizza box and ignored him.

'Hawaiian pizza?' I asked. 'I suppose you think you're funny.'

'I want to hear about it – Amy wouldn't tell me anything.' Charlie handed me a piece of kitchen towel in lieu of a plate and grabbed a huge, gooey slice of pizza before settling back onto the sofa. 'Actually, she kept saying I was a

40

cockwomble and told me to stop calling her. Was it amazing?'

'It was amazing.' I chose my words carefully, focusing on my memories of the sea and the sand and the smell of morning pastries and pretty pink flowers and pineapple that tasted nothing like the pineapple on this pizza. 'It's really beautiful.'

'I still can't believe you did it, Tess,' he said. 'Packed up, flew halfway round the world. It's so not you.'

I shrugged, picking pieces of sad, tinned pineapple off my pizza. He didn't know the half of it.

'Being me wasn't getting me very far, was it?' I said, wiping my hands on a paper napkin and wrapping my hair around itself in a bun on the back of my head. 'And I needed to get away from everything.'

The skinny blonde elephant in the corner of the room coughed delicately and tossed its hair.

'Everything?' Charlie repeated.

'You know, work and everything,' I said, attempting to clarify without using the V word. If I never heard the V word again as long as I lived, it would be too soon.

Charlie wrapped his huge hand around his delicate wine glass and nodded. 'Vanessa.'

And we'd managed fifteen seconds. Not bad going.

'You know . . .' He cleared his throat and took a drink. 'Me and her, it was nothing to do with me and you.'

'I don't want to talk about it,' I said, meaning it entirely.

41

'It was a thing.' For some reason, he hadn't stopped talking. 'It was not a clever thing, I know, but it was like she was in one box and you were in another and I never even thought about you being in that box because you're you and she's her and you were in a more important box anyway. Does that make sense?'

'None, not even a little bit,' I replied. 'I really, really don't want to talk about it.'

'I never had feelings for her,' he said, continuing to talk in spite of specific instructions to the contrary. gesticulating wildly and using his pizza as a prop. 'It was all, well, it was all that it was.'

'It was just sex,' I said, my mind wandering over to the last time I'd heard those words.

'I know I'm an idiot and I know I was dick-led and I know you'll never forgive me . . .' I looked away but heard the clink of the wine bottle on the rim of the glass. 'But yeah, it was just sex. I'm a bloke. I was drunk and a fit girl came on to me and I am fully aware that it was the worst decision I've ever made.'

Sipping my wine, I considered his words for a moment. Two weeks ago, that sort of defence would have made my head explode but now, having made my own bad decisions, with my own fit bloke, I could almost understand. Almost.

'If I could take it back, I would.' Charlie climbed off the settee, his long legs kneeling in the lid of the pizza box before he pushed it away and I watched it skate across the room and disappear

42

under an armchair. 'If I'd known what might happen with you, I would never—'

'You're drunk,' I said, half-hopefully. 'We don't have to have this conversation now.'

'I've had two weeks to think about this, Tess,' he said, taking the wine glass and paper-towel pizza plate out of my hands.

His breath was warm and sharp from the wine but he smelled the way he had smelled since the very first day I had met him. A mixture of Head & Shoulders, the Issey Miyake aftershave he had spritzed on before he left the flat this morning and underneath all that, the same comforting Charlieness that had wrapped itself around me a thousand times.

'I know I fucked up. And not just by what I did and who I did it with, but by not realizing how amazing you are bloody years ago. You're my best friend. You make me laugh, you take care of me; you're the one who is always there. You're shit at beat-em-ups but I don't care. There are too many awesome things about you. I can't believe I didn't work this out before.'

'Like what?' I said, nervous laughter in my voice. 'What's so awesome about me?'

'Everything,' he said, grinning. 'We like all the same films, we like all the same TV shows, we like the same music. God, it's like we were made for each other. You're basically me and I'm basically you.'

I wanted my wine back. Was that true, really? *Did* we like all the same things? And did I want

43

to be with someone who liked me because I was exactly like him? I hated to admit it but I had a feeling it would be more true to say I liked the things he liked so we would have more reasons to spend time together. We never, ever did anything I suggested – because I never suggested anything.

'I need you in my life,' Charlie said, not put off by my contemplative silence. 'And not as a mate. I didn't realize how much I needed you until now. Just don't tell me it's too late.'

As it was, he didn't give me a chance to tell him anything. Instead he took my hands in his and pulled me towards him.

'Tess,' he whispered. 'My Tess.'

It was what I wanted: to be his, to belong.

Softly, slowly he pressed his lips against mine and I was full of wine and butterflies, so I kissed him back. I closed my eyes, let myself drift and kissed Charlie Wilder as though there wasn't a single other man on the planet.

Only, I knew that wasn't true.

CHAPTER 3

It was very early the next morning when I woke up in Charlie's bed. With Charlie, but without any clothes. The night before, it had seemed like such a good idea, the getting naked thing. I hadn't had a good day by anyone's standards and nothing seemed to take my mind off bigger problems like a good seeing-to. It was one of the fun new things I'd learned about myself of late. Unfortunately, for everything I'd learned, I seemed to have forgotten how much trouble dropping my knickers tended to land me in. Twelve hours earlier, the idea of sleeping with Charlie was warm and reassuring and comforting but when I woke up at dawn, the sunlight slicing across his blue-for-a-boy bedroom, there was one thought I couldn't get rid of, no matter how many times I tossed and turned.

Nick Miller.

Here I was, nestled in the nook of the man I'd been achingly in love with for ten long years, and all I could think about was how different it felt to waking up beside Nick. I kept trying to close my eyes but every time I began to drift off, there he was. His ashy blond hair and blue eyes staring right at me, making me shiver from head to toe.

Strangely enough, waking up naked with one man but only being able to think of another was a bit confusing and so, as quietly as I could, I slid out of bed, grabbed my clothes from last night and tiptoed towards the bedroom door. All I needed was ten minutes to make a cup of tea. Or maybe I could go for a quick walk, blow away the cobwebs. Actually, it might be a good idea to pop back to Amy's. I could leave Charlie a note. Yeah, that was a good idea. As long as I left a note it was OK. Everyone loved a note . . .

'Morning.'

I froze in the doorway, pulling my borrowed T-shirt past the hem of my knickers with one hand and trying to push my hair into some sort of shape with the other. Charlie rubbed at his face with the back of his hand and smiled.

'Hello.'

Well, at least I didn't have to worry about what to put in the note.

'Where do you think you're off to?' he asked, stretching his entire body down the length of the bed as I averted my eyes. Even now, even at twenty-eight years old, I still couldn't make direct eye contact with a penis. At least not in daylight. Definitely not sober.

'Uh, just putting the kettle on,' I replied, my hair flopping down over one eye. I can pull off sexy, I

46

thought, planting my hand on my waist and dropping my hip. Then immediately standing up straight and feeling like a twat. 'I'll be back in a minute.'

'Not in the mood for a cup of tea,' he said, pulling back the covers and patting the mattress. Once the duvet had been removed, it wasn't hard to see what he was in the mood for. I coloured up from head to toe and averted my eyes. I had been fantasizing about Charlie for a decade and we'd had actual sex twice now, but seeing his actual peen with my actual eyes was still too much.

'I need a wee,' I said, the words falling out of my mouth before I could consider how incredibly unsexy they were. Charlie frowned and waved me away. 'Back in a minute.'

Once the bathroom door was safely locked behind me, I sat down on the loo and pressed both hands against my face. What was wrong with me? Why was this weird?

If only I could stop thinking about Nick.

'I'm not thinking about him at all,' I corrected myself and ran the cold water over a dubious-looking flannel. 'Not at all.'

Why would I be thinking about him? I had just woken up in the arms of a wonderful man who was over six feet tall, had all his own teeth and had bought me pizza. In an online dating world, Charlie was the catch of the century.

'So I'm not thinking about Nick.' I slapped myself around the chops with the icy flannel. 'I am wishing

I had never met him, but I am not thinking about him.'

There was nothing to think about anyway. So what if he was so attractive he made Matthew McConaughey look like he'd fallen out of the ugly tree and hit every branch on the way down? So what if he was intelligent and passionate and fascinating? So what if the sex was intense and so all-consuming that I still have pale yellow traces of his fingerprints on my arms and shoulders and hips and even thinking about our time together made me forget to breathe.

Nick was a *fling*. I had a fling and now that fling was over. And not just because he sent a heart-stoppingly brief 'call me' email a week ago and then failed to pick up his phone or answer anything subsequently, but because I had decided it was over. Hawaii was a fantasy; this was real life. And it wasn't a bad trade by any stretch of the imagination.

'Totally over the Nick situation.' I was resolute underneath the flannel. 'The fling has been flung.'

Not that I wasn't a bit pissed off. Yes, he had good reason to be annoyed at me, but when a man sent you an email that said 'call me' and then didn't actually answer your calls, that was enough to slot him firmly into the 'douchebag' category.

'Why tell me to call if he didn't want to speak to me?' I asked the flannel.

It didn't answer. It just smelled damp and sad.

'Everything all right in there?' Charlie knocked on the door. 'You setting up shop or something?'

'I'm was just, you know,' I stood up and flushed for the want of a better response, 'doing stuff.'

'Oh,' he replied. 'Oh. Right, uh, I'll let you get on with that then.'

'I'm not doing that,' I shrieked, realizing he had added two and two and got something very unladylike. 'I was just washing my face.'

I threw the door open and waved the damp flannel around to prove my innocence.

'You didn't use that, did you?' Charlie asked, taking it from me with his thumb and forefinger and sniffing gingerly.

I pressed my fingers to my face. The skin was still all there. 'Why?'

'No reason.' He threw it over my shoulder into the bath and wiped his hand on the back of his boxer shorts. 'Come here.'

Before I could protest, Charlie wrapped his arms around me and rested his chin on the top of my head. I clasped my hands behind his back and made myself smile, trying to relax into him. I'd always found Charlie hugs reassuring. He was so tall, he even dwarfed me when I wore heels and I was five ten. In bare feet, it was like being cuddled by a considerably cuter Bigfoot. I felt his chin on the top of my head and heard a purr-like noise emanate from his entire being.

'Let's go back to bed . . .' His hands slid down my back and up underneath my borrowed T-shirt.

'This is the first time I've been happy to not have a job since we got fired.'

'I can't,' I said, writhing out of his reach and grabbing hold of both of his hands before I got carried away. Again. 'I've got a meeting.'

Even though I was congratulating myself for listening to my brain instead of my vagina, it was still hard not to fall right into Charlie's arms and let him carry me back to bed. This was what happened when you didn't have sex forever and then had all of the sex at once – you lost control of every single sensible impulse in your body.

'A meeting?' Charlie casually pushed his erection down like a bad dog. 'Who have you got a meeting with? At this time in the morning?'

'It's an agent,' I replied, my eyes squarely locked on his. 'So . . . I was taking photos in Hawaii. For a magazine.'

'You were taking photos?' he asked, finally leaving his penis alone. 'Like a photographer?'

'Just like a photographer,' I nodded and looked at my hands. How did I keep this as brief as possible? 'I didn't just decide to go to Hawaii. I went to take pictures of this man for *Gloss* magazine. He owns a fancy department store in New York and he's retiring so they were doing a feature.'

'And you were the photographer?' Charlie crossed his arms, making his biceps pop. '*You* took the pictures?'

'I took the pictures,' I said, not looking at his arms at all. 'I was the photographer.'

'But you're not a photographer,' he pointed out. 'You're a creative director at an ad agency.'

'Technically, I'm more of a photographer than a creative director right now,' I replied. 'You know I was always interested in photography.'

'Do I?'

'Anyway, they really like the photos – the magazine, and Al, the guy I was taking the photos of. So now he wants me to go to Milan and take some more photos for a project he's working on. I guess it's a career retrospective or something?'

'Woah.' Charlie breathed out, sitting down on the edge of the sofa. 'That's bloody amazing. Mental but amazing.'

'I can see how you would get to mental,' I said, wiggling one big toe and then the other. 'But I really love taking photos and it turns out I'm good at it.'

'Are you going to go?' he asked. 'To Milan?'

I scrunched up my face and shrugged. 'I don't know.'

'Do you want to go?'

'I want a cup of tea,' I answered, standing up and walking straight into the kitchen. I knew his flat as well as I knew him and before he had even followed me, I had two cups on the counter, his instant boil kettle bubbling away.

'You always want a cup of tea,' Charlie said, opening the fridge and taking out the milk. 'But do you really want to do it? This photo thing?'

'I honestly don't know.' I couldn't look at him while I spoke. Why was this so hard? I placed a teabag in each cup and felt my eyes prickle with the tears of an awkward conversation.

'When do you have to make a decision?' he asked. This was why he was a great account manager, always on the details. 'When would you have to go? Do you know how long you'd be away?'

'Soon,' I said, splashing my moo juice onto the kitchen top. 'And I'd be away for a little bit.'

'And how long is a little bit?' He put the milk back in the fridge and took his tea. 'Three days? Four?'

I stirred my tea with a teaspoon that didn't match any of his other cutlery and watched the milk swirl away into an evenly coloured cuppa.

'I'm not sure.'

I was lying. I did know. Agent Veronica had sent me several long and detailed emails about the job, each with an increasing degree of foul language. Agent Veronica did not believe in mincing words.

The job would take at least three months, probably more. The rest of July, August, September and some of October. I could easily be away until Christmas. Stood there in Charlie's kitchen in my pants, holding a hot cup of tea, everything seemed to slow down to a complete standstill and I couldn't quite seem to find the right words to tell him that. So I didn't tell him anything. It was a serious problem I appeared to have developed.

'Sounds like an amazing opportunity,' Charlie said, heaping mounds of white sugar into his mug. I wasn't allowed to put sugar in Charlie's tea, I never added enough. 'I mean, you never went travelling or anything after uni. It might be fun.'

'It's not just as easy as packing a bag and getting on a plane.' I breathed in and felt the world shift back to a normal speed, rattling off the excuses I'd been telling myself, every time the tiniest buzz of excitement swelled up in my stomach. 'I don't have anywhere to live, I don't have any money, I don't even have a camera. And yes, the pictures from Hawaii worked out but this is a much bigger deal. It's not a fun thing, it's a proper job that a real photographer would kill for. I honestly don't know if I'm up to it.'

'You, Tess Brookes, are up to anything you put your mind to,' Charlie said, his dark brown eyes clear and resolute. 'You know that. Or at least *I* know that. How many times do I have to tell you?'

I looked up at him with a half-smile hidden behind my mug. Of course, he had to go and remind me that he wasn't just a great shag and my lifelong crush, but my best friend as well.

'A camera is easy enough to get, isn't it? And you haven't bloody shown me the pictures from Hawaii yet but I don't believe you would do anything less than a perfect job. You always do.'

'You mean because I'm OCD?' I asked.

'I mean because you work hard and you're good at whatever you do,' he said, splashing his tea around his bare feet. 'As for the not-having-anywhere-to-live thing – you could always stay here.'

'I'm not a very good roommate, as I'm sure Amy would tell you,' I said, tearing off some kitchen towel and wiping up his mess, vaguely impressed in the back of my mind that he actually had kitchen towel. 'And really, your spare room isn't big enough to swing a cat. Plus you've got a surfboard in it. When was the last time you surfed?'

'I didn't mean move in as a roommate,' Charlie said. 'I don't want you in the spare room.'

I stood up slowly, clutching the grubby kitchen towel. His floors needed cleaning. 'What?'

'How's your tea?' he asked.

Leaning against his kitchen cabinets, resplendent in a creased-to-buggery boy's T-shirt, with bird's nest hair and a handful of dirty paper towel, I searched for the right words. Charlie crossed his legs, leaning against the fridge in an impressively casual display.

'Did you just ask me to move in with you, in a non-roommate capacity?' I asked, scrunching the paper towel into a tiny ball in my fist. 'Seriously?'

'I'd say "I know it seems a bit quick" but it doesn't.' He put his tea down and took the paper towel out of my hand before throwing it at the bin. And missing. 'I've had two weeks to think about this and it was two weeks too many. I know how I feel about you. You're my best mate and I reckon last night proved the amazing sex wasn't just a one off, so why mess about?'

'I can think of a few reasons,' I replied. Actually, I couldn't. I could only think of one but this really didn't seem like the time to tell him I'd been shagging someone else the whole time I was in Hawaii, especially since he'd apparently been sitting on his arse in London, doing some pretty epic soul-searching. 'It . . . it is a bit quick, Charlie. I feel a bit bleurgh about everything.'

'Bleurgh?' He looked understandably deflated.

'Overwhelmed,' I clarified. 'Confused.'

'So this wouldn't be the right time to tell you I've accepted a pitch for our agency, then?' he asked, wincing.

'But we haven't got an agency?' I said. 'What have you done?'

'Don't be mad at me.' He held his hands out to defend himself against whatever puny attack he thought I might launch and grabbed a sneakily hidden copy of *Marketing Week* from the top of the microwave. 'But I saw Perito's were looking for a new agency and one of the blokes in their marketing department is on my football team and I knew you'd come up with an amazing campaign, so I asked him if we could pitch. And he said yes, because he totally loves your work.'

'He loves my work?' my ego asked on my behalf.

'He was totally obsessed with you,' Charlie nodded. 'Knew loads of your campaigns.'

'So just like that? We've got a pitch?' I wondered if there was any wine left. Tea clearly was not strong enough for this conversation.

'Yes,' he said. 'But . . .'

'But?'

'He needs to see the pitch by next Friday because they're seeing agencies the following Monday. And we're going to be one of those agencies.'

'That's not even a week!' I loved stating the obvious. 'We would have to come up with an entire marketing campaign, just me and you, by next week?'

'Yeah, but Tess, Perito's Chicken as our first account? Our own agency?' Charlie looked so excited. I recognized the enthusiasm; I used to share it. 'How amazing would that be?'

Worryingly, if anyone had asked me that question two weeks ago, I wouldn't have been able to describe how amazing it would be. I'd have been like a pig in peri peri sauce.

Charlie Wilder was asking me to move in with him. Charlie Wilder was asking me to pitch an advertising campaign for a Portuguese chicken cook-in sauce. Charlie Wilder was asking me to start a brand new advertising agency with him. But no, I had to go off to Hawaii on a voyage of pissing self-discovery and meet a tosspot of a man who would be rolling around on the floor, sides positively splitting, at the sound of any of this.

'And it isn't just Perito's.' Charlie was still talking, still trying to win me round. 'I talked to some of our old accounts and they're interested. Squiggles' Kitchen Towels wants to come with us.'

At least that explained why he had so much kitchen towel.

'And there's Brookes & Bryan, the jewellers we just signed; they're up for it too. And I reckon I can totally get Noodle Pots. You're the best creative director there is, Tess, and I can't do this without you. They all want you, not some knobhead account manager. I need you.'

Charlie took a step towards me and reached out to run a hand through my hair.

'Tell me you're not just the littlest bit interested?' he said, his hand getting stuck somewhere around my ear.

I shivered, trying to separate out my feelings of professional pride and sexual desire. I wasn't sure whether or not I could. It was a bit disconcerting.

'I've got to go to my meeting,' I said in a weak voice. 'Can we talk about this later?'

Sensing defeat, Charlie stopped. Part of me was so disappointed that he hadn't grabbed hold of my hair, bent me over the oven and shagged me senseless until I agreed to all of his demands; but the part of me that got up at seven every morning, got dressed and went about her daily business in a sensible fashion, respected him for giving me the time and space to make a considered decision. After all, this was sweet, loving Charlie we were talking about, not filthy, tosspot Nick.

Not that I was thinking about Nick.

'Tess-motherfucking-Brookes!'

Agent Veronica stood up, put out her fag and grabbed me for a stale, non-optional hug as soon as I set foot in her office.

57

'Sit your arse down. Cup of tea? Cup of tea.' She strode over to the door and coughed delicately. 'Two cups of fucking tea when you're ready, if it's not too much fucking trouble?'

Slamming the door behind her, she shook her head and sat back down behind her desk. 'Can't get the staff,' she lamented. 'Now, do I need to slap some sense into you or have you just come to confirm your flights?'

Veronica, it was fair to say, was something of an imposing woman. Very blonde with very red lipstick and an ever-present fug of cigarette smoke that tended to knock the breath out of your lungs before you had a chance to get a word in edgeways. Not that you ever really had a chance to get a word in edgeways. She stubbed out a crimson-ringed dog-end with matching pointy nails and sat back in her seat. Perched on the edge of my chair, my bag safely on my knee, I waited for her to say something. It never hurt to put a potential weapon between Veronica and your vital organs.

Given that she hadn't spoken in four seconds, I took it that I was safe to begin.

'Well—'

'I don't want to hear "well"!' she shouted, slapping her desk with her hand and grabbing a fresh pack of Silk Cut out of her drawer. 'I want to hear, "sorry I've been such an ungrateful shithead all week, Veronica. You're amazing, Veronica. When does my flight to Milan leave, Veronica?"'

'I've had a lot of thinking to do,' I protested as she savaged the plastic film around the cigarettes.

'Wandering around in the rain? Staring out over the river and wondering "What if?"' she asked. 'Fuck that. You're leaving on Sunday.'

'It hasn't rained this week . . .' I muttered, confused. Then realized what she had said. '*What?*'

'Sunday, you leave on Sunday.' Veronica took care to enunciate each word very carefully, as though I were simple or slow. I was fairly certain she believed I was both. 'You start work on Monday, so it seemed like a good idea to get you on a flight on Sunday. You *comprende?*'

'I can't leave on Sunday,' I said, holding my bag closer into my body. 'That's in two days. I'm not ready.'

'So what are you doing sat there like a bastard lemon then?' she asked. 'Go home, wash your fucking hair, pack a fucking bag, find your fucking passport. You're going.'

'Veronica . . .' I started, reaching a hand up to touch my hair. 'I can't just up and leave on Sunday for three months.'

'Why? You haven't got a job, have you? You haven't got anywhere to live . . .' She paused to light up again, either oblivious or unconcerned by the laws about smoking in the workplace. I assumed the latter. 'From what I've heard, you're lucky you're not having this conversation with me in a fetching orange onesie. Thank God they didn't send you down, girl. Some butch bitch'd

59

be wearing you like a glove puppet inside half an hour.'

'Who told you . . .? You know what, never mind.' I blinked, trying to erase the terrifying image she had just planted indelibly in my mind. 'It's still a lot. To go off to Italy for three months in two days. I can't even speak Italian.'

'They all speak English,' she said, dismissing my fears with a sweep of her ignited arm.

'Really?' I asked.

'Well, no, but if they don't speak it, I doubt very much that they've got anything fucking interesting to say anyway.' She pointed at me, making stabbing motions with her lit cigarette on every word. 'You. Are. Going. To. Milan. On. Sunday.'

'I can't go for three months,' I replied, my head full of Charlie's morning erection and Perito's spicy chicken. Not together though, eww. 'I can't.'

With a loud, fragrant sigh, Veronica leaned back in her chair and fixed me with a narrow-eyed stare as her assistant shuffled through the door and placed two cups of tea on the desk with a barely smothered cough.

'You know you're not supposed to smoke in the workplace, don't you?' I asked, chugging my tea so there would be one less hot thing for her to throw at me.

'I eat here, I sleep here, I shit, shower and shag here.' Veronica ground the half-smoked cig into her ashtray, leaning forward and gripping the edge of the desk with her blood-red talons. 'Can't imagine anyone's going to tell me to put my fag out. Unless it's bothering you?'

'No,' I said quickly. 'I find it quite comforting.'

'Your parents smoke?'

'No,' I replied, feeling the fear of God in my gut. 'Just, you don't see it enough these days, do you?'

She sat back again, reaching behind her and shoving the window open. It wasn't until I heard the amplified buzz of traffic outside that I realized I'd been holding my breath. Sweet Baby Jesus in the manger.

'So you don't want to go to Italy for three months?' she asked, clicking her mouse a couple of times and looking over at the screen of her Mac.

Thank God, we were back to business.

'Three months is so long. A lot can happen in three months,' I said.

'Oh, are you expecting some other fashion icon to appear from the heavens and offer you a once-in-a-life-time opportunity?' she asked, her hands clasped together in prayer.

'I don't want to agree to three months,' I replied, as staunchly as possible. Playing hardball had never been my thing. Actually, playing any kind of ball had never been my thing, euphemistically or otherwise.

'I'll tell them you'll go for a week, do a recce and then make a decision,' she said. 'And if that decision is anything other than "thanks for giving me this opportunity, Mr Bennett, now may I kiss your arse?" I'll have you fucking killed.'

A week. I felt relief roll off my shoulders. I could do a week. I'd know how I felt in a week. Probably.

'Thank you,' I said, visions of *Roman Holiday* and big plates of pasta suddenly rushing through my head. Everything I'd held at bay until now crashed over me on one big Italiano-gasm. I was going to Milan.

'That would be amazing. It's just that I've got other stuff, maybe. I don't want to commit to something I might not be able to do.'

Veronica's head snapped round towards me so quickly, her hair almost moved. 'You know I'm your agent? You can't book a job without me because then I'd have to fucking kill you and I hate having to sort that out. Right pain in the tits.'

'It's not a photography job, it's advertising,' I said quickly, preparing for a slap. 'Like I was doing before.'

'Can you see me right now, Tess Brookes?' Veronica pushed her massive leather chair over to the wall behind her and began knocking her head against the wallpaper harder than I could imagine was comfortable. 'This is me, banging my head against a brick wall. And why do you think I'm doing that?'

'Is it because I'm a fucking idiot?'

I thought it was worth a guess.

'Ding ding ding!' She waved her arms above her head like Kermit the Frog and thankfully stopped bashing her head against the wall. 'You're a fucking idiot. This is a chance that will never come around again. You are a twenty-eight-year-old untested, unproven, rookie photographer. You ought to be spending the next five years trekking around shit weddings in Bracknell, taking pictures over dinner because the main photographer can't be arsed.'

It was a fair point.

'At best, you'd be looking the other way while some big-shit fashion photographer got a blow job from some underage model while you changed the flash and spent so long holding up reflectors that you had a right bicep bigger than a world champion wanker.'

Again, not untrue.

'Am I getting through to you? Shall we just go over what exactly is on the fucking table here?'

I didn't feel like we especially needed to but I didn't think it would be in my best interests to tell her no and so I went with a noncommittal half-shrug and made an awkward mewing noise in the back of my throat. Veronica sat forward and held out her hand, ticking off each of her points with so much force, I was worried she was going to break off her own fingers.

'One first-class fucking trip to Italy, a base in Bertie-cocking-Bennett's private apartments in Milan, a job working personally with Bennett himself that a million other photographers would happily bum a goat to get, and a proposed fee that is twice what I would have even attempted to get for you – and I, Tess Brookes, am a fucking ballbreaker when it comes to fees. So what, pray

63

tell, is your opportunity? Because if it's anything other than Jesus-fucking-Christ asking you to rebrand his bell-end, I'm afraid I'm not going to understand.'

I bit my lip and pulled my handbag closer to my chest.

'Do you know Perito's Portuguese Chicken?'

CHAPTER 4

Accdording to a hastily scribbled note on the back of a Domino's Pizza napkin, Amy was out at a job interview when I got back to the house and where her other five flatmates were, I didn't care to know. Seizing my chance, I grabbed a semi-clean towel from Amy's radiator and ran into the bathroom, locking the door. Sharing a bathroom with six other people, even temporarily, was enough to do terrible things to your sanity.

'What am I going to do about Charlie?' I asked my liberated rubber duck, who had insisted on accompanying me into the shower as I turned on the blessed hot water. 'I do want to go to Milan but I really want to try for the pitch too.'

'Can't have it all,' he replied with a silent quack. 'But shouldn't you try to clear your messes up here before you go gallivanting off to Italy? Are you moving in with Charlie? Why haven't you called your mum? And how long has it been since you shaved your legs?'

'I don't think me or Charlie are ready to move in,' I said, wondering whether or not that was actually true. It was only now that I realized how long it had been since I'd shaved my legs and he hadn't complained about them once. 'And my mum hasn't called *me*, has she?'

It was fair to say my mother and I hadn't exactly parted on the best of terms the last time I'd been to visit.

'You need to call her and you know it,' the duck said.

Annoyingly, he was right. She might be a passive-aggressive pain in the arse but she was *my* passive-aggressive pain in the arse and the fact that we hadn't spoken since our argument was starting to weigh on me.

'And of course,' Rubber Ducky wasn't finished with his truth bombs, 'you're still thinking about Nick. Even though he hasn't called you back.'

'I am not!' I snapped before realizing I was lying, not only to a rubber duck but also to myself. 'But so what if I am? He told me to call and now he won't speak to me. What if something has happened to him?'

'Is that what you're telling yourself now?' he asked.

'Fuck off.'

The 'he must have died or he would have called' rationale. Keeping single women delusional since the invention of the telephone.

'I just don't understand why he would ask me to call him and then not call me back.'

'Could always move in here,' Rubber Ducky suggested, changing the subject. 'There'll be a free room at the end of the month.'

'I can't live here.' I shuddered at the thought as the water began to cool without me touching the thermostat. With still unshaven legs, I conceded defeat and turned off the shower. 'No one should have to live here. Amy should have moved out years ago.'

'I'm not arguing with that,' he said. 'This bathroom is disgusting. You're going to have to make a decision about something and soon. I'm not showering in here again.'

Wrapped in my not-really-big-enough towel, I opened the bathroom door, trying to keep my vagina covered, and gave the rubber duck my best side eye.

'Duly noted,' I replied. 'I'll see what I can do.'

'Hello?'

Somewhere on Parsons Green high street, en route to meet Paige on a shoot, I found the courage to call my mother. But my mother didn't answer. Even though their voices were almost identical, I knew at once it was my younger sister, the eternally put-upon middle child, Mel.

'All right,' I said with a cough. 'It's Tess.'
'Well.'

The ability to put that much weight behind that one word was a skill she had learned from our mother. I only got the boobs and the hair; Mel had inherited the whole passive-aggressive package.

'Is Mum there?' I was trying to keep my voice light in the hope that they had all forgotten me storming out of the house two weeks ago. Of course, it would have made more sense to hope I would bear witness to the second coming of Jesus but still, it was nice to be an optimist.

'She is.' She quickly switched to a yell that was entirely unnecessary given the size of my mother's house. 'Mum! It's Tess!'

'And what does Tess want?' I heard Mum yell back.

'She wants to know what you want,' Mel relayed faithfully.

'Can I just speak to her, please?' I asked. My tolerance levels were dropping with every passing second. 'It'll be quicker.'

'I'm very well, thanks for asking,' she said. I had not caught my favourite sister in a good mood. 'She says she wants to speak to you!'

'Maybe I don't want to speak to her,' Mum replied, sounding very pleased with herself. 'I haven't forgotten what she said when she walked out of this house.'

'She says—'

'I heard what she bloody said.' I cut Mel off before she could finish, wondering whether it wouldn't be easier to just throw myself off the Westway and hope a passing bus was there to finish me off. 'And I haven't forgotten. I'm sorry for losing my temper and I shouldn't have walked out without explaining what was going on but I was upset.'

'She says she's really sorry and she shouldn't have walked out.'

'That's not exactly what I said, is it? Put her on the bloody phone, Mel.'

'Don't swear at your sister,' my mum said, finally on the line without an interpreter. 'You're not in the position to be calling my house and being all high and mighty.'

I closed my eyes and rubbed the spot in the middle of my forehead that felt a tiny bit like it might actually explode. Still, better an aneurysm than an apology – that was the Brookes motto. Or at least it should be.

'I wasn't swearing at my sister—'

'Yes, you were. I've got ears, you know.'

Breathe, Tess, breathe.

'I didn't mean to,' I corrected myself. 'How are you?'

'As if you're bothered,' Mum huffed audibly down the phone. 'After that scene you caused.'

The scene she was referring to wasn't so much 'a scene I had caused' as a scene caused by my sisters hanging me out to dry by telling my mother I had lost my job at Donovan & Dunning, at which point she had chucked a glass of red wine across the room and got into a screaming row with Amy. In the middle of a christening. Amy had of course diffused the situation by climbing onto a table and holding the baby aloft while singing *The Circle of Life*. Amy was wonderful.

'And you're the one who walked out and said you were never coming back.'

It was good to know she'd run everything through

her own filter and come up with her own version of events. History was written by the winner. The winners and their mums.

'I'm sorry,' I said as calmly as possible. There was no point in getting into another row; the only thing that would work here was blanket apologies. 'I didn't mean it. I was being stupid.'

'Yes, you were.' Clearly not enough apologies yet. 'You sounded like you were off your head. Charlie says you're not doing the heroin, though.'

And if Charlie said so, it must be true. The only person who had had a bigger crush on Charlie for the last decade was my mum. Mostly, it only manifested itself in overly maternal smothering when he went with me to visit, but I always felt a bit bad for my stepdad whenever she started pawing my best friend. Poor, lovely Brian. Patience of a saint, that man has.

'I'm not doing heroin, I was just made redundant,' I explained, the words still sticking in my throat. Me. Redundant. Bleurgh. 'And it wasn't only me, the whole company went under, so it wasn't anything I did.'

'There's no need to be defensive,' Mum sniffed. 'No one said it was your fault.'

Another historical revision: that was exactly what she had said. Loudly, while throwing wine glasses around at a christening.

'Hang on, if the company has gone under, what is Charlie doing?'

Deep, cleansing breaths.

'Charlie is fine, Mum,' I said. She was practically hyperventilating on the end of the line. 'He's setting up his own agency. We're actually talking about doing it together.'

'Oh, Tess!' And just like that, her tone of voice altered completely. 'Your own business? With Charlie? Well, that sounds like a very good idea. Would he be your boss, then?'

'No, Mum, we'd be partners,' I said as calmly as possible. Why had I called her again? Was I worried that my inevitable stroke wasn't coming on quick enough? 'He would run the client side and I would do the creative.'

'I'm sure Charlie knows what he's doing,' she said, entirely turned around. 'Mel, have you heard this? Charlie is starting his own advertising agency and giving Tess a job. She's going to be the head of his creative.'

I heard some approving, disinterested noises in the background and decided it was time to wrap things up while I was, relatively speaking, ahead.

'OK, that's really all I called for,' I started. 'To say sorry and—'

'You should both come for Sunday dinner,' Mum declared, cutting me off mid-escape. 'You should drive up and tell me all about it.'

'I can't Sunday.' Oh, there was that throbbing in the forehead again. I stopped short on the edge of the pavement to let the number 85 bus go by.

'And why not?' she asked.

'I won't be here,' I said, wondering whether or

not throwing myself under the number 85 bus might not have been a bit easier than having this conversation.

'Not here? What does that mean?'

Don't tell her about Milan, don't tell her about Milan, don't tell her about Milan . . .

'I'm going to Milan.'

Oh, fuck me.

'What are you going to Milan for?' Mum shrieked so loudly that even the nice old lady coming out of Costa could hear her. 'You haven't got time to be gallivanting around on holiday when Charlie's trying to start a business.'

'I'm actually going for work,' I said, taking a deep breath and trying to work out how to phrase this. 'I'm taking some photos for someone.'

'What have I told you about this photography nonsense, Tess?' she said after one too many moments of silence. 'You don't let a hobby get in the way of a career. We had this conversation a long time ago.'

In truth, there had never really been much of a conversation. I had loved taking pictures when I was growing up – it was one of the few things I had shared with my dad before he left us to have another go at starting a family – and I'd begged my mum to buy me a camera of my own when I turned eighteen. But whenever she found me poring over photography books, or looking at my pictures, she would pop up with a snide comment or a stark reminder of how hard it was to make

72

it in a creative field, that a proper job was much more secure and the right thing to do. I'd believed her, of course, and put my camera to one side to concentrate on my marketing degree, but the passion had always been there. Maybe it was buried deep under PowerPoint presentations and the desire for a company pension, but it was there.

'And they're paying you to take photos, are they?' she asked.

'Yes,' I said, hoping for another number 85 bus.

'With what, magic beans?'

'Honestly, Mum, it's a long story.' At least she couldn't accuse me of lying on that one. 'And I really have to go now but I'll call you later and tell you all about it, yeah?'

As if it was going to be that easy.

'I've got to say, I think you're making a very big mistake. Charlie's offering you a job on a plate and you want to fanny off to Italy and take photos. Italy!'

She applied the same emphasis to 'take photos' as someone else's mum might to 'sacrifice virgins'.

'But if you want to waste your time on silly adventures, you go ahead and do it,' she said with a cluck, apparently done with the conversation. 'Give my love to Charlie.'

As if it was going to be that easy.

CHAPTER 5

'I'm glad you've been keeping busy,' Paige said, completely ignoring the four half-naked men to her left, after I brought her up to speed on my current predicament. 'You can't help but get into trouble, can you?'

'You know me,' I replied, staring at the four half-naked men to Paige's left. 'I like to keep myself occupied.'

'What was it like, getting arrested?' she asked. 'Did you have to wear an orange onesie? Orange would look terrible on you.'

I nodded, not entirely sure what I was agreeing about while four of the most handsome men I had ever seen, all wearing black eye masks and very little else, hoisted one of the most beautiful women I had ever seen high above their heads. I gazed at the photographer's big, beautiful Nikon camera with so much envy, I thought that it might fly up into the air and land in my hands. It didn't.

'You know, this is incredibly distracting,' I said, turning fully in my chair to peer over the mezzanine onto the set below. We were in a very fancy studio on a very fancy street in a very fancy area and I was terrified of touching anything. 'How do you ever get any work done?'

'This, my love, is work,' Paige said, curving her scarlet lips into a very happy smile. 'I'm the art director. I'm directing the art.'

I nodded, resting my chin on the balcony and trying not to gawp. Paige worked for *Gloss* magazine, coming up with the ideas for photoshoots and executing the creative. We had met in Hawaii and, after a few teething problems, she had come to my rescue more than once and, as everyone knows, a friendship forged in the fires of adversity is as strong as one that has weathered the test of time. Or something. One of the models caught me staring and flexed his pecs while flashing me a grin. This was the best reason I had come up with to get into fashion photography so far.

'What are they doing exactly?'

'It's a lingerie shoot for the October issue,' she explained. 'Halloween vibe – hence the masks. But given that most women will never look like that girl in just their knickers, I thought it might soften the blow to chuck in something easy on the eye.'

'Or four somethings,' I clarified. 'Are they their *actual* abs? They're not drawn on or anything?'

'You know, sometimes the photographer casts the models,' she said. 'And that photographer could be you.'

I gulped.

'Look, only you know what you really want to do,' Paige said, slapping me gently on the arm. 'I really haven't known you that long and I've only seen you as a photographer so I can only comment on that; and my comment is, you've got a raw talent not many people have. If it's something you really want to pursue, now is the time. There won't be many more opportunities like this. Make the most of it.'

I tried to make myself look away from the orgy of muscles and hair gel below and concentrate, my heart thrumming at the words 'raw talent'.

'I know it looks obvious from the outside,' I said, playing with the hem of my stripy T-shirt. 'But I really do love advertising. Maybe it doesn't sound as sexy and exciting as being a photographer, but it is to me. It's not like I was looking for something to save me from the dark, depressing days of a real job. Starting my own agency was something I used to dream about and let's be real, it's a more sensible option than starting out as a photographer at twenty-eight; it's definitely more secure.'

Paige nodded slowly. 'Starting out in the business isn't easy,' she admitted. 'I'd hire you though.'

'Thanks,' I said with a smile.

'You'd be cheap,' she added.

'Thanks,' I said without a smile.

'So, only you can answer the question.' Paige shrugged her shoulders, sending her long curtain of blonde hair cascading down her back. I made a mental note to ask her which conditioner she used before I left. And then to scalp her. 'Is it going to be photography or advertising?'

'That's not really the question though, is it?' Amy barrelled up the stairs behind me and blew into Paige with a hug so aggressive, anyone would have been forgiven for thinking she hadn't seen her in ten years. It had been three days. And that was the first time they had ever met. Five seconds later, she dropped Paige in a heap and hurled herself across the sofa to treat me to the same hello.

'You got my text then?' I choked when she finally let me go. Amy nodded, her black hair glossy under the studio lights and her polka-dot shorts riding up dangerously high as she leapt up and threw herself towards the mezzanine railings.

'Fuck me,' She spun around to face us and pointed down at the shoot below. 'I'll take the blond. Or the brunette.'

'Which one?' Paige asked.

'I don't care,' Amy replied. 'This is *amazing*.'

'Didn't you have a job interview today?' I asked. 'How did it go?'

'Shit,' she said, pinching the tight skin above her exposed belly button. 'It was for TopShop. They wanted me to work weekends. And they kept asking me whether or not I thought I was reliable and professional.'

'Well, yeah, I think most Topshops are open on the weekend.' I didn't bother to ask if that was what she had worn to the interview because I already knew that it was. But what did I know? Maybe nothing said 'please give me a job in fashion retail' more than denim polka-dot shorts and a cropped pink T-shirt bearing the slogan 'It's not me, it's you'. I think you're reliable and professional.'

It was a lie. I thought she was reliable when it came to turning up on my doorstep with a bag full of Galaxy and three bottles of wine, but I thought she was horribly unreliable and, if possible, even more unprofessional when it came to keeping a job. And mostly I thought that because it was true. In and out of retail jobs, a brief flirtation with teacher training and a puppy love infatuation with the idea of becoming a twenty-first century Avon lady, Amy had a commitment problem when it came to work. And men. And everything else on earth.

However, that didn't seem like a helpful opinion in that moment so I kept my mouth shut and smiled. Amy gave me a cheerful grin in return and slipped her arm through mine. Ours was a long-term love affair. We'd been friends since before we could talk and some days I wished we could go back to those times. Like now.

'That is very good to know,' she said with a big grin. 'Because I've been thinking. You clearly can't work out whether to shit or wind your watch without help so I'm coming to Milan with you.'

'No you aren't,' I said, stunned.

'I am,' she corrected. 'I'm going to be your assistant. Like that lady down there.'

I peered over the balcony and saw an exhausted, harangued-looking girl rubbing oil into one of the model's chests.

78

'You might actually need an assistant,' Paige said, shrugging. 'And god knows, you do need a life coach. Like, all the time.'

'And that's what I'm here for.' Amy spread out her arms with a flourish. 'I can fetch, carry and make sure you don't ruin your life, all at the same time.'

'Amy, I—'

'I'm a great multitasker,' she added, nodding at Paige.

I sat and stared at my best friend, clicking the tips of my bitten-down fingernails together.

'Tess . . .' Amy reached across the sofa and took both my hands in hers. 'It's going to be awesome.'

Why did her words sound more like a threat than a promise?

'I'll have to clear it with my agent,' I muttered, accepting defeat far too easily. I'd never been able to say no to Amy. It was like denying a pitbull puppy a treat. So little and cute, you couldn't bear to turn it down and you kind of knew that if you did, it would rip your hand off and take it anyway.

'Now, are we still pretending to talk about work? Is this yours?' she asked me, letting go of my hands and reaching over to grab a full-to-the-brim glass of white wine from the coffee table. 'Amazing, thank you.'

'What else would we be talking about?' Paige asked, straightening her pink silk top and grabbing her own wine to get it out of Amy's reach. It was nice to see the new friends had at least one thing in common: getting hammered in the middle of a work day.

'Nothing,' I replied as fast as I could, quietly glad that Amy had taken away my wine. I was not a good drinker. 'One hundred per cent work talk only.'

'If you really want to go for the advertising job as much as you say you do, maybe you should go for it.' Paige casually glanced over at the shirtless men, flickered an eyebrow and shook her head. 'Photography won't be the easy option.'

'Yeah, and maybe you could even go from working six days a week to the full seven?' Amy replied. 'I'm sure it would only freak you out to have to spend your birthday with your friends instead of in the office. Or Christmas. Or New Year.'

'You work over Christmas?' Paige looked horrified. Then took a drink. Then looked horrified again.

'No, it's fine,' Amy said, waving her hands and her wine around in the air. 'Tess isn't normal. Tess is a martyr. She's happiest when she's miserable.'

Paige nodded. 'That explains why she went for Nick.'

'I'm happiest when I'm busy,' I said before Amy could pounce on the mention of his name. 'There's a difference.'

For the want of a better plan, I picked up an empty glass and poured in a couple of slugs of wine. I was not a big drinker for good reason. More than three drinks and I could not be held responsible for my actions. More than four and I couldn't remember them anyway. But this definitely felt like a legitimate wine-to-the-rescue moment. Amy took hold of my wrist, raising the glass to my mouth, and I drank obediently, disappointed in my appalling lack of willpower.

'How do you feel right now?' Paige asked. 'If you had to make the decision right now, pick one and never do the other ever again, which would it be?'

'I don't know,' I said, wishing I didn't see Nick and Charlie in my head when she asked that question. 'I had a plan, you know? I knew where I was going and I knew what I wanted. And now it's like, boom! decision time. But if I make the wrong decision, what happens then? I'm buggered. Completely buggered and miserable and I die alone with seventeen cats all called Steve. It's too hard.'

'Have I missed something? How does picking the wrong job leave you as a crazy cat lady?' Paige looked swiftly from me to Amy and back again. 'Were you drinking before you got here?'

'She's not drunk,' Amy said, patting my hand as though I was a deranged nana. 'She's just not really thinking about the jobs, are you?'

'Oh, bloody hell.' Paige rolled her eyes. 'And we were doing so well at avoiding the subject of cock. OK. Hang on a sec, I just need to set up this last shot and then we can get trashed and talk about this properly.'

Trashed? I looked at my watch. It was barely even three o'clock.

Amy looked at me with a 'well?' expression, an already empty wine glass in her hand. I genuinely didn't know where she put it; the woman was miniscule and drank more than Lindsay Lohan on the average Thursday.

'What?' I picked up my glass and gave my wine one more sip. 'Spit it out.'

'Have you explained it all to Charlie?' she asked.

'No.'

'Have you heard from the other one?'

'No.'

Just then, my text message alert sounded loudly in the bottom of my handbag and every internal organ jumped. Even my spleen wanted to know who was it was from. It was Charlie.

One by one, my organs settled back into their usual positions, consoling each other on their way down. I didn't know why I was surprised. Nick wasn't going to call. Nick wasn't going to call. Nick wasn't going to call. And no matter how many times I told myself that, it did not feel any better.

'Speak of the devil,' I said, my voice unexpectedly scratchy. 'Charlie wants to know where we are.'

'Tell him to fuck the fuck off, we're talking *about* him, not *to* him,' Amy replied. 'You thought it was Nick, didn't you?'

'It's fine,' I said for the millionth time, tapping out a quick message to Charlie. 'Everything is fine.'

'So,' Paige reappeared at the top of the stairs with her hands on her annoyingly slim hips, 'can we please get to the bottom of this?'

'Yes please.' Amy cocked her head to one side and squinted at me. 'But we've been going too easy on her. Tess, quick-fire decision time: Charlie or Nick?'

'There *is* no decision to make.' I could hear my voice rising along with my blood pressure as I spoke every syllable. 'You know we're not talking about him.'

'The name Nick is *verboten*,' Amy explained to Paige. 'I'm not allowed to mention him, even though she's been checking her phone to see if he's called every other second since Monday night.'

'Well, *I* haven't agreed to that,' Paige replied. 'So she's going to *have* to talk about it, isn't she?'

'Can I have another drink, please?' I asked, holding out my suddenly empty glass.

'What do you want?' She reached over to the small fridge beside her. 'Wine, champagne, beer, Pimm's in a can – ick – or I think there's some vodka in the freezer? I bet one of the models is holding, if you want anything else.'

'Holding what?' I asked.

'Bless her, she's very naïve,' Amy said, rolling off the settee and crawling into the fridge to grab the other bottle of white. 'So, Nick or Charlie? If you had to marry one and throw the other off the side of a boat?'

'Why are we having this conversation when there is no Nick in the equation?' I asked. I hated myself for it but even saying his name out loud made me want to do a little cry. The sharp 'k' sound at the end of his name seemed to hang in the air forever and I felt like I'd been punched. 'There is only Charlie.'

'And if this was three weeks ago, you would be jumping up and down and picking out Tiffany engagement rings by now,' Amy replied. 'So how come you're sitting here, drinking Paige's wine with a face like an arse instead of at Charlie's, drinking his wine and throwing out all his porn?'

All four of the male models looked up at us with their blank, handsome faces. The female model didn't even blink.

I blinked. I refilled my glass. I sighed. My daydreams of being in love with Charlie and Charlie being in love with me rarely got as far as domesticity and I felt like a dog that had been chasing a car – I finally had what I'd always wanted and now what was I supposed to do with it?

'I know I should be stashing my pink toothbrush next to Charlie's toothbrush and doing a happy dance,' I said. 'I don't know what's going on with me.'

'You're such a liar.' Was it just me or did Paige look a little bit annoyed? 'Just admit it.'

'I need time to think about things.' I was not going to say it. 'Charlie was totally cool about it.'

'Good for Charlie,' she replied. 'I don't want to be biased or anything, but I've got to be honest, I really don't see any competition. I know Nick is hot and everything but Tess, he's such a twat.'

'I know,' I nodded. There was that sick feeling

again. Why did I want to defend him? She was right, after all.

'And Charlie fucked up, he did, but he's only a man,' she went on. 'Vanessa is hot and we've only got to look at Angelina Jolie to know that men have no control over themselves when it comes to hot women. Brad cheated on Jen because of a hot woman. On *Jen*, Tess, Rachel from *Friends*. Do you see what I'm saying?'

'Sort of . . .' I frowned.

'You weren't together when it happened, you know. You can't hold this against him forever.'

'I bet I could,' Amy said. 'Charlie's not good enough for you.'

'And what's not good enough?' I asked, coming over all spikey and defensive on Charlie's behalf. I was giving myself emotional whiplash. 'The fact that he's sweet and caring and funny? That he's always been there for you and me whenever we've really needed him? That he comes home with me so I don't have to deal with my mum on my own? Shit, the fact that he's met my mum and still wants to be with me should be reason enough to put a bloody ring on it.'

'Fine, I'm convinced,' she replied. 'After ten years of you giving him the puppy dog eyes, Charlie Wilder is the world's most amazing man, apart from when he's being a thoughtless shithead, and has finally woken up and realized that you are the absolute dog's bollocks and that he wants to make an honest woman out of you, conveniently

85

at the exact time you're looking elsewhere. He wants what he suddenly might not be able to have. Awesome.'

'It's not like that,' I said, wondering whether or not it might not be a little bit like that.

But Amy wasn't finished. 'And regardless of how you feel about Charlie and regardless of how many phone calls or emails you have not received, you cannot sit there and tell me you don't have feelings for Nick which, at the very least, says something about your feelings for Charlie.'

It was altogether too close to home.

'What have I told you about using the "N" word?' I pulled my feet up underneath me, burrowing into the settee.

'And you can't keep referring to him as "the N word",' she said. 'People really aren't going to be OK with that.'

'What's happening with him anyway? You called him and he hasn't called you back?' Paige was trying to look supportive but I knew it was a strain. After all, she had history with Nick and much more of a history than I did, even if it was a history of rejection.

'Pretty much.' I shook my head. 'But what's the point anyway? It was a holiday fling. He didn't even know my real name, for God's sake. This is real life: Charlie and the agency and chicken cook-in sauces. Maybe that doesn't seem as glamorous and exciting to everyone as Milan and photoshoots, but it's exciting to me. And the

Charlie thing . . . It's throwing me because I've wanted this for so long and now maybe I have it. How would that not be confusing? To anyone?'

'That's how I felt when I got my first Chanel 2.55 bag,' Paige nodded with genuine sympathy this time. 'It was like "can I actually take this out? Can I actually use this?" It's hard.'

'You're both fucking mental.' Amy was not big on Chanel bags or metaphors. 'And Tess, I know how long you've been in love with that cockwomble, but you're not the kind of girl who only wants what she can't have. I should know, because I am. So if you're not champing at the bit to shack up with Mr Wonderful, there's a good reason for it and I don't believe it's just nerves. I think you've got real feelings for Nick and I don't think you can ignore that.'

'How can I have real feelings for him?' I asked, burning up. 'I only knew him for a week. And he didn't really know me at all.'

It was a question I'd been asking myself a lot, only Amy and Paige didn't realize it was rhetorical. I did have feelings for him – big, scary feelings that I didn't understand and, in all honesty, did not want to. I'd always been so safe and secure in my feelings for Charlie but every time I thought about Nick, my stomach clenched and my hands made tiny fists and I wanted to hit something. Preferably him. I wanted to go to sleep and wake up with nothing but my über-crush on Charlie back the way it was. Everything would be so much simpler.

'To be fair, you did lie to the man about your entire existence while merrily shagging him senseless,' Amy said. 'Even after he bared his soul to you. I might take a few days to call you back for a chat, to be fair.'

'He bared his soul?' Paige looked less than impressed. 'You mean, he pulled out some of his cheesy old lines?'

'There were cheesy lines in the beginning,' I admitted, not wanting to come to his defence but entirely incapable of stopping myself, 'but there was a certain degree of soul-baring after a bit. Maybe not baring, maybe it was more like soul-flashing.'

'What a knob,' she breathed, taking a big deep drink of her wine. 'Him, not you.'

'It's starting to feel like it never happened.' I flipped to the sent messages in my phone and saw his name over and over. I wondered what would give out first, his refusal to reply or my dignity. 'Every morning when I wake up, it feels more and more like I was never in Hawaii, like he never existed.'

'Don't upset yourself over it,' Paige said, shifting in her seat. 'I'm sure it was all bullshit. I don't know if that man is capable of anything other than trying to get into a woman's pants.'

Paige had known Nick a lot longer than I had and I was fully aware that she had tried very hard to get into his pants, and not the other way around. And that didn't make this conversation awkward at all.

'Bottom line is,' Amy shrugged and emptied her second glass of wine, 'something is stopping you from moving on with Charlie. Something's got you stuck. That something is Nick.'

'Paige, can you come and check these shots?' the photographer bellowed from the set below. With a very grumpy look on her face, Paige dutifully stood up and marched down the stairs.

'Shout if the models need oiling. The male models,' Amy yelled as she went before turning her attention back to me. 'I know I haven't been entirely Team Charlie when it comes to you two being together-together but if you tell me this is what you really, really want, I will shut my mouth, buy you a shit housewarming present and never say the "N" word again. But you have to be entirely honest before you get yourself into something you might regret.'

'You really have got to stop calling him that,' I sighed.

There it was again. What did I want? 'I don't want to ruin everything because of a holiday romance hangover.

'Life isn't a Choose-Your-Own-Adventure book, Amy,' I said. 'If I cock this up, I can't just go back to the end of the last chapter and try something else.'

'Oh, Tess,' She smiled and hugged me, squeezing my shoulders tightly. 'That's *exactly* what life is: nothing is set in stone, nothing has already been decided. That's where you've been going wrong all these years.'

'Am I interrupting something beautiful?' Charlie's

voice broke through our Kodak moment, making Amy jump and spill my wine before I could drink it. Which was probably best. 'Don't let me stop you, I always knew there was something going on with you two.'

'Didn't I tell you not to tell him where we were?' Amy jumped to her feet, kissed him on the cheek and bounced off downstairs to the set. 'Just because she'd rather be in bed with me than you. No need to be jealous, Wilder.'

'Amy,' Charlie nodded. 'Always a pleasure.'

He clambered onto the settee, all arms and legs and coppery curls, looking like a sexy hipster Bambi man.

'I see she's taking this well?' he said, pulling the strap of his man-bag over his head and setting it carefully on the cushion between us. 'Everything all right?'

'Everything's fine.' I nodded with too much enthusiasm, not sure what to do. Normally we'd have hugged by now or I'd have taken the piss out of him for his jeans being too skinny or unfastened the second button of his T-shirt because one wasn't enough and three would be too many. Instead, I put my wine glass down and sat on my hands. 'You had a busy day?'

'I played football manager for about three hours and then I remembered outside existed so I went out and got you this.' He pulled a blue carrier bag out of his messenger bag and handed it to me with a flourish. 'Sorry it's not wrapped.'

'What is it?' I asked. I bloody loved presents. Surprises not so much, but presents? Yes, please.

'Open it,' he said, his smile almost bigger than mine. 'I hope it's right.'

Inside the bag was a box and inside that box, was a camera.

'Oh, Charlie, you didn't!' I tore away the packaging as carefully as I could and pulled out a brand-new Canon camera. It was almost identical to my old one, lighter and shinier and with fewer bumps and bruises on the body, but the buttons were all in the same places and she fell into my hands as though I'd known her forever. 'You can't have!'

He inched over on the sofa and squeezed my knee, his huge hand covering half my thigh in the process. 'I can and I did,' he said in a low voice that made every inch of my skin prickle. 'And you're going to go to Milan and take amazing photos of Mr – I forget his first name – Bennett and his clothes and whatever else you want to take amazing photos of and you're going to be amazing at it.'

'But the pitch?' I looked up at him and then at my camera, my beautiful camera; beautiful, beautiful Charlie. 'It's only a week away.'

'Yes it is,' he said as I reached out to unfasten his second button; I couldn't look at it for a moment longer. Charlie covered my hand with his and I felt a warmth wash over my entire body. 'But I don't want to wake up next to you every morning, not knowing whether or not you're wondering "what if?" because I know you'd never say anything. So I'm not giving you the chance to regret this. OK?'

Just when you thought you knew everything about someone, they had to go one better.

'This is amazing,' I said, cradling the camera in my lap and leaning over to give Charlie the biggest hug I could muster. 'You're amazing.'

'I'm all right,' he replied. 'And let's be honest, I'm just trying to warm you up for later.'

I looked away so he wouldn't see me blush. We'd always flirted with each other but now I knew I was going to have to follow through, I couldn't seem to keep the colour out of my cheeks.

'I talked to my mate at Perito's this morning,' he said, squeezing my knee. 'He's going over to Portugal with his team on Monday and he asked if we wanted to go along, meet the founders of the company and all that.'

'But Milan?' I held my camera tightly. 'And you hate flying?'

'I told him you were already otherwise engaged,' he said, fiddling with his newly opened button. 'But I said I'd go. Double scotch and some positive thinking and I'll be OK. It's got to be a good sign, hasn't it?'

'It's an amazing sign,' I agreed, a twinge of jealousy in my chest that I wouldn't get to go along. Not that I didn't have an adventure of my own to worry about. 'I'm really excited.'

Admittedly, I didn't sound *that* excited but I was

somewhat distracted by what was happening below us in the studio.

'Is there any point in asking what's going on down there?' Charlie asked, nodding at the set downstairs.

Amy had done a fine job of making herself useful. I watched as she merrily rubbed moisturizer into the chest of one of the male models, bouncing from foot to foot, while Paige was on all fours on the bed, demonstrating a particularly uncomfortable-looking pose for the female model, who still looked bored. Gorgeous, but bored.

'There is not,' I replied, turning my back on it all and looking back down at my lovely camera again. 'This really is amazing, you know.'

'Doesn't really feel like the right time to get all heavy . . .' He gestured over to where Amy was now rubbing lotion into the chests of two men at once with her eyes closed. 'But I wanted you to know I'm serious about this. And that I'm going to do whatever I can do to make you happy. It's all I can think about, that we should be together. You're what I care about.'

I still couldn't quite believe what I was hearing. 'More than Arsenal?' I asked, doubtful.

'Let's not go completely crazy.' He ran his hand through his already messy hair and grinned. It was so fucking adorable, my heart almost exploded. 'But getting there, at the very least. So, can we go?'

'Go?'

'Home?' he said, taking the camera out of my

hands and slipping it back inside the box. I fought the urge to slap his hands away – given that he had paid for it in the first place I supposed he was allowed to touch it. 'I've cleared out two entire drawers. For you.'

Oh yeah, he'd asked me to move in. And while I hadn't said no, I hadn't said yes, either. In fact, if I recalled correctly, I'd said I needed time to think. I rested my hand on the camera box and breathed out slowly, confused by the thought that it might not be a lovely, thoughtful gift but a very expensive pat on the head. Had he just assumed I was going to move in? That I was going to say yes to joining the agency?

'I said I'd stay with Amy tonight,' I said. 'She had a job interview today and it didn't go very well and she's stressing out so . . .'

'She doesn't look that stressed,' Charlie said, disappointment all over his face. 'Are you sure? I was going to cook for you.'

'Now I'm definitely sure!' I took the camera, safely back in its plastic bag, and gripped the handles tightly. My precious camera. My precious, emotionally loaded, symbolic camera. 'No offence.'

'None taken. I know I can't cook for shit,' he said with a shrug. 'To be honest, I was hoping you'd take over halfway through anyway.'

'Because I'm such a domestic goddess?' I stood when he stood, leaning into a kiss that still felt strange. Lovely, but strange. 'I'll call you tomorrow.'

'Will you though?' Charlie pulled his Oyster card

94

out of his bag and stuck it in his back pocket. 'Because I've heard that one before.'

'Odds are good,' I confirmed. 'I'd say better than fifty per cent.'

'OK. Tess?' He stopped halfway down the stairs and looked back up at me, all pale skin and big eyes and wide, happy mouth.

'Charlie?' I sat back down on the settee, happily stroking my camera. I was probably overreacting. He wasn't trying to force me into a decision I wasn't ready to make. That wasn't Charlie at all. He wouldn't do something like that.

'I love you.'

My eyebrows shot up so high I assumed they were forever lost in orbit around the earth.

It was hardly the first time the 'L' word had left Charlie's lips and found my ears but this was different. This wasn't the same as when I brought him an Egg McMuffin because he had a hangover or called him an Addison Lee because he was too lazy to get the night bus from mine. This was a legitimate 'I Love You'. This was my first ever 'I Love You'. I had no idea what to do.

'OK,' I replied, nodding and trying not to be sick. 'That's brilliant.'

Charlie scratched his head and I knew he was waiting for me to say something else but my mind was completely blank. Charlie Wilder had told me he loved me and I had no words. None of them.

'OK,' I said again.

And then it was happening again. I felt myself

95

leaving my body and floating up into the corner of the room, watching as I stared blankly at the first man to tell me he loved me.

This is where you're meant to say 'I love you too,' my brain whispered.

And I knew that. I'd been waiting for this moment forever. But I didn't say it. Instead, I smiled brightly and gave him a double thumbs up.

'That's brilliant,' I said.

'OK,' he echoed, staring at me from the top of the stairs. 'Brilliant.'

And then he was gone.

CHAPTER 6

'**I** cannot believe you gave him a thumbs up!'
Out of everything I'd ever done, nothing had tickled Amy quite like this.

'*Double* thumbs up,' I corrected. 'It was a double thumbs up.'

'I'd take that if it were me,' she said, heaving her first enormous suitcase off the luggage carousel at Malpensa airport, barely blinking at the fact it weighed almost as much as she did. Agent Veronica had assented to my bringing her to Milan as my assistant with only four 'fuck you's and one use of the 'c' word. It was as though she was starting to like me. 'Charlie Wilder finally drops the L bomb and you give him the double thumbs up and say thank you. Thank you!'

'I didn't say "thank you",' I said, looking for my own sad little bag. A hasty patch-up job with duct tape meant it was very, very recognisable. 'I said, "brilliant" and I haven't heard from him since. Now, can we agree to never speak of it again?'

'What did you expect him to do?' she asked as she pulled up the suitcase handle and leaned forward, using it as a chin rest. 'Propose? "Oh, I

97

just told a girl I love her and she said 'Brilliant' so I should totes put a ring on it?"'

I thought about it for a second. 'Yes.'

'And you gave him a double thumbs up,' Amy stretched her arms over her head and smiled. 'Good job on getting the camera out of him first.' The camera. He gave me a camera, told me loved me and I gave him the thumbs up. What a knobhead. 'You can't really be surprised that he's pissed off, can you?'

I shrugged, eyeing my case as it rattled along the conveyor belt towards me. Half the size and a third the weight of Amy's case; I couldn't even begin to work out what she had brought with her.

'No,' I protested, grabbing my case and wrenching my still-sore shoulder as I pulled it from the belt. 'Of course not. But I didn't think he'd be so flippant about the whole thing.'

'He isn't being flippant.' She pushed her hair out of her face and sighed. 'He's being *hurt*. This is what hurt looks like. Isn't it obvious?'

Honestly, my hurting Charlie was an entirely new concept. I'd spent so long nursing my unrequited crush that the thought that I could actually damage his feelings was a bit of a mind-blower. But she was right.

We'd spoken on Saturday night when I called, determined to make things right between us before I left for Italy. Unlike a certain other man I would not name, Charlie answered his phone when I called it. But similarly to Mr Unmentionable, he wasn't best pleased with me. I was met with a variety of one-word responses to my every question, and when I finally suggested we get together for dinner as I was leaving for Milan in the morning, he declined, citing prior plans for his mate's birthday. Since I had been his social secretary forever, I knew it really was Robbo's birthday, but I also knew when Charlie was pissed off. And above all else, I knew a man would never put the thirty-second birthday of a passing acquaintance above the opportunity for a shag. Not that I was planning to shag him, but clearly my track record of declining a sleepover wasn't fantastic in these situations. After blowing me off, he switched to the pitch, telling me he was leaving for Portugal on Monday morning and that I should email him my stuff for the pitch so he could work everything up for Friday, then hung up. No 'have fun', no mention of us living together, no mention of his declaration of love, no mention of my appalling response to said declaration. He was all business.

As was quite obvious to everyone alive, I was not an expert in men but I was an expert in Charlie. He was clearly furious. The only time he'd been this cold to me in the last decade was when I accidentally washed a pair of his jeans that had tickets to the FA Cup final in the back pocket. That resulted in almost a week of stony silence but he soon came round when he needed help picking a birthday present for his then girlfriend. Suffering the indignity of trying on lingerie that was going to be worn by a woman who was sleeping with the man I believed was the only possible father to my future children felt like more than enough punishment for denying Charlie the opportunity to see Arsenal lose on penalties in extra time.

But knowing he was perfectly justified in his huff didn't help me. It still felt overwhelming – starting a business, moving in together, the first 'I Love You' *and* a chicken cook-in sauce? Who did he think I was, Beyoncé? I was an organized person who liked a plan, and in my head I had always imagined these things happening in a timely, organized fashion. I'd waited ten years – why did they all have to appear at once?

'This is good timing,' I said, wiping away an errant tear that had crept out of nowhere before Amy saw. Stupid eyes. 'This slows things down. We'll both be so busy this week, we won't have time to stew on stuff. And when I get back, it'll all be OK.'

'Totally healthy reaction,' Amy said, shoving her passport in the back pocket of her hot-pink jeans. 'You're so on top of this.'

'I'm a grown woman,' I replied, pulling her passport out of her back pocket without her even noticing and placing it safely into into my travel wallet with my passport. 'I can make my own decisions.'

My suitcase was light to the point of embarrassment, compared to Amy's gargantuan twosome. All I had packed were comfy jeans, a few T-shirts and shirts and a couple of jumpers in case it got cold at night, even though I had been soundly assured by Agent Veronica that Milan in July would be 'fucking roasting red hot like the seventh circle of hell' and that she would rather hang herself by her own ovaries than 'spend a second in that shithole'. It wasn't all boring though; I had been to M&S and bought two new packs of pants especially for the trip. It hardly mattered what I wore on my nether regions, since Amy was the only person who was likely to see them and, given my natural tendency to be a never-nude, that tended to be unplanned and against my will anyway.

'So,' Amy waved at a driver holding a board showing my name and waited for me to find my feet, 'what would you do if you turned around and Charlie was stood on one side of the airport and Nick was on the other?'

'Turn back around and keep walking?' I said, still breathless. 'Oh Jesus Christ, they're not are they?' I hardly dared move.

'Well, Charlie isn't,' she shrugged. 'And since you apparently managed to spend a week in playing photographer without taking a single bloody shot of Mr Miller, I don't know what he looks like, do I?'

'If you're going to tell me you haven't googled him,' I nodded at the driver as we trotted towards him, overly excited to see my own name badly written in wonky black marker, 'I'm going to call you a liar.'

'Do you have any idea how many Nick Millers there are in the world?' Amy said. 'Not including a character in a very popular sitcom?'

'A few?'

Secretly, I was pleased that she'd had a hard time finding him. If Amy had got so much as a peek at Nick, we wouldn't be in Milan right now. We'd be wherever in the world he might be so she could hunt him down and force us down the aisle with a shotgun.

'You're a pain in my arse, Brookes,' she muttered. 'I never tell you a story without visual aids.'

'Yeah, and if you could stop texting me pictures of your one-night stands while they're sleeping, that would be brilliant,' I replied.

With a big wide smile, Amy turned and gave me a double thumbs up.

'OK,' she said. 'That's brilliant.'

'Remind me again why I brought you with me?' I asked my alleged best friend, fighting the urge to punch her in the face.

'Because you love me,' she said, weaving her arm through mine, as our driver piled our bags onto a trolley. 'And you couldn't possibly survive another adventure without me.'

'Totally should have brought Paige,' I mumbled to myself as we walked out of the air-conditioned airport into a heat that almost made me crumble to my denim-clad knees. So this was the seventh circle of ovary-hanging hell Veronica had talked about.

'Warm out,' Amy said, sliding on her sunglasses. 'This is going to be fun.'

'It's going to be something,' I replied, looking for my own sunglasses in my handbag and having a sudden flashback to leaving them on top of Amy's dresser in the rush to get her out and into the taxi that had been waiting for us for twenty minutes. 'It's definitely going to be something.'

'Oh my God!'

Amy hadn't stopped talking since customs so it was a testament to just how impressive Bertie Bennett's Italian home was that it had managed to shut her up so successfully. Even when I had explained that the clouds that looked so much like mountains were, in fact, mountains, she hadn't stopped for breath so the look of dazed amazement that had come over her now was wonderful to behold for many reasons. From a best-friend perspective, I was happy to see her look so happy. From a human-being perspective, I could have cried with joy at the first moment of silence in over an hour.

As the car pulled off the road and a pair of huge iron gates swung open to allow us inside, I pressed my fingertips against the window of the car. When I'd arrived at Bertie Bennett's house in Hawaii, I thought I had accidentally wandered into heaven. The wonderful modernist architecture, the sea, the sand, the way the air smelled so sweet and welcoming. But this was something else; this was like something I had only seen in fairytales. One moment we were on a perfectly normal-looking city street while Amy regaled the driver with tales of her latest urinary tract infection and the next we were sitting in complete silence and rolling into the courtyard of the most beautiful, stately building I had ever seen.

When I was sixteen, my entire class had gone on a school trip to London and I distinctly remembered being more than a little bit disappointed by Buckingham Palace. Not that it wasn't impressive; but my imagination had been ruined by too many Disney movies, so it had too many corners and not enough turrets for my liking. But this place? Al's Milan pied-à-terre made Buck House look like a two-up, two-down council house.

It wasn't that it was enormous or sprawling or set in acres of artfully landscaped grounds, it was just impossibly beautiful. The house was elegant and simple with so many big, sparkling windows I couldn't even count them all. Everything was symmetrical, which brought out the ecstatic OCD in me and I kept looking up to the top floor, expecting to see a princess combing out her hair on one of the balconies. Passing through the gate, the car came to a halt in the courtyard, a stone fountain bubbling away in the centre, more archways leading off to small but perfectly formed manicured lawns, decorated with trees and plants. Gorgeous to look at, but just like his super-modern home in Hawaii, entirely inviting. Nothing about this storybook palace said 'do not touch'; it was far more 'feel free to take off your shoes and run around barefoot and would you like a bottle of wine and a straw while you're doing that?'

A white-glove-wearing footman opened the passenger door and I climbed out of the car, eyes still skyward, taking in each of the three levels of Al's second home. Unlike Hawaii, there was endless activity behind each of the arched windows. I could see people rushing around from one room to the next, curtains pulled back and windows thrown open. Clearly, someone was in a rush to get ready for something.

'Tess?' Amy peered at me over the top of the car, wavering on her tiptoes. 'Are we in the right place?'

'I don't know about you,' I replied, watching the huge wooden double door creak open to reveal a familiar face. 'But I'm pretty bloody sure that I am.'

'My darling!' A short, handsome man with coffee-coloured skin and impeccably parted jet-black hair rushed across the courtyard, barrelling past assorted staff members who were trying to go about their business, and scooped me up in an impressive hug. Mostly impressive because I was at least five inches taller than him. *Aloha!*

'Kekipi!' I hoped he wouldn't find the fact I still had my feet on the ground as awkward as I did. *'Aloha.'*

Nestling his head into my boobs, he looked up at me and grinned. Apparently he did not find it awkward at all. 'Now are we Tess or Vanessa today?'

'Tess,' I said quickly. 'Today, tomorrow and until the end of the world.'

'That could be tomorrow if things don't calm down in there.' He gestured back towards the house before turning his attention to Amy.

My bestie was vibrating with barely restrained giddiness and not for the first time since I'd invited her along on this trip, I wondered whether introducing the two of them was, in fact, an incredibly bad idea.

'You must be Amy the Assistant.' He decided to forego the formalities of introductions and planted two big kisses on Amy's cheeks. 'I like you already, you make me look tall.'

The first time I met Kekipi, it had been in an entirely official capacity and even though the pretence of professionalism fell by the wayside relatively quickly, something was definitely different this time. Gone was the black uniform he had sported as the estate manager of Bertie Bennett's Hawaiian hideout, and in its place was a bright aqua-blue trousers and hot-pink shirt combo. In fact, Kekipi's shirt coordinated with Amy's jeans so well, you would have been forgiven for thinking they had planned their outfits together. Which I imagined would be happening daily from tomorrow morning.

'We're so glad you decided to come,' Kekipi said, waving for two men in light grey trousers and white shirts, apparently the official ensembles of the Milanese Bennett household, to whisk our

106

suitcases out of sight. 'It's been a very dramatic week. Senior and Junior have not been getting along at all and Senior is having what can only be described as one of his "artistic" moments.'

'Is that good?' I asked, following him into the entranceway of the house. Kekipi pursed his lips and shook his head.

I'd met Al's son, Artie, in Hawaii and he was a curious man to say the least. There was a lot of tension between them, and while I loved Al with a fierce and fiery passion reserved for the very best grandpa substitutes the world had to offer, clearly something was up between father and son. Plus, Artie had a handlebar moustache, and given that he did not work at a circus, that made me immediately suspicious.

'While I am pleased to see him so active after such a long time,' he replied with an arched eyebrow, 'he needs to calm down a little. He isn't as young as he used to be and Mr Bennett the younger isn't nearly as tolerant of his father's whims as we might all like.'

'Where is Al?' I asked, trying not to trip over my feet as I tiptoed across the beautiful, intricately tiled floors, my shoulders unrolling as the air conditioning washed over me. 'Is he here?'

'We arrived yesterday,' Kekipi confirmed. 'He's in his room, working, working, working. He'll be at dinner later.'

When I finally forced my eyes off the floor, I saw that there were flowers everywhere. Every surface held vases upon vases of beautiful, freshly cut blooms, all of them in shades of white and peach.

'Are these for me?' Amy asked, plucking a white rose from a vase and placing it behind her ear. Reaching out to grab the banister of an elaborate, twisting staircase, I fought off a flashback. Nick, a single flower, the waterfall . . . 'You shouldn't have.'

'I didn't,' Kekipi said with unmistakable disdain. 'Don't get me wrong, I know the value of a good floral arrangement but this is all Domenico's doing.'

'Domenico?' I asked.

'Miss Brookes.'

A tall, slender man descended the staircase in the requisite grey trousers, a matching jacket and added slim black tie. How he was wearing a suit and tie in this weather was beyond me – I was sweating so much I looked as though I had entered a wet T-shirt competition. But while he looked every inch the perfect butler, his stiff demeanour felt at odds with the make-yourself-at-home atmosphere of Al's palazzo.

'Domenico,' Kekipi said with a flourish. 'The estate manager here in Milan.'

'He's the Italian you?' I asked, wiping my hand on the back of my jeans and achieving nothing more than making a sticky situation stickier.

'Please,' Kekipi sniffed. 'I've never been so offended.'

'Miss Brookes.' The tall man greeted me with three air kisses, very carefully avoiding touching any part of my actual being. Not that I blamed

108

him but it did make things feel ever so slightly awkward. 'I am Domenico, Mr Bennett's number two here at the Palazzo Della Stelline; we are so pleased that you have arrived.'

He turned to Amy and gave her a small bow, no kisses.

'And you are Miss Brooke's assistant?'

She looked at me, looked back at him and shrugged. 'I suppose I am.'

Uh-oh. Clearly not impressed.

'Excellent. I have rooms prepared for both of you in Mr Bennett's most beautiful guest apartments. I would be very happy to show them to you if you would be so kind as to follow me.' Domenico gestured up the stairs with an elaborate flourish of his arm and a far-too-wide smile. I'd seen waxworks show more authenticity.

'I'll take the ladies to their rooms,' Kekipi said, knocking Domenico's hand to his side and sweeping his hair from his forehead. 'What time is dinner?'

'Mr Bennett has suggested the ladies dine with him in the grand salon at seven,' he replied, bowing his head graciously. 'If you require anything at all before that time, please do let me know. Pressing 1 on the phone in your room will connect you directly to housekeeping and they will be happy to help you with whatever you might need.'

Kekipi stood on the first step of the staircase behind his Italian counterpart and clutched the wooden banister, eyes narrowed, knuckles white. He was seething.

'And we will dine downstairs.' Domenico turned to give Kekipi the full weight of his stare. Even though he was standing on the stairs, Kekipi was still the shorter of the two but height difference wasn't going to be enough to win this battle. 'Afterwards.'

'OK, Mr *Downton*,' he said, hand on hip. 'Maybe Artie likes to keep things upstairs downstairs but I'll be eating with Mr Bennett and the ladies in the dining room at seven. And I'm lactose intolerant, so keep that in mind while you're preparing your feast. Ladies.' He snapped his fingers and pointed up the stairs. 'Follow me.'

'Tess, he's fabulous,' Amy whispered. 'He's the most best gay man I've ever met. And I've met all the gay men, fabulous or otherwise.'

'I think he might actually be the best man, gay or otherwise,' I replied. 'Just wait until you get him to do karaoke. He's a God.'

'Thank you so much, Domenico,' I said, repeatedly dipping in mini bows as we scooted around him and up the stairs after Kekipi. 'I'm sure we'll be fine. But thank you. And for dinner. Thanks.'

'Stop thanking him,' Kekipi yelled without looking back. 'It's his job.'

'Thank you,' I mouthed.

'*Prego*,' Domenico said with a small smile. 'You're welcome.'

'So what was that all about?' Amy asked as she and Kekipi bounced up a second staircase and along the hallway on the third floor. 'You two don't get on, I take it?'

'I've been with Al for a very long time,' Kekipi explained, linking arms with Amy as they trotted on in front of me. I dawdled behind, running my fingertips along the heavy patterned silk that lined the walls.

'When the Bennetts purchased this palazzo in the late seventies, it was Jane, Mrs Bennett's, passion project. She renovated the entire place, designed the gardens, the colour schemes. She spent years pulling together the furniture . . .' His voice grew soft with recollection as we turned a corner into an identical hallway. It was like being lost in a beautiful hall of mirrors.

'But when Jane became sick, Al wanted to keep her in New York, near the best doctors, and eventually, they retreated to Hawaii almost altogether. Since he lost Jane, Al has barely left the island. He spends a little time in New York when he must and I always travel with him to ensure he is well looked after in a manner he finds comfortable but Mr Bennett Junior, for the last fifteen or so years, has spent the majority of the year here in Milan, tending to the business. He hired Domenico.'

'So this is Al's son's house?' Amy asked as Kekipi came to a halt at the end of the hallway in front of a pair of white double doors. 'And Domenico is his guy?'

'The house still belongs to Al,' Kekipi clarified, pulling a key out of his pocket. 'But without Jane, he hasn't seemed interested in visiting for a very long time. Domenico does a very good job of looking after the house while we are away and he takes excellent care of Mr Bennett Junior but we have differing management styles. As I said, Al and I have worked together for a very long time, we have been through so much. Domenico thinks he's top dog because he manages a palazzo. He thinks I'm some simple islander who is only good for organizing a luau and mixing drinks.'

'You are very good at both of those things,' I said. 'But you know you're more than that. Don't rise to it.'

'So wise for one so young,' he sighed. 'I knew I liked you.'

'How come Al wanted to come back now?' Amy asked. 'What's happening here that has convinced him to leave Hawaii? Because I'm totally happy to get on a plane to Hawaii and help out over there if he changes his mind.'

Kekipi gave us both a small smile and slipped the key into the elaborate gold lock on the door before him.

'I imagine all will be revealed at dinner,' he said, turning the key and pushing open the door. 'Or at least, all that Al is ready to tell us. Are you ready to see your rooms, ladies?'

'Oh. My. God!'

It was the second time in the same hour that the building had silenced Amy. I was really starting to like this place. Following her into the bedroom

– and only jumping very slightly at Kekipi's friendly slap on my arse – I understood what had got her so excited. Our 'rooms' were incredible. The ceilings were twice as high as mine at home and huge, airy windows opened out onto the street below, standing watch over the park across the way. Just like the house in Hawaii, most of the furniture was white and overstuffed but in every corner, I spotted a different antique – a beautiful wooden writing desk, an elegant mirror, a painting that clearly hadn't come from Ikea; Jane Bennett's signature style was everywhere I looked. But where were the beds?

'Tess, I have you in this room,' Kekipi said, opening a second set of double doors on his left. Oh. The beds were in the bedrooms. Of course. My room was dominated by a beautiful wooden four-poster bed, draped in the softest-looking white linens, and over by the window was another beautiful-looking antique desk, topped by a brand-new shiny Mac. 'I had them install whatever photography software it didn't have,' Kekipi said, waving at the computer. 'I wasn't sure whether or not you would have everything you needed.'

I crouched down to peel off my Primark ballet flats and let my feet sink into the plush carpeting. It was like walking on a polar bear. Not that I had ever walked on a polar bear.

'And Amy, you are across the salon.' He gestured towards the other set of double doors on the opposite side of the room. Amy ran across and threw the doors open, squealing in incomprehensible delight. 'As Domenico mentioned, you only need to press 1 to reach the housekeeper should you need anything at all, and I'm on 219 if there is anything only *I* can help you with.'

'What's the karaoke scene like around here?' I asked, ignoring Amy's screeches.

'Abysmal,' he sniffed. 'But we'll make our own fun. Besides, you've got tales to tell me before we start singing songs. Unless you're going to begin with the Ballad of Mr Miller?'

'Unlikely,' I said with a wan smile. 'But I could give you a catchy disco number called "my best friend told me he loved me but I didn't say it back and now I'm dead confused".'

'Most of Beyoncé's songs have one-word titles now but I'm sure we can work with it,' he said. 'That's definitely a story that needs a cocktail. Meet me downstairs in a little while? An adult beverage after dinner, perhaps?'

'Sounds wonderful,' I agreed. 'And you can tell me more stories about Domenico because I know you have them.'

'Quite.' Kekipi kissed both my cheeks with two very noisy, very non-Domenico smacks, handed me two suite keys, one for me, one for Amy, and closed the salon doors behind him.

'Tess, get in here!' Amy bellowed from her room. 'Come and look at my bath! It's massive! I can swim in it! Can we swim in it?'

'I'm not coming in if you're naked.' I hesitated

in the doorway, waiting for confirmation that she was still at least semi-dressed. 'We've talked about this.'

'I'm not in there yet, knobber.'

And she wasn't. She was bouncing on her bed, trying to touch the canopy with her fingertips.

'I feel like I'm in *Beauty and the Beast*,' she breathed, dropping onto her arse and falling backwards to spread eagle across the enormous mattress. 'Do you think they'll adopt me?'

'Maybe you could marry Artie,' I suggested.

Amy shot upright, eyes wide open.

'Is he single? Is he straight? Actually, that doesn't matter – is he single?'

'I will be in my room, working,' I said, ignoring the question. Sometimes it was all you could do. 'Try to stay out of trouble.'

'You don't need me to help?' she asked, looking a little crestfallen. 'Because I'm totally ready to assist the shit out of you.'

'Go for a swim in your bath,' I said, heading back into my own room. 'I'll see you in a bit.'

Closing the door, I took in a very deep breath and let it out as slowly as I could. Across the room, a huge mirror showed me a picture of a girl who looked just like me, only not quite. I smiled and she smiled back but it wasn't the confident, self-assured look I was hoping to project. I hoped that would come in time. I was calm. I had this.

Pulling my phone out of my handbag and setting

up the charger by my bedside, I checked quickly to make sure Charlie hadn't tried to call. Of course, he hadn't. When I thought about the look on his face after I gave him a bloody thumbs up, I felt sick. He had every right to be furious with me. By the time I saw him again, he would understand and I would be over the shock of the whole thing. After all, I did love Charlie. I'd loved Charlie before he had loved me, I was so in love with him that I couldn't remember what it felt like not to be in love with him. So why couldn't I say it back?

Once my workstation and bedside table were all set up, I threw my suitcase onto the bed. Compared to Amy's bags, it felt completely empty. It was only when I unzipped it, I realized it felt like it was completely empty because, aside from two packs of Marks & Spencer's knickers, it *was* completely empty.

'Amy!' I was shouting. I knew I was shouting but I could not stop myself from shouting. I stared at the bare black lining of the suitcase. 'Where the fuck are all my fucking clothes?'

'Calm down, potty mouth,' she trotted into my room, calmly dragging one of her enormous cases behind her. 'Don't be angry with me but I had a look at what you'd packed while you were in the shower this morning and honestly, I didn't think you were doing yourself any favours, so I packed another case for you. Ta-da! And you're welcome.'

I stood, I stared, I did not speak.

'I know you were all about monochrome

116

non-statements in the office,' she went on, dropping into a cross-legged pile in front of her suitcase and reaching around, giving it a huge hug as she fiddled with the zip, tongue sticking out the side of her mouth in her best Miley impression. 'But we're in Milan now, Tess. This is fashion, right? I talked to Paige when we were at the shoot the other day and she was telling me how Milan has all the amazing, out-there couture and that it's like, the most fashion-forward city and then I looked in your case and it was just a bit sad.'

'So you thought I could make a fashion-forward statement by going out in my pants?' I picked up one of the five packs and threw it at her as hard as I could. Which sadly wasn't nearly hard enough.

'You've got to have pants,' she replied, throwing them right back. 'I'm not completely mental.'

'And what about my bras? And my pyjamas? And all my fucking clothes, Amy?' I was not calm. I did not have this. More importantly, I did not have any clothes. 'Oh my God, Amy, oh my God.'

'You're wearing a bra.'

'Women need more than one bra,' I shouted.

'That's crazy,' she replied, shuffling her own, perfectly formed, bra-less A-cup boobs inside her T-shirt and pushing up the lid of her case to reveal a rainbow fancydress box of nightmares. 'I told you; I packed a case for you from my stuff. This is going to be loads of fun. Take you out of your comfort zone a bit.'

'It might have escaped your notice but I'm

already outside my comfort zone!' I was shouting again. 'I'm in *Milan*. And since when were you an expert in *haute couture*?'

She pouted. 'Did someone in this room not have an interview at Topshop two days ago?'

'Oh, that's it, I'm going to kill you!' I raised my hands and let them clap back against my sides before I could actually attack. It would be a crime to get blood on this gorgeous carpet. 'I can't believe you've done this to me.'

'I'm going to go back to my room and let you look through this stuff.' Amy shuffled onto her feet and folded her arms in front of her. 'You can thank me when you've calmed down. Oh, and so you know, I did pack your sad toiletry bag in there so you know, you're welcome.'

All I could think was that Amy was very lucky that my shoulder was still sore from falling out of a window or she would have been waking up at the bottom of a river, inside her bloody suitcase. This was ridiculous. I pawed through her outfit selections, trying not to cry. There wasn't a single thing in here that I would ever, ever choose to put on my body, even if it had fitted me, which next to none of it would. Amy had once described traditional clothes sizing as 'fascist' and refused to be boxed into a number or a letter 'dictated by the man' but that was a very easy stance to take when you were a size six and had what could be loosely defined as an eclectic fashion sense.

At five ten with a little waist, big arse and giant

boobs, I tended to have a bit more respect for the difference between a size six and a size sixteen. Unless I was planning to wear a hessian sack, I couldn't just throw something on and belt it in the middle. Mounds of glitter, neon, sequins, feathers, leather and pleather oozed out of the suitcase like the magic porridge pot but I might as well have been sitting here with a bag full of Christmas crackers. I couldn't wear any of these clothes; Al and Kekipi would think I'd lost my mind. I also couldn't wear any of these clothes if I wanted to keep my midriff and the bottom third of my arse cheeks covered. Oh, and wait for it, right at the bottom was the bloody neon unicorn T-shirt. Of course. I pulled it out and looked at the gurning quadruped, my bottom lip quivering.

'Better wash this out,' I said, peeling off my white V-neck and closing the suitcase, blinking back tears. 'Every night for the next week.'

Brilliant. My first week as a professional fashion photographer and everyone was going to think my fashion icons were either Ian McShane in *Lovejoy* or a poorly dressed drag queen. It was the stuff dreams were made of.

Incapable of even looking at Amy without being moved to violence, I avoided her for the rest of the afternoon. Wearing my jeans and her friendly, ill-fitting unicorn T-shirt, I decided to spend my time getting to grips with my new camera in the gardens instead. Al's Italian home-away-from-home was truly wonderful. When I marched out of the bedroom, slamming the door behind me, I was certain nothing short of ritual sacrifice would calm me down but as soon as I was outside, in the courtyard, I felt better. For a moment, I wondered if I'd finally had that aneurysm I'd been worrying about and if this was actually heaven – but it couldn't be. Surely, if there *was* a benevolent God, he wouldn't make anyone spend eternity in this T-shirt?

Stepping into the sunshine and looking back on the building's façade made me feel like a princess. And not the real-life Kate Middleton variety; no, the legit, wide-eyed, long-shiny-hair-and-a-waist-too-slim-to-contain-all-the-necessary-vital-organs Disney variety. Actually, maybe they were the same, it was very hard to tell. The gardens were made up of small squares of courtyard, some laid with flagstones and decorated with fountains and urns filled with beautiful trees and plants and others were laid with lush grass and had vines running all over the walls that surrounded them. Almost all of them had narrow arcades running down the sides, with endless repeated archways supporting the palazzo above and providing shady spaces to hide from the sun.

My favourite was the smallest of all the spaces I discovered. Unlike the rest of the gardens that flowed into each other, this one was hidden behind a wooden door and a sandy yellow wall. Inside it looked as though no one had been in here for centuries, even though, from the look of the shiny sprinkler system and ashtray with two dead cigarette butts, clearly someone had. But still, even if there had been other visitors, I couldn't help but be reminded of *The Secret Garden*, one of my favourite books when I was little. I loved reading about Mary and Colin and Dickon, working away in their own private hideaway, bringing the garden back to life.

Sometimes, when my parents were arguing or my sisters were being less than sisterly, I would go to the bottom of our garden and climb over my dad's wheelbarrow and the old pots of paint he still hadn't taken to the tip, and pretend that the little square of scrub between the shed and the hedge was my very own secret garden. It was a perfect plan until our neighbour busted me 'borrowing' a couple of pansies from his back garden and grassed me up to my mum. But now my mum was far away and there was no one to drag me inside and make me scrub my hands until the dirt had washed away from under my fingernails and the skin was red and raw. I snapped away, working out the setting on my new camera, fiddling with the flash, the exposure, trying to get used to the bright summer light. Even though Hawaii had its share of sunshine, it hadn't seemed as harsh as it did here in Milan. At least here in my garden, there was enough shade to stop me from burning off every layer of skin. Note to self: buy sunscreen. Along with sunglasses and an entirely new wardrobe.

Glancing upwards, I noticed a balcony at the end of the building on the third floor. My room was at the end of the building on the third floor. With all the nonsense over my case, I hadn't even looked out of my own window. Retracing my steps through the courtyards, I finally found my way back to the main entrance of the house and bolted back up the stairs and down the hallway to my suite. Panting more than I would have liked, I ran over to my window and pulled aside the curtains, blinking down into the sunshine. There it was, my secret garden, right outside my bedroom. Only it seemed it wasn't just my secret any more. There was a man sitting at the small, wrought-iron table in the corner, flicking his cigarette into the ashtray I had found.

I slipped back behind my curtains, not hiding but not wanting to be seen. Had he been outside my garden the whole time? Had he heard me singing 'A Whole New World' considerably louder than I would have if I'd known there was another human within fifty feet? Something in my stomach tightened as he rested his cigarette in the ashtray and stretched his arms up high, linking his hands behind his ashy blond head.

It couldn't be.

'Get your shit together, Tess,' I told myself, forcing my shaking hands to steady themselves, and held my camera up to my face. 'And now open your eyes, you daft cow.'

I prised my left eye open and forced myself to

122

look through the viewfinder, trembling as I zoomed in. The focus blurred in and out, settling into sharp reality just as the man in the garden looked up towards my window. Pressing my back against my bedroom wall, I breathed in and closed my eyes. That was how you made yourself invisible, wasn't it? I heard my pulse pounding in my ears, the blood rushing around my body so fast and making me so dizzy that I couldn't trust my legs. I grabbed at the camera strap around my neck, pawing desperately. I threw it onto the bed and bolted into the bathroom just in time. My knees gave way and I fell in front of the toilet, just in time to be so incredibly sick.

Panting heavily and wiping my clammy forehead with the back of my hand, I tried to turn and wedge myself in between the toilet and the corner bath. Well, I thought, still shaking and wiping my mouth with the back of my hand. Surely it couldn't be the first time a girl had thrown up at the mere sight of Nick Miller?

CHAPTER 7

'Hello, my girl.'

I heard a warm, deep voice speak from the end of the table before I saw him. It was Al, my fairy godfather, resplendent in a dark three-piece suit and white shirt. Beside him sat Kekipi, similarly suited and booted but opting for a more Kekipi-ish cream-coloured fabric that set off his tan a treat. Apparently we were dressing for dinner.

And when I said we, I did not mean me.

I was wearing my jeans and a long-sleeved black T-shirt with a low back and, formerly, a sequin trim on the sleeves that had been relatively easily hacked off with a pair of nails scissors. It was the only half-decent option I had found in Amy's suitcase of horrors and incredibly upset about it I was too. This was not the outfit I would have chosen to be wearing when I went one-on-one with Nick Miller. Obviously, the outfit I would have chosen would be the dress I had worn at my recent wedding to Ryan Gosling. Sadly, I was stuck in baggy old jeans and Amy's T-shirt. Score.

'Hello!' I opened up my arms to Al for one of

the best hugs in the business, keeping one eye open to scan the rest of the room over his shoulder but there was no one lurking in the shadows, no one waiting with a snarky comment, just Kekipi, tipping me the wink.

Nick wasn't there.

I breathed out for what felt like the first time in hours, relieved, disappointed, sick to my stomach. I wanted to see him so badly, I could taste it; I wanted to take my eyeballs out and rub them all over him so I would never forget exactly how he looked, sitting in the garden, smoking that cigarette.

'I am very glad to see you here.' Al pulled out the chair beside him and waited for me to sit down, his eyes twinkling in the candlelight and late evening sun. 'And how lovely you look.'

'I didn't know we were dressing up,' I replied, taking my seat as a waiter appeared to pour my water before disappearing just as quickly. There seemed to be an awful lot of cutlery surrounding my eighteen million plates and four glasses. What was I going to do with four glasses?

'I had a bit of a luggage malfunction.' I gestured down at my jeans and pulled a face. 'Fingers crossed I can do better tomorrow.'

'Luggage malfunction?' Kekipi asked, slapping another waiter's hand away to pour my glass of prosecco himself. 'Sounds scandalous.'

As with the rest of the house, the dining room was predictably beautiful, but instead of the high ceilings everywhere else in the palazzo, I looked

125

up to see the sky. The dining room was outside. Even though it was inside. Mind. Blown. The dining table was right in the middle of the room, covered in more white and peach flowers, roses this time, and the whole space was lit with candles.

'Amy decided to pack for me,' I said. 'So I need to go shopping. Without her.'

'Milan's best boutiques are right on our door-step,' he said. 'We'll go in the morning.'

I nodded, deciding now wasn't the time to get into the difference between Milan's best boutiques and the nearest H&M. Sipping my water, rather than the prosecco, I tried to peep around the room as subtly as possible. Definitely just us. And the invisible waiters.

'Are you looking for someone in particular?' Kekipi asked.

I looked at him sharply.

'Should I be?' I asked, combing my hair behind my ear and lowering my voice into a hiss. I'd been calling his extension for hours and he hadn't replied once. It was hard to concentrate on half an Italian episode of *Game of Thrones* when you were as pissed off as I was. I had not had a restful afternoon.

Kekipi shrugged and I dug my fingernails into my palms so sharply, I was worried I had magic-ally developed Wolverine powers.

The double doors opened once more to reveal Amy, wearing the leftovers from Molly Ringwald's prom dress in *Pretty in Pink*. Her polka-dot skirt

126

entered a full three seconds before she did, clashing impressively with the peachy tones of the dinner table.

'Hi!' She tiptoed over to the table in matching pink Mary Janes and white ankle socks. 'I'm not late, am I?'

'Not at all.' Al rounded the table to kiss the back of Amy's hand and pull out her chair. 'I apologize for not being here to meet you earlier; I am Albert Bennett, and please call me Al. So happy that you were able to come along on the adventure.'

'How could I not?' she said, settling into her chair with a prolonged rustle. 'Tess had such amazing stories about her visit to Hawaii that I wouldn't have missed this for anything. And you know, she needs a chaperone.'

'So this is Amy.' I glanced over at Kekipi who was clearly already utterly in love. He was so fickle.

'What are you wearing?' she whispered as the main doors opened again to allow four waiters carrying elaborate platters to the table. 'That's supposed to be a dress.'

'Maybe on you,' I hissed back. 'But unless everyone at the table wants to see my womb, it's a shirt on me.'

'Still, you could have dressed up a bit,' she muttered. 'I love Al's beard.'

'It's a brilliant beard and don't you start,' I warned her as the platters were placed on the table, full of cold meats and cheese and God knows what else. 'Are we waiting for anyone else?'

'Artie can't join us this evening,' Al replied with a barely detectable edge to his voice. I couldn't work out if he was annoyed or relieved. 'So I believe I have you two ladies all to myself. So, Tess, remind me exactly where we left things in Hawaii? What's been happening with you?'

'I'm sure no one wants to hear about that.' I waved my hand, waiting for someone else to start eating so I could stuff my face with prosciutto. The service might be super formal but I was happy to see the actual meal was going to be suitably casual.

'She came home, she made up with Paige, called Nick like a million times but he hasn't called her back, so now she's sort of going out with her mate, Charlie, and he wants to start an advertising agency but I think she's mental to do that when she could be doing this. Oh, and Charlie told her he loved her and she gave him a double thumbs up.' Amy paused to take a breath. Just one. 'And, oh, she got kicked out of her flat and then arrested for breaking and entering and fell out of a window, which sounds worse than it is because it's actually quite a funny story. I swear to God.'

The entire table stared at her in silence.

She raised her glass to her lips, peering at me over the edge. 'What?'

'Thanks,' I said with a bright smile. 'That was concise.'

'What?' she reached over and grabbed a piece of bread, much to Kekipi's delight. 'You didn't break your neck or anything. They didn't put you in prison; you're not in Holloway. Or Rampton.'

'What's a Rampton?' Kekipi asked, nothing on his plate and rapture in his eyes.

'Prison for mentals,' Amy answered.

'It's a maximum-security hospital for the criminally insane,' I said, piling my plate high with meat. 'So yeah, we're all relieved I'm not there.'

'Yet,' Amy added.

'It sounds as though you've done a fine job of keeping yourself busy,' Al said, spooning some olives onto his plate. 'I'm glad you could fit me in.'

'It wasn't a difficult decision,' I lied, not wanting Al to think I didn't want to be there. 'There's a lot of stuff going on but I'm really excited to be here. Super excited about your project.'

'As am I,' he replied. 'It's something I've been thinking about for a long time but I needed someone to give me a kick up the backside to get it started.'

'Kekipi?' I said.

Al smiled as he swallowed an olive. 'Of course not, it was you.'

It was me?

'It was *me*?'

'Of course you.' Al set down his knife and fork while Amy and I ploughed through the cheese platter. 'All those talks we had, you really made me think, Miss Brookes. Life is too short not to take chances when you get to my age and so I've decided to go for it.'

'Go for what, exactly?' asked Amy, through a mouthful of burrata. 'If you don't mind me asking.'

'Originally, when I asked you to come here, it was to shoot a retrospective of sorts,' Al explained. 'Taking those photos of Jane's clothes, it was wonderful. Really, it was the first time I've been able to take pleasure in fashion since I lost her.'

Amy sniffed loudly, pulled a very sad face and then shovelled another forkful of cheese into her gob.

'I thought what a glorious idea,' he went on, after offering Amy a consoling pat on the wrist. 'A beautiful book to catalogue all of my Janey's glorious clothes, all the fashions she chose for the store, all of the outfits that were important to us. Janey always said that clothes tell a story and what better story to tell?'

'I think that's a brilliant idea,' I said. He was right, I'd never been much of a clotheshorse but I remembered every last detail of every important outfit I had ever worn, good or bad. 'But, what are you thinking now?'

'I still want to do the book one day, a full retrospective, the history of it all,' he replied as the servers reappeared to take away the food, much to my dismay. 'But looking back made me look forward. I might have seen my best years but I'm not for the knackers' yard just yet. I'm not quite ready to go gentle into that good night.'

'What he's trying to say is, you created a monster,' Kekipi interrupted. 'I find him huddled over his

130

desk at two, three in the morning. He won't go to sleep, he won't rest in the day, it's all quite frustrating.'

'He's worse than having a wife,' Al said, scratching his beard and shaking his head. 'As you know, my son Artie is set on taking over the Bennett's retail business.'

'I do know that,' I confirmed. Artie had been quite clear about his ambitions the last time we had met. He had also been an obnoxious wanker, a trait he did not inherit from his father. 'So what does that mean for you?'

'It means starting again,' he said, the twinkle in his eyes turning into a burn. 'AJB.'

Amy looked at me, concerned. 'Isn't that something you can catch?'

'The initials stand for Albert and Jane Bennett.' Al sat back in his chair and unfastened the bottom two buttons on his waistcoat. 'My new fashion line.'

'That's amazing.' I said, both to Al and the servers who had reappeared carrying lots more food. 'You're really going to do it?'

'Janey always wanted to start her own line but we got so caught up running the shops and then Artie came along and before we knew what was happening, we were old and she got so poorly.' He nodded to a tall, dark-haired waiter to fill one of the glasses beside his plate with red wine. I wondered how many members of staff were rattling around the place; I had yet to see the same person twice.

131

'I was game at the time but once things had moved on,' Al said, swirling the wine around in his glass, 'I felt out of step with things. And Artie was quick to confirm that for me, as you can imagine.'

I smiled politely as the waiter filled another of my glasses with red wine and then drained my prosecco, so that I wouldn't have two full glasses of booze in front of me. Two glasses of wine would be fine. I couldn't possibly get throw-up drunk when I'd eaten a bakery's worth of bread and was about to go to town on what looked like the most delicious pasta I'd ever seen. My biggest worry was that my jeans wouldn't fit in the morning and then I really would have to wear the stretchy green and blue paisley mini skirt I'd found in my suitcase.

'But looking at Jane's clothes for the first time in so long, it occurred to me that maybe fashion hasn't changed that much. Or maybe I'm so old that my eye has come back in style, I'm not sure.' He spun a forkful of tagliatelle into his mouth, miraculously missing his beard. 'The idea of putting together a history of Bennett's made me think that we should be documenting this new venture from the very beginning. And that's why I need you.'

I felt myself flush a little, whether it was from the wine, the compliment, or the fact that it was still almost thirty degrees out and I was wearing jeans and a long-sleeved T-shirt, I wasn't sure.

'Not that I'm trying to talk myself out of the

job,' I said pushing my pasta around the plate. 'But you do know I'm not a real photographer, don't you? You could get anyone for this. Like – like a proper one.'

The fact that I could not actually name any proper photographers only confirmed to me that I was not one.

'I know you may not be as experienced as some photographers,' he corrected me, 'but I've seen your work and, more importantly, I've seen your passion. Do you remember that first day we met on the beach?'

I thought back. 'The day I wasn't watching where I was going and fell flat on my arse?'

'The day you were so engrossed in your pictures that you didn't even see me sat right in front of you,' Al said. 'You have a talent, Tess. And what's more, you bloody well make me laugh. I can't think of anyone else I'd rather have poking around in my business with a camera. I don't want a gang of strangers documenting my every move. I've thought about this. I only want people I trust in on this, people I like.'

'And there's nothing I would love more,' I said, meaning every word. 'But I don't want to let you down. I love taking pictures, I just don't know if I'm experienced enough to do you justice.'

Al reached across the table to take my hand. 'You are so determined to deny your passion. Why would you wish your life away on anything other than the thing you love?'

'Good question.' Amy spoke from behind her wine glass, her eyes rolling skyward.

'Amy hates my job,' I explained. 'In case you were wondering.'

'I don't hate her job,' she said, turning to address the gents. 'I hate that she has no life. I hate that I'll call her on a Saturday morning to go to the pictures that night and she's in the office and I hate that I call her on Sunday to see if she wants to go for lunch and she's in the office. Do you know she missed her own surprise birthday party two years ago? Tell them why.'

'They don't want to know why,' I said.

'Tell us why immediately,' Kekipi countered.

'My boss asked me to work on a special project,' I said, flashing Amy a warning which she duly ignored. 'That's all.'

'She cat-sat his incontinent Persian for three bloody days,' she shouted, slapping the table. 'Over her own birthday.'

I rubbed a hand over my face, only to get a palmful of smudged mascara. Brilliant.

'Professionalism and self-sacrifice are great strengths,' Al said, taking my panda hand in his. 'But perhaps it wouldn't hurt for you to take a little bit more time to see what makes you really happy, work out what lights the fire.'

He let go of my hand and patted it lightly, before turning his attention to the rest of the table.

'So, Amy.' She perked up at the mention of her name like a neglected puppy. 'I'm assuming you haven't been assisting my favourite photographer for very long. Tell me, what were you doing before she convinced you to run away to Milano?'

'Me and Tess grew up together and then we went to uni and I was going to be a teacher but I hated it and then I was engaged to this guy Dave who was lovely but it didn't work out and I probably should have broken it off earlier but you don't really know until you know, do you?'

Al and Kekipi stared at her, shell-shocked once more. Amy took a deep breath and started again.

'So we broke up just before the wedding, actually, but he's fine, he's engaged again and she's having a baby and I've been working retail mostly but at the moment I'm in between jobs, so Tess said, come to Milan and help, so I thought, why not go to Milan and help! So yeah, that's it really. Any other questions?'

I sipped my wine and sat back in my chair, smiling at my shoes, while Al and Kekipi stared at my best friend, completely speechless. There were only three things to know when dealing with Amy. One, never wear anything dry-clean only, two, never order anything you weren't prepared to share and three, never, ever, ask her a question.

Once she got started, she did not stop.

'Al's right though,' Amy said, following me along the hallway, Mary Janes in one hand, a full glass of red wine in the other. I couldn't bear to look in case she was spilling it on the carpet. I wasn't her mother; she wasn't my problem.

Oh God, I thought, fidding around in my pocket for the suite key, she so was.

'You're so dead set on doing what you think is the right thing you've actually convinced yourself it's what you want.'

I breathed in through my nose and reminded myself I was only moments away from locking the door to my bedroom, with Amy on the other side of that door.

'I'm not saying starting an agency wouldn't be exciting, I'm not saying Charlie isn't exciting,' she said with a look that suggested that was exactly what she was saying. 'I'm only thinking about how excited you were when you got your first camera. You were so happy. I can't think of anything else you've ever loved that much. Apart from me. And *The Little Mermaid.*'

'It is a genuinely good film with an important message,' I replied, unlocking the door to our suite. Someone had been in to straighten up. There was nothing I didn't love about this place.

'Yes, I know! It's about pursuing your passions.' Amy rapped me on the side of the head. 'Ariel takes a chance and risks everything to get what she loves.'

'No it isn't,' I said, pushing her away and kicking off my Primark flats. 'It's about determination. It's about knowing what you want and refusing to give up on it.'

Amy glugged her wine and attempted to place

the empty glass on a side table and missed. 'So you're saying that working eighty hours a week is the same as selling your voice to a sea witch?'

I picked the glass up and placed it down carefully. 'So you're saying that trading my voice for legs is the same as turning my back on my career to fanny about trying to be a photographer?'

'She's got legs!' Amy yelled as I turned and walked straight into my bedroom. 'Human legs! And we've only got three days!'

Closing the door behind me, I undid the top button on my jeans before it pinged off across the room and broke something. It would have been great to get some advance warning that there were going to be four courses at dinner before I stuffed my face with half a loaf of bread and hoovered up all the pasta. Not that the steak that followed wasn't delicious. Or the tiramisu. I just didn't need to eat again for another week.

'Tess!' Amy pounded at my door. So much for peace and quiet.

I opened it an inch, peeping through the crack.

'Me and Kekipi are going out for a drink, do you want to come?' Amy stood smiling sweetly with the living room phone in her hand.

I did want to go.

I wanted to ask Kekipi what was going on with Nick. Had I really seen him in the garden earlier or did I need to book myself in for a CAT scan? All though dinner, every time I'd try to raise the subject, Kekipi had moved the conversation on to something else. But now it was late, I was tired, I had more mascara on the back of my hands than on my face and so it was a no.

'You go,' I said, shaking my head. 'Don't take him to a karaoke bar though, I'm warning you.'

'You're sure?' she asked, looking more than a bit sad. 'Come on, we haven't had a night out in ages.'

'I've got to be up in the morning,' I reasoned. Al and I had made breakfast plans to talk business and I didn't think rolling in, stinking of late night McDonald's with sick in my hair would be a good way to start. Not that I'd ever done that. Cough. 'I wouldn't be a lot of fun. You go and bond with Kekipi, keep him out of trouble.'

She saluted and leaned in to plant a jammy goodnight kiss on my cheek. 'Understood, so get some sleep. Love you.'

'Love you too,' I said. 'Have fun.'

I watched as she skipped out the front door and waited to hear it close before shutting my own. She was exhausting but she was still the best. Shimmying out of my jeans, I picked up a hair tie and pulled as much of my hair as I could up behind my head.

'Tess!'

More pounding on the door.

'Amy?'

'Nice pants,' she commented, glancing downwards when I opened the door. 'I can't find my key. Can I borrow yours?'

'Yeah, of course,' I picked my room key up from its home on the nightstand and handed it over, knowing I would probably never see it ever again. 'See you tomorrow.'

More kisses, more love, and Amy and her polka-dot prom dress were gone.

Standing by the door, I played around with the five light switches I had found until I decided on my favourite arrangement: chandeliers off, desk lamp off, lamp on my side on, lamp on the other side off. Pretty lamp in the corner of the room on but dimmed. I wondered if Jane had put all these options in herself. Not for the first time since I'd met Al, I wished I could have met her.

'Tess!'

'Oh, for fuck's sake,' I muttered, opening the bedroom door on my best friend. 'What now?'

'You haven't got any cash on you, have you?' she asked. At least she had the decency to flutter her eyelashes at me. Her unsmudged eyelashes. 'I've got my credit card but I don't want to be a dick and have to go out to find a cash machine if we end up somewhere that doesn't take cards.'

I silently stalked over to my handbag and counted out the euros I had picked up at the airport while Amy had been busy trying every perfume in Duty Free.

'Thank you.' She took the cash and backed away without going in for a kiss. 'I'll bring you a present.'

'Don't bring me a present, just don't lose my key,' I replied, closing the door behind her with not quite a slam. If the stuff she'd put in my

139

suitcase was anything to go by, I really didn't want a present.

I sat on the edge of the bed in my knickers, counting slowly and waiting for the next knock. Knowing Amy, there would be at least one more thing. Sure enough, a few moments later there was another knock. I covered my hands with my face and tried not to laugh. This time she was getting a slap. A lovely, well-meaning slap.

I opened the door, ready to impart the slap of love but it wasn't Amy.

'Hi,' I said.

Nick didn't say anything.

Instead, he took a step forwards, forcing me to back up into my bedroom, and shut the door behind him. I looked up at him; with my bare feet he was just a little taller than me, setting us face to face, only inches apart. But staring into his eyes was too hard. His expression was impossible to read, hard and unsmiling. No one was going to accuse him of being in a good mood. And he still wasn't saying anything.

I tried to move my feet but I couldn't, tried to open my mouth but nothing came out. Instead I stayed where I was, arms glued to my sides and wishing more than anything that I was wearing something other than Amy's T-shirt dress and my M&S pants. Breathing in sharply, Nick took another step towards me and slowly exhaled, his breath warm on my neck. I realized my breathing wasn't quite so even, and as he raised a hand up

140

to my waist, I felt it becoming more and more ragged, more uncontrolled. He wasn't even touching me and I couldn't hold it together. His hand settled underneath my T-shirt, on my hip and burned through my skin. He always seemed to run a few degrees warmer than me but this time, it felt like he was melting right through me, as though I was turning to liquid where he touched me. I couldn't walk away but I could stand still. Ish. My toes curled underneath my feet and I padded on the spot, crossing my legs and making incoherent noises as Nick tightened his grip on me and raised his other hand up to my face. He traced his finger-tips along my cheekbone and reached around to the back of my head, searching for my hair tie. I stretched up to help him, needing the comfort of my hair to hide in but before I could find it, he pulled away sharply and slapped my arms back down to my sides.

'No,' he said, his voice low and dark. 'Stand still.'

I made a noise, not quite sure what it was, but entirely incapable of controlling it, and pressed my arms against my sides, my fingers digging into my thighs, and waited for him to take out my hair. I felt it before I saw it, because at some point I'd closed my eyes, but it didn't make it any easier, not being able to see him. I could feel him, I could smell him, that top layer of soapy freshness – shower gel, shampoo, fabric detergent, all tempered with something real and warm and unrelenting underneath it all. He smelled so wholly like himself

I would have known it was Nick in front of me if I had been wearing a blindfold.

With my hair loose and arms by my sides, I waited for his next move, but instead, his touch disappeared. Slowing my breathing, I opened my eyes to see him unbuttoning his light blue shirt, slowly and purposefully, looking at me the whole time. I made myself keep my own eyes open and looked up, as boldly as I dared. I took in his hair, ash blond and newly cut, revealing his Hawaii tan line where he was starting to go grey at the temples. His wide mouth was still unsmiling and his jaw firm as he peeled away his shirt and dropped it on the floor behind him. Next came his shoes, his brown leather lace-ups, and as he bent down to remove them, the muscles in his broad back moved underneath his skin. Shirt, shoes, socks, gone. All that was left was his belt, his jeans and whatever was underneath.

Then something inside me snapped. What was I doing? I wasn't some ridiculous virgin about to be devoured by the big bad man. I was pissed off. I hadn't heard from him in over a week. I had called and called and left messages and sent emails and he had ignored every one of them. I had chased after him a week ago, asked for one chance to explain and he had walked away from me. And now he thought he could just walk into my room, take off his clothes and – do what, exactly?

His eyes firmly on mine as he unbuckled his belt, it didn't really seem like he was being terribly coy in his intentions.

'I called you,' I said, forcing my lips to make more coherent sounds than a whimper. 'You didn't call me back.'

Nick pulled his belt out of its loops with a snap and held it in both hands. Blinking slowly, he looked down at the length of leather in his hands and then back up at me.

'Do you want me to go?' he asked, moving closer to me until I felt myself backed up against the bed. 'Tell me to go.'

I didn't want him to go. I wanted him to never have shown up in the first place. I wanted him in New York, across a sea and an ocean and several time zones away.

But instead of saying all of that, I reached out and took the belt from his hands, throwing it down somewhere behind me. Nick reached out and grabbed the back of my head, pulling me towards him with a handful of hair, and kissed me hard. It was like nothing I'd ever known, the feeling of his skin against mine, one hand caught in my curls, the other wrapped around my throat. I clutched his shoulders, trying to hang on for dear life until he broke away and pushed me backwards onto the bed.

'I didn't think so,' he said, unbuttoning his jeans and dropping them to the floor.

Now he was smiling.

CHAPTER 8

'Are you OK?' Amy asked at breakfast the next morning. She added two sugars to my tea without asking. If you'd asked anyone else on earth, they'd have told you I didn't take sugar but she knew when I needed it. 'What's wrong?'

I fiddled with my teaspoon, tapping it on the table, and offered her a tight, happy smile.

'Nothing. I'm fine.'

It was the biggest, boldest lie I had ever told.

I took the tea and tried to smile. I really wanted to talk to her but I couldn't, not in front of Al. He was so excited about our planned trip to visit some amazing pattern cutter that it was difficult to find the right time to mention that Nick had turned up outside my door, shagged me senseless, and then vanished before I woke up.

I was mad at myself for letting him in my room. I was even more mad at myself for letting him in my knickers. And I was positively furious about the activities that had occurred once he was inside said knickers. But nothing had got my goat more than the fact that he had done a Miller Houdini and vanished in the middle of the night.

Of course, Amy wasn't going to settle for a 'nothing'. She knew me far too well.

'Yeah, whatever,' she whispered when Al turned his attention to one of the waiters. We had a table full of delicious food and he wanted a bowl of Coco Pops. 'Something's going on. You haven't been right since you got here. And why are you wearing that white T-shirt again, you skank? I gave you a suitcase full of perfectly good clothes.'

'You gave me a suitcase full of perfectly good circus costumes,' I said, tearing into a croissant with displaced rage. 'And I can't talk about it right now. I'll tell you in a bit, I promise.'

She pouted for a moment and then nodded.

'Has something happened?' She stirred my tea on my behalf.

'I said I'd tell you in a bit,' I said, shoving so much buttery baked goodness into my mouth, I could barely breathe. The more croissant in my mouth, the less likely I was to start screaming. 'So, I'll tell you in a bit.'

'It's not Charlie, is it?' she asked. 'Did he call you?'

Oh, bugger me. *Charlie*.

I was officially the worst.

'Good morning, all.'

Actually, I couldn't be the worst because the worst had just walked into the room.

Strolling towards the table, Nick showed no signs of having lost any sleep at all. In fact, he looked really quite well. His beautifully tailored white shirt was rolled up to his elbows, showing off his tan and his jeans fitted him in the most irritatingly wonderful fashion. And like the total twat he was, he was barefoot. I wondered how Al would react if I were to get up from the table and punch him. Just once, I told myself, and not that hard. Not hard enough to cause any permanent damage. I had Amy for that. For the first time since we stepped foot on Italian soil, I was so pleased that she was with me. She might be a bundle of bad ideas and ADHD but she was also the person I trusted most in the world when I needed someone in my corner. She wouldn't be swayed by a pretty face.

'Fuck me,' she breathed. 'Don't look now but my future ex-husband just walked in.'

Or maybe she would.

'Mr Bennett, good to see you again.'

The two men went on for the über-hetero hand-shake-hug combo, clapping one another on the back and laughing heartily. It was like watching Daniel Craig hug it out with Father Christmas, if Father Christmas had been wearing neon-green board shorts and a Grateful Dead T-shirt and Daniel Craig, was in fact, the devil. Once they broke away, Nick turned to look at me, hands on hips, smirk on face, begging for a kick in the balls.

'My stellar photography team,' Al said, waving to Amy and me. 'Miss Amy Smith and of course you know Tess.'

146

'Actually, we haven't been properly introduced, have we?' he said to me, holding out his hand. 'Nick Miller, nice to meet you.'

'Fuck. Off!' Amy shouted at the top of her voice, before clapping her hand across her mouth. 'Sorry, Al.'

Our host blinked slowly and tried not to smile. I wasn't having the same problem.

'Hello,' I replied through a mouth full of pastry, ignoring the outstretched hand. Partly because I didn't want to shake his hand and partly because I was afraid that a shake would lead to a slap, that would lead to strangling the life out of him. 'Tess Brookes.'

'Right, OK.' It seemed like he was putting as much effort into not laughing as I was putting into not killing him. 'And Amy, lovely to meet you too. It is Amy? Just checking; there's been confusion with names before.'

'Last time I checked,' she replied, still utterly awestruck. 'You're Nick?'

'You've heard of me?' he asked, taking a seat beside her while I folded my arms across my chest and crossed my legs, staring at my reflection in the coffee pot on the table. It wasn't possible for me to look pissed off enough but I was giving it a really good attempt.

'I've heard of *a* Nick,' she said, emphasis on the 'a'. 'You're Nick Nick?'

'I am going to get changed,' Al announced, springing out of his seat with surprising vigour for a seventysomething-year-old man. It was amazing what an awkward conversation could achieve. 'Leave you youngsters to get better acquainted, as it were. I'll meet you out front in half an hour.'

'So, Tess is it? Tell me about yourself,' Nick reached for the coffee pot and poured himself a cup, still smiling. 'What brings you to Milan?'

I picked up my cup of tea and stared straight ahead, ignoring the aching in my inner thighs. Actually, no, don't ignore it, I told myself; you deserve to be in pain. And Nick deserved to be ignored. And we should both be flogged . . . unless he enjoyed that kind of thing.

'Not talking to me?' He turned his attention and crinkled blue eyes on Amy, who immediately spat out her orange juice. 'Amy. What about you? Excited to be in Milano?'

'Don't pronounce it like you're Italian; it makes you sound like a tit.' The words were out of my mouth before I could stop them. I never had been very good at keeping a dignified silence around him. 'Aren't you supposed to be off "travelling" somewhere?'

God help me, I loved an air quote when I was irate.

'I was "travelling".' Nick mimicked my bunny ears, sipped his coffee and took a moment to peruse the pastries. Not in any rush to answer me at all. 'I "travelled" to Hawaii and to New York and to London and now I'm in Milan.'

'You were in London? When were you in London?'

I wanted to be cool and calm and collected but I didn't know how. I shoved another mini pastry in my mouth, hoping it would slow down my snappy responses. When in doubt, eat.

'Last week,' he said. 'Why? Did you miss me?'

Across the table, I saw Amy finally snap out of her Nick trance and blink back at me before opening her mouth as far as it would go, pointing at me, pointing at Nick and then miming shooting herself in the head.

'I called you,' I said as coolly as possible given how very sweaty and naked we had been a few hours ago. 'I emailed you.'

'And my out of office said I wasn't replying to messages.' He shrugged, sipping his black coffee. 'So what's the problem?'

'But you must have seen the missed calls!' I was starting to spin out. Maybe mainlining sugar at breakfast wasn't such a good idea. 'You gave me your number, you told me to call.'

'I don't answer numbers I don't know,' Nick rubbed his hand across his eyes and yawned. 'Sorry.'

'You told me to call you!' I shouted.

'You should have left me a message,' he said.

'You just said you weren't listening to messages!'

'I wasn't.'

Placing my teacup gently on the table, I stood up, blinded by rage, sleeplessness, and badly applied eye make-up, and marched straight into the server bringing out Al's Coco Pops.

'Priceless,' Nick laughed as I pawed at a bra full

of cold milk. 'Where's a photographer when you need one?'

I turned back to beg Amy for help but she was already on her feet.

'Ow!' Nick yelped at the perfectly timed slap she delivered to the back of his head on her way past. 'What was that for?'

'Nothing specific,' Amy replied, handing me her napkin and propping me up. 'But we're here for a week – let's assume I'm going to need a couple in the bank.'

'So that's Nick.' I rubbed at the pale chocolatey stain spreading across my white T-shirt as we all but ran back to my room. Amy raced to keep up with my long legs, breaking out into a gallop every few steps, altogether far too excited.

'Oh my God, Tess,' she said, grabbing hold of my forearm and shaking it. 'Oh my God!'

'Don't,' I warned, waiting for her to produce my key to our rooms. Hers was still missing. 'Just don't.'

'You've seriously had a go on that?' she asked. 'Really?'

'It's not something I'm proud of.' I stomped into my bedroom, tossing the ruined T-shirt onto the bed. 'He's an arsehole.'

'You should be proud! He is literally one of the sexiest men I've ever seen with my own eyes.' Amy opened up the suitcase of nightmares and started looking for something for me to wear that wouldn't get her punched in the face. 'I thought my knickers were going to melt right off.'

'I told you he was hot,' I muttered, shaking my head at a gold lamé crop top.

'Yeah, no offence but you think *Charlie* is hot,' she replied offering a neon-pink sweatshirt with a diamanté bunny face. Amy loved her neons.

'Charlie *is* hot!' I grabbed the sweatshirt out of her hand and threw it across the room.

'Charlie is good-looking,' Amy acknowledged. 'But in that bloke-down-the-pub-who-you-have-a-bit-of-flirty-banter-with-after-your-third-drink way. Nick is break-the-bed, don't-come-up-for-air-for-two-weeks hot. H-O-T. I wanted to get *on* him. It was like, *primal*. I think I might actually be pregnant from looking at him.'

'Yes, he's hot but he's also arrogant and pretentious and smug and self-absorbed and selfish and mean and impatient and—'

Amy had stopped rummaging through the suitcase and turned a pair of enormous blue eyes on me.

'You had sex with him!' she shouted, hurling T-shirts and blouses and assorted faux furs at my face. 'You had sex with him last night!'

'What are you talking about?' I tried not to sound impossibly flustered through a mouthful of angora.

'*You had sex with him,*' she repeated, eyes narrowing as she Sherlocked the room. 'You were all mardy and weird this morning and you wouldn't say why, then you weren't surprised when he showed up at

151

breakfast and – Oh. My. God! – there are condom wrappers sticking out from underneath the bed!'

She bent down to grab the shiny foil squares and waved them in my face. 'Magnums? Tess? Fuck off. There's no way someone gets to be that scorching red hot *and* be hung like a horse. It's not fair. Tell me *everything*.'

On my knees by the edge of the bed, I pressed my face into my hands and shook my head. 'I don't want to.'

'Well, you're going to,' she said, giving me the same slap around the head that she had given Nick. 'And since we're supposed to be back downstairs meeting Al in fifteen minutes, I'd imagine you'd want to get it out the way now. Before I tell Kekipi.'

I looked up, fully aware of the pathetic expression on my face and sniffed. 'He turned up last night, after you left,' I said, aimlessly sorting through her clothes. 'And it just happened.'

'What, was he naked? You fell on his penis and it slipped in?'

'Sort of . . .' I said.

'You didn't ask him why he hadn't called you back?' she asked. 'You know, before you shagged him rotten?'

'There wasn't a lot of talking,' I admitted, rubbing my itchy nose. My nose always itched when I was about to cry. 'It was just all a bit, well, you know – you've met him now. Knicker-melting.'

Amy pulled off the plain black vest she was

wearing and handed it to me before picking up the pink rabbit sweater and slipping it over her head. It went perfectly with her polka-dot hot pants. 'And you didn't talk to him after?'

'There was some panting and then some silent cuddling,' I mumbled, feeling tears stinging my eyes. Why was it so much more awkward reliving the tender moments than the getting shagged rotten moments? 'Then I must have fallen asleep and when I woke up, he wasn't here.'

'He fucked off while you were asleep and he didn't take his own condom wrappers with him?' Amy asked. 'That is the worst thing I've ever heard.'

'That's the worst thing you've ever heard?' I pulled the vest over my head and pretended it wasn't very snug. 'Honestly?'

'He could have at least cleaned up after himself if he was going to shag and run,' she said. 'Now come on, I'm not having you sitting around heartbroken when you've got important things to do. You're not going to let him ruin today, are you?'

'I'm not heartbroken,' I said, utterly heartbroken. 'I feel stupid. And angry. And awful. I mean, what about Charlie?'

'First things first.' Amy held up her hand to tick off her very important points on her fingers. 'One, you shouldn't feel stupid. You were seduced by Michael Fassbender's better-looking younger brother. Anyone with a vagina would drop trou for him so you can't be held responsible. Two, you are allowed to be angry. The condom thing has got me raging, let alone his vanishing in the middle of the night. And I know three isn't going to make me popular but, what about Charlie? You're not married to the man, you're not even technically going out with him, are you?'

'I suppose not,' I said, pouting. 'But I don't think I'm supposed to be shagging some random man, either.'

'This is going to come as a bit of a shock . . .' She took my hand in hers and squeezed. 'I know you've been in love with Charlie forever, but you know all those years you've spent pining over him and building up that lovely little fantasy world in your head?'

I nodded.

'*He* wasn't doing the same thing.'

I hated it when Amy was right.

'He was out shagging other women left, right and centre. So you might be ten years into this thing with him but he's spent, what, two weeks thinking about you as anything other than his mate? You told him you needed time to think and you're thinking. You haven't done anything wrong other than have regrettable sex with a twat and Tess, believe me, we've all done that. Charlie included.'

I swallowed, slapped both hands on my thighs, pretended it didn't sting like a motherfucker, and stood up straight.

'I know you don't believe me,' Amy said, bouncing

upright and drowning in her sweatshirt. 'But you didn't cheat on Charlie. You don't have to feel guilty.'

'I'm OK, I really am,' I said, fluffing out my hair until it was roughly the size of Africa and grabbing my camera bag from the desk. 'Shall we get this show on the road?'

'Yeah, after you throw these away, skank.' Amy threw the torn condom wrappers at me, flapping her fingers in midair. 'I need to wash my hands about a million times.'

'Milan is pretty,' Amy whispered to me as we moved swiftly through the streets in the backseat of Al's SUV. 'And sometimes a bit like Leicester. But mostly really pretty.'

I smiled back in lieu of a reply and carried on staring out of the window. I knew what she meant: one moment we'd be driving past some ridiculously elegant building, all sparkling rows of identical windows and gorgeous columns, and the next, we were circling around a grey sixties concrete office block. It was unsettling, but not nearly as unsettling as the feeling of someone staring at the back of my head. Nick was in the back of the car, beside a very vocal Kekipi. Al had taken the passenger seat and, other than the insistent rhythmic tapping of his fingers on his knee, had been silent for the entire trip. I took random snaps out the window, of Al's nervous tic, of my feet. Anything to distract myself.

'Who are we meeting this morning?' Amy asked, twisting underneath her seatbelt to address Kekipi

155

directly. And to give Nick a very, very dirty look. 'Are we nearly there yet?'

'This morning, it's Edward Warren,' Kekipi replied after consulting his iPad. 'He's a pattern cutter. And yes, sit down properly.'

'What does a pattern cutter do?' she asked, ignoring him and shifting onto her knees.

'A pattern cutter is the most important part of the puzzle,' Al answered Amy's question in a loud voice, cut with excitement. 'He is the translator between the designer and the manufacturer.'

'I'm going to assume you don't mean translator as in English to French?' I asked. Nick laughed. Amy doubled her efforts in the filthy look department. Nick shushed.

'Actually, it's very similar. The pattern cutter takes the sketches from the designer – in this instance me – and turns them into samples, working patterns, to send to the manufacturer,' he explained. 'The pattern cutter takes the dream and turns it into a reality.'

'Sounds hard,' Amy said. 'He's basically a magician.'

'A very technically skilled magician who can take very vague sketches from the alleged designer and turn them into something someone might actually want to wear, without offending said designer.' Al upped the pace of his nervous tapping. 'So you can imagine, the best in the business are in high demand. I am incredibly lucky that Mr Warren has agreed to see us today.'

'He's good then?' I asked.

'Edward Warren is the best,' Al nodded, brushing his beard. 'I have known him for a very long time but I'm still very lucky that he's agreeing to even discuss this with me. Where it goes from there, we shall see.'

'He's worked for everyone,' Kekipi said, flashing his eyebrows towards the roof. 'Seriously, anyone you can think of—'

'Let's not be indelicate . . .' Al issued a caution from the front of the car. 'Edward is a very private man. It was all that I could do to convince him to let me bring you all along in the first place, without your spreading gossip about him before we even get to his studio.'

'Versace, D&G, Armani, Prada,' Kekipi mouthed. '*Everyone.*'

Al cleared his throat loudly. 'You do know I can see you in the mirror, don't you?'

'And?' Kekipi asked. 'I didn't say a word.'

I looked over at Amy and wondered if we would still be bickering in the back of other people's luxury cars in fifty years time.

'What?' she stared back at me, confused. 'What are you looking at?'

'Your face,' I said, turning my attention back to my camera and smiling.

Edward Warren's office was no more than a ten-minute drive from the palazzo, but we had been up and down and in and out of so many tiny winding streets, that I had no concept of how far we had driven. We arrived outside an odd building, somewhere in between the charm of old Milan and the misery of its sixties expansion. Complete with square windows and iron bar balconies, it looked like a council house version of Al's home. Only the heavy, warm wooden door suggested something interesting might be going on inside. One by one, our awkward group trailed inside: Al in the front, Amy right behind him with Nick holding rank in the middle, while Kekipi and I brought up the back.

'Is it worth asking what on earth is going on with you and Mr Miller?' he whispered as Al announced us to the receptionist. 'Or are you still dreadfully angry that I didn't tell you he was here?'

'I'm so far past angry,' I replied, smiling politely as Al introduced each of us in turn for the purpose of the visitors' book, 'that I'm not going to tell you. That's your punishment.'

'What if I take you shopping once we're done here?' he bargained. 'Miss Smith filled me in on her well-meaning wardrobe snafu and without Miss Sullivan here to dress you, someone is clearly going to have to help.'

'That would be the best thing ever.' I even amazed myself at how quickly I rolled over sometimes. 'Is there an H&M in Milan?'

Kekipi pulled away sharply and scrunched up his features.

'How would I know?' he sniffed, slipping his arm

through mine. 'I said I would take you shopping, not trawling for rags with the unwashed masses.'

I immediately had visions of myself rolling around on the floor with my camera, trying to get a good shot in a full-length ballgown.

Before I could reply, we were ushered through the nondescript lobby and into a lift that clearly wasn't big enough for the five of us, the receptionist, and Nick's ego. Or whatever else was pushing into my hip when I squeezed in front of him. Clamping my hands tightly around my camera, I kept my eyes front and centre.

Given that I was concentrating so hard on keeping quiet, it might not have been immediately obvious as to how overwhelmed I was by Edward Warren's office. As the lift doors slid open, I immediately cast my eyes downwards, assuming we had accidentally arrived on the set of a period porno but, as the receptionist ushered us out and I made myself look around, I realized the room wasn't full of naked women, just incredibly graphic, life-sized photographs of naked women.

Al strode down the room, ignoring the copious vaginas on display, laughing heartily at a man who sat on what appeared to be a throne, his pointy ankle boots thrown up on his enormous desk. Kekipi attempted to keep pace with his boss while Amy wandered along behind them, all wide eyes and wandering hands. The room was huge, but it was crammed with furniture; a leopard-print chaise longue by the window, an oversized work table draped in silks, satins and various velvets by the door and, for a reason best known to Edward Warren, at least a dozen statues of big cats. The walls were lined with red silk and I counted fourteen enormous nude photographs on the walls. It was definitely an acquired taste – even Hugh Hefner might have called it a bit much.

'Edward bloody Warren!' Al's voice boomed across the room.

Filling the space with the world's most expensive shit did nothing to dull its acoustics. Possibly something to do with the enormously high ceilings, complete with their own version of the Sistine Chapel frescoes, redrawn to include a man who looked ever so much like Warren, of course.

'Mr Bennett!' Edward rose to his feet and met Bertie in a very aggressive-looking hug. For some reason, I'd expected him to be a short man; however he was anything but. Al had to be almost six feet tall, maybe even more before his age had brought him down an inch or two, but Warren towered over him. Yes, there was a touch of help in his Cuban heels but this was not a Tom Cruise situation. He was enormous. Stooping to trade air kisses with Kekipi, I saw that he was starting to lose his hair on the top of his head but what was there was jet black and stylishly cut and when he looked up to fix Nick, Amy and myself with a sharp, level gaze, I couldn't quite work out how old he was.

'And the back-up dancers,' he commented, making no move towards us. 'They are adorable, Al.'

'My photographer, Tess Brookes, and her assistant, Amy Smith,' Al turned to introduce us. I waved my camera in an attempt to verify my profession. 'And Nick Miller, our esteemed writer – perhaps you've read some of his work?'

'No, I haven't.' Edward gestured for Al and Kekipi to take the two seats in front of his desk before waving the rest of us towards the many other seating options in the room. 'Please sit.'

I took a seat next to Amy on the leopard-print chaise while Nick glowered on a black velvet armchair opposite. I frowned, bouncing the weight of my camera between my hands, waiting to feel good about him feeling bad. My brain wanted to laugh right in his face but my ovaries wanted to go over and give him a hug. What was all that about?

'So, what's all this I hear about the House of Bennett finally happening?' Edward might have been a total tosspot to us but he smiled so warmly at Al, I could almost forgive him. At least my brain could; my ovaries were still a bit offended on Nick's behalf – stupid reproductive organs. 'I'm all ears, Al.'

'It's just as I explained on the phone,' Al said, unfastening the bottom button of his suit jacket. Today's three-piece was a gorgeous charcoal grey. I had to admit, as much as I loved Santa Surfer Al, he did look very dapper in his suit. 'It's time to do something different.'

The receptionist who had shown us in reappeared

161

as the lift doors slid open in silence, carrying a tray with three cups of espresso and some very promising-looking biscuits. Of course, she sailed right by us and placed them on Edward's desk. It was only when she sailed right back again that I recognized her. There she was, completely starkers, two photos in on the right-hand side of the room. Crikey. I shook off my English awkwardness and held my camera up to my face to cover my blushes, hoping that Warren wouldn't ask me and Amy to pose for his wall of nudes: me, because I wouldn't, Amy, because she would.

'I think it's time we both did something different,' Edward said, taking a leather folder from Kekipi. 'Preferably on a beach with a cocktail.'

'You'd be surprised at how boring that can get after a while,' Al replied. 'And you've been telling me you're ready to retire for the last twenty years. I'm sure you've got a couple of months in you to help an old friend out with one last favour.'

Edward opened the folder and pulled out a dozen or so sketches. Trying to be inconspicuous, I left the safety of my sofa and stood at the side of the desk, snapping away, focusing on the delicate watercolour paintings.

'Does she have to do that?' Edward asked Al, seizing up at the sound of the shutter.

'She does,' Al replied. 'But she's very lovely so don't worry about it at all.'

Focusing in on the sketches again, I couldn't help but be surprised at how beautiful they were.

Most were watercolour paintings of dresses, all nipped-in waists and full skirts in delicate colours. Zooming in, I saw that these images were not recent. All of them were dated in the bottom left-hand corner and went back as far as the 1970s, the newest from 2006.

'These are Jane's?' Ed asked, his voice softening.

'We did them together,' Al confirmed. 'She did most of the sketches and I did the painting. It was something she always wanted to do. Now it's something that I *will* do.'

'They're very beautiful.' Ed carefully replaced all of the sketches in the folder and handed it back to Kekipi, who took it with the kind of reverence I had only seen him show for a strawberry daiquiri. 'And timeless. You're intending to take the couture route, I assume?'

'I'd like them to be worn, not admired from afar,' Al said, his tiny coffee cup disappearing into his beard. 'But I do want to create something special.'

Edward templed his fingers and rested his chin on top. 'And you'll distribute through Bennett's, of course?'

'There's very little point having a clothes shop in the family if you can't sell your own clothes,' Al nodded. 'But ultimately, I would like to open standalone stores. I'm looking at locations in New York, London, Paris and Milan. They wouldn't roll out until phase two, of course.'

Leaning back, Edward whistled as I took a couple of gratuitous photos of his throne. His actual throne.

'No point in half measures,' he said, scratching a bushy black eyebrow. If he could have transplanted both eyebrows onto the bald patch on top of his head, he would have been absolutely golden.

'Absolutely,' Al agreed. 'Which is why I'm here. No point going to anyone but the best.'

'I am flattered of course,' he replied. 'And I'd love to work with you. What are you looking at, timings-wise?'

'We have everything in place.' Al sat up, straightened his tie and beamed. 'And I'm not getting any younger. I want to show next spring.'

'You want to show Spring Summer next September?' Even through the viewfinder of my camera, I could tell that Edward didn't look nearly as convinced as Al. 'That's awfully soon.'

'And the Autumn Winter shows in spring are even sooner,' Al nodded. 'And that's what I'm talking about. A twelve-piece capsule collection to show in February.'

'But it's already July!' Edward looked as though Al had just told him he was planning to knock up his grandmother. 'It's not possible.'

'I thought that too,' Al said, glancing over at Kekipi. 'But I made a few calls, Kekipi made a few calls and it turns out most things are achievable with the right connections and an open cheque book. So what would it take to get your team on board?'

'No one from my team is available.' Edward held out his arms with a puppy dog sadness. 'But you don't want one of my team, do you? You want me. And I am entirely at your disposal.'

With a slap on the desk as loud as thunder, Al stood up and reached across to shake Edward's hand as Kekipi rolled his eyes.

'Drama queens,' he muttered while I captured the Kodak moment.

'Kekipi, why don't you take the ladies out to see the sights,' Al said, giving Kekipi a good-natured shove. 'Edward and I can manage the business side of this without boring the four of you.'

Glad to get out of Liberace's playroom, I nodded, and dragged Kekipi out of his seat.

'And the "writer"?' Edward asked, raising an eyebrow in Nick's direction.

'I think he might want to stay,' Al said without asking. 'You three can take the car, Nick and I will walk back.'

'Have the best time,' Amy said to Nick in a low voice, waving with both hands.

'She's a delight,' he said as I stowed my camera in its bag. 'It's interesting how much you can tell about someone from their friends.'

'It's interesting how much you can tell about someone who has none,' I replied. 'Like she said, have the best time.'

'Oh, I will,' he assured me, grabbing my arm as I passed. I swallowed hard and froze. 'I usually enjoy myself, no matter how substandard the material is I'm given to work with.'

Wrenching my arm away and feeling somewhere

between whitely furious and get-me-a-bin nauseus, I slid my feet through the ankle-deep carpeting and into the waiting lift, punching the button for the lobby. I needed to put as much distance between myself and that man as possible, both vertical and horizontal.

'Shopping, then?' Kekipi asked.

'Sure,' I nodded. 'Shopping.'

Prison never seemed like a preferable option but thinking about it, I would much rather end up there for not paying my credit card bills than for ripping Nick's heart out of his chest and ramming it down his throat.

So, shopping it was.

CHAPTER 9

'I think I'm going to be sick.'

I sat down on small wooden chair, dropping shopping bags all over the floor and collapsing onto the table in front of me.

'*Buongiorno.*'

A waiter smiled politely at Kekipi as he seated himself with considerably more grace, taking off his grey checked jacket and hanging it on the back of his chair.

'*Buongiorno,*' he replied. '*Due caffe, per favore. Grazie.*'

'*Prego.*' The waiter waltzed wearily back inside the café, leaving me and my enabler to wallow in the spoils of our shopping trip.

'I don't know what you're complaining about; you've got what, four bags? Five? It's nothing.' Kekipi whipped out his phone, furrowed his brow for a moment and then popped it back in his pocket. 'And they're all fabulous investment pieces.'

'I was completely broke before I got here,' I replied, pushing one of the bags with the tip of my toe and trying not to convert the many euros

I had parted with into pounds. As long as they were euros, it didn't count, did it?

I took my own phone out and placed it on the table, waiting for the inevitable call from the credit card company to confirm that I had, in fact, been killed by a desperate shopaholic who was now trying to calm her murderous impulse by spending money that I didn't have in assorted Milanese boutiques. 'Now I'm completely broke and horribly in debt.'

'But you're completely broke, horribly in debt and the owner of some very beautiful shoes,' he reasoned. 'Those little black pumps you were insisting on wearing made me so sad. They looked as though they were about to crawl off your feet and throw themselves into a volcano.'

While we were shopping, everything he had suggested had made so much sense. I did need new flats and maybe spending money on a pair of handmade Italian shoes rather than picking up three identical pairs from Primark for a tenner was an investment. And I couldn't walk around Milan with one pair of jeans, one stained T-shirt and one borrowed too-tight vest, could I? So, the new J Brand jeans were vital. And what with the weather being so unpredictable, I definitely needed the adorable printed Red Valentino cropped trousers for when it was too hot to wear my jeans. If I thought about it, I could rationalize all of it, from the Cosabella lingerie, past the satin-front Vince sweater, down to the Sergio Rossi black patent pumps, but sitting here looking at it all, I had epic shopper's remorse. Al was paying me well for this job but I was hardly on *Pretty Woman* money and Kekipi wasn't about to pony up any cash in return for my sexual favours. In fact, he'd probably chuck me a few quid to keep my clothes on. In this version of the story, I was the one who had made the *huge* mistake.

'Any dessert?' The waiter popped back up with an impressive display of elaborate cakes and a "please buy these, I'm on commission" smile.

'We'll take one very fruity thing and one very chocolatey thing,' Kekipi replied without looking. 'You need some sugar, you look tired.'

'I need my head looking at,' I mumbled, eyes on a particularly lovely and especially expensive stripy, teal Missoni dress. I could always take it back, I thought, reaching down to stroke it gently. Although, it was very nice . . . Maybe prostitution wasn't the worst way to make a living if it kept me in pretty things.

'Right, I held my water while we took care of business,' Kekipi waved towards the bags, still looking very pleased with himself, 'but enough is enough. Spill. I want all of it.'

'All of it?' I asked, wondering how quickly I could heterosexually gross him out. 'Really?'

'Right up until something goes in somewhere I never want to think about,' he confirmed. 'But as soon as it comes out, you can pick up the story again.'

I pulled a hair tie out of my handbag and wrapped my hair up and away from my face before I started my story. It was absolutely roasting out and I was thankful that Kekipi had chosen this place for our coffee stop. We were inside what I had to imagine was the world's most beautiful shopping centre, all high glass-domed ceilings and intricately tiled floors. Where Meadowhall had a Paperchase, this place had a Prada. It was fancy.

'You can skip over the part where you fell out of a window but leave in the bit where you got arrested, Amy filled me in on all of that,' he said as our coffee and cakes arrived. 'I want all the stories about boys but remember to leave out the actual penetration. I know, I'm such a prude.'

Such a prude?

Whatever Kekipi and Amy had got up to the night before had exhausted her to the point of turning down our shopping-slash-gossiping trip in favour of an afternoon on her arse. Without her to interpret, I was able to get through my story relatively quickly. Kekipi, for all his dramatics, really was a great listener. He shook his head, gasped and nodded in all the right places, sneakily encouraging me to reveal far more than I had originally intended. No wonder Al kept him so close over the years: he must know where all the bodies were buried.

'And that takes us up to this morning, which I suppose takes us up until now.' I stuck a tiny silver fork into a giant chocolate-covered pastry and tried not to drool as a mountain of cream oozed onto my plate. 'So what do I do?'

Kekipi speared a glazed strawberry on his fruit tart and chewed thoughtfully.

'Tell me why you slept with Charlie,' he said, moving on to a raspberry.

'Because I love him,' I replied automatically.

'But why did it happen when it did?' he asked. 'Why didn't you rush straight from the airport and into his arms? Really think about it.'

I inhaled a forkful of cream while I thought about my answer. 'When I was in the police station, I called Charlie because he I knew he would come and get me without being all dramatic about it. He makes me feel safe and comfortable and it's easy. He knows me.'

Kekipi flicked a packet of brown sugar before ripping the top and dumping it into his coffee.

'Fine,' he said after a moment's consideration. 'Now tell me why you slept with Nick last night.'

Eurgh, I thought.

'Eurgh,' I said.

'First thing that pops into your head,' Kekipi said. 'Don't overthink it.'

'That's the problem,' I replied, shifting from thigh to thigh in my seat. 'I didn't think about it at all. If I had, I wouldn't have bloody done it.'

My fairy gayfather smiled into his coffee cup and sipped. I frowned at the chocolate pastry in front of me and helped myself to his fruit tart.

'Someone wants to have her cake and eat mine?'

He rapped my knuckles with his pastry fork. 'I think we're uncovering a major character flaw in you, young lady.'

Harsh, but fair.

'Once upon a time, I was involved with two men.' Kekipi pushed his plate towards me and took a forkful of chocolatey goodness in exchange before starting his story. 'One was older than me, such a smart man. Educated, considerate, caring . . . All he wanted was to take care of me, start a family, be together. I don't think anyone has ever loved me as much as he did.'

'What about the other one?' I asked. I couldn't imagine Kekipi with a sugar daddy.

My interest was officially piqued.

'He was younger, my age, and just about the most wonderful man I have ever known.' He loosened his tie and cleared his throat, his elegant fingers lingering on the buttons that fastened his collar. 'I had never loved someone the way I loved him. We were young and reckless and all the other words older people use to describe two people in love when they know it won't work out. But I couldn't bear to be away from him. Every time he was near, it was like I had rolled around in poison oak. He didn't make me feel alive; he made me feel immortal. I thought we were invincible, him and me.'

It was strange to think of Kekipi as a young man in love. It was hard to think of Kekipi as anything other than Al's sidekick and my confidant. I

172

realized I knew next to nothing about him and suddenly felt terribly guilty for never stopping to ask questions.

'If you were so in love with him, where was the competition?' I asked. 'I don't follow.'

'He was married.' He tightened his tie again and turned his attention to organizing the sugar bowl by packet colour. 'To a woman.'

'Bit of a road bump,' I said. Kekipi let out a quick, hollow laugh and nodded.

'Every time we were together, me breaking my heart over him going back to his wife, his family, I told myself it was the last time. I knew the other man was better for me. He loved me, he cared about me . . .' He paused his sorting and looked me in the eye. 'He made me feel safe.'

'But you didn't love him, did you?' I said, seeing exactly where this story was going. 'He was just a rebound, wasn't he?'

'No, I did. I did love him,' Kekipi countered. 'In a different way. He was like the ocean: when he left, I knew he would come back, I knew he was forever. The other man, he was a volcano: explosive, unpredictable. That kind of relationship sounds more exciting but it can burn, will consume you, if you let it.'

'Nice Hawaiian metaphors,' I smiled and sipped my coffee. 'What happened?'

'Everyone said the same, don't mistake passion for love.' He looked off down the arcade. It was strange to watch someone tell a story that still

173

caused them such upset after so long, especially someone so generally positive and happy. 'And after many hours of contemplation, many conversations with our friend, Mr Bennett, I made my choice.'

I slipped my camera out of its case and took a few quick pics while he wasn't looking. His expression was so beautiful, something I'd never seen on him before and I couldn't help myself.

'Who did you choose?' I asked.

'I chose the ocean,' he said, shaking his head back into the present. 'I wanted to be with someone who would take care of me. I wanted to be with the man who said I love you every night when we fell asleep together.'

I couldn't wipe the surprise off my face. 'Then what happened?'

'What always happens when you aren't true to your heart,' Kekipi replied. 'We were happy for a while until I began to resent him. And then the arguments began, arguments, drinking, cheating. That was the beginning of the end, really.'

'You never thought about going back to the other man?' I asked softly.

Kekipi gave a decisive shake of his head. 'He left the island. Moved his family to California, I think. When I told him it was over, he went crazy, threatened all kinds of things. It was only when I ended it that I really understood that he loved me just as much as I loved him but it was too late.'

'And he was married all that time?'

'Yes,' Kekipi nodded. 'But you have to understand, this was a different time. Our community was very conservative, it wasn't easy to be out back then and not that long since it was illegal to be gay in Hawaii. I never blamed him for getting married, and I was never angry with his wife, the poor woman. She knew all about it. It must have been awful for her. But in the end, he wasn't the one who made the decision that kept us from being together, I was. Now stop taking my photo before I Britney you with someone's umbrella.'

I pursed my lips, camera in hand, and considered his story.

'So you if you could do it all over again, you would choose the volcano?' I said, rolling my aching shoulder and squeezing my sore thighs. 'Even though it seemed like the dangerous decision?'

'I wouldn't want to do it all over again, at any cost,' he said. 'But I do know you shouldn't make decisions based on what makes you feel safe. Make your decisions on what makes you feel alive. Life might be too short for regrets – but it's far too long to live with a compromise.'

It was a fair point. It felt like a lifetime since I'd first seen Charlie sauntering across the university campus with a sticker-covered guitar strapped to his back, but when I thought about how quickly a whole decade had gone by, it made me catch my breath.

'Just out of interest,' I said, scooping up the last

bits of pastry with my fork. 'What did Al say? When you broke up with your boyfriend?'

'He didn't say anything,' Kekipi replied. 'But I wished I had listened to his advice in the first place.'

'He told you to choose the married man?' I asked, not sure whether to be surprised or not. Al had an unnerving tendency to be right about things.

Kekipi nodded and tapped the table twice.

'Now, have you finished? There's a lovely mosaic of a bull over there and if we stand on his testicles and do a shimmy and a spin, it's meant to be good luck.'

'We have to shimmy?' I asked.

'I added the shimmy,' he said, standing and brushing off his immaculate suit. 'No one has any flair these days.'

'This is really beautiful,' Amy said, pulling a white silk sleeveless blouse covered in delicate polka dots out of a stiff cardboard carrier bag. 'Kekipi has the best taste ever.'

'How do you know I didn't choose it?' I asked, hanging up my new clothes and trying very hard not to look at the price tags.

Amy raised a dismissive eyebrow and handed me the shirt. 'Do you think he would take me shopping? Do you think he would pay?'

'Do you?' I stroked a baby blue T-shirt that was softer than the basket full of kittens I would inevitably grow old with and yawned. 'You OK?'

'Yeah.' She draped herself over the arm of the big squishy chair closest to my wardrobe. 'Charlie called me while you were out.'

'He did?' My heart stopped for a moment. He hadn't called me. Or texted. Or emailed. Or faxed. Or carrier pigeoned. 'To say what?'

'Just wanted to know if we'd got here all right,' Amy said, stretching and arching her back like one of my future cats, her minuscule bum rising off the seat as she did so. 'He said he hadn't heard from you.'

It was fair, he hadn't. I wasn't quite sure what to say and I couldn't imagine he was desperate for me to FaceTime him to give him the double guns again.

'What did you tell him?' I asked, terribly interested in the hanging loops on a pair of white denim Rag & Bone shorts, covered in tiny motorcycles – an incredibly practical purchase on my part.

'I said we were so fine that you'd shagged Nick all night long and now you were too knackered to bother texting him so he should probably go and throw himself off Tower Bridge,' she said, kicking me in the arse. 'What do you think I said?'

'I'm sorry,' I said, closing the wardrobe and rubbing my bum cheek. 'I don't want you to be in the middle of all of this. You didn't actually say that though, did you?'

'I told him Al had been working you like a slave and that I'd knocked you out with Night Nurse last night because you weren't feeling very well,' she replied. 'He bought it, obviously. But yeah, you owe me.'

The number of times we had exchanged those words.

'Anything from Mr Miller?' she asked.

I folded in on myself, collapsing onto the floor like a grumpy giraffe and lay flat on my back. Things always looked better when there wasn't any further to fall.

'I still can't get over how offensively sexy he is,' Amy sighed.

'Don't call him sexy,' I said with a wince. 'No one says sexy any more. It sounds so nineties.'

'But he is sexy,' she argued, twisting upside down so that her head dangled down in front of me. 'He's not just *handsome*; he's got that "grr" thing. Like when Daniel Craig came out of the ocean in James Bond, only fully dressed. Imagine him in swimming trunks. Oh God, imagine him *naked*.'

I held my breath and waited.

'Oh my God, of course, you've seen him naked!' Amy shouted, holding her hands over her face. 'It's too much for my tiny mind. You have literally blown it to pieces.'

'But you have seen what a twat he is,' I said, stretching my arm out for my handbag. I couldn't quite reach it, meaning the universe didn't want me to text Charlie just yet. I'd text him later, just as soon as I could reach my bag without having to move – and just as soon as I had worked out what I wanted to say. 'So you know why it's a no go.'

'I know, I know,' she said, rolling down onto the floor at the side of me, 'but there's definitely something going on with you two. You're all jumpy and sketchy around him.'

'I am not sketchy.' I didn't bother to try to refute jumpy. 'He makes me uncomfortable.'

'Yeah he does, all night long,' she replied, snapping her fingers and singing what I knew for a fact was her favourite Lionel Richie song. 'When we were in the car on the way to that weirdo's place, he was just, like, staring at you. The whole time. Didn't look out the window once. He just sat there, really enjoying the back of your head.'

'That's because Milan can't compete with my incomparable beauty,' I said, sniffing my armpits and wondering if I could get away without a shower before dinner. 'I am a goddess.'

'Yeah,' she nodded, 'definitely that. Also, he can't put his dick in Milan.'

'As eloquent as ever,' I said. 'Did anyone say anything to you about dinner tonight?'

'Nope,' she said, rolling onto her front and dragging herself up to her feet. 'I got the car back, I saw the lovely Domenico, confirmed for the millionth time that we had everything we needed and then came up here for a nap. Now you're back.'

'I was gone for five hours,' I pointed out. 'And that's all you did?'

'It was a hell of a nap,' Amy said, pumping her hands over her head and swinging her hips. 'Can we go out tonight?'

'I should call Charlie,' I said, staring sadly at my handbag. 'And I need to look at the photos from this morning. And talk to Al about what we're doing next. And God, look at the Perito's pitch.'

She lowered her arms slowly, sadly. 'So that's a no, is it?'

'We'll go out tomorrow night,' I promised, the words sounding awkwardly familiar. 'I'm sorry.'

'Fine, I'll go and find out about dinner, I'm rav.' She patted her flat stomach and trotted out the door. 'Go and have a shower, you stink.'

You couldn't put a price on the value of an honest friend, I told myself, as I rolled to my knees and crawled into the bathroom.

'You've got to be kidding me.'

After a very long, very hot shower, I'd found a note from Kekipi shoved under my door, telling me that dinner would be in the dining room at eight before giving very explicit directions as to how I was to prepare. I did as I was told, worried that if my efforts weren't up to scratch, he'd withhold food, and since I hadn't eaten anything other than a few bites of breakfast and the pastries at lunchtime, I really wanted my dinner. And so I dutifully made sure I'd shaved my legs below and above the knee, dried my hair properly, put on make-up, and, as the note explicitly instructed, slipped into the little black dress he had chosen for me in the Valentino boutique. There was no way I could have ever afforded it if he hadn't flirted

180

his way to a sixty per cent discount, and for that I would be eternally grateful. It was the most perfectly fitting dress I had ever owned. Short but not too short as to show my knickers, it was nipped in at the waist and had a perfect straight-across slash of a neckline that tethered my unmanageable boobs in place without making them look like they'd been bound down for netball practice. It was a miracle.

I assumed I was being preened by proxy so he could show off his fabulous styling to Amy and Al over dinner but instead of finding a table full of friendly faces, there was only one guest at the table and his face wasn't friendly at all.

'I take that look to mean you were expecting other people to be here as well.' Nick poured himself a glass of red wine from one of the four open bottles of booze on the table and kicked his feet up on one of the empty chairs. 'Excellent.'

His bare feet.

Although I was annoyed at being set up, I couldn't help but take a little perverse pleasure in the fact that Kekipi had got one over on Nick the genius. Even if it did mean I had to sit through dinner with him, all on my own. Immediately I felt my skin begin to prickle.

'You don't have to stay,' I said, striding over to the table as confidently as my untested new heels would allow. At least I was bloody well wearing shoes. 'I'm not forcing you.'

Nick watched as I reached for the white wine,

moving extra slowly so as not to knock anything over, break anything or somehow manage to set myself on fire. I suspected Amy had had a hand in the table design: there were candles everywhere and she was a little firebug. Swirling the wine in his glass, he didn't say anything, just sat and watched while I poured out an inelegant quantity of Pinot Grigio and took a massive swig. Placing the glass back on the table and out of easy reach, I crossed my legs and folded my arms, wishing I hadn't put my hair up. It would have been nice to have something to hide behind while he continued his famous silent treatment.

'So you're going to sit there and stare at me all night, are you? Fine.' I refused to be drawn into his mind games again. 'I'll just entertain myself.'

Happily, the table was loaded with enough bread, cheese, meats and salads to cater every one of Kim Kardashian's weddings and all of it looked divine. At least I had something to distract me while I was busy ignoring him.

Halfway through my attempt to saw a particularly tasty looking loaf in half, Nick gave a loud, violent sigh before knocking back his entire glass of red and slamming down his glass. It wobbled for a moment as he stood up and stared at me across the table while I stared back at him, one paw full of cheese and the other full of bread. Without so much as another grunt, he stormed back into the house, slamming the door behind him.

His glass wobbled again, before falling over and rolling off the table, shattering the instant it struck the courtyard floor.

'Fucking hell,' I whispered, breathing out for the first time in what felt like forever. As quickly as it had closed, the door flew open again, Nick striding back over to the table, his forehead all creased and his jaw heavy and tense.

'What I want to know,' he said, noisily pulling out his seat amongst the shards of broken glass, grabbing the bottle of red and starting the process all over again. 'Is where you get off, being angry with me.'

'What?' I couldn't quite believe what I was hearing.

'You're the one who lied about your name, your job, who you are. You're the one who lied about everything to everyone and now you're angry with me because I didn't return your fucking phone call?' he said, his voice getting louder as he went on. 'Well, I'm very sorry, Tess or Vanessa or whatever your name is, but I'm not an eccentric old man who did so many drugs in the Sixties that he's confusing giving someone a chance with letting someone take advantage of him. I don't let people take advantage of me. And I don't like liars. And you're a liar.'

Well, that was me told.

I placed my bread and cheese on my plate, making a silent promise to come back to them and picked up my wine glass with a shaky hand. I wanted to come back with something really snappy, something searing and brutal and personal and vicious. But it was hard to get up on my high horse when at least half of what he had said was true. Or that was to say, factually accurate.

'You didn't seem to mind me last night,' I said, as calmly as possible, after I had drained the last drop of wine in my glass. 'Or do you have an evil twin I should know about?'

Nick ran a hand over his face then reached around to rub the back of his neck. I watched his white T-shirt strain against his bicep and felt nothing other than the desire to pull the T-shirt off his body and strangle him with it. Enough was enough. The prickle of anger was enough to remind me why I *was* mad at him.

'And more to the point, how could I explain if you wouldn't let me?' I asked, folding my arms over my perfectly positioned bosom. This dress was incredible. 'I tried to talk to you. I tried in Hawaii and I tried to call you. I emailed you, I sent you texts.'

Still, he said nothing, his grey-blue eyes empty.

'You told me to call you and then you didn't call back. And then last night . . .' I spoke slowly, not sure what my voice was going to do. Balanced and even might have been the goal but I was only ever seconds away from incredibly shrill or desperate sobbing whenever I spoke to him and neither of those had ever done a woman any good in an argument. 'And then last night happened. And I woke up and you weren't there. What do you want me to say? To do? You're going to have to tell me because I really don't know.'

I heard the last word fade off and was proud of myself for getting it out without losing it. This was progress. Old Tess would have dissolved into an emotional puddle shortly after showing him an incredible PowerPoint presentation that explained, in ten slides or fewer, why he was the most offensive dickhead on the market for English women aged twenty-eight and over.

Without anything else to add, I turned my attention back to the cheese and hoped there would never come a day when dairy turned on me too.

'I emailed you because I needed an explanation,' Nick said, pushing pieces of crystal around on the floor with his toe. 'But then when I thought about it, I couldn't see what use there would be in getting one.'

Wonderful, reliable, noncomplex cheese. I chewed while I worked out what to say, tearing my chunk of bread into tiny little pieces.

'What now?' I asked, chasing the cheese with a big gulp of wine – the internationally recognized dietary choice of scorned women. 'Are you going to keep on punishing me? Keep saying really horrible things to me in public? Because that's been brilliant so far.'

'I don't know you,' he replied without a moment's hesitation. 'I don't know anything about you. As far as I knew, you were a photographer called Vanessa Kittler who had shagged at least half of London but for some reason, you decided to show another side to me, and then I find out that you're not Vanessa, that you've lied to me the entire time, but I still see that other side to you and that's got me really confused.'

'That's what this is about?' I felt a little bit sick and it had nothing to do with the cheese or the wine. 'You thought I was some massive slag and that you were the only super stud who could get through to me? And now what, you're angry that I'm not actually that slag?'

'No.' Nick leaned forwards, resting his arms on the table, shuffling a salami out of the way. His being surrounded by cured meat did nothing to dispel the tension or the queasy feeling in my stomach. 'I just don't like being lied to.'

'That's funny,' I replied. 'Me neither.'

Turning away and shaking his head at something I hadn't said, Nick sipped his wine and fiddled with the edge of the white tablecloth. Still stunned into pukiness, I waited for him to say something, utterly out of my own words for the moment.

'I don't think I need to explain that I had feelings for you,' he said, eventually settling back into his chair to look at me. 'And I don't think it would be difficult for anyone to understand why I might have reacted harshly when I found out you were lying about, well, everything.'

I sucked in my cheeks and forced myself to nod, even though I felt I would definitely like his feelings explained.

'But we're here now and we've got to work together, sort of.' He scratched his nose and took a cleansing breath. 'Maybe we should agree to start over. I can be professional if you can.'

'Last night was professional, was it?' I asked. More wine. I needed more wine.

'Last night was a mistake,' Nick replied, his voice smooth and deep where mine was thick and uneven. 'Sorry about that.'

I had managed to get through twenty years feeling approximately seven feelings: love for Charlie, complete adoration for Amy, tolerance for my family, a bedwetting fear of Vanessa, blind ambition, constant peckishness and the desperate need to sleep. I wasn't sure if peckishness actually counted as a feeling but it had played a big part in my life, so it felt wrong to discount it now, but here, sitting at the table across from Nick, I had never felt so confused in all my life. I was furious with him for being so self-righteous and embarrassed that he was right about so many things. But at the same time, it hurt me that I could have hurt him in this way and, as much as I tried to deny it, there was a sad, angry sinking feeling that was threatening to overwhelm my peckishness. He didn't want me.

'I don't want things to be difficult for everyone else,' Nick said, finishing off his wine and pouring more. 'So we'll start over, and like I said, I don't know you.'

'This is so stupid,' I said, refolding my arms and

looking up to the stars that were just starting to prick through the night sky. I thought back to all the time we had spent talking, all the things I had told him that I had never told anyone else. 'You *do* know me.'

'Just because I know what you want in bed, doesn't mean I know anything about you as a person,' he said. 'And clearly, that works both ways.'

Ouch. Just ouch.

'But I'll give it a go. Let's see how well I know the real Tess.' The light was back in his eyes but it wasn't the playful sparkle I liked so much, it was a dark, angry fire. 'Are you really a photographer?'

'Yes.' I really needed to start believing that myself. 'But before I got my agent, I worked in advertising.'

'Makes sense,' Nick replied, his half-smile blossoming into a full smirk. 'What with you being such a good liar.'

I felt my toes curl inside my shoes. How much abuse was I supposed to take? 'And this is starting over and being professional, is it?'

'I'm sorry, I've just never liked people in advertising,' he said with a shrug. 'They sell lies for a living. You can't argue with that, can you?'

'I don't know if I can do this,' I said, clutching my wine glass and waiting for something inside to break. 'All I did was tell you a different name. Everything else I said was true. Everything that happened, happened. You know everything about me, Nick. Please don't do this.'

He looked at me from across the table, his eyes running over every inch of me. I shuffled uncomfortably in my seat. My dress covered me up from neck to knee but when he looked at me, I might as well have been sitting there in my pants. Not even my pants; I felt like I was wearing nothing but one of those awful candy thongs you saw in Ann Summers. It was worse than being naked. I grabbed a thick linen napkin from the table and laid it across my lap and one of the tea lights near me flickered as I remembered to breathe. The flame guttered for a second before going out.

Nick stood up, slowly this time, and walked around the table towards me.

'Tess.'

He crouched down until he was bouncing on his toes at the side of my chair, his hands gripping the armrest so tightly, I could see his knuckles turning white.

'It feels so wrong, calling you that.'

I pursed my lips and screwed my napkin up in my hands.

'You're right, I do know something about you,' he said, his lips so close to my ear that I felt his words before I heard them. 'I know I don't trust you. And I could never be with someone I don't trust.'

He stood up and walked away, grabbing a bottle of red wine from the table as he went.

I watched two big smoky tears drop into my lap,

veins of mascara creeping along the fabric of the napkin.

Probably not the most successful date in history, I thought, wiping away my tears and picking up a huge chunk of cheese. But at least he hadn't taken all of the wine with him.

CHAPTER 10

I couldn't face going back to my room. It was more or less impossible to navigate the hall-ways and staircases without bumping into someone and I knew that Amy would be waiting for me, either to get the gossip or catch Nick and me in the act. As much as I knew she had meant well with the dinner date set-up, I didn't want to talk to anyone until I could open my mouth without crying. I felt so cold and heavy and broken.

Hauling myself to my feet, I tipped the bread and cheese from my plate into a napkin that I hadn't ruined and picked up the bottle of white wine. What I wouldn't give to be one of those girls who starved herself through upset. One Saturday, a few years ago, Charlie took me to look at engage-ment rings with him. Afterwards, I had gone straight back to the office, locked myself in the stationary cupboard and eaten an entire birthday cake. Ever since then, when I was having a bad day, I'd wonder whether or not I could make my millions by selling women a plain cake that came with ready-made icing letters so you could write your own message. Like, 'Sorry the man you love is considering marrying a twenty-two-year-old stripper!' or 'Surprise! That bloke you shagged hates you!'

Who wouldn't buy three of those a week?

My secret garden was all closed up for the night but that was nothing a good shove wouldn't fix. With my heels and bottle under my bad arm, I gave the door a bash with my good shoulder and stumbled inside when it gave way too easily. I dropped my shoes and tiptoed onto the closest patch of grass, letting my legs sink underneath me. I'd never been much of a crier and now I knew why. It wasn't a lot of fun. My eyes were sore and my nose felt raw and swollen. Of all the glitches in human design, crying had to be the worst. It served no physical purpose I could think of and I certainly didn't feel any better for getting it all out, no matter what anyone's nan might think.

I lay down and stared up at the stars for as long as I could stand to do nothing. The evening was still warm and the grass smelled delicious, sweet against the salty taste of tears in my mouth. Had things taken a different turn, it could have been such a romantic evening. If only Nick hadn't decided to make it one of the most painful, upsetting experiences of my life, the little scamp, everything would have been great.

That and the fact that Charlie is still waiting to hear from you, the voice in my head reminded me. You know, Charlie? Tall, brown eyes, love of your life?

I groaned out loud, rolling onto my front because it was too hard to drink wine on my back, and pulled my phone out of my tiny black shoulder bag. I jabbed my finger at the screen and brought up Charlie's last email, about the Perito's pitch. It was warm and funny and there were kisses at the end of it. Of course, he'd sent that before he gave me a camera, said I should follow my dreams and then told me he loved me. Before I gave him a double thumbs up, said thanks and then ran away to Milan to jump into bed with another man.

That's what anyone would do under the circumstances, wasn't it?

It was all very confusing, I thought, drinking more wine directly out of the bottle. It's all too much.

No it isn't, the voice piped up again. Nick doesn't want you. Charlie does. You've wanted Charlie forever, Nick is a flash-in-the-pan fling who's only bothering you because your pride is hurt. This is easy; this is obvious. There's nothing complicated about it.

Gnawing on a piece of bread, I considered my subconscious. Maybe it was right. Maybe the Nick thing really was just all ego. After all, it was Charlie I called when I was in trouble, wasn't it? And all Nick's bullshit, it went both ways. He kept saying he didn't know me but really, it was me who didn't know him. I was hurt at the way he was reacting but maybe this was the real him, at last. Why should I be so upset about someone who could treat me so badly? This wasn't me. I wasn't about to let him bring me down. I tried to remember what had happened the last time I'd lost a pitch, hitting myself in the mouth with the wine bottle. It was hard to concentrate on two things at once sometimes.

It was two years ago, Sparkle paper towels, and what happened then? They gave the account to Eskum so I went after Squiggle and now Squiggle outsells Sparkle three to one. Because you don't give up, I told myself, if you lose something, you go after something better.

And this time, I already have something better, I realized, dropping the almost empty wine bottle and watching it trickle away into the lawn. I have Charlie and Charlie was worth a million Millers.

Pressing the home button over and over until my phone finally woke up, I opened my texts and carefully tapped out a new message before pressing send. Smiling, I stuffed the last handful of cheese into my chipmunk cheeks and staggered to my feet, feeling impossibly pleased with myself.

Give me a problem, I thought, dropping my phone into my clutch bag as I headed back into the house, and I will give you a solution. I was a genius. Tess Brookes, problem solver.

Tuesday morning shot through my unclosed curtains like a knife, slicing across my room, my bed and eventually my face. No matter how many times I tossed and turned, I could not escape the sunshine. I was awake. And I was hung over. I inched across

194

the bed, feeling for the edge and hoping I found it before I threw up in the covers but I was not going to be that lucky. This wasn't a puke-it-all-better hangover, this was a constant-thud-in-the-side-of-your-brain-because-you-downed-a-bottle-of-wine-and-didn't-even-attempt-to-drink-any-water-before-you-crawled-into-bed hangover.

Tess Brooke, problem drinker.

I vaguely remembered finding Amy asleep on the sofa in the living room that linked our bedrooms and vaguely remembered putting on my new pyjamas even though apparently I hadn't bothered to remove the price tag before I got into bed. Or bothered to put them on the right way round.

This was why I didn't drink. I could not be trusted.

A knock at the door made me look up altogether too quickly. Holding my head, I stuck my furry tongue out as far as it would go, opening and closing my mouth a few times until felt like it might start working again.

'Yes?' I called, staring at the dirt under my finger-nails. Where had that come from?

'Good morning.' Al poked his white, fluffy head around my bedroom door and smiled. 'You're indisposed. I'll come back later.'

Oh shit.

'No!' I flapped my arms around like a confused Muppet. The back-to-front pyjamas probably weren't helping me look more composed. 'I'm sorry, it's fine, come in. What time is it? My alarm didn't go off.'

I left off the 'because I didn't set it' part of that sentence.

'Almost ten,' he said, entering the room with a pair of black patent shoes in his hands. Why did they look so familiar? 'I believe these are yours.'

Oh shit. Times two.

'It's ten?' I asked, accepting the shoes before Al disappeared into the living room and came back with a large silver tray. He had brought me coffee. He was literally the best man alive. And I hated people who misused the word 'literally' almost as much as Amy hated it when I used air quotes. 'We missed you at breakfast.'

And that was when it all came flooding back. Oh, bollocks.

'I'm sorry.' I took the cup of coffee he held out and watched as he poured his own before taking a chair beside the bed. 'Last night was a bit strange and I must have forgotten to set my alarm and I can sleep through anything and I'm really sorry, I'll be ready to go in, like, ten minutes.'

'We're not going anywhere today, so please don't apologize,' he said, dismissing my concerns like the big-bearded wonderman that he was. 'A little bird told me they organized a surprise dinner for you and Mr Miller last night. Two little birds actually.'

'A little English bird and a slightly bigger Hawaiian bird, both of whom should know better?' I asked.

196

'Quite,' he nodded. 'Mr Miller appeared to be in quite the black mood this morning.'

'He was?' Oddly, the news of his bad mood brightened mine somewhat.

'Oh, terrible,' Al said. 'Not that I would want to interfere but can I assume dinner wasn't quite the romantic occasion the little birds had planned?'

'It was not,' I confirmed, gulping the coffee altogether too quickly. 'He shouted at me, walked out, came back in and shouted at me again and then told me he would try to be professional. Oh, and he dropped a glass but he didn't do it on purpose. I don't think. And then I ate some cheese in one of the gardens.'

'Jane's favourite garden,' he said, passing me a plate of buttery toast. Literally the best man. 'When we bought this place, there was a painting of it in one of the bedrooms and she became obsessed with restoring it to its former glory. The previous owners had been using it for storage. My Janey spent hours in there, sketching, reading. She did her fair share of cheese eating in there too.'

I wondered how much drinking she'd done in there, shying away from the sunlight as it shifted across my bed again. 'I'm really sorry.'

'You must stop apologizing,' Al insisted. 'It does an old man good to see some young people running around, living. Kekipi and I have been holed up in Hawaii for so long, I'd forgotten all the fun of watching other people's stories unfold until you came along.'

197

'You could just watch *EastEnders*,' I suggested. 'Or *Hollyoaks* if you really hated yourself.'

'The course of true love never did run smooth,' he replied, dusting off his hands before topping up our cups. I didn't know if it was because we were in Italy or because I was so hung over I made Lindsay Lohan look like someone who made good choices, but the coffee really was amazing. 'Relationships will always be complicated, I suppose.'

'Sometimes I wonder how the human race still exists,' I said, allowing myself a moment of grumpy self-pity. 'How does anyone even get together in the first place?'

Al frowned. 'I hear the internet has a lot to do with it these days. The internet and alcopops. Is Cilla Black still on the scene?'

I shook my head and frowned. 'I don't think so.'

'Great pair of legs, Cilla,' he said. 'Janey was always going on about Cilla's legs whenever she came over.'

'But how do you know if you're making the right decision?' I asked, bypassing the Cilla conversation – one inconceivable thing at a time. 'It seems like my mum can barely stand the sight of Brian sometimes but they're still together. Kekipi told me what happened with him, how he thought he was making the sensible decision and he ended up with no one. Amy left her fiancé because it was too sensible and now she's on her own.'

'And I spent fifty years with my soulmate and

I'm on my own as well,' Al added. 'How does that fit into your equation?'

'But that's different,' I said, trying to work out the sensitive way to say 'she died'. There wasn't one. I stayed quiet.

'What I'm trying to explain is that you never know how things will work out,' he said. Al was so wise. I attributed it all to his beard. 'I wouldn't trade a hundred years with anyone else for the time I had with Jane. You should never give your life to someone if you can't give them your heart.'

'What if they don't want my heart?' I asked.

'Then they don't deserve it,' he said sagely. 'But that doesn't mean you should give it to the first person who asks for it. You're a special girl, Tess. You're bright, you're talented, you're ambitious. You remind me so much of Janey sometimes. You know, she always wanted a daughter and I think the two of you would have got along very well.'

It was hard to know what to say to that. I smiled and drank my coffee, hoping I looked appropriately moved.

'I can only tell you what I told Kekipi a very long time ago. A life is too long to live with regrets.' He patted my shoulder and finished off a bite of toast. 'What you want today might not be what you want tomorrow but only you know what you really need. And that might not be what's on offer right now, but that doesn't mean you should take what is.'

'Well, that makes sense,' I assured him. And not

just about Charlie and Nick. Beginning to feel a little closer to human with several gulps of coffee running through my veins, I cleared my throat and smiled as brightly as possible. 'What's on the agenda for today?'

'I have another meeting with Edward,' Al said, pulling on his lapels like a particularly proud barrow boy. 'And I thought you and Amy might like to take some photos of Jane's studio. All the original sketches are in there, along with a lot of her clothes, all the pieces she designed herself with her seamstress. I'd like to make sure everyone knows where the inspiration for the line came from.'

'I think it's really amazing.' I looked across at my camera, waiting patiently on the desk. 'It's so great that you're going to actually have clothes in shops from her designs. Artie must be so excited to carry his mother's line in the store.'

'Artie doesn't get excited about anything I do unless it involves signing something over to him.' Al's mouth disappeared into a thin line inside his beard. 'But he's agreed to consider carrying the line at least.'

'Consider?' I asked. 'He's not going to just take them?'

'Artie feels that he has spent a long time proving himself to me,' Al said, standing up and straightening his suit. 'I believe this is retribution of sorts. Now I must prove myself to him.'

'That is messed up,' I said, growling. 'Is it wrong that I sort of want to punch him?'

'It probably wouldn't make matters any easier,' he laughed. 'But regardless, I'm hoping the party on Friday night will improve his mood.'

'Party?' I asked, ears perking up. 'There's a party?'

'I knew I'd forgotten something,' Al muttered, hands deep in his pockets. 'I *am* getting on. We're having a party on Friday night to announce the line. Big do, lots of razzmatazz, get the industry excited – drunk and excited. Kekipi will tell you all about it – he and Domenico are taking care of the arrangements as we speak.'

'A match made in heaven,' I said. 'I'm sure they'll love the opportunity to work so closely together.'

'Won't they just?' he agreed with his own brand of chuckle. 'Oh, and tonight I've got a box at the opera. I was very much hoping you and Miss Smith would join me. You're such a civilizing influence on Kekipi.'

'Really?' If I was a civilizing influence on Kekipi, I hated to think what he was like when I wasn't around. 'Of course, we'd love to go to the opera. Thank you for asking.'

In reality, I was not sure we would love to go to the opera at all. Or at least, I was not sure that either Amy or myself could be trusted at the opera. Apparently, I couldn't even be trusted to get myself back to my room after dinner and I always tried to avoid taking Amy anywhere that she needed to be still and silent for more than fifteen minutes. We hadn't been to the cinema together since *Titanic*.

'Domenico will show you to the studio, just call

201

him when you're ready.' Al filled up my coffee cup one more time before he made for the door. 'And I took the liberty of asking Kekipi to borrow some dresses for you ladies this evening. I'm assuming you didn't bring an awful lot of formal wear with you for a week taking photos.'

Formal wear? I'd assumed a nice frock and proper shoes. This was a *formal wear* occasion?

'*Arrivederci*,' Al bowed at the door. 'Remember, the easy path is rarely the right one.'

'Right,' I muttered, dropping back against the pillows as I heard the door click shut. 'Which means I probably shouldn't just go back to sleep.'

Sometimes, life was a real challenge.

'Look at you two.' Kekipi clapped both hands to his face as Amy and I appeared at the top of the staircase in all our opera-going finery. 'Goddesses. Beautifully dressed and expertly styled goddesses.'

'Shall I tell him that you've already fallen over twice?' Amy whispered.

'Let's save that for later,' I replied under my breath, trying to kick my gown out of the way as I walked. 'These things tend to come in threes.'

'You do look utterly charming,' Al said as Amy skipped down the last few stairs and planted a kiss on his cheek. She did a spin for the assembled crowd, entirely comfortable in her four-inch heels. There had to be an upside to being very short and it certainly wasn't getting a good view at concerts. While I stumbled around in heels like a stoned

Bambi, Amy had been wearing four inches and up ever since she turned fifteen. 'It's not usually quite so formal an affair but tonight is some grand premiere or charity event or something. I forget.'

'I feel like Eliza-fucking-Doolittle,' Amy replied, giving the boys another spin. 'This is batshit amazing.'

'Perhaps Eliza Doolittle at the beginning of the story,' Kekipi replied, patting her shoulder.

The second Amy had slipped into the dress Kekipi had chosen for her, she had been transformed. Unfortunately, her mouth hadn't. But still, swapping the black and green striped strappy playsuit she'd worn all day for a floor length, nude-coloured Carmen Marc Valvo gown with a high neck, long sleeves and endless handsewn sparkles had turned Amy into something unearthly. Smoothing her hair and adding a flick of black eyeliner finished the look perfectly. I had never seen her so breathtaking.

'And Tess, look at you.'

Al, Kekipi, Domenico and two silent men in what I recognized as the chauffeur's uniforms waited patiently as I clung to the banister and tiptoed down the stairs. I wasn't especially scared of falling again but Kekipi had been very clear that if I ripped the dress, he would rip me a new arsehole, and I didn't like the sound of that at all.

'Didn't I say you would look incredible?' Kekipi said, more to everyone else than to me. 'You look incredible.'

To agree with him would have seemed a little conceited but to argue would have been total bullshit. There was nothing else for it: Kekipi was going to have to dress me every day for the rest of my life. He had arrived at our suite two hours earlier with a bag full of deep blue-green Monique Lhuillier tulle and I had been incredibly suspicious. It was tight, it had a high neck and tiny little cap sleeves that threatened to make the most of even the slightest of bingo wings but once I had been properly trussed up, I couldn't imagine ever wearing anything else. The colour of the dress made my hair and eyes glow and the crossover bodice pushed everything into positions my body had long since given up on ever achieving naturally again. At the bottom of the tight mermaid skirt, a semi-sheer skirt fell in clouds around my feet. I never wanted to take it off. I wanted to wear it to do the washing-up, I wanted to wear it to go to the post office, I wanted to wear it to the gym. And I didn't even go to the gym.

'Quite beautiful,' Al commented, holding out his arm. 'Shall we?'

I felt myself colour up a little, hoping it came off as a blush of modesty and not the sweaty flush of someone who had been sitting too close to a radiator. There was a lot of internal structuring to the dress.

'I'm not late, am I?'

I turned to see Nick jogging down towards us, two stairs at a time, one hand running along the banister.

'Sorry, I got carried away working, totally lost

track of time,' he said, rubbing his chin and looking straight through me. 'Can we pretend it's designer stubble?'

'How very George Michael of you,' Amy commented, tossing her head like an angry pony. Nick ignored her. He was very good at ignoring people.

'Not late at all,' Al told him, giving my arm a squeeze and pointing me towards the door. 'Nothing is more Milan than being fashionably late.'

It was pointless to pretend Nick didn't look devastatingly handsome in his midnight-blue tuxedo, and it was even more pointless to pretend my heart hadn't dropped to the floor as soon as I saw him. While we were shooting Jane's studio, I'd filled Amy in on our dining disaster and somehow managed to get through the entire story without crying once. Granted, I'd had to throw up twice but I was pretty sure that had more to do with the bottle of wine I had drunk on a stomach full of burrata than how upset I was about Nick.

'How cheesy does he look?' Amy asked as we climbed into the first waiting car. 'I thought every man looked better in a suit but he looks like a crap stripper.'

He didn't. He looked like a God and he made me feel like I was wearing a dishrag. But I knew she was still feeling guilty and so I smiled and kept my mouth shut.

'You're not going to slag him off with me?' She looked sad. 'Come on, you'll feel loads better. Say it with me: Nick is a cockweasel.'

'I just want to get to the opera,' I said, watching his spectacular arse climb into the second SUV. 'He's not worth talking about.'

'All I'm saying is, no one gets this upset over someone they don't care about.' Amy held up her hands in surrender before switching to a fist pump. 'And now, not another word. Let's get our opera on.'

Banging my head gently against the cool glass of the car window, I crossed every available appendage and prayed that we would all get through this night without showing Al up, getting thrown out or arrested. Once a week was quite enough for me.

'Oh man, it's ridiculous,' Amy breathed when we rolled to a standstill ten minutes later. 'Tess, look!'

But I was already looking. The opera house really was beautiful. Standing proudly opposite a large square that seemed to have emptied itself as a courtesy to *La Scala,* the exterior was dramatically lit with huge golden spotlights that shone upwards onto its grand white exterior. The building itself reminded me a little of Buckingham Palace, as if it were her maj's sexy Italian cousin, but the people stepping out of the cars and walking inside made every single person who had ever stepped foot inside the palace look like a right old set of tramps. And that included any and all royal weddings.

'Is this seriously where we're going?' Amy asked as a man strolled past us carrying a cane. 'That man is wearing a cape.'

206

'Maybe it's Batman?' I offered, really wishing I'd bothered to do something more impressive to my hair than wash it. 'Why is there so much fur? It's July.'

'I think all these people are on their way home from their weddings,' Amy said. 'Or maybe they moved the Oscars. This can't just be a Tuesday night on the town, can it?'

'Who knows?' I spotted Al exiting his car across the street and unbuckled myself quickly as our driver opened my door. 'But can you please make sure I don't fall over and make a total twat of myself?'

'No, I can't,' Amy said, full of regret. 'But don't worry. All the best people fall over these days. Jennifer Lawrence falls over all the time and everyone loves her.'

'And me and Jennifer Lawrence are basically the same person, so we're sorted,' I muttered, taking the driver's hand and pulling myself out of the car. 'I'm going to die here, I can tell.'

In my heels, I was easily pushing six feet which made concentrating on remaining upright and joining a conversation with the vertically chal-lenged Amy and Kekipi virtually impossible. Al was merrily chatting away to assorted strangers in rapid-fire Italian, throwing out air kisses and laughing heartily at every other thing every other person said. Anxious, I tried to hang back, afraid of being drawn into a conversation when I didn't speak the language and afraid that I was not going to be able to take off my heels when they started to hurt beyond the telling of it in approximately seven seconds.

As someone who had barely left the country her entire adult life, it was strange to be surrounded by another language. My ears prickled at the dance and rhythm of words I didn't understand and inside I heard instruments tuning up, the discordant notes clashing against each other but harmonizing completely with the din outside.

'Nice dress.'

I wasn't sure how long Nick had been stood in front of me as I was very busy staring at a woman in a floor-length red gown that was so huge, she had two men carrying her skirts, but when I came to my senses, there he was.

'Thanks,' I said, finding my voice somewhere in the pit of my stomach and dragging it up whether it liked it or not. 'Nice suit.'

'I thought it might come in handy,' he replied, shaking out his arms until the white cuffs of his shirt appeared at the end of his sleeves, 'coming to Milan, working with a fashion designer and all that shit.'

'You have a beautiful way with words,' I said, shifting my weight from foot to foot. I really wanted to get inside and I really wanted to get away from Nick. 'You should be a writer.'

'I'll consider it.' He held out one arm and waved towards the entrance of the theatre with the other. 'May I?'

Across the road, I saw Amy already wrapping herself around Kekipi's arm and laughing wildly at whatever disgraceful thing he was saying. I had never been so jealous in my whole life.

I brushed my hair out of my face and shook my head. No. I was strong. I was woman. Or something. 'This is you being professional, is it?'

'Really?' His expression was about as comprehensible as the Italian I heard all around me. 'Just shut up and take my arm.'

Stubbornly, I crossed my arms and breathed out heavily.

'Oh, for Christ's sake!'

Nick grabbed hold of my arm, threaded it through his and began to walk towards the entrance, giving me very little choice but to follow him. I was already unsteady on my spindly heels and I would not fall over in front of all of Milan high society because someone was having another of his bipolar moments.

'Do you know the Katy Perry song "Hot and Cold"?' I asked him, tottering along a few paces behind.

'Of course not,' Nick replied, producing two tickets and handing them to a man wearing an incredibly impressive top hat. 'Should I?'

'No,' I admitted. I knew it because Amy always sang it at karaoke and by the time I got out of work on most Friday nights, Amy was so drunk she always wanted to sing karaoke. 'Silly question, really, it's not jazz.'

'I don't only listen to jazz,' he said as we dodged the kissing crowds and found ourselves in a huge foyer with beautiful crystal chandeliers hanging from the ceiling. The parquet floor shone so brilliantly that I could see reflections of the white columns that separated us from the opera boxes. 'I listen to all kinds of music.'

'Such as?'

'Leonard Cohen. Joy Division. Radiohead.'

'Oh, all the modern chart toppers,' I said, ducking my head to hide a smile. 'No wonder you're so happy all the time.'

'When Katy Perry has been around as long as Leonard Cohen, you can take the piss out of me,' Nick replied, something like a smile hovering on his face for a moment. 'How on earth are you going to get through an evening of opera if you can only manage to listen to three minutes of beeps and screeches and call that music?'

'I'm sure I'll manage, Granddad,' I reassured him, pretending that the warm fluttery feeling in my stomach had nothing to do with the fact that Nick was smiling at me and everything to do with the fact that I hadn't eaten anything since breakfast for fear of not getting into this dress. 'Where are we going?'

'To Al's box.' He checked the tickets and pointed to a dimly lit archway. 'Should be right over here.'

The atmosphere outside *La Scala* was excitable, like everyone was just a little bit drunk, but inside it was completely overwhelming. I couldn't think of another time when I had been so overcome by a space. Hawaii had been spectacular, all that sea and sand and sky, but this was something else, something man-made and almost as beautiful. The theatre curved around the stage and the red, velvet-lined boxes above and below us seemed to go on forever. From where I stood, every surface seemed to have been touched with gold.

'It's so beautiful,' I said, almost too scared to take a seat. 'Look at it!'

I glanced over my shoulder but Nick wasn't looking at the theatre below us, he was looking at me. The warm fluttery feeling in my stomach hatched into a fully blown case of butterflies.

'Amy wanted snacks,' I said, taking a step away from him, holding one elbow with the other hand and trying to work out where was safe to look. It certainly wasn't anywhere in the vicinity of Nick Miller. 'Do you think there's a concession stand?'

'Do I think there is a concession stand in *La Scala*?' Nick asked, his eyes flickering back up to meet mine. 'Are you serious? You're not in the Odeon.'

'I don't know, do I?' I mumbled as we reached our box, taking a seat in the back row. 'I've totally had snacks in the theatre before.'

'Whatever there is, you can't eat or drink in the boxes,' he pointed at a very polite sign that suggested proper theatre etiquette. 'So, no snacks, no flash photography and phones on silent.'

211

Pulling my iPhone out of my little black bag, I flicked the buzzer on to silent. Through the shattered glass, I could just made out a new text message. It was from Charlie and appeared to be a row of smiley face emojis. Either Portugal was going very well or he'd been spending altogether too much time with Amy, I thought, putting my phone away. While I sat in an empty opera box next to Nick, mentally singing 'LALALALALA' as loud as I could to drown out my sobbing ovaries, I didn't feel quite right, trying to resolve my Charlie situation. One regrettable shag at a time, Tess, one regrettable shag at a time.

'Here you are!' Kekipi and Amy barrelled around the corner, faces flushed and short of breath. 'We were wondering what you were getting up to.'

'And if I didn't know better, I'd ask what exactly you two have been up to,' I said, leaning over the back of my red velvet chair, forehead furrowing. 'Snogging in a broom cupboard? Kekipi, has she turned you?'

'If I could bear the thought of a woman's vagina, Amy's would be the first on my list,' he replied, shuffling down to the front row of the box and pulling Amy along behind him. 'After yours, of course. And Britney's. I owe her and she needs the love of a good man.'

'What have you been up to?' I asked. Nick busied himself with his own mobile, actively ignoring our box buddies. Hmm. I really hadn't thought about him in all of last night's nonsense but it seemed as though he was pretty pissed off with the whole set-up and the setter-uppers. Interesting.

'Can you keep a secret?' Amy leaned back and whispered, her breath heavy with whisky.

'You know I can't and – Jesus Christ, you stink!' I said, pushing her away. 'How did you manage to get tanked between here and the car?'

Kekipi opened his tux jacket for a split second, revealing a shiny silver hip flask, before whipping it shut just as fast. 'None for you, Ms Brookes, if you're going to be a buzzkill.'

'I totally called her a buzzkill in the car!' Amy shrieked loudly enough to turn heads three boxes away. 'High five!'

'She was a lot more fun in Hawaii,' Kekipi stage whispered, unscrewing the cap of his flask. 'Italy does not suit her temperament.'

'I'm so glad we brought the kids.' Nick looked away while Amy and Kekipi crouched down below the front of the box to take another drink. I smiled, reaching over to squeeze his forearm before I realized what I was doing. He stiffened as the lights around us lowered.

'Sorry,' I whispered, pulling away but before I could move my hand, he had covered it with his own. Even in the semi-darkness, I could see his eyes on me again. Not nearly as brave as the last time, I raised my brown eyes to meet his blue and tried very hard not to throw up. The butterflies had turned into something altogether less romantic and manageable and I was very, very close to freaking out.

'Sorry, everyone.'

A white-gloved hand pulled back the scarlet curtain to our box and bathed Al in the light of a tiny torch. He followed it down to the front row and took a seat beside Amy, brushing his hair down.

'My mullet isn't in the way, is it?' he asked, turning towards Nick and me. I wasn't sure whether it was the look on Nick's face, the confusion on mine or just the fact that we were holding hands but something caused Al to slap his thigh and laugh out loud before turning back towards the stage.

'Tell me you brought an old man a drink,' he whispered to Kekipi as the orchestra started up. 'You know I can't get through one of these things without a nip of something.'

And with Nick's cool hand still holding onto my sweaty one, I knew exactly how he felt.

CHAPTER 11

Everything I'd ever heard about the opera was true. It was dramatic and emotional and passionate, and if you didn't have a clue what was going on, it was incredibly boring. For the first fifteen minutes, I sat patiently, waiting to get it. After that, I started looking around at the other boxes, frowning at the captivated looks on everyone else's faces. What was wrong with me? Even Julia Roberts was moved to tears in *Pretty Woman*. Did I really have less emotional and cultural depth than a Hollywood Boulevard hooker?

On top of everything, it was nigh on impossible to pay proper attention to what was happening on stage when Nick had been holding on to my hand for fifty-six minutes exactly. Even though my shoulder was killing me, I was too scared to move more than an inch and every time Nick shifted in his seat, I felt a wave of warmth roll all the way over my body. It was like the lining of my dress had been replaced with a malfunctioning electric blanket. My mouth was dry but my palms were damp and I was terrified of sweating irreparably in my dress. I actually felt bad for the performers.

No matter what else was happening, it was nothing compared to what wasn't happening between Nick and me. Every breath, every movement, every time his eyelid flickered, I was aware of it all and it was all too much.

Halfway through a high note so impressive that I almost forgot to worry about whether or not I was ruining thousands of euros of borrowed silk with my mere existence, Nick suddenly pushed my hand away and shot up out of his seat. I watched, open-mouthed, as he fought with the velvet curtain for a moment before disappearing altogether. Well, I wasn't the opera's biggest fan either, but anyway you cut it, that was just rude. I flexed my suddenly cold, clammy hand and circled my shoulder in its socket. What had just happened? Where had he gone? Was he coming back? Amy and Kekipi seemed to be too busy giggling amongst themselves to have noticed anything and unless the occasional snore was how one was supposed to show proper appreciation for a well-presented aria, it looked like Al was fast asleep.

Fuck it! I was going after him.

The foyer was almost empty, presumably because everyone inside had spent an awful lot of money to come to the opera and they were going to stick it out until the bitter end whether they liked it or not. A bit like ordering a disappointing curry and making yourself finish it, even though every mouthful made you sad. Stepping out of my shoes, I padded around on the cool wooden floor for a moment, my feet sighing with relief as I looked for Nick. There wasn't an overly dramatic man-child to be seen for miles.

'Excuse me . . .' I reached out to tap a passing gentleman on the arm and gave him what I hoped was a winning smile. 'I don't suppose you saw a man pass by just now? In a dinner jacket?'

I didn't know if it was the language barrier or the fact that at least fifty per cent of people in the building were men wearing dinner jackets but he gave me a quick once-over and then followed up with the internationally recognized expression for 'get off me, you mental' and disappeared into one of the boxes. I glanced down at the black patent stilettos in my hand and reluctantly shoved them back onto my feet. If carrying your uncomfortable shoes made you an undesirable in Milan, I hoped that man never made it to Clapham on a Saturday night.

'Because *that's* likely,' I muttered, heading for the exit and some fresh air.

But fresh air was hard to find when, right outside the exit, I found Nick pacing up and down and dragging deeply on an already half-smoked cigarette.

'Since when do you smoke?' I asked, hacking out a feeble cough.

'I don't.' He threw his cigarette down and ground it out with his heel. 'I quit.'

'Looks like it,' I said, tightening my grip on my bag in case I needed to use it as a weapon. 'I'm so impressed by your willpower.'

'I smoke when I'm stressed.' Nick raked his fingers through his ashy blond hair, still pacing. 'Is that all right?'

I shrugged, leaning against the archway that lead back inside to take the weight off my feet. 'I'll admit tonight wasn't the captivating experience I was hoping for, but it's hardly driven me to drugs.'

Nick stopped moving and stared at the ground. I followed his eyes, landing on the dying embers of his cigarette. The sun wasn't quite set all the way but the theatre cast a shadow over the two of us and the tiny orange glow on the floor. I watched as it faded away into nothing.

'I've got no idea what I'm doing,' Nick said, finally.

Swallowing hard, I kept my eyes on the floor. 'About what?'

'Everything,' he replied. 'Work. Life. Everything.'

'You're doing this,' I said, waving my hands around in the air. 'For Al. This project.'

'Yeah,' he laughed. 'This is not what I do. I'm a journalist, I tell stories that need to be told. This is a trumped-up scrapbook, not a real job. I shouldn't be here.'

'Then why are you?' I asked, wanting to know the answer and not wanting him to say another word in case it wasn't what I wanted to hear.

'Because I cannot stop thinking about you!' His voice cracked and creaked in all the right places and when I looked up, he was right in front of me. 'I must have lost my fucking mind.'

I sucked in my bottom lip and bit down hard. 'Just what every girl wants to hear.'

'I promised myself, after all the shit with my ex, I wouldn't get involved with another crazy bitch.' Nick rolled his eyes upwards, as if he was giving his own brain a filthy look. He breathed out heavily, the air in his lungs still coloured with smoke. 'And look at me; I'm in Milan, chasing a girl across the ocean, a girl who can't even give me her real name. Nice work, Nick.'

His body was so close to mine, I could hear the tulle of my skirts rustling. So this was why there were never any pre-marital shenanigans in the olden days. You couldn't get away with anything without half the house hearing it.

'You know none of that had anything to do with you,' I said, unexpected tears swelling against the rims of my eyes, my nose prickling. 'And I'm not crazy or a bitch, thank you very much. But, tell me honestly, for the last time, are you going to keep beating me over the head with this? Because if you are, I don't think I want to do this any more. This "professional" thing.'

To hell with Amy and her forbidden air quotes.

Nick reached his hand up to my face and held it, running his thumb along my cheekbone to wipe away the one wily tear that had escaped. My temper had dissolved into rapid breathing and I was coming dangerously close to hyperventilating. This dress was not designed for overly emotional situations; there was altogether too much boning. Which was ironic, when you thought about it.

'Is this what you call being professional?' Nick asked before pressing his lips to mine.

I gave in before I even knew, pressing my forearms against his chest, my hands wrapped around his neck. It was the closest I had ever come to a swoon in my life. With the cold stone of the opera house behind me and the solid warmth of Nick pushing up in front of me, I was completely trapped and I loved it. His kiss was softer than it had been before, still as insistent, still as passionate but altogether less certain. Through all the layers of fabric in my dress, I felt his thigh slip between mine and heard a tiny gasp escape my lips as he broke away to draw breath.

'This is ridiculous.' Nick pulled his arms away from me and loosened his tie, unfastening his top two buttons. I pressed a hand to my chest, holding my heart in place and putting something, even if it was one of my own limbs, between us. His skin smelled like cigarettes and shaving lotion and salt. He turned away, pulling a small white box out of his pocket and shaking out another cigarette.

'I do wish you two would stop trying to lose us.'

Kekipi bounded down the steps like a bow-tie-wearing Labrador, breaking the painful tension between Nick and me. Amy followed him, a little less light on her feet than when we had arrived and, looking at her eyes, a lot less sober. Behind them, Al brought up the rear, scratching his head.

220

'What's wrong?' I shifted my attention and was very thankful that ladyboners weren't a real thing or I would have given myself away completely. 'Is it over?'

'It's not over for another two hours,' Kekipi declared with a shudder. 'I couldn't stand it for another second. Bored now.'

'And we ran out of whisky,' Amy added with a hiccup. 'Which was a major problem.'

'Yes, well . . .' Al stuck his hands deep into his pockets and wrinkled his forehead. 'It has been a while since I've attended the opera. Perhaps nostalgia has clouded my memory a little.'

'Oh, thank God,' I said. 'I thought it was just me. It was really nice though, Al, getting dressed up and coming to the theatre and everything. It's so beautiful inside.'

'And you're outside because?' Amy raised a questioning eyebrow and flicked her eyes over towards Nick. 'Bit of fresh air?'

'Something like that,' I said. 'God knows.' God being Nick, obviously.

'I don't know about you, but I need a drink.' Kekipi wrapped his arms around mine and Amy's shoulders and directed me towards our waiting cars by the kerb. 'Al, a nightcap?'

'It's seven-thirty,' Al replied, looking at the cheap plastic watch under his dinner jacket. 'I don't think this counts as a nightcap.'

'Fine. Al, lots of shots at a dirty dive bar I know?'

Al opened the door to the first car and jumped

inside. 'I think I'm going to pass,' he said with a quick salute. 'I don't need to spend a second longer than necessary in this penguin suit. See you in the morning, gang.'

'Should we not go home and get changed?' I asked, concerned once again for my dress and potential new arsehole.

'Hell, no.' Kekipi took my hand and pushed me, bum first, into the car. 'Tuesday nights are always more fun in formal wear. Are you joining us, Mr Miller?'

Nick still stood a way away from the action, inhaled on his cigarette once more and then threw it into the street. 'Why not?' he replied, striding over to the car. 'I could use a drink.'

'This should be fun!' Amy quickly clambered into the car next to me before Nick could take his seat, forcing him round to the front. 'Let's get hammered.'

'You know, I'm really tired,' I whispered in her ear while Kekipi gave the driver directions in perfect Italian. 'And there's some weird stuff going on with Nick. I think we should just have one and then head back; we've got an early start in the morning.'

'Totally,' Amy agreed, patting my knee. 'That's exactly what we'll do. One quick drink, in bed by ten.'

'Perfect.' I settled in and smiled, relieved. 'I love it when you see sense.'

★   ★   ★

222

'I love this song so much!' I yelled, clinging to Kekipi's neck and throwing back my shot. 'I tried to get it for a commercial I was working on but they wouldn't give the rights, the bastards.'

'You're so rock and roll, it hurts,' he replied, handing me another miniature glass full of good times. 'Are you having fun?'

'So much fun,' I nodded, before doing the second shot and banging the empty glass down on the bar. Or was it my third? Might have been my fourth. I couldn't quite remember. 'This place is great! Milan is great! Italy is great! Being a photographer is great!'

'You're great,' he said while I clicked my invisible camera all around the bar. At Amy, dancing on a table; at my new friends Gino and Francesca, who I had met in the queue for the toilets; at the laughing bartenders; at the half-empty bottle of champagne in Kekipi's hand. And at Nick, leaning against the bar, chatting to a random brunette. Hmm. Lowering my camera, I reached out for my champagne glass and sipped in the most ladylike fashion I could muster. Which wasn't that ladylike.

'Have you given any more thought to what you'll do at the end of the week?' Kekipi asked, snapping his fingers in front of my face. 'To what you're going to tell your friend?'

'It's haaaaaaard.' I stretched out the 'a' as far as I could to make sure Kekipi knew I was serious. 'Because I love advertising but I really love photography too.'

I stretched out the 'ooooooo' in love as well, just in case I wasn't making myself completely clear.

'I can see how the lure of sitting behind a desk and trying to negotiate the rights to Miley Cyrus songs could be just as creatively fulfilling as travelling the world and taking beautiful photographs,' Kekipi nodded. 'It must be a nightmare for you.'

'No one understands,' I said, shaking my head firmly from side to side. 'I *do* love it. It's good. It's like, you get a brief or someone says "make my baked beans exciting" and no one thinks baked beans can be exciting but you find a way to make them the most exciting baked beans ever . . .' I paused to give him a good poke in the chest. '*Ever* though, like the most exciting in the world. And you win! You win the job and then you see your ad on telly in the middle of *Coronation Street* and it's brilliant and you know you've done a good job. I like knowing I've done a good job.'

'Then explain to me,' he removed the finger that was still jabbing him in the chest and pushed my arm back down to my side, 'why you like photography so much.'

'Because it's good too.' I took another tiny sip of champagne and hiccupped immediately. 'Because it's just the camera and me showing everyone else what we can see. It's the same. But different.'

'The same but different?'

'It's telling stories,' I said. 'It's all telling stories.'

'And speaking of stories,' Kekipi unfastened his

224

bow tie and began wrapping it around his fingers into a tidy bundle before popping it into his jacket pocket, 'what on earth happened with you and Mr Miller last night?'

'I am still very angry about that.' I resumed pointing. And then drinking. And then pointing. 'That was a shitty thing to do.'

'Amy and I consulted and we felt that a conversation needed to occur.' He pushed my arm back down again. 'I apologize for my devious nature – just this once. But seriously, dish. What happened?'

'He went mental.' I looked back across the bar to see Nick still talking to the random brunette. She was far too pretty for me to be OK with the situation. Very long legs. Really good tits. Clearly the devil.

'Expand?'

'He's angry that I lied to him.' I forced my eyes back to my big gay bestie and away from Nick's Sophia Loren-lookalike. 'And he said he could never be with me. But then tonight, outside the opera . . .'

'Go on?'

'We had a bit of a snog-type thing,' I admitted to a round of delighted applause. 'I don't know what's going on. Can I have another drink?'

'You can have two.' He filled my champagne glass until the bubbles overflowed and trickled down my fingers. 'It's quite obvious what's going on here: he's punishing you. He's hurt, his ego is in tatters and he's punishing you. Straight men are so cliché.'

'You think?' I puckered up my lips to meet the champagne glass as early as possible and still managed to spill it down the front of my dress. Thankfully, Kekipi had his eyes on Nick and Sophia.

'Honey,' he topped off his own champers and smiled, 'I told you once that you were my hero; you're playing this just right.'

'Wasn't that the time I kicked that awful man in the balls and then threw up in my hair?'

'He was a terrible homophobe,' Kekipi reasoned. 'You threw up in your hair? I'm sure you just had half a McChicken sandwich in there.'

'Either way . . .' I stared at the champagne flute in my hand, glanced over at Amy on the tabletop and suddenly realized this was all a huge mistake.

'No, you've been perfect until now,' Kekipi continued. 'You stay detached and distant, show how much you don't care, and it'll drive him crazy. Don't give an inch.'

'But I passed out in a garden last night and woke up without my shoes,' I stage-whispered over the music. 'I think maybe I do care.'

'Yes, but he doesn't need to know that, does he?' he said with a sigh. 'You're so lucky you found me. Now drink that drink and get your bestie off that table before she breaks her neck and kills herself. Or worse, tears her dress.'

Taking my orders, I marched across the bar, only bashing my hip against two chairs as I went. The bar was already dark and tiny and aside from our awkward foursome, Gino, Francesca and Sophia

Loren, the only other patrons were three older Italian gentlemen who really didn't look to me like they cared for random English girls dancing on their tables. Or gay Hawaiian men paying the bartender two hundred euros to play music from his iPhone. They just did not come off as Miley Cyrus fans.

'Amy!' I shouted, holding on to the back of a chair so that I didn't fall down when I looked up. My centre of gravity was seriously compromised by my heels. And the shots. And the champagne. 'Get down, you're going to break your neck.'

'Fuck off, Mum,' she shouted back, kicking in the general direction of my face and thankfully missing. 'I'm having fun.'

'Please?'

'No.'

'For me?'

'No.'

'Kekipi wants to tell us some stories about secret gay celebrities.'

Scrambling to her knees and then her down onto her bum and finally her feet, Amy grabbed her handbag from underneath the table and gripped my arm as though it was about to fall off.

'Tell me it's neither of the Ryans?' she pleaded with big blue eyes.

I gave her an elaborate and dramatic shrug and watched her scuttle across the bar as fast as her feet would carry her. Which was, to be fair, much faster than mine would, even out of heels.

Sinking into the nearest seat, I couldn't stop myself from staring over at Nick. There he was, all smiles and charm, still talking to the Italian woman. He had taken off his tie in the car and the top three buttons of his shirt were undone and even though I couldn't see it, I knew the woman he was talking to was being treated to flashes of his toned, tanned skin and the light scattering of blond hair across his chest and it made me crazy.

Just admit it, the voice in my head was back again. You're gagging for it.

'Where is the rubber duck when you need him?' I said, wishing I'd brought my drink with me, even though the room was already starting to spin. 'I am so not gagging for it.'

And I wasn't. I was in so much deeper than that. Every second that I sat there, watching Nick chat up another woman, I could feel myself getting darker and darker. I couldn't bear it. It was making my skin crawl. I had sat in student unions, in bars, in restaurants, at weddings, at work and even slept in the same room as Charlie and his assorted girlfriends over the years and it had made me sad. I'd been disappointed. But did I do anything? No. I threw myself into my work and ignored it, hoping it wouldn't last long. It never did. But this . . . this was terrifying. I felt a hair's breadth away from frenzy. If that woman touched so much as a hair on Nick's head, I didn't know what I would do. And in that moment, it was all so clear. I saw him, I saw myself, I saw everything.

The woman leaned over and rested her hand on Nick's arm and, laughing like a madwoman while I stared like a psycho, I was on my feet before I even knew where my feet were.

'Right, that's it!' I shouted, kicking my shoes across the room. 'Get off him. Get right off!'

Since there were only thirteen people in the bar, including the staff, it wasn't hard to get everyone's attention, even over Miley. In fact, she probably could have walked through the door and twerked herself silly and no one would have noticed.

'*Scusi?*' The woman looked appropriately startled as I threw myself in between her and Nick, elbowing him backwards to make room. 'Nick, this is your friend?'

'No,' I answered for him. 'I'm not his bloody friend.'

'She's not,' he confirmed. 'Definitely not. Tess, what are you doing?'

'I don't know,' I could hear myself slurring and couldn't quite work out why. Everything sounded fine in my head. 'But I know what I'm not doing. I'm not sitting over there while you stand here, being all Mr Charming Arse and flirting with this woman!'

I patted her on the shoulder and smiled as apologetically as I could.

'I'm sorry,' I said. 'This is a whole big thing. It's not your fault you're the sea witch.'

'The sea witch?' She was confused. It was sad.

'Yeah, it's this whole Disney thing,' I explained,

waving my arms around in the air. Was it me or had my hair got bigger? 'Amy will explain it to you.'

'Amy?'

'Really, this doesn't concern you,' I said, turning my attention to Nick. 'It concerns you. And your "I'm not interested but I am interested but I'm not interested" bollocks.'

'Are we really going to do this now?' Nick asked through gritted teeth. 'Because I'd really rather not.'

'I don't give two shits about what you'd rather do,' I wailed. 'I waited for someone to make his mind up for ten years, Nick. *Ten years*. And now I'm supposed to sit there like some twat and wait for you to decide what you want? No way. Forget that.'

Somewhere in the bar, I heard Amy cheering.

'You told me how you felt and I listened and I've gone along with your hot-and-cold headfuck of an attitude until now but enough is enough!' I stamped my bare foot on the bar floor to prove my point. 'I like you. I more than like you. Actually, I think I probably might that other word you, but I can't say it here and I'm not going to say it because you're awful and you can't make your mind up and you're just messing with me and my foot hurts.'

I looked down at the floor, trying to pick up my foot and bend down to check it out, all at the same time. First mistake. The second was grabbing hold of the front of Sophia Loren's dress to stop myself from falling when I inevitably went over.

'Oh shit,' I yelped as we both toppled to the floor, me with a handful of frock, her with both boobs popping out as we went.

'I think that's our cue to leave.'

On my hands and knees, surrounded by too much tulle, my own blood and an empty bottle of limoncello I faintly recognized, I felt at least one pair of tiny fists beating me around the head while two bigger hands grabbed me around my waist and yanked me upwards.

'Sorry,' I shouted as I was hoisted onto someone's shoulder and carried towards the door. *'Mi scusi. Ciao Ciao!'*

The cold night air was a shock. It had been so hot in the bar, and from my unconventional upside-down view, I could see it had rained while we had been inside. No wonder it was so lovely and fresh. With blood rushing to my ears, it was hard to follow the exact conversation but there were definitely two male voices involved and what-ever they were discussing, we were not standing still to do it.

'Could you please put me down, please?' I asked, the contents of my stomach, almost entirely liquid, beginning to churn.

'No.'

'But I might do a sick.'

Without another word, I was immediately turned the right way round.

'I need Amy to hold my hair,' I said, brushing my hair out of my face and laughing as it sprang right back. 'She holds my hair best.'

'Amy is still in the bar, retrieving your shoes and Kekipi's phone,' Nick said, turning a corner and finally setting me down on the damp ground. 'What the fuck just happened in there?'

I pouted and shrugged.

'I got the shoes!' I heard Amy and looked over to see her holding my heels over her head triumphantly. Altogether less triumphant was the huge red stain in the middle of her chest. Kekipi's jaw dropped as we all stared at her. 'Don't worry, I haven't been shot – that chick threw a glass of red wine at me. Probably fair.'

'The dress!' Kekipi reached out to lean one hand against the wall. 'I think I'm going to faint.'

'I'm definitely going to be sick,' I said, kneeling down and gathering my hair behind my head.

'They wouldn't give me your phone,' Amy told Kekipi, rummaging in her own tiny evening bag. 'And I think I've forgotten mine.'

'Thank you,' I whispered to Nick as he took hold of my handheld ponytail as I leaned over and threw up delicately in the gutter. Wiping my mouth on the sleeve of my dress I smiled at him. 'I love you.'

'Jesus Christ!' Nick crouched in front of me, his hands still holding my hair, not quite beaming back. 'Have you got your phone to call the car?'

'Yeah,' I muttered, sitting up straight and pawing through my purse. 'Here.'

Nick passed my phone to Kekipi and sighed.

'What am I going to do with you?' he asked. 'What was that?'

'You're supposed to say "I love you" back,' I pointed out, trying not to throw up again. My body did not care for lemon-flavoured liqueurs. 'Or at least give me a thumbs up.'

'No, you're not supposed to give someone a thumbs up when they tell you they love you,' Nick replied. 'Not ever.'

'Now you tell me,' I said, taking my phone back and holding it in my hand. Squeezing the hard, sharp brick helped me focus. 'Can we go home?'

'The car will be here in two minutes,' Kekipi said, bending down to rest his hand against my forehead. 'We'll be home in fifteen, sweetcheeks. I really do have to stop getting you drunk, don't I?'

'No,' I said with much seriousness. 'I think my tolerance is improving.'

'You really are my hero,' he smiled back at me. 'Come on, let's get you to your feet.'

It felt like we waited forever for the car to arrive but I put that down to the fact that everyone else seemed very concerned that the people from the bar were going to hunt us down and kill us. Once we were safely inside and motoring through he streets of Milan, I pulled out my phone, remembering the weird emoji-filled text from Charlie.

Not for the first time, my phone did not want to play fair. It took forever to open up the conversation and even longer before it allowed me to scan up to my last sent message. 'Oh, fuck off,' I muttered, pulling my hair into my face so I couldn't see my phone. It was the perfect plan.

'What's wrong?' Nick asked, stroking my hair away from my head. 'Are you going to be sick again? Do we need to stop?'

'No, it's fine,' I promised, lying through my back teeth. 'It's nothing.'

Impressively, I had lied twice in that short sentence. I was absolutely going to be sick again and it really wasn't fine. Lying on the backseat of the car, resting my head in Nick's lap, I flashed back to the night before, back to my secret garden. The reason Charlie had sent me a text message full of smiley-faced emojis was because he was happy. And the reason he was happy was because I had sent him a text message of my own.

A text message that said 'I love you too' and there was not a single thumbs up emoji to be seen.

CHAPTER 12

'I can't believe you made me walk this morning.' Amy reached up and grabbed the sunglasses from my face, slapping them over her own eyes. 'I think I'm dying. I didn't think limoncello was that strong.'

'If we'd got in the car, I would have thrown up,' I said, squinting down the street and checking numbers on the buildings. 'And I don't think limoncello is any stronger than anything else but it probably doesn't go that well with whisky and champagne.'

'This bag is heavy – being an assistant is rubbish,' she moaned. 'I'm leaning towards the agency, right now. Could I be your secretary? I could answer the phones and fetch sandwiches and find a husband.'

Sixty-seven, sixty-nine, seventy-one.

'Not sure the agency is going to be an option,' I said, shifting my genuinely heavy backpack and stopping to check the directions on my phone. 'I have to talk to Charlie about last night.'

'You're going to tell him you threw up in a gutter?'

'I don't know exactly what I'm going to tell him but I do have to talk to him. And Nick.'

'Yeah, what's that all about?' she asked, pushing her sunglasses back up her shiny nose. 'He was practically pleasant last night. Is he ill? Does he have some sort of syndrome?'

'That's offensive to people who have some sort of syndrome,' I said. 'Any sort of syndrome. Nick isn't mentally ill; he's just a knob. But then, so am I, so there we go.'

I was relatively hazy on what had happened after we got home. I remembered Nick helping me up to my room and getting me out of my dress but since I woke up in an empty bed with my knickers on, I was fairly certain he had done the gentlemanly thing and vacated the room as soon as I was under the covers. And I wasn't sure how I felt about that.

'I can't decide if this is a better situation or a worse one,' Amy replied, switching her backpack to the other shoulder. 'Now you've got both of them trying it on? Maybe you should send them on a quest or something. Make them prove their love. First one to come back with the Heart of the Ocean is the winner.'

'The problem is, Nick didn't exactly throw himself at my feet, did he?' I said, shepherding her to the pedestrian crossing and trying not to trip over someone's sausage dog. Milan was full of sausage dogs. 'And – I can't quite believe I'm saying this – but even if Charlie went to the bottom of the ocean and found the necklace, I don't know what I would do with it.'

'Woah,' Amy breathed. 'You're serious. You would never take *Titanic* in vain.'

'I know.' I turned down the alleyway that I hoped would bring us out at Edward Warren's studio. It didn't. 'It feels weird. I've had this crush for so long and I don't know how to explain it, but something has shifted. Can you be in love with two people at once?'

'Asked every shitty romcom ever,' Amy said. 'Unfortunately for you, yes, I think you can but I don't think it can be the same kind of love. And just so you know, a crush isn't the same as being in love.'

I rolled my shoulder and it stung like a bitch. I might have slept on it funny. Or I might have fallen down and grabbed someone's boobs to hold me up. One or the other.

'I do have feelings for both of them,' I said, pressing the aching muscles in my neck. 'But it's different.'

Amy skipped in front of me, clutching her hands to her chest. 'Charlie is the moon and Nick is the sun? Charlie is a daisy and Nick is a luscious red rose? Charlie is Liam Hemsworth and Nick is Chris Hemsworth?'

'Is Chris hotter than Liam?' I asked.

'Eh.' She waved her hand from side to side. 'It's pretty fifty-fifty looks-wise but Liam loses points for the Miley Cyrus engagement thing.'

'I do worry about you,' I said, still struggling to choose a favourite Hemsworth.

'I only wish I'd known it was going to be this easy for you to get over him,' she said, following me back out of the alley without a peep of complaint. 'I could have found some random hot fuck-knuckle to bang some sense into you ten years ago.'

'I can't believe I told Nick I loved him,' I said, checking the map one more time. 'I can't believe I pulled that woman's dress down.'

'The dress part I can believe,' she went on, trotting along behind me. 'I should have cut you off after the champagne but yeah, I think the "I love you" part was a shock to everyone. Even if it is completely obvious.'

'It's so not obvious,' I said, quite aware that it was.

'Yeah, it is.' Amy pulled her polka-dot shorts down to cover her knickers as we arrived outside the studio. 'This is *wild*. I thought you just wanted to shag the arse off him but you properly love him.'

'Mmm.' I was as noncommittal as possible. 'I think this is it.'

I still wasn't completely ready to talk about it. If only I could have had my life-hanging epiphany when I wasn't completely tanked, I might feel better. Telling someone you loved them and then throwing up on their shoes was not the beginning of a love story to echo through the ages.

I pressed the doorbell then pinched my cheeks to bring a colour to my face other than green. 'We can talk about this later. Actually, no, we can't.'

'I just want to get this done as quickly as possible,' she muttered, rubbing her temples. 'I need a Berocca mixed with Red Bull and half a packet of Nurofen Plus. What's the Italian equivalent of Nurofen Plus?'

I turned to give her a look but there really was no point. We were both so hung over that anything other than express verbal communication was a waste of time.

'It shouldn't take long.' I took a step back to stare up at the unassuming façade of Warren's building, waiting to be buzzed in. 'We're just here to get a few shots of whatever Edward has done so far.'

'Thank God we're in Italy though,' Amy said as the door opened and a different slender secretary indifferently ushered us inside. 'I need to eat all the carbs.'

'All of them,' I agreed, thinking of the amazing spread on the breakfast table that neither of us had been able to touch. 'It'll be fine; he can't have done that much, can he? We were only here on Monday. We'll get in, take a few shots and be out in no time, I promise.'

'As you can see, I have been quite busy.'

Edward Warren, resplendent in head-to-toe emerald green, highlighted with a leopard-print tie, threw open the door to his workroom with a flourish.

'Fucking hell,' Amy breathed. 'Have you got elves working for you?'

239

'I tend to get a little carried away when I'm invested in a project,' he said, waving us past an army of tailors' dummies, some half-dressed, some draped with fabric, others in what seemed to be finished designs. 'I haven't really slept since I last saw you. When I was working on my collection, I had all the samples at the factory within a week.'

'This is *amazing*.' I set my backpack down on one of the few bare surfaces, and tried to count the dummies but my hangover had them dancing all over the room. There had to be at least a dozen in varying states of undress. 'Has Al – I mean, Mr Bennett – seen them yet?'

'He's coming by tomorrow.' Edward frowned at the closest dummy, removed a pin and replaced it, smiling at an imperceptible difference in the design. 'He tells me you're to take photographs of whatever you like, of everything. Do I need to be in them?'

'It would be great to get you in a couple of shots if you don't mind?' I said, looking at the room again with my photographer's head on. 'Ideally, it's all supposed to be pretty natural so maybe we could get you to work on one of the dummies while we shoot?'

'I don't like to work in front of strangers,' he said stiffly, adjusting his tie. 'But as this is for Al, I'll try. Where do you want me?'

'The light is really nice over there.' I pointed to the huge arched windows in the front of the building and away from the extensive collection of explicit nude photographs on the walls. It was nice to see he was consistent in his decorating. 'How about that?'

'I love your tie,' Amy said as she unfolded the reflector from my kit, jumping as it popped into shape. 'It's so leopardy.'

'I never really loved leopard print until I moved to Milan,' Edward explained, flipping the end of his tie happily. 'But the Italians have a taste for it and I have to say it's catching.'

'Very D&G,' Amy replied as though she knew exactly what she was talking about. 'I like the mafia widow look myself.'

'Yes,' Edward replied, reviewing her spotted shorts and pink cropped top for evidence. 'It is a classic.'

I rubbed my knuckles over my forehead, driving my hangover into the back of my head as I rifled around for my light meter. If there was one thing that Amy was great at, it was making friends. She could make anyone feel comfortable and usually knew his or her darkest secrets inside half an hour. It was a gift I wished I shared; strangers usually made me feel awkward and uncomfortable. That was one of the reasons I'd been so happy in my Charlie bubble for so long: I was rubbish at chatting people up and even worse at being the chattee. The last time a guy had had a crack at me in a bar, he ended up breaking down in tears and confessing that he was gay. I was quite proud of myself but Amy had been disappointed to say the least, especially when he confessed his feelings for the guy she was talking to. I think everyone went home alone that night.

'You've really done all this since Monday?' I asked Edward as he began to adjust the fabric on a beautiful pale silk shirtdress with a huge, full skirt. At least I found it easier to talk to people when I had a camera in my hands. 'It's incredible.'

'Without wanting to sound disparaging, they weren't complicated designs,' he said, turning a little towards the light without even being asked. For someone who didn't like having his photograph taken, he seemed to know exactly what he was doing. 'They are beautiful and classic and it's a long time since I worked on anything like this, but they weren't difficult for me. The beauty of these clothes will be in the detail and the execution. They're timeless.'

'Amy, can you lift that up a bit?' I asked. She gave a faint whimper and raised the circular reflector over her head, baring her belly. 'So, Mr Warren, you've known Mr Bennett a long time?'

'Sorry?' He blinked twice, clearly distracted by Amy's bare flesh. 'Oh, it's Edward, please. And yes, I've known him for . . . goodness, it must be forty years. I was an assistant to a very famous designer in the seventies and we spent a great deal of time with the Bennetts. Jane actually introduced me to my ex-wife. In fact, she introduced me to two of them.'

'I've heard so many lovely stories about her,' I said, crouching down and zooming in. 'She must have been amazing.'

'She was a very kind woman, very gracious,' he nodded. 'But she was a powerhouse. God help you if you ever got in her way. Or divorced one of her friends. Or two of them.'

'How many times have you been married?' Amy asked.

'Lift that up again, Amy,' I interrupted. 'She sounds amazing. And terrifying.'

'Oh, she was,' Edward laughed, folding the fabric on the dummy and pinning it in place. 'It was almost worth upsetting her to watch her go. I remember once, during fashion week, she and Al were holding a party at their palazzo and an up-and-coming shoe designer – I won't name names – came over to talk to Al about his new line, but everyone knew Jane ruled the roost when it came to the shoe department, everyone except this young man. Anyway, Al tells him he'll have to speak to his wife and the designer mistakenly thinks he means to get an opinion because, you know, she's a woman, she must be shoe crazy. So, he turns to Jane and says, "Tell me, *madam*, what do you look for in a shoe?" and Jane says "Something that sells one thousand units a month" and walks away. Never spoke to him again, refused to even look at the samples.'

Amy and I stared at him.

'Maybe you had to be there,' he muttered. 'But

it was a very long time until you could walk into one of their stores and buy a pair of shoes with a certain colour sole. Never cross a Bennett.'

'Al just doesn't seem like the sort of man to hold a grudge,' I mused, shifting positions to get a wider shot.

'Don't underestimate him,' Edward said, smoothing out his epic eyebrows. 'And Artie inherited his mother's temper.'

'I know he and his dad don't necessarily get on brilliantly,' I replied, wrinkling my nose. 'I shot him in Hawaii a couple of weeks ago but I haven't seen him here yet.'

'All the better that you don't,' he said, adjusting his cufflink. 'You know what a difficult character he can be. I'm glad they're talking again – it would have broken Jane's heart to see them at each other's throats the way that they were.'

I signalled for Amy to lift up the reflector again, getting a high-pitched whine in response. 'I don't think I realized it was that bad. They really fell out then?'

'I don't like to gossip,' Edward said before deciding that he was more than happy to make an exception. 'But it was very unpleasant for a while. Al was in Hawaii; Artie was here in Milan or out in New York. As I understood it, Artie felt that he was doing all the work on the business and should be made CEO of the company.'

I snapped a couple of shots to keep him talking. 'But that's happened now, hasn't it?' I asked.

'Yes.' He clambered to his feet and dusted off his emerald knees. 'And now they're talking again, but I wouldn't be surprised to see another tiff. Artie inherited Jane's temper but he failed to develop some of her more gracious habits and he was always such a mummy's boy. But like I said, I'm not one to gossip.'

'Clearly,' Amy said, dropping the reflector to the floor. 'Dreadful habit.'

'It's a shame you aren't taller, you would make a wonderful model,' Edward said, looking up from the dummy to consider my friend. 'Such an interesting face.'

'Interesting?' she returned his gaze with as serious an expression as she could muster. 'Bugger. If only I could grow a foot overnight.'

'Perhaps you would be interested in modelling for me?' Edward asked, gesturing to the huge black-and-white photos on the walls. 'I actually took all of the pictures in this room.'

'I reckon we can get the rest of it done without you,' I said before Amy could punch him in the balls or accept. 'Thank you so much, Mr Warren.'

'Right, yes.' He pulled a business card out of his back pocket and handed it to Amy. 'Think about it.'

'Tess could model for you,' Amy said, immediately putting the card down on the table beside her. 'She's tall.'

Warren cast his eyes my way, looked me up and down and screwed up his face.

'You are tall,' he said, hand already on the door handle. 'Good for you.'

'I'm going to Photoshop his bald patch even bigger,' I whispered as the door closed behind him. 'Wanker.'

'Please tell me we're done?' Amy begged, two hours later, poking her head out from underneath one of the unfinished dresses. She had been flat on her back underneath her *haute couture* tent for the last twenty minutes and I was well aware that she was losing patience. Amy wasn't someone who suffered in silence. Ever. 'You must have taken a photo of every stitch in every dress.'

'I'm trying to be thorough,' I said as I adjusted the flash. I *was* trying to be thorough but really, I was just enjoying myself so much I'd been messing around for at least the last forty minutes. There didn't seem an awful lot of point in sharing that information with Amy.

'Look at you.' Amy gave me a tired smile. 'You're so excited. You really do love this, don't you?'

I smiled right back and carried on clicking.

'I can't imagine not having a camera in my hands now,' I said. 'It's so weird. I never thought I'd be able to fall in love with something so quickly.'

'Are you talking about photography or Nick?'

'How many times do I have to tell you to shut up?'

'I can't wait to see the pictures,' she said with a yawn. 'Which is a thinly veiled hint that I really think we could have been finished by now.'

'This is my job, you know,' I replied, clicking through my last shot. 'And it is supposed to be yours as well, at least for this week.'

'Don't remind me.' She shuffled out from underneath the dummy and began trying to roll up the reflector. I wondered how many times she would attempt it before giving up. 'Although it'll be fun to have someone to go to the Jobcentre with for a change.'

'Nice.' I turned off my camera and stashed it safely in its bag, feeling a pang of Charlie-related guilt. Would I have to give him the camera back? Would it really count as a break-up if we were never really going out? 'Have you got everything?'

'Everything except my sanity,' she replied, holding up her backpack. The reflector was shoved in the top, not even nearly properly folded. 'Can we please get a car back to the palazzo?'

'You can call it the house, you know,' I said as I nodded, pulling out my phone and dialling Domenico and asking him to send someone to pick us up. 'I would know what you mean.'

'But it isn't a house,' she gushed, following me into the lift, waving goodbye to the naked women on the walls. 'It's a palazzo and I love it. It's so beautiful and I love going back to find my bed already made and dinner already cooked – and they're sending us a car, Tess! You just called and they're sending a car. I think I was Italian in a former life, I feel so at home here.'

I raised both eyebrows. 'Yeah, it's definitely

because you were Italian in a former life and not because you're lazy.'

'I can't help that I was made to enjoy the finer things in life,' Amy said. 'I don't know what I'm going to do when we have to leave.'

'Well, that makes two of us,' I said, whipping my brand new sunglasses off the top of her head and sliding them up my nose. 'Come on, the car will be here in a minute.'

Incapable of standing in one place for more than two minutes, Amy bounced around the street while we waited outside. I pushed up the long sleeves on my striped T-shirt and leaned my head back, letting the sunshine wash over my face and give me as many premature wrinkles as it liked, while she pawed the window of an incredibly expensive lingerie shop.

'There are loads of knicker shops here,' she shouted back at me. 'Do you think Italian people do it more than English people?'

'Just because you're not speaking Italian doesn't mean you can shout things like that across the street,' I pointed out, refusing to make eye contact with her and hoping none of the straight-to-the-point-of-po-faced people walking quickly by could understand.

A large black SUV I recognized from Al's Milanese harem of cars pulled up across the street.

'Amy,' I shouted, waving her over. 'The car is here.'

But before she could scoot back from ogling the window of the neighbouring shoe store, the

248

door of the car opened and a tall, grey-haired man stepped out. Twisting the ends of his handlebar moustache, he pressed the buzzer on Edward Warren's studio. I took a step backwards into the doorway of one of the knicker shops.

'Where is it going?' Amy wailed as the car pulled away. 'Please don't leave us.'

'That's not for us,' I said, grabbing her collar and dragging her into the doorway beside me. 'That's Artie Bennett.'

'Al's son?' she whispered, eyes wide. 'Nice tash.'

'It does make him a bit conspicuous,' I agreed. 'What's he doing here?'

'I got the impression Mr Warren wasn't that keen on him,' Amy said, wrinkling her nose. 'He certainly doesn't look like it's a social call, does he?'

A second black SUV pulled up just as Artie disappeared inside the studio. Taking Amy by the hand, I dashed across the street and hopped straight into the back seat of the car.

'What do you reckon that was all about?' Amy asked as we pulled away and into the busy midday traffic.

'I don't know,' I said, looking through the back window of the car and wishing I could be a fly on the wall in that studio. 'But he certainly didn't look very happy.'

'Maybe he told two men that he loved them and has to work out what he's going to do with his life as well?' Amy suggested, pre-emptively cowering in the corner of the backseat.

'Yeah, probably,' I replied, punching her in the arm. 'There's a lot of that going around.'

'Just the ladies I wanted to see.'

Before we had even pulled all of the equipment out of the car, Al was jogging down the front steps and taking the backpack out of Amy's hands, throwing it onto his back. Back in his comfy clothes, knee-length board shorts and a faded Led Zepplin T-shirt, he looked altogether more like himself than he had yawning his way through the opera.

'Hello.' I couldn't help but smile when Al was around. My mum's father had died when I was very young and since my dad hadn't ever really been around, I'd never met his parents. I'd been in the market for a surrogate grandpa for a long time and I couldn't think of a better candidate. 'Nice shorts.'

'So glad to be out of a suit.' He pulled at the neck of his T-shirt and stuck out his tongue. 'It's too bloody hot.'

I nodded, desperate to get out of my super-cute printed trousers and T-shirt combo and into the shower.

'Have you spoken to Artie this morning?' I asked, not quite sure what to say. 'Only I thought I saw him just now, when we were leaving Mr Warren's studio.'

'I haven't seen him today,' Al said, looking a little uncomfortable. He always looked a little bit uncomfortable when he was talking about his son. 'Probably out shopping. He's worse than his mother for spending money on clothes.'

'You don't think he'd be visiting the studio?' I suggested.

'Unlikely.' He shook his head and chuckled. 'There's very little love lost between Artie and Edward. Artie has never forgiven him for putting him over his knee at Paris Fashion Week when he was seven.'

'I can see how that might leave some mental scars,' I replied, perfectly happy to change the subject. Their domestics were none of my business. 'I don't suppose you've seen Nick around, have you?'

I thought I'd done quite a good job of sounding terribly casual but according to the look that passed between Amy and Al, I wasn't quite as blasé as I had hoped.

'He's out all day,' Al confirmed. 'Left me a message. We were supposed to have lunch together but apparently there is some journalistic emergency that must be tended to.'

'Totally gone to buy a ring,' Amy said.

'So what's on the agenda for today?' I asked, digging an elbow into her ribs. 'Well-deserved day off?'

'No rest for the wicked,' Al said, shaking his head. 'Off to look at the retail space the estate agent has found. Care to come along?'

'I was going to look over this morning's shoot

actually. Can you manage without us?' I shifted my own backpack onto both shoulders. Why did everyone always take Amy's bag from her? She was little but she was as strong as an ox. So what if I was five foot ten? I was as weak as a kitten and twice as pathetic.

'Oh, I'm sure I'll cope,' he said with a wink. 'How is everything looking?'

'We'd tell you but we'd have to kill you,' Amy said. 'And *I'm* not doing anything, I could come and look at the shop with you. I've worked in enough of them.'

'Fabulous.' Al offered Amy his arm. 'I could use an expert eye. And Tess, I was thinking, it would be lovely to blow up some of the photos you took in Hawaii for the party, the ones of Janey's dresses. What do you think?'

'Sure,' I shrugged, trying not to scream out loud. My pictures? My pictures on display at one of Bertie Bennett's famous parties? 'Did you want to pick some?'

'You're the photographer,' he said, opening the car door for Amy. 'Whatever you choose will be perfect, I'm sure. Perhaps pick eight or so and email them to Kekipi? He'll get them sorted out in time for Friday.'

The two of them jumped straight back into the car Amy and I had just stepped out of, leaving me in the courtyard waving like I might never see them again. As the car disappeared down the road, I turned to look at the palazzo. It really was beautiful.

I knew that if I chose photography it wouldn't always be glamorous locations and swanky jobs on this kind of money, but the alternative was starting to look a lot less appealing. Even if I got to spend one week a year somewhere as beautiful as this, a blank, beige office in the cheapest part of East London could hardly compete. We might have a water fountain if we were lucky. This place had an actual fountain.

'I could get used to it if I tried,' I said, starting up the staircase.

It wasn't that I was in love with climbing three flights of stairs up to my room, although it was probably brilliant exercise for my arse, but every time I stepped foot in the palazzo, I expected to see bluebirds hovering around me and adorable squirrels running ahead of me down the hallways. It was magical. And enormous. Amy and I only took up one suite at one end of one floor. I didn't even know where Nick was staying, let alone Al and Artie. Three floors of stories, hidden behind locked doors. Me and my camera were itching to get inside some of them. Instead, I headed up to my own room, riffling around for my suite key, and noting the glow of my phone in the bottom of my bag.

Opening the door, I dropped my bag on the sofa in the living room and dropped myself into the armchair closest to the window. I had fallen in love with the street below, the park across the road, and promised myself I would make time to go and get lost in it as soon as I'd got some work out of the way. But who knew when that would be?

I settled at my desk, taking the memory card from my camera and slotting it into the card reader that was already plugged into my laptop. While I waited for the morning's photos to download, I checked my phone, finding dozens of exciting spam emails offering to help me enhance my penis and two text messages, one from Paige and one from Charlie.

Paige's text was lovely, *All right, slag, managed to keep your knickers on this time?* Without a wittier response in me, I replied *No* and pressed send. Hopefully she would have some words of wisdom for me. The text from Charlie wasn't quite so easy to deal with. *You around to talk for a bit?*

Hmm. In all fairness, I was around but I didn't really have time to talk. I needed to edit a load of pictures and work out a way to say: 'I know I said I was in love with you for ten years but it turns out I sort of love someone else now, and so it's a thanks but no thanks from me' in a way that wouldn't make him want to beat me around the head with a sackful of Perito's Chicken cook-in sauce. And every time I tried to think about it, my brain started to melt.

A holding text was the only thing for it. Fighting with my shattered screen, I told him I was out on a shoot and would call him tomorrow. I always worked best on a deadline. Now I had twenty-four hours to sort things out with Nick and work out how to tell Charlie that I still wasn't sure about the agency but I was pretty certain that I didn't want to move in with him or spend any more one-on-one time with his penis but I still totally considered him to be one of my very best friends. Because men loved hearing that, didn't they?

Staring at my laptop, I felt myself spacing out. Maybe if I started on the Perito's pitch and came up with something amazing, I'd feel less guilty. At least then I would only be fucking up half of Charlie's life – and nothing took the edge off having your heartbroken like winning the account for Britain's second most successful cook-in sauce, did it?

'Or maybe that's just me.' I gave myself a concerned glance in the big, gold mirror that hung above the desk. 'Bugger.'

CHAPTER 13

'Here you are,' Amy said, skipping into my room. 'Should have known I'd find you behind a desk.'

'Hey, what time is it?' I waved behind me and rubbed my screen-sore eyes. It felt as though I had been staring at the same blank page forever but I still had nothing for the Perito's pitch but a notebook full of scribbled out statements and lots of Pinterest boards of badly cooked chickens. 'How was the shop thing?'

'It's nearly seven and the shop thing was great and you need to get dressed for dinner.' She walked straight over to my wardrobe and pulled out a pair of jeans and a black silk long-sleeved top. 'Come on. I've got loads of exciting things to tell you.'

'I think I'm just going to get this finished,' I said, nodding at the computer. 'I need another hour or so.'

'Have you spoken to Charlie?'

'No.'

'Have you spoken to Nick?'

'No.'

'Let's go out and get something to eat,' she said,

holding up the black top and waving the arms around. 'Kekipi is downstairs, waiting. You've got to eat, woman.'

I flicked my eyes over to my peacefully charging iPhone. She wanted to go out? We weren't all eating dinner together?

'I'm not really in the mood to go out,' I said, rolling my shoulders and flicking attention back to my blank PowerPoint presentation. 'You go. Have something yummy for me.'

'So I saw Domenico on my way up.' Amy walked over to the desk and leaned against my shoulders. 'He reckons Nick's still not back from wherever he went this morning.'

'Must be something important then.' I sucked in my cheeks and pursed my lips at the computer monitor. How could he go missing after what had happened? What kind of person reacted to a declaration of love by vanishing? Other than me?

Amy rested her chin on the top of my head. 'You've been sitting at this desk since I left, haven't you?'

'Yes?'

'Which was six hours ago.'

'Yes?'

'Wow, it's almost like we've travelled back in time.'

'I've got work to do.'

'Fine.' She wrapped herself around me from the back of my chair, squeezing my arms against my body and leaning over my chair. 'You're forcing me to do this, you realize.'

Before I could move, she pressed Apple and 'S' then jabbed the power key on the monitor.

'Amy, you shit!' I exhaled hard. 'I'm halfway through something.'

'And you'll always be halfway through something until someone makes you stop,' she said, diving across the floor to pull the plug on my computer altogether. I gasped as the little white light in the front faded into darkness. 'This is for your own good.'

The way I looked at it, I had two choices. I could throw Amy out of the window and tell everyone that she fell, or I could punch her in the boob, get changed and eat some dinner.

'Just so you know,' I said, picking up the jeans and top and heading for the bathroom. 'I'm going to punch you in the boob as soon as I've had a wee.'

'Excellent!' She flopped onto my bed and raised her arms in victory. 'Can't wait.'

'*Buona sera.*'

The world's happiest waiter greeted our little gang as we walked into the restaurant. Al had declined our dinner invitation for reasons unknown and Nick was still AWOL, leaving me, Amy and Kekipi to fend for ourselves.

'*Buona sera,*' Kekipi replied in his gentle, lilting Italian. '*Tavolo per tre, per favore?*'

Our waiter waved us forward, guiding us through a tidy maze of square tables covered with sharp white linens and populated by stately looking older gentlemen in suits, and elegantly dressed middle-aged women who spoke to each other in rapid Italian. I ran the backs of my hands lightly over my nose and forehead, hoping to dispel as much shine as possible. How did they look so well put together? And there wasn't a natural look in the place: every woman had their hair and make-up done and no one looked like they were about to melt. My hair was already piled high on top of my head but the jeans and long-sleeved top had been a mistake. If it hadn't been for all the mirrors on the walls, I would have stripped down to my pants but we were planning to eat and I didn't want to be put off my own dinner.

Once I had been shamed by every woman in the restaurant, we finally arrived at our table, right at the back of the room, tucked away from the classy diners near the window.

'Are they ashamed of us or something?' Amy asked, taking her seat as the waiter pulled out her dark-wood chair. 'Shoving us in the back?'

'I booked under Al's name,' Kekipi explained with a nod to the waiter. 'This is the best table in the restaurant. Away from the riffraff.'

'Amy's so used to being the riffraff, she didn't realize,' I said, dabbing myself down with my napkin. 'It's lovely.'

'So what?' She smiled brilliantly at the waiter as he flicked her napkin onto her lap. 'They don't have a seating hierarchy in Pizza Hut.'

'There is a time and a place for Pizza Hut but this is a little nicer.' Kekipi said something to the waiter that included the word *vino* and made my stomach turn ever so slightly. 'Make sure you save room for dessert. Or make yourself sick in between courses. The choice is yours but you won't want to miss out.'

'I don't think I'd have to force myself to throw up if there's wine involved,' I said, my face turning green just from looking at the empty glasses on the table. 'I think I'm going to be sober sister tonight.'

'All the more for us,' Kekipi said with a friendly shrug. 'So, tell me stories. I spent all day shackled to Domenico the Dull planning the party for Friday night and honestly, that man wouldn't know a good time if it crawled up his butt and did the *merengue*. Hopefully some fun will be had, but believe me when I tell you it was an uphill struggle.'

'Sounds like it's going well?' I gave the waiter what I hoped was an internationally recognized smile for 'I don't speak your language but I appreciate your service' as he poured me a glass of water.

'Jane planned all Bennett bashes,' he said a little sadly. 'We haven't really had a party since she passed, but Al is determined to go all out with this. You know what they say: behind every great man is a strong woman. And behind every strong woman is an entire gang of fantastic homosexuals with the perfect snappy comeback and an even better colour scheme. It'll be as good as it can possibly be.'

'I can't wait,' I said, chugging my water. 'All I did today was work, so you win.'

'I worked too,' Amy said. 'We went to Edward Warren's studio this morning and then me and Al went to look at a shop he's thinking about renting.'

'And how was Mr Warren this morning?' Kekipi asked, nodding at the wine our waiter had brought over for his approval. 'It's been such a long time since I've seen him, I'd forgotten how delightfully sleazy he is.'

'That just about covers it,' I said, shuddering at the memory of his not-so-tasteful nudes. 'He offered to take some pictures of Amy in the buff.'

'Not that I'm encouraging you . . .' He paused, sipped the wine and swilled thoughtfully before giving thc waiter a second nod. 'But that man is richer than Croesus.'

'Was Jesus rich?' Amy asked. 'I thought he was supposed to be poor.'

Kekipi shook his head and tasted the wine before the waiter poured him a full a glass.

'And to be fair, you don't have a job,' I said, covering my wine glass with my hand, equally proud and disappointed in myself.

'Actually, I kind of do,' Amy said, exclusively proud.

I blinked and then remembered to smile. 'Topshop called?'

'No.' She cleared her throat and shuffled in her seat, throwing back her shoulders and pulling

261

herself up to her full five feet. 'Al offered me a job and I said yes.'

'You're joining the family?' Kekipi clapped, clearly delighted. 'Oh, young Padawan, I will teach you all I know.'

'Al offered you a job doing what exactly?'

As soon as the words were out of my mouth, I realized I did not sound as supportive as I could have been.

'I mean, yay,' I added. 'Woo.'

The grin on her face wavered for a moment before she regrouped and turned her attention to Kekipi.

'We were walking around the shop and he was asking me what I'd do if it were mine,' she said, after a big sip of wine. I could see she was trying to play down her excitement and I felt terrible. 'And you know, I had loads of ideas and Al really loved them all and he said it would be brilliant if I would help him, you know, bring those ideas to life and I agreed and I'm going to work with him on realizing his concept stores. I'm, like, a consultant.'

'Well, cheers to that.' Kekipi raised his glass. 'To Amy the consultant.'

'Amy the consultant,' I echoed. 'That's amazing.'

'*You* can't cheers,' Amy said, pulling her glass away from mine. 'It's bad luck to toast with water. I don't want your bad luck.'

'Yeah, that's the last thing you need,' I said, still struggling to get my head around her new job.

'So, what are you actually going to be doing? And where are you going to be doing it?'

'We're still working it all out.' The edges of her mouth tensed slightly. 'But it'll most likely be based in Milan for now. We're going to be looking at concept stores in other cities eventually.'

'This is so exciting,' Kekipi said quickly, raising his glass again. 'I didn't realize you were such a retail guru.'

'Oh yeah, I've worked in loads of shops. This is basically what I've spent my entire career working towards. Totally meant to be.'

Even though every atom of my body knew it was a horrible thing to do, I sat back in my chair and let out the tiniest, quietest snort.

'Excuse me?' Amy pulled up the strap of her neon-green sundress and gave me a look. 'What was that for?'

'Oh, you know what?' Kekipi pushed out his chair and quickly stood up. 'I might just use the restroom before we order.'

'Did you just laugh at me?' Amy asked, her smile gone.

'No, I didn't laugh.' I closed my eyes and gave myself a mental slap. 'I accidentally made a badly timed noise. It didn't mean anything.'

'I know you're the super amazing career girl and I'm the hilarious unemployed fuck-up,' she replied, folding and refolding the napkin in her lap. 'But I can do this. You weren't there – Al really liked my ideas.'

'I didn't say you couldn't do this,' I replied. 'I don't think that at all. I'm just as hilariously unemployed as you right now, aren't I?'

'No,' she said calmly, 'last time I checked, you had two jobs to choose from. Because it always works out for you and it never works out for me, does it?'

'I've only ever had one job,' I pointed out, not nearly as calmly. 'So I think "it always works out for me" is a bit of an exaggeration. And maybe it hasn't worked out for you yet because you haven't found something you want to stick at.'

She pursed her lips and ran a finger round the rim of her wine glass. 'So now I'm a slacker who can't stick to anything?'

Oh, fuck a duck. I bit my thumbnail, trying to work out how I had managed to dig myself into such a deep hole so incredibly quickly.

'I feel like you haven't really loved any of the jobs you've had before,' I was trying so hard to choose my words carefully but all I could hear was the sound of a shovel hitting the soil. 'And all those jobs have been retail.'

She stared at me while raising her glass to her lips.

'Apart from that one where you dressed up as a fox outside the bingo hall. That wasn't retail. And you actually did that for ages.'

She finished her entire glass of wine in two gulps and placed the glass back on the table.

'So you think I should go back to handing out

fliers in a sweaty second-hand animal costume?' she asked.

'That's clearly not what I said,' I replied, waving my hands in the air and fitting right in with everyone else in the restaurant. 'No one should have to hand out fliers in a sweaty second-hand animal costume.'

'I'm sorry my previous career choices weren't good enough for you,' she snapped. 'But I never wanted to sit chained to a desk, being miserable and wasting my life. If I'm unhappy, I don't stay in a job and convince myself it's OK for seven years.'

'Then what happens when you get sick of this job after three months?' I said, with a slight snap of my own. 'You just going to call Al and tell him you're poorly then never show up for work? Again?'

She picked up her menu and flicked her fringe away from her forehead. 'That's not going to happen.'

'Because it's never happened before,' I said, picking up my own menu and pretending to read about the specials. 'Obviously.'

'Oh, shut up!' Amy slapped her menu back on the table, making the cutlery bounce and rattle. 'I'm going to do this, I'm going to be great at it and you are going to owe me a massive apology.'

'I hope you're right,' I replied, straightening my knife and fork. 'For Al's sake.'

'For Al's sake,' she repeated. 'Glad you're so worried about me.'

'Of course I'm worried about you,' I said. 'I'm

always worried about you, but Al has been really good to me and I don't want you to get into this without thinking it through and then pack it in. This is a really big deal to him and he doesn't know you and you don't know him and I know you've done loads of retail but you haven't ever really done anything like this, have you?'

'I've spent more hours working in shops than you've spent taking pictures,' she said, looking me dead in the eye. 'Al took a chance on you and it worked out, didn't it? Did you have this conversation with yourself before you came out here? Because as I remember it, you were pretty happy to come and fanny about in Milan for a week and then sod off back to London and Charlie and the agency if it didn't work out, weren't you? Wouldn't that qualify as letting Al down?'

I felt my cheeks redden and looked away.

'I'm going to do this, Tess, and I'm going to be good at it. The reason I haven't stuck to stuff before was because I was bored. The jobs were boring. This is going to be a challenge and Al is going to help me and teach me, not just send me to the stockroom with a tagging gun and a load of manky, sweaty boob tubes that some twat of a teenager who doesn't use deodorant wore out once and then brought back.'

'I'm sorry . . .' I blew out a big, heavy breath. 'If you want to do this, you should do it. It sounds really exciting.'

'It *is* really exciting,' she said, casually swiping her hand across her cheek. *'I'm* really excited.'

Oh God, I'd made her cry. What an absolute shitbag. I silently willed her eyes to dry up while she concentrated on her menu with glossy eyes.

'So tell me about the shop – where is it?' I asked with far more enthusiasm than necessary. 'What are you planning?'

'It's on Via della Spiga,' she replied with a sniffle. 'And I don't know yet. I just suggested some stuff and Al thought it would be good. Whatever.'

'What are we all having?' Kekipi arrived back at the table just as the tension simmered down to quiet resentment and an awkward silence. 'Have you decided?'

'I might start with the *Caprese* salad,' I said, trying to communicate everything that had happened in the last four minutes with my eyebrows. Sadly, while they were plentiful, they were not magical. 'What about you, Amy?'

'Dunno,' she replied with a sullen look.

'Excellent.' Kekipi laid his napkin across his knee and gave me a stern look. 'Fantastic. More wine, anyone?'

'I might have a half,' I said, holding out my glass.

Kekipi filled it almost to the brim before emptying the rest of the bottle into Amy's and then waving it at the waiter.

'Wine makes everything better,' he explained. 'And anyway, it's impossible to get drunk when you're eating pasta. Soaks it all up. Now, Tess, the *Caprese* salad, you said? Sounds delicious.'

I nodded, sipping my wine very, very slowly while Amy chugged half the glass right away. Maybe I should have stayed in my room, after all.

Kekipi had been right about one thing: the food was delicious. Unfortunately he had been either misinformed or lying through his back teeth about everything else. Wine did not make everything better and the pasta did not soak it right up. Two bottles later and Amy was struggling to wind her spaghetti onto her fork and Kekipi's eyes had taken on a distinctly glazed look. I was still nursing my first glass, very keen not to throw up or lose my shoes again. I could only abandon them so many times before they started to take it personally.

'Still no word from Nick?' Amy asked, attempting to spear a slice of sausage from her plate before giving up and diving in with her fingers. 'Nothing at all?'

I shook my head and filled my mouth with fish.

'You two are fantastic,' Kekipi contributed while sawing up his steak. 'You're my second favourite couple after Kim and Kanye. Why can't you see what's so obvious to everyone else?'

'It's confusing,' I said, pushing up my long sleeves for the thousandth time. Silk might look pretty but it did not stay put. 'One minute he says he hates me, the next minute we're kissing.'

'The next minute you're shagging like rabbits,' Amy added. 'The next minute he has vanished without a trace. Oh my God, do you think he's married? That he's got three kids and a wife? Two wives? Seven kids?'

I dropped my knife and fork on my plate and stared while she shovelled food into her mouth. 'I didn't before but I do now.'

'Just a theory,' she shrugged. 'It's that or he is just actually properly mental.'

'He's got some trust issues,' I said. 'Things were bad with the ex, I think.'

'You think? You don't *know*?' Kekipi clicked his tongue. 'Honey, you need to talk to that man and get some sense out of him. We can all see he likes you, we can all see that you like him. Call him. Call him right now.'

'Ooh, yes, call him!' Amy came to life, clapping like a toddler who had eaten an entire tube of Smarties. 'Put him on speakerphone, I've got some questions for him.'

'I'm clearly not going to do that,' I said, sitting on my bag to prevent Amy from doing it for me. 'I'll speak to him tomorrow.'

'And say what?' Kekipi asked. 'Not to be difficult, but you said he has trust issues, no?'

I nodded, assuming I would not like where this was going.

'Have you told him about your suitor back in London?'

And I was correct.

'He knows bits,' I said, eyes down. 'We haven't really had a thorough update on the situation. Mostly because he keeps bloody disappearing before we can have a proper conversation.'

'And when you have that proper conversation, what exactly are you going to say?' He popped a huge piece of cow in his mouth, giving me a five-second respite. 'Hmm?'

Hmm, indeed.

'I was sort of planning to wing it?'

'No, you're being a pussy,' Amy said, in between swallows of wine. 'About all of it. Make a bloody decision, Tess.'

'You've got to love the mouth on this girl,' Kekipi said, his mouth still full.

'First you love Charlie, then you love Nick. First you love advertising, now you love photography.' She swung her hands from side to side to illustrate her point but only succeeded in knocking a basket of bread out of the hands of a passing waiter. 'You can't have everything and you can't just stay there on the fence. What do you want?' She narrowed her eyes. Payback time.

Surrounded by a shower of bread rolls, for the wont of a snappier comeback, I shrugged. What I really wanted to do was whine and cry and ask her why she was being so mean before going to my room and taking all my toys with me. But I was twenty-eight and sitting in a restaurant in Milan and I didn't have any toys with me, so that wasn't really an option.

270

'Life isn't just about what you want,' I said, shifting on top of my clutch bag. Beading was not comfortable to sit on. 'You can't just do what you want and hope everything will turn out for the best. You've got to plan for the future, think ahead. It's not about what might sound like the most fun now.'

'Wow!' Amy closed her eyes and smiled. 'It's like sitting here listening to your mum.'

All the colour drained from my face and suddenly, I felt very, very sick.

'Can you even hear yourself?' Amy asked. 'You're actually sitting there, telling me that what you want doesn't matter, what makes you happy doesn't matter. Is that what you want? Marry Charlie, give up your dreams and slog away day in and day out at the agency so you can turn into a bitter, resentful old cow like your mum?'

'Do I need to go to the restroom again?' Kekipi asked, switching his stare from me to Amy and back again. 'Because I didn't really need to go last time and I'm worried one of the waiters thinks I'm trying to pick him up.'

'No,' Amy threw her arm out in front of him, effectively sticking him to his seat, 'you don't need to do anything. *She's* the one who needs to think about what she just said. You don't know, Nick or Charlie. You can't decide, agency or photos. You *can* decide and you do *know* but you've spent so long listening to, and believing, all your mother's shit that you don't believe it.'

271

She paused for breath and wine.

'You don't trust your gut. This is the first time in your entire life you've had to make a difficult decision and you're trying to wimp out of it, but you can't. If I lived by your logic, I'd be married to Dave and as miserable as sin, maybe even divorced by now. Or worse, I'd be your mum and Brian, sitting around the house, hating each other. Is that what you want? Just be fucking brave for once in your life.'

I stared across the table at the girl who had been my best friend for as long as I'd been alive. When Gareth Hunter pulled her skirt out of her knickers while we were doing handstands, I was the one who chased him round the playground and kicked him in the balls. When I was too embarrassed to get changed for swimming in year nine because my boobs were already enormous, Amy was the one who had performed a Spice Girls' song-and-dance routine on the other side of the changing room so I could put my cossie on in peace. When Caitlin McGarry, my year ten nemesis, told everyone in the village that Amy had called off said wedding because we were secret lesbians, Amy turned around, grabbed my boobs and announced to the whole church that she could do a lot worse. Which would have been bad enough if we hadn't been in church at the time. At midnight mass. Completely stinking drunk.

But at that exact moment, I didn't know her at all. Or at least I didn't want to know her.

'I'm really sorry,' I said, pushing my chair away and standing up, suddenly too hot and too confined and too desperate to be anywhere other than there. 'I need to go.'

'Tess . . .' Amy stood up to follow me but Kekipi blocked her path. 'Come on, I'm sorry. Sit down.'

'No, it's fine,' I called out behind me, ricocheting through the tables and grabbing hold of the backs of empty chairs on my way out. 'Sorry.'

It was dark outside but still so humid that I could feel the sweat trickling down between my shoulder blades and pooling in the small of my back. I felt sick and dizzy and confused and I needed to not be there. The pavement was practically deserted and motorbikes and push bikes lined the streets, suggesting that the bars and restaurants and grand old houses all around me were filled with all the cheering, laughing people I could hear somewhere outside my head. Every so often, I lifted my head and saw lights flickering on in high up windows, or curtains being drawn, closing me out of the happiness inside. Or maybe that was just how it felt. Perhaps they were closing the curtains on their own arguments and dramas. Everyone had their own crises, didn't they? And everyone felt as though theirs was the most important in the whole wide world.

After a few minutes of careening blindly down the street, I saw a park appear to my left. I had accidentally found my way home, or at least I had found my way to the palazzo. It wasn't my home; I didn't actually have one of those. With the park on my left and the palazzo on my right, I did exactly what Amy wanted me to do. I made a decision. Even though I was tired and upset, I was still me and being raped and murdered in an unknown city park in the dark wasn't at the top of my list of things to do in Milan so I slipped through the gate and sat on the first bench I found, close to the railings that separated the park from the street and let myself breathe.

Why were things never easy? Why were they always either boring, exhausting or so hard I wanted to run into the nearest wall, headfirst, and have the hospital put me in a medically induced coma until it was all better? I rubbed my clammy hands up and down my jeans and tried to clear my head. Everything was shouting in there and I couldn't concentrate. Charlie and his chickens and Nick and Al and the photos for the party and what was Artie doing at Edward Warren's and what if Amy let Al down and poor Kekipi, losing his one true love all those years ago?

'One thing at a time, Tess,' I whispered, my voice strange against the quiet of the trees around me, and the passing scooters that whirred down the Corso Venezia. 'One thing at a time.'

Without knowing why, I put my hand into the back pocket of my jeans and pulled out a napkin that I'd scribbled on the night before Milan to try to marshall my thoughts. A four-point plan. Get a camera, go to Milan, come home, win the Perito's pitch. Had I been smoking crack that day? Had I really thought it would be that easy?

It almost made me laugh that the one thing that I had been so sure of, the Perito's pitch, was the one thing I felt the most defeated by. No one was ever going to accuse me of being an expert in how to deal with men, and even fewer people would send you my way if you needed a top photographer, but advertising was the one thing I knew. Only not this time. I'd spent all afternoon reading the brief over and over and I had nothing. I didn't want to let Charlie down, but even more than that, I didn't want to fail. I never failed at anything. But then again, how many things had I actually tried?

At the same time, I was having the best time taking the photos for Al's project. Shooting Jane's clothes, their designs, Warren's samples – every time my right finger clicked the camera, I felt a buzz. It was exciting. But did that mean I should give up everything I'd ever known? A career I'd worked hard for? You didn't walk away from something just because it wasn't exciting any more or because something else seemed shiny and new. But there had to be a compromise, a middle ground between the Amy way, chasing after life like a kitten with a ping pong ball, and my old way. Or, as much as I hated to admit it, my mother's way.

Amy was right, life was supposed to be lived, not endured. If Al hadn't chased after Jane when

275

she was engaged to another man, I wouldn't be sitting in this slightly creepy park in Milan on my own in the dark. OK, that wasn't the best example, but if Al hadn't taken his chance when it came along, I would never have got the call to work for him in the first place, I would never have borrowed-slash-stolen my camera and I would never have met Nick. Maybe it was time to give the path less travelled a proper look.

I stood up, screwed the napkin up into a ball and tossed it in the bin at the side of the bench.

'Don't be a wimp, Tess,' I told myself, biting colour back into my lips and heading back to the palazzo. 'It's time to be brave. Don't be such a chicken.'

I stopped dead in my tracks, feeling my eyes widen with delight.

'Don't be a chicken,' I repeated, the smile that had started in my eyes finding its way down to my mouth. 'Be brave.'

Sometimes, I thought as I raced across the street and ran through the gates of the palazzo, I was so good, I scared myself.

CHAPTER 14

It was late when I finally turned off my computer but I was incredibly happy. One problem down, only about fourteen left to figure out and I would be sorted. I had been working in the dark, in too much of a hurry to even bother turning on my bedroom light, so I knew Amy had come home a while ago. The lights in the living room had flickered on, sending a sandy gold beam under my bedroom door before they went out again just as quickly. I felt sick to my stomach at arguing with Amy; I never felt myself when things weren't right between us and while I knew waking her up would mean taking my life in my hands, I wouldn't be able to sleep until I'd said I was sorry.

Tiptoeing out of my room and across the living room, I tapped gently on her door before letting myself in.

'You awake?' I asked, trying not to bump into any more furniture. I already had glorious bruises blossoming on both hips from my pinball-esque exit from the restaurant. 'Skankface?'

'No,' she replied, the duvet pulled right up over her head. 'Piss off.'

'I would but I need to say sorry,' I said, settling on the edge of her bed, just about managing not to shove my bum in her face. 'There's this really annoying thing where I can't sleep if you're mad at me.'

'I'm always mad at you and you sleep like a baby.' Amy pulled the covers down, her mascara all smudged and her eyes red raw. 'A giant baby with stupid boobs.'

'You're the baby,' I said, a relieved half-laugh burbling out of my mouth, mixed with a fresh rush of tears. 'When are you going to start taking your make-up off before bed?'

'Last night's eyeliner is good enough for Debbie Harry so it's good enough for me,' she said, rolling over the bed and making room for me to put my cold feet under the covers. No matter how hot it was outside, the bedrooms in the palazzo were air conditioned to the point of frigidity. 'I'm sorry I was such a cow.'

'I'm sorry I freaked out.' I wiped my own mascara smears away with the sleeve of my shirt. 'And you know, you were right. My brain got stuck and it needed a bit of a shake. Maybe not quite such a loud one in a restaurant before I'd even had my pudding, but still . . .'

'The pudding was amazing,' she replied, reaching out for my hand and giving it a squeeze.

'You actually stayed and had pudding after I walked out?' I shook my head in the darkness. 'Honestly.'

'Yeah, what are you going to do?' Amy said with a sniff. 'Now either shut up and go to sleep or sod off back to your own room. I'm tired.'

'I'll see you in the morning,' I said, kissing the top of her head and padding back to my own bedroom, the knot in my stomach feeling considerably looser, if not entirely undone. Without looking at the clock, I picked up the phone and dialled Kekipi's extension.

'What's wrong?' he answered in a voice thick with sleep.

'I'd feel bad about waking you up but I heard you still had dessert after I left so I don't,' I said.

'Well, I'm not getting up to get it for you now,' he yawned. 'Are you OK?'

'Yes, sorry for making a scene,' I said, resting the handset between my ear and my shoulder and retying my ponytail. 'Um, do you know which room Nick is in?'

'He's directly underneath you,' Kekipi replied, a smile in his sleepy voice. 'The irony.'

'Thanks, goodnight,' I replaced the handset and took a deep breath. Two apologies down, one to go. At least, the last one until morning.

The house was still in the middle of the night, but it didn't feel sinister like big old houses usually did. If anything, it felt more open, as though I could walk through any of the doors and find myself in a fairytale. As much as I wanted to, I fought the urge, given that there was every chance

I'd find myself in someone's bedroom while they were asleep and that was generally frowned upon.

At the bottom of the staircase on the second floor, I paused across from a pair of double doors. They were the same as the doors to my suite, white with delicate gilt edging, but whatever was going on inside was certainly not the same as what was happening upstairs. Someone was talking, shouting, but not in English or Italian. If I had to guess at a language, I would have said Chinese or Japanese but since my ability to discern the different between languages of the Far East began and ended with Wagamama and The Golden Dragon, I was at a bit of an ignorant loss. Before I could decide what to do, one of the doors opened and someone slipped out. Domenico.

Once he had slipped away down the dark staircase, I stared at the closed door for a couple more seconds. Before Domenico had even made it to the bottom of the stairs, the shouting started up again. Sadly, the ability to translate through sheer willpower alone didn't come any more easily than telepathy, and so I continued on my mission, marching down to the end of the hallway, certain, determined and only ever so slightly terrified.

I knocked on Nick's door, half-hoping that he wouldn't be there. He'd been AWOL all day after all; maybe Amy was right, perhaps he'd had to pop home and pick the kids up from school. Turning a terrified giggle into an awkward cough, I stepped back, startled when the door did open. There he was, not missing, no kids, just Nick, holding on to the door handle and looking very confused.

'Do you know what time it is?' he asked, his voice gruff and worn.

'I don't actually, I was working.' I pushed past him into the room and noted that it was half the size of mine. Ha. 'Where were you today?'

'Working,' he replied as he rubbed his eyes with the heel of his hand. 'What's going on?'

I let myself take one quick look at his bare chest and snugly fitting boxer shorts before giving myself a shake and remembering why I was there.

'I need to apologize,' I said. 'For last night.'

'Oh. Right.' Nick held out his hands and let them fall back to his sides with a slap. 'We'll just pretend it never happened. Hardly the first time a drunk girl declared her love for me.'

'I really only wanted to apologize about the puking part.' I was suddenly very interested in my toes. 'That part kind of still stands. I think. Sort of.'

'It does?' He raised an eyebrow and a hint of a sleepy smirk appeared on his face. 'Well, well, well.'

'Don't well, well, well me, Nick Miller.' I looked over my shoulder at the bed and then back at the man in front of me. 'Is it OK if I sleep here tonight?'

'Depends. Do you really want to sleep?' he asked, turning the lock on the door and walking over to me, taking both my hands in his. 'I'm all awake now.'

Averting my eyes, I smothered my own smile and let the heat from his body warm me through.

281

'I'm tired,' I said, pulling him towards the bed. 'And we need to talk about stuff. In the morning.'

'Talk about stuff? Can't wait.' He kissed the back of my neck as I turned away. 'But you're a terrible tease, you know.'

'I'm sure you'll survive.' I sat on the edge of the bed to strip down to my underwear, thankful for the forgiving cover of darkness that kept me in flattering shadows until I slipped under the covers.

Shuffling backwards, I kept going until my back was pressed right up against Nick's chest and his legs were curled around mine and his breath was blowing evenly over my right ear. I closed my eyes and curled my hands over his, basking in the calm, easy warmth of the moment.

Perhaps I had walked in on a fairytale after all.

I woke up to a phone ringing, face down in my pillow and uncomfortably disoriented. Reaching out for my nightstand, my hand slashed through empty air and the phone continued to ring. Altogether too quickly, I realized I wasn't in my bed and so the phone wasn't where it was supposed to be. The phone was on Nick's side of the bed. Only Nick wasn't. Rolling over, I squinted into the semi-darkness of the closed curtains and looked for signs of life. Nothing.

'Not again,' I mumbled, crawling across the bed to stop the phone from ringing, either by answering it or throwing it through the window, I wasn't quite sure yet.

'Hello?'

'Oh, um, Tess? Did I dial you by mistake?' Al sounded confused at first and then wildly pleased with himself. 'I was trying to reach Mr Miller.'

'No, this is Nick's room,' I replied, face-palming myself for answering the phone in the first place. Which was more embarrassing? Pretending it was perfectly normal for me to be answering a man's phone at the crack of dawn or telling your *de facto* granddad and boss that you honestly didn't let the man whose phone you're answering put any appendage in any part of you. Well, at least not in the last twenty-four hours. 'I'm just visiting.'

'Of course,' Al said, doing his best Patrick Stewart impression. 'Good to see my collaborators collaborating.'

Hmm.

'If you could let Mr Miller know this morning's field trip has been postponed, that would be fabulous.'

'Yeah, no problem.' I clutched the duvet tightly around myself and looked around the empty room. 'I'll tell him. Did you see the photos I sent to Kekipi?'

'The photos, dear?'

'Of Jane's dresses,' I reminded him. 'For the party?'

'Oh yes. They were marvellous.'

Even though I was plenty confused myself, I couldn't help but notice he sounded distracted. 'Is everything OK?' I asked. 'Is there anything I can do?'

'Just some hiccups,' he said, smoothing out his

voice and my nerves. 'Teething problems I probably should have expected with a new business. Nothing to worry about at all. Let's all catch up this evening at dinner, yes?'

'Sounds brilliant. See you then.'

I hung up the phone, pulling my knees up to my chest, and sighed. All I had to do was get through the rest of the day without killing anyone and I'd be just fine.

'Well, bugger me backwards, look who it is. How's your vagina?'

'Morning, Paige,' I smiled into my iPhone in spite of myself. 'My vagina is fine. How's yours?'

'Grown over,' she replied, the line crackling very slightly. 'Sealed up. There are tumbleweeds up there, I think. Tell me everything.'

'I would if I had any idea what's going on,' I said, turning on my computer and pressing a hand over the speakers before it could bust out its irritating Apple chime. 'But I need a favour and you're the only person I trust to help.'

'Are you trying to flatter me because you know I won't want to do it?' she asked. 'Because I'm very lazy and if it means getting off my arse, I won't lie, I'm probably going to say no.'

'There is the slightest getting-off-the-arse element,' I admitted, 'but only to walk to the printer. Mostly, it just involves using your eyes and pressing, like, four buttons.'

'Four is a lot,' Paige said. 'You're clearly taking

liberties but luckily for you, the printer is next to my desk.'

'I need someone to look over the Perito's pitch for me and then print it out,' I explained, opening up my PowerPoint document from the night before and scanning to make sure I hadn't gone completely mad. 'I'm emailing it all to Charlie but he's shit at presentation boards and I'm worried I won't have time to get it done properly before Monday.'

'You're still going ahead with this then?' she asked. 'Because someone might have told me that a certain tallish, blondish shagger had made an appearance in Milan and that the two of you were getting along quite well.'

'How are you in touch with Amy?' I opened an email and clicked on the attachments. 'That girl cannot be trusted to relay the facts.'

'Facebook, innit?' Paige said. 'And Twitter. And Snapchat. She loves an app, that girl.'

'She's sending you Snapchats?' I pressed send and tried very hard not to think what she was sending photos of. 'Yes, I am still doing this and yes, Nick is here but no, I haven't got a clue what's going on. I thought I had for half a second but you know what he's like.'

'You know what?' she said. 'I really don't. I only know Nick the Knobhead. I know the character he puts about, the arrogant, full-of-himself shagger, but that's not really him, is it? Or is it? Because I'll be so happy if it is.'

'I honestly don't know,' I said, wishing it wasn't

the truth. 'He changes his mind more often than I change my knickers and I know you don't know me that well, but believe me, I am fastidious about clean knickers.'

'Good to know,' Paige replied. 'Back to Nick: you could do something incredibly wacky and ask him what's going on?'

I looked over my monitor and checked out my reflection in the mirror. Thank God Nick hadn't been there when I woke up, I looked like a panda on meth.

'It is starting to look like I'm going to have to take such drastic measures,' I said, trying to wipe away some of the mascara that was crusted all around my eyes. I didn't care what Amy said: there was no way Debbie Harry walked around looking this shit. 'Terrifying.'

'And not to make matters more difficult but where does this leave taller, darker and quite frankly as far as I'm concerned, handsomer, Charlie?'

'It leaves him as my best friend,' I said, hoping it was still true. 'I haven't quite worked that part out yet.'

'At least you're sending him a brilliant ad campaign for chicken,' she reasoned. 'That's bound to cushion the blow. Sorry I'm dumping you, darling, but ta-da! Here's a big old boost up the career ladder.'

'Are you taking the piss?' I asked.

'I'm not sure, to be honest,' she replied, 'but I'm looking at this presentation and it is *brilliant*. Don't be a chicken! Eat one. Really funny.'

'Because Perito's is spicy,' I said, excited. 'So people need to be brave to eat it! And we'll have a man in a shit chicken suit running around with a load of blokes doing Evel Knievel stuff – you know, stupid things that men think are cool.'

'Yeah, it wasn't a difficult concept to grasp,' she sighed. 'But thanks for assuming I'm an idiot. I'll check it, print it out, and courier it over. Send me his address?'

'Sending it now,' I said, still very pleased with myself. It wasn't often I managed to take someone hurling insults at me and turn them into a killer ad campaign. I was a glass of whisky and two married mistresses from feeling just like Don Draper. And it was a bit early in the day for the whisky. 'Thanks so much for this, you're a lifesaver.'

'So you're still coming back at the weekend?' she asked. 'Do you want to get lunch on Sunday or something? Catch me up on how your very many difficult conversations go?'

'Yeah, I'll let you know when we're back,' I looked around my bedroom, feeling incredibly possessive all of a sudden. 'We'll make a plan.'

'Fine, glamorous photography lady,' she said before blowing me two kisses. 'Talk to you later.'

'Paige?' I squeaked before she could hang up.

'Tess?'

'Thank you,' I said, feeling silly and grateful and sad and happy all at the same time, 'for not sending me home in Hawaii. You could have kicked me off that shoot right at the beginning. If it weren't for you, I wouldn't be here now.'

'Don't thank me too soon,' she warned. 'And don't do yourself down. You're good, Tess. You're a good photographer, and I'm only going to say this once, but you're a hot piece and a nice person.'

'Thank you,' I said, wanting to give the phone a hug.

'I mean, a bit *too* nice sometimes, probably. Almost erring on the side of martyr. And you'd do a lot better if you put a bit more effort into the hot piece part of that compliment but in general, all the raw materials are there for a shit-hot, shit-kicker of a woman.'

'Thank you,' I said, wanting to hang up.

'No worries.' This time I got three kisses. '*Ciao ciao, bella.*'

Peering back into the mirror, I frowned, peeling off my shirt and heading for the shower. It was hard to be annoyed with someone when you looked like Alice Cooper's ugly twin sister but somehow I found a way.

The showers in the palazzo weren't the most modern or luxurious in the world but any kind of hot running water was pretty wonderful when you had woken up alone in a bed that wasn't your own. I wasn't quite sure how it happened but almost an hour had passed since my chat with Paige when I finally found myself fully dressed. Amy was hanging out in the living room, knees first on the sofa,

leaning out of the window and staring at the beautiful, sunny day outside.

'You look nice,' she said, giving me a slightly
surprised but approving glance. I curtsied,
holding out the skirt of my little red sundress
and accidentally showing her my knickers. It was
shorter than I might have liked, but that's what I
got for letting a gay man choose my clothes.
'You've done something with your hair.'

'Washed it *and* dried it,' I declared, joining her
on the settee. 'Fancy, I know.'

'What's the occasion?' she asked. 'Is the Queen
coming for dinner?'

I shrugged, trying to find my bench in the park.
'Could be. You never know with Al, do you?'

Three sharp knocks announced Nick's entrance.
He walked right in before we could invite him,
without waiting for anyone to come to the door.
I knew it was really my fault for not locking it
behind me on my way in but I was still annoyed
enough to blame him for anything and everything
that came to mind. The door not being locked,
apartheid, Justin Bieber's breakdown, whatever.

'There you are.' Nick strode into the middle of
the room in a beautiful light blue shirt that almost
matched his eyes, his hair darker than usual, still
damp from a shower maybe, and his jeans were
perfectly tight in the arse and loose in the leg. I
wondered how many pairs he had tried on before
he bought them. I hoped it was at least nine. Jeans
shopping was soul-destroying.

'You're just so bloody good-looking,' Amy sighed loudly, sliding down onto her backside and sighing. 'Could you wear a bag over your head or something?'

'Is there anywhere else I should be?' I asked him, ignoring Amy. It was something that took a lot of practice and he seemed to be struggling with it, his attention constantly flickering over to her stony expression.

'You're not where I left you,' he said. 'Does she need to be here for this?'

'Not where you left me?' I was confused. 'I'm not your car keys.'

'No, she's not,' Amy agreed. 'And yes, Nicholas, I do need to be here. It's my room.'

'You said you were tired and I woke up early so I went for a run,' Nick said, rolling up the arms of his sleeves as he spoke. He did not seem to be enjoying his audience. 'And I got back and you weren't there.'

'I was tired last night,' I said, so glad I had washed my hair. Clean hair was much better for self-righteous flicking. 'That didn't mean I was tired this morning.'

Nick stared across the room and out of the window, his jaw tight and his expression dark. Our living room had gorgeous high ceilings and huge, bright windows but Nick managed to suck all the air out of the room and replace it with tension in a heartbeat. Someone had turned the volume up on the cars driving by on the street below and every dog bark made me jump.

'Ooh!'

One too many seconds of awkward silence were broken by Amy.

'So, you slept in his bed last night but didn't put out?' she asked, pointing at me. 'And then he woke up this morning with a hard-on, as you do, but thought you didn't want to eff him so he went for a run, or he had a wank but doesn't want to say that in front of me, and when he got back, you'd disappeared. So now he's being mardy?'

I looked at Nick and shrugged, the sounds outside returning to normal volume, the room relaxing around me. 'Sounds about right.'

'And *you're* annoyed because he wasn't there when you woke up and *he's* annoyed because you'd gone when he got back from his run, which had to be really difficult with a hard-on. Just saying.' Amy rolled her eyes and rested her head on the back of the settee. 'Do you two need a full-time translator or what?'

'It would seem so,' Nick replied, carefully folded sleeves now folded right across his chest.

'It's not Tess's fault,' Amy said, hopping up off the settee and patting Nick on the shoulder as she passed. 'She's never really had to deal with a proper wanker like you. She's probably going to fuck this up another couple of times . . . just so you know.'

'Duly noted,' he said, the suggestion of a smile crinkling around his eyes while Amy backed into her bedroom while theatrically staring at Nick's arse.

'I was annoyed that you weren't there when I woke up,' I said as her door closed. 'You should have woken me up.'

'And I was annoyed that you weren't there when I got back,' he replied. 'Now that's cleared up, can we talk? Without an intermediary?'

I looked out the window and immediately found my bench. It looked different in the daytime.

'Apparently not well but we can try,' I said. 'Why don't you start?'

'Not here.' Nick held out a hand and cocked his head towards the door. 'I want to show you something.'

'Maybe he didn't run off the erection,' Amy shouted through her closed bedroom door. 'Be safe.'

'She doesn't get out much,' I said, my body fizzing as his fingers wove themselves through mine. 'Where are we going?'

'Somewhere erections are frowned upon,' he replied. 'So Amy doesn't have to worry.'

I made a small half-laughing sound but I couldn't help but be a little bit disappointed. Maybe I shouldn't have bothered washing my hair after all.

CHAPTER 15

'I can't believe you made me get on a motorbike,' I said, my arms still wrapped around Nick's waist minutes after we had come to a standstill. 'My legs don't work.'

'Your legs do work,' Nick said, calmly peeling away my arms and knocking down the kickstand with his boot. 'Can you stand up?'

'No.' I was not lying.

In twenty-eight years, I had never been on a motorbike. When I was little, my uncle had come off his and spent an entire summer in traction. While I found his agony hilarious at the time – very few things were as funny to a seven-year-old girl as a grown man in a full-body plaster cast – the message was clear: get on a motorbike and you will die. My mother had been quite vocal about it, my uncle had been lucky but every single other person who came within fifteen feet of a motorbike was absolutely, definitely, one hundred per cent guaranteed to die. And like everything else my mother had banged on about over and over and over, I took the message to heart and considered it gospel.

Until an attractive man asked me to get on the back of his bike . . .

'It's the best way to see Milan,' Nick explained, manoeuvring himself out of his seat and attempting to loosen my vice-like grip on the handles behind me. 'Didn't you love it?'

I stared at him with wide-open eyes. 'I have had my eyes closed for the last twenty minutes.'

'We were only on the bike for five,' he replied. 'Come on, it's safe now.'

'I'm not getting back on it,' I said, letting him lift me off the leather seat of the bike, holding my breath until I felt solid ground beneath my feet.

'Then you'll walk home,' he said without flinching. 'Now look, wasn't that worth it?'

The sun was so strong, it was hard to see exactly where I was until Nick pulled the sunglasses off the top of my head and slid them over my eyes.

'Honestly,' he sighed and tilted my head upwards. 'Look up there.'

We were parked beside what looked like a big church until I raised my eyes up and realized that it just kept going. And going and going and going.

'Woah.'

'I think that's what the new pope said when he came here for the first time,' Nick commented. 'It's the *duomo*. Isn't it amazing?'

The blinding white spires of the cathedral stretched so high, it looked like they would split the sky and make it bleed. Back on the ground, I stumbled backwards, dizzy from looking upwards and still trying to find a spot where I could take it all in. It was basically the size of the village I had grown up in. I was impressed. I'd never been especially religious – me and my sisters hadn't been raised to believe in anything other than being home in time for tea – but I'd always been impressed by churches and cathedrals. The idea that someone, or rather a lot of someones, would dedicate their lives to building something so epic without so much as an iPhone to help them blew my mind. I couldn't even put up a picture without the spirit level app. Not that I ever put up my own pictures, but I did like playing with the app.

'It's beautiful,' I said, feeling as though I could look at it for days and never get bored. 'How have I not seen this before now?'

'You've been walking around with your eyes closed?' Nick pulled on my arm. 'Let's go.'

I pulled up my shades to show him that my eyes were wide open. 'We're going in?'

'No.' He leaned in and pressed his lips against mine, quickly enough for it not to be a big deal to anyone around us, but long enough to make all the blood rush to my head. 'We're going up.'

As much as I hated how arrogant and self-righteous Nick could be, I loved the fact that he took charge and made plans. I was so used to being the Boss of Everything at work and waiting for Charlie to plan anything more exciting than a lunchtime trip to Subway that it made a nice change. He made me feel like a girl, rather than a bossy loser.

'This way.' He pushed me through a metal detector, surrounded by very tall men in very impressive uniforms, carrying very big guns. I cowered, keeping my eyes down and praying that they wouldn't shoot me. Nick gave them all manly nods and kept on going. 'You don't mind a few stairs, do you?'

'No . . .' I wasn't entirely sure. How many stairs were a few?

'Ladies first, then.'

In front of me was a very narrow, very dark, stone staircase. I peered around the corner, only to see it twist upwards into the darkness after four or five steps, and looked back at Nick. He gave me a bright sunny smile, followed by a gentle push on the arse.

'Is there not a lift?' I asked.

'Yes,' he replied. 'But we're not using it.'

'Gotcha,' I said, turning my back to him and trying to delicately dab away the sweat that was already speckling my forehead from being out in the morning sun. 'How many steps is it?'

'To the top?' he asked, turning to squint at a sign in Italian behind him. 'That would be nine hundred and nineteen.'

'Brilliant,' I said. 'Great workout. I haven't had my run today.'

'You run?' he asked.

'No.' I replied. 'I don't.'

'One foot in front of the other, Tess.' Nick gave me a second, considerably less gentle shove. 'There are people waiting.'

'Easy,' I said, my legs already protesting. 'Piece of cake.'

'You enjoying yourself?' he asked as we rounded the second corner. 'With the project, I mean?'

'Yeah,' I said, pleased to discover I could speak and climb upstairs at the same time. Tess Brookes, multitasker. 'I'm loving it, actually, and I've got so many great shots. It's fun, documenting Al's new baby.'

'More fun than advertising?'

I reached out to run my hand along the cold stone wall of the staircase and kept going.

'It's different,' I said, not wanting to start a row in such an enclosed space. 'I know you don't approve but I love working in advertising. It's a different kind of challenge, though.'

'Explain it to me,' Nick's voice sounded so close but I didn't dare turn around to look at him in case I fell. The staircase was narrow and winding and stiflingly hot. 'I want to understand.'

'To me, both jobs are about telling a story,' I said, turning another blank corner. Oh good, some more stairs. 'With advertising, you have a blank page or fifteen seconds of airtime, and someone wants you to tell the story of their product as clearly and convincingly as possible. With photography, it's the same. There's a story in every picture and it's up to you to tell it. It's really easy for me to see a concept in my head, advertising or photograph, but to put it on paper or on TV and have everyone else get exactly what I was trying to say? That's the challenge. And I love that.'

'OK, I get that.' There wasn't even a trace of exertion in Nick's voice. 'But it sounds like a creative thing, not something you should be whoring out for a Pot Noodle.'

'I don't consider it whoring.' I was concentrating too hard to make air quotes but I was still thinking them. 'I consider it a challenge.'

'Convincing people their lives aren't complete until they've bought whatever you're selling is a challenge?' he went on. 'Telling them they aren't good enough until they've bought a new pair of trainers? I don't think I'll ever get that.'

'Maybe I'm just not as precious about things,' I said, my breath coming shorter, my thighs starting to burn. It was all very sexy. 'And I don't think about it that way. I'm just trying to do a good job.'

'But you're a photographer now, right?' His transatlantic lilt came in at the end of the sentence. If I hadn't been heaving for breath, I might have made a sarcastic comment. 'Surely you can see that working in advertising eats away at the soul?'

'Mm-hmm,' I said, panting. 'What if I haven't given up advertising?'

He didn't reply and I was fairly certain it had nothing to do with his being out of breath. Didn't he say he'd been for a run this morning? How was he still upright? My legs were so heavy but I refused to give him the satisfaction of asking if we could slow down.

'Are we nearly at the top yet?' I asked.

'No.' he replied. 'Not even close.'

I wondered how they would get my body back down if I died in the staircase. Hopefully, they would make Nick carry it back down to teach him a lesson but I assumed he would probably just chuck me out a window and leave me for the Alsatians. Except I hadn't seen any Alsatians in Italy and I didn't think I could cope with the indignity of being eaten by a group of dachshunds. So I kept on going. Sweating, heaving and staggering onwards, ever onwards.

Just as I was considering giving up on Nick, life and breathing in general, I turned the last corner and caught a glimpse of a painfully bright sky ahead of me.

'Thank you Sweet Baby Jesus and all the angels,' I whispered, scraping the sweat from my forehead and searching for something sacred-looking to kiss. Somewhere along the last one hundred steps, I'd gone from lightly glowing to looking like I'd been in a spinning class for fourteen hours. Which was actually a ridiculous thing to say – I mean, as if I'd ever been in a spinning class in my entire life?

'Isn't it amazing?' Nick grabbed my hand and stepped in front of me, pulling me along a narrow walkway. I was so busy putting one foot in front of the other and waiting for the sparkles in front of my eyes to go away that it took me a moment to look up and realize where we were. 'Milan might not be the most classically beautiful city in Italy but this is pretty bloody impressive.'

'We're on the actual roof,' I said, my fingers tightening around Nick's. 'That is the actual edge of the actual roof!'

'I know.' He stopped in front of another, shorter but steeper, open-air staircase. 'Where did you think we were going?'

'Somewhere that passed health and safety codes?' I suggested, pointing at the steps in front of me. 'I'm not going up there!'

'Yes, you are,' Nick said. 'Because you can't sit down on this part; pretty easy to fall over the edge, too. That's much harder up there. You can sit down when we get to the top.'

It was all I needed to hear. Shoving him out of the way, I scrambled up the last twenty steps and emerged on the glowing white roof of the cathedral.

'It looks a bit like a sci-fi Houses of Parliament,' I said, staggering along the slanted roof and sitting down on the first stable-looking surface I could find. 'Don't you think?'

'No.' Nick sat down in front of me and pulled out his phone.

'Well, I'm not in a rush to go back down.' I leaned backwards and stared up at the sunny sky while my leg muscles tried to relax. 'I'm knackered.'

'Don't worry,' he said, pointing his phone directly at me. 'We'll take the lift. Smile for the camera.'

'The lift?' The few muscles that had managed

to calm down tensed right back up. The camera phone clicked and Nick grinned. 'Delete that immediately, it is not my best angle.'

'I'd have to agree,' he replied. Thankfully, I was already so red in the face from my climb, he couldn't tell I was blushing. 'So what, you're not a big fan of heights?'

'Not the biggest,' I said, still pissed off about the lift revelation. It was a bit of an understatement, but I didn't want to embarrass myself, like I had the time Amy made me go on the big wheel at the village funfair and they had to stop it to get me off, mid-panic attack. Not even slightly humiliating for the sixteen-year-old me. 'But it is nice and quiet up here.'

Nick held up one hand and started ticking things off. 'You don't like motorbikes, you don't like heights, you don't like climbing stairs—'

'I didn't say I didn't like climbing stairs,' I interrupted, my chest still heaving.

He didn't even bother to say anything, just raised his eyebrows and carried on.

'You don't like the opera, you like a drink – but from what I can tell, drink most certainly does not like you – you're jealous, impulsive and can't walk in high heels for more than five minutes.'

'Quite the catch.' I pulled my knees up under my chin, tucking my skirt around my thighs so as not to show all the statues of saints my knickers and wrapped my arms around myself. 'I'd totally go out with me.'

'Last night you said you wanted to talk about stuff,' Nick shoved his phone back into the pocket of his jeans. 'So, stuff. Go for it.'

'I'm not very good at talking about myself.' I dropped my eyes, partly because it was so bloody bright on the roof of the *duomo* and partly because I didn't know if I could talk to him and look at him at the same time. 'Can you give me a brief or something?'

'You could sell me three different kinds of kitchen cleaner but you can't tell me what you're thinking?' he asked.

I shrugged. 'You're the professional question asker, I think you should start.'

'Tess Brookes . . .' He cleared his throat and held out an imaginary microphone. 'If you could be anywhere in the world, doing anything at all, with anyone at all, where would you be and what would you be doing and who would you be with?'

'I think I'd be here, doing this,' I replied, surprised at my own answer. 'I think I'd be with you.'

'Not with the mountain climber from London?' he asked, something difficult to read crossing his face.

'You mean Charlie?'

Nick pressed a finger against a seam in the roof. 'Charlie . . . sounds like a solid sort of bloke.'

'He – he is.' I felt sick, talking about him with Nick. Charlie didn't even know Nick existed. Nick didn't know I'd slept with Charlie a week ago. I couldn't think of a time when I'd felt more like

302

Vanessa, even when I was pretending to be her. 'He's brilliant. But things change, don't they?'

Nick flicked his head in an indeterminate gesture, as though he couldn't decide whether or not to agree, and looked out over radiating streets of Milan.

'People change,' I said. 'Sometimes I think they don't know they're changing until it's already happened, though. You get so used to being one person, its weird when you wake up and everything is different.'

'Do people change though?' He turned back to me, the sky making his eyes seem more blue than grey today. 'Can people fundamentally change who they are?'

I rested my chin on my knees and felt a trickle of sweat down my spine. 'I don't know,' I admitted. 'But the things they want can change, even if they're the same person deep down.'

'My mum always told me, I want never gets,' he said with a rueful smile. 'I think she just meant biscuits at the time but Christ Almighty, that was an important life lesson.'

'My mum told me a lot of things,' A montage of tellings-off and head shaking and disappointed expressions ran through my head to a sad soundtrack. 'Turns out I probably shouldn't have been listening to her quite so much. What was it you wanted that you didn't get?'

'We're doing you now,' Nick said, skilfully avoiding the question. This was why he was the

303

professional question asker. 'So the Charlie thing, you're telling me you were in love with a man for ten years, you shagged him, he rejected you and now you're totally over him?'

'When you put it like that, it does make me sound like a bit of a shallow twat,' I pointed out. 'But in a nutshell . . . I don't know what to think. I love Charlie; he's one of my best friends. But maybe that's all he was meant to be. Someone I love, not someone I'm *in* love with.'

He pulled a pair of Ray-Bans out of his shirt pocket and slid them over his eyes, even though he had his back to the sun.

'Because you're in love with someone else?' he asked.

Even though I'd said it once, said it and meant it, I opened my mouth and the words wouldn't come out. I shut it quickly as my stomach flipped, just in case something did come out. Something I liked to call . . . vomit.

'Excuse me, could you take our picture?'

A tiny Asian woman tapped me on the shoulder and handed me a camera without waiting for me to agree. A little befuddled, I stood up, wobbling on the slanted roof, and tried to focus on the happy family in front of me.

'Sorry it's taking so long,' Nick shouted. 'She's a professional.'

'Professional what?' the father replied as everyone in the photo chuckled.

'Assassin,' Nick answered and their laughter

stopped abruptly. 'And pastry chef. And do you still babysit on weekends?'

'Here you go.' I handed back the camera as the father snatched it from me and hurried his family away from us as quickly as possible, which, given the steep slant of the roof, was not an easy escape. 'Do you like making people feel uncomfortable?'

'Me?' He looked surprised. 'Yeah, actually, I think I do. I spend so much time trying to make them feel comfortable and getting them to spill their guts, it's fun to mess with someone a little bit.'

'Ah . . .' I sat back down carefully, combing my damp hair over one shoulder and out of my way. 'You like manipulating people.'

'Says the girl who convinces people to pay over the odds for hand sanitizer.'

Ooh, I'd touched a nerve.

'I've never worked on a hand sanitizer campaign,' I replied as coolly as possible. 'I was just making an observation.'

'This is the problem,' he said, eyes hidden behind the safety of his sunglasses, 'you don't really know anything about me.'

I didn't reply right away but sat staring at him, without a tinted barrier of my own, and thought about my conversation with Paige the day before. I didn't know him. I didn't know his favourite film; I didn't know his middle name or where he grew up or what his dad did for a living. But that didn't change the way I felt.

'What do you want me to say?' I asked. 'You're right. I know everything there is to know about Charlie, from his shoe size to when he lost his virginity, but I never felt this way about him. Or anyone. It's not based on what you like to eat for breakfast – and God knows it's not an intellectual decision that I'm making. It's just how I feel. When I'm with you, I feel like me.'

Nick took a deep breath in and breathed it out heavily, rubbing his temples, tanned forearms flexing. 'I'm older than you, you know.'

'Good God, no,' I flung my arm against my forehead in mock horror. 'Someone call the police!'

A couple nearby looked startled and the man pulled out his phone.

'Oh no, no,' I shouted, flinging my arms out wide. 'It was a joke. No police. *No polizia.*'

The woman reluctantly lowered her husband's hand, giving me a 'just say the word' look before staring at Nick like she wanted to turn him into stone.

'I've been through this before.' Nick, oblivious to the drama unfolding around us, carried on talking about his favourite subject. Himself. 'And it's all well and good to have feelings but attraction isn't enough to make a relationship work. What happens when the sex burns out? What's left then?'

'The feelings?' I was confused. 'Aren't they separate to the sex?'

'Are they?' Nick asked.

'Wow!' I felt my eyes widen, combined with a

sudden need to punch him really hard. 'It sounds to me like you're saying I have an irrational teenage crush on you because you're good in bed and you're just in it for the sex.'

'That's not what I said.' He looked away, rubbing his knuckles over his stubbly chin. I shifted around from cheek to cheek. Sitting on a hard, hot roof was not comfortable. 'But you tell me, what is all this really based on? How can it actually work?'

I closed my eyes and tried to come up with an answer that didn't involve physical violence. When I was a kid, Amy and I were obsessed with Disney movies and I had always been cynical of how quickly the princesses fell head over heels in love. Yes, Prince Eric was a hot piece but really, Ariel, you're going to give up your entire life and *the ability to breathe underwater* to shack up with some bloke you barely know at sixteen?

But with Nick, I felt something I'd never felt before. Not the irresistible urge to make a deal with a sea witch, but there was a pull, a friction. Something that got under my skin and made me want to be near him, even though I sort of wanted to slap the taste right out of his mouth at the same time. And when I was with him, I felt different: calmer and more grounded but still like fireworks were going off in my brain . . . and in other places. When I was with him, I felt more like myself than I ever had before.

And that was what I wanted to say to him, up there on the roof of the *duomo* while he patronized me about his advanced age. But instead, I felt myself go hard and cold and pulled away.

'Someone really fucked you over, didn't she?' I heard the words come out of my mouth before I really thought about saying them. 'Doesn't being so damaged get exhausting?'

'That would be an easy answer for you, wouldn't it?' Nick replied, laughing. 'That I had a bad experience with some other woman, that it's nothing to do with me and you?'

'You didn't have a bad experience?' I asked. I knew that he had, he'd already told me. I just didn't know the details but I was bloody well going to get them.

'You've got no idea what you're talking about,' Nick said. 'And thanks for proving my point.'

I could feel my temper starting to get the better of me. I'd let him call all the shots so far and enough was enough. What was the worst that could happen? Apart from him breaking my heart and me throwing myself off the roof of a cathedral?

'No way!' I leaned forward on my knees and snatched the sunglasses off his face and chucked them behind me.

Somewhere on the level below, I heard a rattle, a clunk and a couple of yelps but nothing sounded fatal so I carried on.

'Fuck you, if you think you can say something like that and walk away,' I said, shoving him hard in the chest. 'I'm sitting here, trying to be honest and talk about actual feelings that I've never even

308

had before and you think you can put your *Top Gun* shades on and laugh at me and treat me like a kid? Fuck off, Nick!'

'You owe me a pair of Wayfarers,' Nick said. He was staring at me like I had lost my mind. And I was worried that I might have. 'I can't believe you just did that.'

'Did you miss the part where my mouth was moving and sound was coming out?' I asked, waving a hand in front of his eyes. 'Because I can repeat myself if you need me to?'

'I got the "fuck you" part,' he said. 'Was there more after that?'

I blinked back into the moment and looked around at the small audience we had gathered. As soon as they saw him staring, they all looked away. And looked right back again when he turned his attention back to me.

'I don't believe you,' I said while trying to get to my feet with a modicum of grace. 'One minute you want me, the next minute you're laughing at me. You want me to tell you the truth and then you don't want to hear it. I'm not the one who can't be honest, Nick. You're so busy covering up all *your* shit, that you can't even hear what *I'm* saying. You can't see me because you're still obsessed with something else but I don't know what that is. I'm going, I can't do this.'

'Oh shit!' He pushed himself up to his feet, Converse proving themselves much more adaptable to a slanted cathedral roof than leather-soled flip-flops, and grabbed my arm. 'Fine, sit down. I'm an emotionally dead dickhead – is that what you want me to say?'

'No,' I said, shaking off his grip. 'I want you to tell me what you're thinking without a bitchy comeback or a patronising bag of wank coming out of your mouth.'

'You really have got a way with words.' Nick took hold of my arm again, his grip tighter this time, and pulled me back towards him. 'I'll admit I'm shit at this. That's why I don't do it.'

I huffed and relaxed my arm. Fighting him was not easy on my messed-up shoulder and I had visions of him suddenly letting go and me tumbling helplessly over the side of the cathedral.

'And that's why you shag girls you meet on assignments and assume you'll never have to see them again?' I asked.

He nodded. 'Assignments. Holidays. Bars I never intend to frequent again. It's easier.'

'Doesn't sound like a lot of fun.' I grudgingly let him guide me back down to a very uncomfortable sitting position.

'And that's how I know you don't have a dick,' he answered. 'It is fun. For a while. And then one day you wake up with a girl in your bed and you don't know her name and all you want is for her to leave so you can pretend she was never there in the first place. That's when it stops being a good time.'

'You wish you'd never met me?' I asked, my old friend nausea turning over my stomach again.

'No,' he replied. 'I wish I'd never met my ex, Amanda.'

I sank sideways, from my knees onto my bum, skirt blowing in the breeze and revealing my pants to everyone on the roof, saints and sinners alike.

It had a name.

'Oh,' I said. I'd used all my words; I was all out. 'She's the ex?'

'I've had a lot of exes.' He stared up at the top of the tallest spire with his hand over his eyes. 'But yeah, I think she's the one you mean.'

'Heartless cow who broke your heart and convinced you all women were untrustworthy bitch faces so you swore that you'd never love again?'

His face cracked into an unwilling smile. 'You've met her then?'

'Read a lot of books,' I shrugged. 'Actually, that's not true. I've watched a lot of telly. There's loads of Amandas on TV. And I lived with one for a long time, so I know those women exist. They cause a lot of problems for the rest of us.'

'Really?' He leaned his head to one side, his hand still covering his face. 'They cause problems for you?'

'It becomes a branding issue,' I said, nodding. 'It only takes one bad apple to ruin the whole barrel. Or bushel. Or whatever apples come in. You get one shitty woman running around and it gives the rest of us a bad name. When really, the other apples are fine.'

'You lost me on the apple metaphor,' Nick

said, inching towards me and resting his hand on my ankle, lightly holding me in place, like I might float away. 'But I think I get what you're saying.'

'It wasn't a very good metaphor,' I admitted. 'One shit woman ruins it for the rest of us. Please continue.'

'It's not a fun story,' he said, hesitating for a moment. 'But I suppose you deserve to hear it. I met her in London, she was from LA – I think I told you that in Hawaii – and it was really intense, right from the beginning.'

'Mmm-hmm.' I pressed my lips together and reminded myself I'd asked for this. Stupid Amanda, the stupid heartbreaker.

'She was in London to audition for something she didn't get and she went back to LA and I couldn't stop thinking about her.' He paused and I rearranged my stony face until I looked more like I was listening attentively and not taking down details for the bounty hunter I was planning to hire to hunt her down and kill her. 'My dad is American, meaning I have dual citizenship, right? So I packed up and followed her to LA and things were amazing for the first year. I loved living in the sun. We had this really amazing flat with a hot tub and you could see the Hollywood sign from our roof deck. It was mental.'

'Sounds brill,' I muttered, adding to my notes. Of course she was an actress. Bleurgh.

'All I wanted was to make her happy.' Nick let

out a half-hearted laugh but he still wasn't smiling. 'But things got tough after a bit. She wasn't getting the roles she wanted and I was getting offered so much work. I turned a lot of stuff down at first but in the end, I had to take jobs so we could pay our rent and that meant quite a bit of travelling. I was back in the UK a lot, out in Australia, in the Far East and she hated it. She wouldn't come with me in case she got an audition – the only time we went away was when we went to Hawaii – but she said she didn't trust me when I was travelling.'

'Why wouldn't she trust you?' I asked, not really wanting to know the answer. I could handle a lot of things but me and Rachel from *Friends* knew there was one absolute truth in this world and that was 'once a cheater, always a cheater'.

'That's the funny thing,' he said. 'She didn't trust me – when really, I shouldn't have trusted her. Came back early from a trip one day and found her shagging some random bloke in the hot tub. She wasn't even having an affair. She didn't even have the decency to go out and fall in love with someone else. She would just go to auditions or to the gym and bring back some random shit and shag him in my house.'

'Oh.'

There wasn't a lot else I could think to say.

'It was my fault, of course, because I kept leaving her.' His grip around my ankle tightened for a second and then relaxed again. 'And after that, it

313

was all downhill. I tried to stay home more but she was angry that I didn't trust her so the more I hung around in LA, the more she would go out and not come home.'

'Hang on a minute,' I frowned, trying to work out what he was telling me. 'You mean, she cheated on you more than once and you didn't dump her?'

'No.' He looked done in. 'I loved her.'

'Right.' I gave him a big, bright sunny smile. 'Just checking.'

Men.

'But in the end, she decided she'd had enough.' He threw his hands up in the air, giving me just enough time to flex my ankle before he grabbed it again. 'She met some rich old fucker with a palace in the hills and I came home one day and she'd gone. Said she couldn't live with my mistrust any more.'

'So you moved to LA to be with her,' I said out loud, piecing the timeline together for my own sanity. 'Then she cheated on you and you put up with it and then she moved out because you didn't trust her?'

He nodded.

'Why didn't you dump her when you found out she was shagging around?' I asked, thinking of all the incredibly feeble reasons my friends and I had been given when being blown off. 'What made you stay?'

'I loved her,' he said again, as though it made

everything make sense. 'That was all there was to it. I couldn't explain it but I loved her. I'd never felt that way about anyone before. So, you know, there's a chance that's why I'm not incredibly keen on rushing into a relationship based on nothing but feelings.'

'Aren't all relationships based on feelings?' I asked, thinking I was fighting a losing battle. 'Isn't that what relationships are?'

'And that's why I don't have relationships,' he replied. 'Ever.'

'Then what is this?' As someone who hadn't even cried when Bambi's mother got shot, I had been crying a lot lately but right now, I had nothing. My eyes were so dry and sore from the sun, from staring at him for so long, my tear ducts were exhausted. *I* was exhausted. 'Why did you bring me up here and make me tell you how I feel, if feelings don't matter? If *my* feelings don't matter?'

'I do care about you.' He moved his hand from my wrist, not holding my hand, but gripping my forearm so tightly I could feel my blood pumping under his fingers. 'But I'm trying to be honest. I don't know if this can work, but that doesn't mean I don't wish it could.'

I closed my eyes, only to see a Nick-shaped silhouette staring back at me.

'Do you even want to try?' I asked.

'I do,' he said. His voice was strong, even if he didn't sound certain. 'Sometimes. Most of the time.'

Pinching the bridge of my nose, I opened my

eyes and stared at my feet, waiting for my eyes to readjust to the sunlight. 'And the rest of the time?'

'I don't know if I trust you.' He wiped a non-existent tear from my cheek. 'And I don't know if I trust myself. I've got really used to my life the way it is and I never expected to want to be with anyone again and then bam, you appear out of nowhere. The thing is, I don't know if we'd be very good for each other. I don't know if I'm any use to you.'

As calmly as I could manage, I peeled his hand off my wrist and took it in mine, squeezing it as tightly as I could.

I felt so powerless, it was all happening to me and I hated it. 'Do I get any say in this?' I asked. 'There's nothing I can do?'

He rested his gaze on our hands and squeezed my hand back.

'I want to try,' he said. 'But I don't want to get fucked over again. I really loved her and that wasn't enough. I don't know what is.'

Never in my entire life had I hated someone I'd never met quite so much. And I lived in a world where *Big Brother* was on the telly every year.

'I'm not her, I wouldn't do what she did,' I said, somewhere between desperation and rage. If only I knew which words to use to convince him that I could make him happy. 'I wouldn't ever cheat or lie.'

'But you did lie. You already lied to me.'

Nick let go of my hand and sat cross-legged right in front of me but in that moment, he might as

316

well have been a million miles away. I tried to think of the right thing to say. I wanted to promise that I would take care of him and make him happy and that I would do all the things that he had wanted to do for Amanda but, deep down, I knew he already knew that. He just didn't believe me. He had already felt the way I felt; he'd been through these exact emotions and had his heart ripped out, torn to pieces, eaten, puked up and then chucked in the wheelie bin for good measure.

Love wasn't rational but neither was fear. He was afraid and as I knew very well, there weren't many things that could keep you locked up in your box as well as fear could. But knowing that and accepting it were two different things. Surely there had to be something?

'Nick.'

I touched the tips of my fingers to the back of his hand and waited. He looked at me for a moment, his eyes too narrow for me to read, his jaw tight and solid. And then he grabbed me, took hold of the back of my head and crashed his lips against mine. I reached out, to hold him, to know it was happening, to make it happen. One hand found a fistful of his shirt, the other was flat against the roof, steadying myself. He kissed me so hard that when he pulled away I could taste blood in my mouth – only I wasn't sure if it was his or mine. I pressed my hand against my mouth, the pulse in my fingers slower than the pulse in my lips.

'What does that mean?' I asked when I found my voice again.

'I'm not sure,' he said, tracing a thumb across his own lips before clambering up to his feet. He held out his hand to help me up and snaked his arm around my waist, holding me to him. 'I'm really happy when I'm with you. That's all I know.'

'I'm happy when I'm with you.' I tried to smile and felt a light in my eyes, even though the corners of my mouth didn't really move. 'Shall we start there and see where we go?'

'I've heard worse ideas,' he said, drawing me in for another kiss, something softer and more socially acceptable on the rooftop of a Catholic church. I copped a quick feel of his arse, hoping that Baby Jesus was looking the other way, but still managed to earn a reprimanding stare from a *nonna* across the way.

It was totally worth it.

CHAPTER 16

I'd never really understood what people meant when they said they were deliriously happy. My only experience of delirium was when I was seven and had the mumps and spent a very unpleasant night in my mum's bed, sweating like there was no tomorrow and waking up every fourteen minutes or so to scream that I was being chased by a giant beach ball. And so, when my friends would describe themselves as delirious, I most often wanted to call a doctor and have them committed – who would want to be in such a state on purpose?

But that afternoon I started to understand. I wasn't being chased by a giant beach ball, but while Nick and I wandered through the city, not talking, just holding hands and stopping every five feet to kiss or touch each other's hair, then laugh at absolutely nothing, I certainly felt like I was losing my mind. It was all I could do not to stop strangers in the street to say hello and tell them how much I loved him. That was how I knew I was losing it. I lived in London; I did not approach strangers, even when the label was sticking out the back of their jumper.

The tiniest part of my brain that was still rational

sat in a corner, tutting and shaking its head, and I did not care. What did it matter that an hour ago, I had thought my heart was going to break into more pieces than one of those impossible spherical jigsaws that some marketing company would give you a million quid to complete? That didn't matter! All that mattered was the hand-holding and the kissing and the being in Italy and the laughing uproariously at that tiny dog over there! It was insane and I loved it.

Eventually, we arrived back at his motorbike full of gelato and happiness and I hopped on the back without a care. Who had time to be terrified when you were presented with a fabulous opportunity to snuggle close to your man? Even the palazzo looked more beautiful when we got home. The fountain seemed to be running in slow motion, the water sparkling away like diamonds, and the stone of the building shone golden in the sun.

'I have to go and do some work,' Nick said as we strolled up the steps, hand in hand. 'See you later?'

My face fell like a three-year-old who had just had her favourite toy taken away and I stretched out my arms as far as they would go, trying to keep the very tips of my fingers in contact with him for as long as humanly possible.

'See you at dinner,' he promised, jogging up the stairs with a smile on his face. A smile I had put there. It felt really good.

I was too high to go back to my room and so I flip-flopped through the grounds, nodding and smiling to everyone I passed, until I found my secret garden. The whole estate was alive with workers; Al clearly wanted to get the place shipshape before his big party. I was excited for him. I was excited for everyone. Hip checking the door to the garden wide open, I skipped inside, feet floating over the grass until I collapsed in a most attractive heap in the middle of the lawn and stared up at the fluffy white clouds high above me. Being in love was so much easier than deciding what to watch on Sky Plus.

But after a while, I'd done so many internal reruns of *Nick and Tess: A Milanese Love Story* that even I was starting to get a little tired of it and did what every girl did in times of intense emotional change. I turned to social media.

I'd never been a big fan of posting my life all over Facebook, mostly because I didn't really have one. Amy, on the other hand, was the queen of social media and had been keeping the internet fully updated on our Italian adventures. There was a shot of her passport at the airport, the driver picking us up in Milan, her first view of the palazzo, me on my hands and knees taking a picture of one of Jane Bennett's dresses. I frowned, wondering whether or not I could untag it, but then saw that our friend Steven had said I had a nice arse, so I left it alone.

But it wasn't just Steven that had been commenting on Amy's pictures. Every single shot since the pic of her passport had a big thumbs up beside it. Charlie Wilder likes this. And just like that, my delirium took a massive blow to the balls.

I flipped to my emails and saw several new messages. A quick one from Paige to let me know she got everything over to Charlie on time, a longer one from Agent Veronica that was not nearly as nice, demanding an update, and a message from Charlie about the pitch.

All right, you,
Portugal was great, flying home tonight. Think they're totally in love with us. They definitely will be when they see your slides. Maybe I should send you off to Milan more often the pitch is amazing. It's one hundred per cent in the bag. What would I do without you?
Thank goodness I don't have to find out.
I love you,
Charlie xx

It had been very easy to forget anything and everything else existed whilst waltzing around the winding streets of Milan, holding hands with a man I wanted to lean over and lick, but when reality crept back in, it did not mess around.

Charlie. Perito's. London. Today was Thursday; I was supposed to be flying home on Sunday for the pitch on Monday. Bollocks.

Flat on my back, the sun remained up in the sky, refusing to vamoose and make way for some dark grey clouds to reflect my mood. I remembered my English A level, I knew what pathetic

322

fallacy was. Damn the height of the Italian summer; clearly I needed to be up on the Yorkshire moors or something. It was hard to hate yourself when the sun had got his hat on.

There was only one thing for it. I'd been brave that morning; I wasn't going to sit around and wait for things to happen to me any more. I would call him. I would pick up my phone and dial his number and tell him everything. He would be upset, he would be hurt, but maybe he would understand. Like Amy said, he hadn't been moping around after me for ten years, it was more like ten minutes. He might even be a bit relieved when he thought about.

And maybe that was a very pretty pig flying past me on its way into the kitchen to become my dinner.

'Be brave, Tess,' I told myself. 'What would Beyoncé do?'

Only, what *would* Beyoncé do? Beyoncé would never find herself in this position, that's what Beyoncé would do. She would be at home with Jay-Z and Blue Ivy watching telly and thinking 'That Tess doesn't half get herself into some situations.'

Without the guidance of an icon and with some resistance from my broken phone, I pressed Charlie's name and hoped something distracting might happen before he picked up, like a runaway train crashing through the walls and crushing me to death, or maybe something a little less dramatic like the end of the world.

'Hi, you've reached Charlie Wilder.'

Oh, for the love of all that was holy, I found the balls to make the most difficult phone call of my life and it went to answerphone? Really?

'I can't take your call right now so leave me a message and I'll get back to you as soon as I can. Cheers.'

'Hello!' I buzzed down the line as soon as I heard the beep. 'It's me. It's Tess. Um, anyway, I got your email. Glad you liked the pitch stuff. I said I'd call you so I'm calling you!'

Nice. Really smooth.

'Anyway,' I went on in my hyper-happy voice. 'I wanted to talk to you about something and I didn't really want to wait but you're not there so I will!'

Insert feeble laugh.

'Sooo, yeah, maybe text me and let me know when's good to chat. Talk. We should have a talk.'

Insert awkward silence.

'Bye then, love you!'

I hung up and immediately hit myself in the forehead with my phone. What was I thinking? Yes, I had ended every phone call to Charlie in the last decade with a 'love you' and 'love you' was very different to 'I love you' but it really wasn't helping me to set the scene that needed to be set. What a knob I was turning out to be.

'Al!'

I had managed to waste a good couple of hours, taking some more photos of the house and the grounds, going through the shots I'd got at Warren's

studios, avoiding thinking about Charlie and generally killing time until I could touch Nick again. It
was past four when I trotted into the lobby and
saw Al sitting on the bottom step of the staircase.
He had a phone in one hand, a worried expression
on his face and a three-piece suit on his back. The
mobile phone looked almost as out of place on
him as the suit. I didn't think I'd ever seen him
holding one before.

'Going somewhere nice?'

'In theory, I should be.' He gave me a welcoming
smile and a kiss on each cheek but he did not look
happy. 'I'm going to see Edward. There's been a
problem with the samples.'

'Everything was fine when I was there yesterday,' I
said, sitting down beside him. 'The samples looked
amazing.'

'I'm not sure what he showed you then,' Al said
with a grimace. 'But he just told me that there's
no way he can go ahead with the project.'

'That's not possible!' I pulled my camera out of
my bag and flipped through to my shots from the
studio. 'See? He had done all this already? I was
sort of expecting him to have everything finished
for the party.'

'As was I.' Al took my camera in his hands and
stared. 'This is all very strange. First the factory,
then the shop and now Edward.'

None of this sounded like good news. 'What's
happening with the factory? And the shop?'

'Things at the shop are relatively simple, red

tape and such.' He waved a hand to show he wasn't too worried, but everything about his demeanor said that was a lie. 'But the factory is more of an issue. I don't know how much you know about the manufacturing business?'

'Oh, loads,' I replied. 'Pretty much everything. But I'm happy to humour you and have you explain it all in very simple terms.'

'Of course,' he said, the corners of his eyes crinkling. 'I very much wanted to work with one specific factory. They don't use child labour and all of their materials are fairly sourced – all of the things that were important to Jane. That are important to me.'

I made myself concentrate on Al's troubles but I couldn't help but worry a little bit about Amy. She was so excited.

'And they can't do it?' I took my camera back and hung it carefully around my neck.

'They say they can't,' he said.

I looked down at the image on the back of my camera, at a dress that might now never exist.

'Do you know why?' I asked. 'Have they explained?'

'They're in China so the time difference is a bit of a pain,' he explained. 'We received an email overnight. I had offered to pay a premium to get things done the way I wanted them done in the time I wanted them doing and initially they agreed but now they're saying they don't have the resources. It's all very frustrating. Perhaps Artie is right: I'm being very foolish thinking I can get into the fashion game at my age.'

'Artie?' My ears pricked up so fast, I felt like Lassie. 'Artie said that?'

'Let's just say he wasn't terribly supportive,' Al said with as much diplomacy as he could muster. 'He has to throw a tantrum from time to time. The trouble with having an only child is that they never learn to share.'

I was so used to seeing Al's face smiling, it hurt my heart to see him sad. His suntanned face wore its wrinkles with pride and I was sure there was a story behind every one, but for all its worn in ways, everything looked wrong when he frowned. His forehead creased against his smile lines and for the first time, I thought he looked old.

'Couldn't he help you?' I asked. 'Couldn't Artie talk to some people for you?'

'Oh, Tess!' Al clapped his hand on my knee and stood up, again, not nearly as light on his feet as he had been in Hawaii. 'You're very sweet to be so concerned for me but it'll all work out for the best. I'm just an old man who is used to getting his own way. It was madness to think that I could turn up in a city that I haven't visited in years and demand to have everything my own way. We'll still have the party tomorrow night – I may have to learn a little humility, that's all.'

'Maybe you should speak to Artie though?' I suggested, really not wanting to push too hard but desperate to find a way to make things work for Al. And for Jane.

'I don't think it would be a lot of help if I did,'

Al said. 'If anything, I imagine he'd try to throw a few more flies in the ointment.'

He dropped his phone in his pocket and combed out his beard.

'I might not make dinner this evening,' he said, giving the driver of the car that had pulled up in front a quick salute. 'But I trust you are excited about the party tomorrow evening?'

'So excited,' I agreed, glad to have another subject to turn to. 'It's going to be all right for me to take photos, isn't it?'

'I would be offended if you didn't.' He gave me a trademark Al twinkly smile and bowed gracefully. 'I hear Kekipi and Miss Smith have been taking care of your fashion choices this afternoon. Any point in asking how you and your collaborator are collaborating?'

I smiled, my brain tipping right back over the edge at the very mention of Nick's name. Actually he hadn't even mentioned his name. Dear God, I was done for.

'Ah, I see,' Al smiled and strode out towards the car. 'Young love, excellent news. Everything as it should be. And all is well with the world.'

I stood up and watched Al go, waving as the car pulled away and thinking how nice it would be for all to be well with the world, just for once.

'Tess!'

But all was not well with the world. All was not even well within my bedroom. I hadn't even closed the door when I heard Amy yelling from her room. Dropping my bag on the sofa and hearing a stomach-churning clunk as it missed its target, I sprinted into her bathroom, led by her screams.

She was definitely being murdered, I told myself, leaping to the worst possible conclusion as quickly as humanly possible.

'What do I do? Help me, Tess!' Amy wailed as I stopped short in front of her bathroom door.

I stood and I stared and then, when I'd had time to process, I laughed – hard and loud and in an incredibly unladylike fashion. Amy was wrapped in a bath towel that was bigger than she was, losing a fight with the most impressive bubble bath monster I had ever, ever seen.

'What is happening?' I asked, gasping for breath and kicking off my flip-flops before wading into the waist-deep foam. Because that would help. 'What did you do?'

'I was going to have a bath because I burnt my shoulders,' she said, tears creeping into her voice. 'You always say if I get sunburnt I should have a bath.'

The fabric of my dress darkened as I fought my way through, feeling my way across the room and searching for the actual bath. Whatever was happening had to stop happening before the foam made its way into the living room. One ruined dress was nothing compared to a destroyed antique carpet.

'You think this is my fault?' I could hear whirring

over Amy's choking sobs. 'You told me to have a bath.'

'I gave you a suggestion and you turned Al's house into a really bad club?' I asked. 'How did you manage this?'

'There wasn't any bubble bath.' She backed away until she was almost out of the room altogether. 'So I put shower gel in and then I turned the Jacuzzi jets on and then – oh, I don't know, this just *happened*. I thought I was going to die.'

'You put shower gel in a Jacuzzi bath?' I gave my best friend my best 'are you kidding me' face and then took a deep breath, diving into the belly of the beast and slapping the side of the bath until I struck gold. Or at least, the off switch. The whirring quieted and the bubbles stopped multiplying and I regained faith that we would all live. 'Seriously, Amy?'

'I don't know, do I?' she ranted, still crying. 'When have I ever been in a Jacuzzi? How could I know it would turn into The Thing?'

'Don't cry.' I waded back through the foam and gave her a hug but Amy didn't want to be consoled. Amy wanted to sit on the floor, surrounded by an admittedly delightful-smelling bubble fog and cry some more.

'I can't do anything,' she sobbed. 'I can't even have a bath without fucking it up.'

'That's not true,' I said, giving in and sitting on the floor next to her. This dress was buggered. 'You can do lots of bloody things. Like you said, you've

330

never had a Jacuzzi bath before, how would you know?'

'Because *you* would know.' She pawed at her face, wiping away her angry tears. 'You wouldn't put shower gel in there, no one would. I'm so stupid. I hate myself. I hate this.'

It was difficult to know where I should and shouldn't touch since she was only wearing a towel and we were still boob-deep in bubbles but this felt like such a supportive patting situation.

'You do not hate yourself, you're not stupid and what are you talking about?' I went with an affectionate punch in the shoulder. It was not especially well received.

'All of it,' she explained, unhelpfully. 'I hate not knowing obvious stuff that everyone else knows. I know you're the clever, serious one and I'm the stupid, wacky one but I'm tired of it, you know? Maybe I want to be taken seriously for a bit. Maybe I want to be the clever one, the one who gets things right.'

'No one thinks that,' I said without stopping to check whether or not I was telling her the truth. 'No one thinks you're stupid.'

'Everyone does.' She hung her head and sniffed. 'Charlie does, my family does, my housemates do. All our friends think that. You even think that a little bit, that's why you don't want me to work with Al, because you think I'll fuck it up.'

She wasn't the only one who hated herself at that moment.

'That's not it at all.' There were times, I decided, when it was perfectly acceptable to lie. 'I only didn't want you to rush into something that you didn't know that much about in case it turned out you didn't like it. If you're excited about it and you're into it, you'll be amazing at it and we both know that.'

'You're a terrible liar.' Amy leaned against me and rested her head against my arm. 'How did you manage to pull off the fake name thing for so long in Hawaii?'

'Everyone was drunk for quite a lot of the time,' I admitted. 'And anyway, shut up. When you want to do something, Amy Smith, you are bloody good at it and I'm being one hundred per cent honest now – I just haven't seen you want to be good at anything for a while. Maybe you've been coasting a little bit.'

'I panicked when I broke up with Dave,' she said. 'Everything was so mapped out and I was so scared that I threw it all out the window. Now I think I'd like to get the map back and just have a quick look and I can't.'

'Or,' I suggested, 'we could get a new map.'

'I suppose,' she replied, her voice a little bit high-pitched but not dolphins-could-hear-her-in-Miami high-pitched. 'I freak out a little bit sometimes. I'm nearly thirty and I've got no idea what I'm doing with my life.'

'Then this is going to be a pretty bloody exciting adventure, isn't it?' I told her. She didn't need to know about Al's logistical nightmares; giving her another reason to question her confidence wasn't going to help anyone. 'So yeah, you had to take a bit of time out to work out what you wanted to do, but Amy, if this was what the universe had waiting for you, isn't it worth a few miserable retail jobs?'

'Yeah . . .' She blew a chunk of floating foam away from her face. 'But don't you start going on about the universe. I'm the one who reads her horoscope and says things like that, not you.'

'Maybe we're not quite as black and white as you think,' I said, the bubbles in the bath starting to pop quietly. 'Maybe we're both a bit brilliant and a bit stupid.'

'You could be on to something.' She let out a sigh and stretched her legs, pressing her toes against the base of the toilet. 'At least about you being a bit stupid.'

'That's the spirit.' I kicked my legs in the mass of foam that still spilled over the bathtub, making the bubbles dance up into the air. 'But so you know, being the clever sensible one can get really boring.'

'Yeah, well, I'm still me,' she said. Now I was paying attention, I saw that her shoulders really were red raw. Ouch. 'Which already makes me loads cooler than you, so I'm not too worried about that.'

'Thank goodness for that,' I said, my sympathy waning fast. 'I'll leave you to clean all this up then.'

'Where have you been all day?' Amy tightened

the towel around her boobs and bent forward onto her knees as if to start cleaning and then stopped. 'How do you tidy up bubbles?'

'I have no idea.' I didn't even attempt to help. 'I was with Nick. We had The Talk.'

'And?'

'And I think we're sort of giving it a try.'

'You think?'

'It's a really long story.' That I had no intention of telling her. 'But the short version is, his ex cheated on him and so he's a bit gun-shy about relationshps.'

'Hmm.'

'What does hmm mean?' I asked as she attempted to smother the bubbles with a spare bath sheet.

'I don't know.' She pulled up the towel, achieving nothing other than sending a load of bubbles wafting around the bathroom. 'You're sure he's not doing the "I'm telling you I'm an arsehole so when I behave like an arsehole, you can't be angry at me for it" thing?'

'Is that a thing?' I asked.

'Oh yeah,' she nodded. 'That's a *massive* thing.'

'He wouldn't do that, would he?' I said, rubbing my itchy nose. 'I don't think he's doing that.'

At least, I didn't until she brought it up.

'I only want you to be careful,' she said. 'You're like a freshly hatched chick or something. Don't let him get away with bullshit just because he's got a massive cock and makes Michael Fassbender look like a right dog.'

'Can we stop talking about his penis?' I said, struggling to get the last word out loud. 'Please?'

Amy turned to give me her best 'are you kidding me?' face.

'Fine, I'm going to get dry. And then showered. And then dry again.' I squeezed out the skirt of my dress and went to leave. 'Can you sort this out from here?'

'You can help if you want,' she called after me as I crawled out of the world's saddest foam party. 'I don't mind.'

'No, you're all right,' I called back. 'You've got it sorted and don't forget to put some aftersun on that sunburn.'

'Yes, Mum,' she shouted.

Even when I was trying not to be the sensible one, I couldn't bloody help myself.

I knew things were getting out of control when I ran down to the dining room at eight and my empty stomach hadn't even crossed my mind. In an attempt to avoid any and all potentially dangerous eventualities, I was wearing flat shoes, a black dress and had woven my hair into the best fishtail plait that several YouTube tutorials had to offer. Amy, exhausted from her one-woman Ibiza tribute, was already in bed and Al was still working, which left me, Nick and Kekipi for dinner.

As much as I wanted Nick all to myself, I was excited to be having dinner with someone else now we were almost officially a couple. The last time I had eaten food with a man I was also sleeping with, it was a 2 a.m. Burger King in Leicester Square with the accountant from Wimbledon who had taken me on three dates and I'd paid for my own burger. And my mum had wondered why that one didn't work out.

'Looks like we've been set up again.'

I opened the door to the outside dining room to find Nick sitting alone at a dinner table laid for five. He was wearing a slim-fitting white shirt and charcoal-grey trousers that pulled over his thighs. If my trousers had been that tight, I'd have wept into a bottomless pit of Ben & Jerry's for three days and nights but on him, they looked wonderful. And the ideas I had for the black belt that was holding them up . . . Bad Tess.

'No Kekipi?' I asked, holding myself at the door. I'd been so excited to see him and now my feet didn't know what to do. God, he was pretty.

'I passed him on my way in but he was running off somewhere with what's-his-name, Domenico?' He poured red wine into the empty glass next to his. 'You're not planning on staying?'

'Thinking about it,' I said. 'I am quite hungry.'

'Then come and sit down.' He patted the table and gave me a grin that hit me right in the womb. 'Or do I have to come over there and get you?'

Just walk, I told myself, padding towards the table and, more importantly, towards the wine.

He stood up and pulled out my chair, confusing the blood that didn't know whether to rush to my head, my heart or my ovaries.

'Did you get all your work done?' I asked, sitting down as carefully as possible and picking up my glass. White wine would have been less dangerous but booze was booze was booze and after Amy's arsehole comments, I wasn't going to turn down a tipple.

'Who wants to talk about work?' he said, his hand creeping along my thigh. 'What have you been up to?'

I took a deep drink and then put my glass down. 'Did you tell me all that stuff this afternoon so that when you act like an arsehole, I can't complain about it?'

Nick looked a little startled for a moment, took his hand away from mine and then laughed.

'So that's what you did this afternoon,' he said, tearing into a piece of bread. 'Bitched about me with your friend and then what, spent an hour overthinking everything I said? Maybe we should talk about work.'

'We didn't bitch about you,' I said, not entirely sure if that was true or not. Did our conversation count as bitching? I was fairly certain that it didn't. 'We discussed.'

'Tess . . .' Nick rested his elbows on the table and bowed his head. My mother would have been raging. 'I was honest with you earlier. I didn't make any promises but no, please tell Amy I'm not planning on banging all the models in Milan and then telling you it's your fault.'

'What made you think of models?' I asked, looking around the empty room for lurking amazons. 'There are models?'

'We're in Milan, there are bloody hundreds of models,' he replied. 'Now tell me, did Amy give you any helpful advice or was it all shrill, sub-*Sex and the City*, you go girl finger-clicking?'

'There wasn't really any finger clicking,' I said. 'And honestly? She probably slagged me off a lot more than she did you. She's protective.'

Nick nodded with his entire upper body. 'And of course you told her what a devilish rogue I am, so she's being extra cautious.'

'If I told her you referred to yourself as a devilish rogue, she would have made me wear a chastity belt to dinner and she would have removed your balls with a rusty cheese grater,' I explained. 'Please never say it again.'

'Fair enough.' He sat up straight and put down his bread. 'I am though, devilish.'

'I'm sure you are.' I took another much-needed drink, eager to change the subject. 'I'm really hungry; are you really hungry?'

He shook his head and shrugged. 'Not really, I ate a couple of of hours ago.

Bastard. 'I thought you had to work,' I said, grabbing a piece of bread from the centre of the table and pulling off what I hoped was a socially acceptable piece and shoving it in my mouth. So, so good. 'I saw Al earlier; things don't seem to be going very well. Has he told you anything?'

'I thought you were taking photos, not taking up investigative journalism?' he replied, pushing a saucer of olive oil over to me. Clearly, this really was true love. 'I'd stick to the illustrative side of this if I were you.'

'You've noticed then?' I sighed, breaking off a slightly bigger piece of bread and dipping it in the oil. 'I wish there was something I could do.'

Nick said nothing, just drank his wine, resting the glass against his chest in between sips and looking at me across the table.

'Maybe I could talk to Artie,' I said. 'Just pop in to say hello, casually let him know his dad could use his support. Doesn't seem right that they're not helping each other out, does it?'

'You really shouldn't get involved in family stuff,' Nick said, tapping his middle finger against the bowl of his glass. 'How would you like it if someone tried to tell you how to act with your parents? Best advice I can give you is let them work it out on their own.'

'If you'd met my parents, you'd know there would be no point in trying,' I said, painfully aware that there was still so much we didn't know about each other. 'Artie should think himself lucky to have Al for a dad.'

'Maybe, but you don't know what goes on behind closed doors,' he argued. 'Never get involved in family stuff. Don't get involved in this. Do your part, take the best bloody photos you can and, at the end of the day, close the door.'

Even though I knew it was probably good advice and definitely came from experience, I was still irritated. I wasn't used to being told what to do and I didn't love it. There was really only one thing to do: more wine, more bread.

'You're so cute when you get annoyed.' Nick stood up, picked up the bottle of red wine and nodded towards the door. 'And really sexy. Let's go upstairs.'

'But . . . *dinner*?' I waved at the empty table, shocked, appalled, hungry and horny.

He took my glass out of my hand and put it down on the table. A broken circle of condensation swelled underneath it on the white linen tablecloth.

'I'm going upstairs,' he said, his fingers playing with the third button on his white shirt. How many white shirts did that man own? Maybe this relationship was a terrible idea – imagine all the washing and ironing! That he would be doing.

'I'm going upstairs,' he repeated, undoing his button before moving on to the next one. My very own *Magic Mike*. Only not. 'And you're coming with me.'

'Am I now?' I asked, knowing full well that I totally was. My knickers seemed to be removing themselves from my person, even as I spoke.

Maybe he was magic, after all.

CHAPTER 17

In the rush to get into bed, or at least on it, I had not worried about closing Nick's curtains properly and so Friday morning announced itself far too early; a golden glow lighting up the room came in from both uncovered windows. Nick lay beside me, belly down, face in his pillows, snoring happily like a baby bulldog. As much as I wanted to wake him up, I let him sleep and settled with sniffing him. We'd been awake most of the night, and not just because I couldn't keep my hands off him. When I had finally found the strength to put him down for more than fifteen minutes at a time, we started talking and it seemed as though he hadn't stopped.

He told me all about growing up with an American dad, spending summers in New York that sounded so glamorous and exciting to his friends that he routinely got the shit kicked out of him every September but which, in truth, were lonely weeks spent inside a too hot apartment because his dad didn't trust him to go out in the city alone. I told him about the summers Amy and I spent hiding in the woods at the back of her house, sleeping through the day, because my parents were arguing so much I couldn't sleep at night and she was spending every evening watching late-night TV, wondering whether or not her dad was going to come home. He never did come back but there wasn't anything that Amy didn't know about *Gladiators* and every movie that had been on Channel Four after 11.00 p.m. between 1994 and 1999.

We talked about our favourite foods, the first time we got drunk, bad fashion choices and delicious snacks. He told me how he wanted to visit Alaska and Russia and I told him how I'd always wanted to see New York and Tokyo and Australia and we promised to take each other to those places and more. I couldn't say when I finally fell asleep or what we were talking about when it happened, only that my voice was sore from talking and Nick was down to a whisper, but I woke up happier than I could remember.

The ceiling in Nick's room didn't seem as high as the ceiling in my room. I traced a crisscross pattern across the room and started counting the squares above me, trying to fall back to sleep so I wouldn't be tired later in the day but I couldn't. Instead, I was playing our conversations over in my head, reliving every last touch, every time he had taken my hand in his and kissed my fingers and every time he had stroked my hair. I memorized every one of his expressions, how his eyes warmed up whenever he talked about travelling, how they burned when he talked about a particular job that he had loved. The way he stared at me when I was talking, a million sparks lighting up his whole face in a different way, every time. There was so much to learn about him and I wanted to know it all at once.

'Go back to sleep . . .' His voice was still raw from its sleepless night when it echoed out from amongst the pillows. 'It's early.'

'But I'm awake,' I said, running my fingers lightly through his hair, sliding down the back of his neck and making circles on his strong back. 'I can't sleep.'

'You clearly aren't trying,' he said gruffly. 'I'll wake you up properly in an hour.'

'I was wondering, have you spoken with Artie at all?' I asked, making a silent note of his offer. 'Since we've been here this week, I mean?'

'Go back to sleep and don't get involved,' he said, turning his head away.

I stopped my circling and rubbed the sleep out of my eyes.

'Don't get involved in what?'

Nick growled, the muscles in his back moving under his skin as he turned his head again. With one eye open, he looked at me.

'What do you know?' he asked.

'What do *you* know?' I asked.

'It's too early for this.' Nick dropped his head back into the pillows, face down. 'I'm a writer. I'm here to tell the story. Never get involved in family business, Tess.'

'So something *is* going on.' I scrambled up into a sitting position and kept shoving him until he turned over with a muffled roar. 'You know something! What's going on?'

'I don't know anything for certain.' He grabbed hold of my wrists to stop my feeble attack and yawned loudly. 'But I heard Artie on the phone to a Chinese factory the other night and he certainly wasn't encouraging them to take his father's business. And I've seen him talking to Warren, the bloke with all the photos of tits on his wall.'

'He's the pattern cutter,' I sniffed. 'But it's good to know what you took away from that meeting.'

'I'm sorry, I have a penis, there were naked woman.' He closed his eyes again and pressed his forearms over his face. 'Can you shut the curtains?'

'I heard someone talking Chinese – was that Artie?' I said, picking up Nick's shirt and slipping it on as I went so as not to flash the entire Corso Venezia below. 'How do you know he was on the phone to China?'

'I speak Cantonese,' he mumbled, 'and some Mandarin. But he was speaking Cantonese and as I'm not a mind reader, I don't know who you heard but it's likely. He's running interference on Al. I don't know why. Yet.'

'Why haven't you told me about this before?' I pulled the curtains to, reminding my reproductive organs that we were in the middle a very important conversation and that now wasn't the time to insist he knock me up with genius, Cantonese-speaking

344

babies, no matter how sexy that was. 'What did Al say? He acted like he didn't know any of this when I spoke to him yesterday.'

'I don't think he does know,' Nick replied from underneath his arms. 'It's fucking tragic. His son is a really nasty piece of work.'

'Wait, what?' I held on to the heavy curtains. 'You haven't told him?'

He let out an impressively exasperated sigh.

'No, I haven't told him,' he said slowly as if he was explaining to a child. 'One, I don't know anything for definite yet and two, I'm the journalist. It's my job to observe and then tell the story. I don't get in the middle.'

My hands curled tightly around the curtains.

'But he's our friend,' I said, just as slowly. 'You've got to tell him.'

'He's your boss,' Nick corrected. 'And I'm a journalist. This is a story.'

I stood in between the two curtains at the window, one leg warmed by the early morning sunlight, the other cold in the shade of the bedroom, and stared back at the bed. Nick was already half-asleep again, breathing steadily and all curled up under the covers. I couldn't quite process what he was saying.

'I don't get it,' I said. 'You're telling me you're not OK with me working in advertising because that's whoring my creativity to the man, but you're totally fine with keeping Al in the dark about his own son trying to sink his new business because it makes a good story?'

'Anything would sound bad when you put it like that,' he replied without moving.

'No, it sounds bad because it *is* bad,' I said. I didn't want to lose my temper and shout at him because, for once, I was entirely in the right and if he gave me that patronizing 'calm down, dear' look, I was very like to strangle him with his own boxer shorts. 'You have to tell Al what you know.'

'I don't know anything.' Nick emphasized the 'I' very carefully. 'And you need to calm down. I'm working on it.'

And there went my temper.

'That's funny,' I snapped, 'because it sounds a lot like you're letting someone I care about, someone who has been nothing but good to both of us, get spectacularly shat on for the sake of a story.'

'Tess . . .' Nick dragged himself upright and pushed his hand through his messy bedhead. 'This could be a big deal, not a bit of a family tiff. Will you please stop being so naïve? You do not get involved in things you do not understand. You're not Lois Lane, you're not going to rush in and save the day.'

'This is ridiculous!' I hated being this angry this early. I hated being this angry at him. 'You're not going to tell Al anything?'

'No,' he said simply. 'I'm going to follow the story and report it.'

'I hope you enjoy your moral high ground,' I said, scooting around the room and collecting my clothes. 'I'll be in my room being naïve and failing to understand how you can look Al in the eye.'

'I really don't want to have this conversation right now.' Nick rolled over, showing me his back and his lack of concern, all at the same time. 'It's too early for this.'

'I don't want to have this conversation either,' I said. 'In fact, I don't think I want to have any conversations with you for a bit. I'll let you sleep.'

'Don't be stupid.' He didn't even attempt to stop me from leaving. 'This is what I *do*. It's my job.'

'Well, I happen to think convincing people to try a new kind of Pot Noodle is less morally compromising than shitting on good people.' I heard the sting in my heart sound out in my voice. 'So this is what *I'm* doing.'

I slammed the door, checked both directions and pulled my knickers on very quickly.

I stomped down the hall and up the stairs to my room, stewing on how easily he'd admitted to all of it and how little he seemed to care. But I didn't have time to dwell on potential heartbreak – I had to find a way to help Al. He was right about one thing at least: I wasn't Lois Lane, intrepid girl reporter. Clearly that was him. I was Superman and I was going to save the day.

Somehow.

As if I wasn't frustrated enough, I couldn't get hold of anyone when I got back to my room. Neither Al nor Kekipi were answering their phones and Domenico reluctantly informed me that they had all left the house already, Artie too, although obviously not at the same time. I took my rage into the bathroom and fumed in the shower, trying to work out what I was going to say when I did get hold of Al and wondering how much Domenico knew. After all, I had seen him coming out of Artie's room the other night. Was he involved?

And as for Nick? I lathered up my hair with previously unknown vigour. How could he be so callous? I was starting to think I had made an epic fuck-up. After all this nonsense, what if the whole Nick or Charlie predicament was pointless? The thought that neither of them was right for me hadn't even crossed my mind until now. Charlie said he loved me, but the girl I was, the girl I'd been for the last ten years, she wasn't around any more. All the things he loved about me weren't real. I didn't love all the same things as he did, I just said I did so he would hang out with me. Coldplay made my skin crawl and, yes, I enjoyed *Star Wars* as much as the next girl but did he really need to watch it every other week? There were so many other movies out there.

But how could anyone choose to be with a man who was so very happy to go back to bed when a good man was about to get shafted so royally? What would happen five, ten years from now? So sorry, darling, can't make parents' evening, I'm very busy selling my mother down the river for a byline in *The Times*. Give whichever child has done well my love and tell the other one I'll ruin his life when I get home.

And so it was down to me. Clearly, I couldn't call the factory in China and have a quick chat with them, and given that my Italian was about as good as my Cantonese, there wasn't much point in trying to get any information out of the people dealing with the lease on the shop, but there was one person in this mess who did speak English. I could definitely speak to him – as long as he was in his office. And he agreed to see me.

I tied up my hair in my best shit-kicking ponytail, grabbed my bag and marched on my enemy.

'*Buongiorno.*'

The receptionist I had already met twice in the last five days stared at me blandly as though she had never seen my face before in her life.

'Bonjouro?' I offered. Italian was never going to be my language. 'Um, hello. I'm here to see Mr Warren.'

I smiled, hoping there was a direct correlation between the number of teeth I showed her and how quickly she let me in.

'No,' she replied without even checking her computer screen. 'No meeting today.'

'I'm working with Bertie Bennett?' I said, taking my camera out of my bag and waving it around until she cowered behind her monitor. Because threatening her with a heavy object was definitely going to change her mind. 'It's very important.'

'No,' she said again. 'No meeting today. *Arrivederci.*'

'Right, I know it's not in the diary,' I leaned over the desk, attempting to look terribly conspiratorial, 'because it's actually a personal meeting. I'm going to be modelling for Mr Warren.'

The receptionist peered over the desk, looked me up and down and then laughed.

'No, no, no!' She gave me a shake of the head as she continued to titter. 'No model.'

I stayed on my side of the desk, making a note of her adorable put-down and adding her to my list. I'd deal with her later, but right now I had to find a way to get to Warren. There was no way I was skulking back to the palazzo, to Nick, defeated. I really should have woken Amy before I left; she would have been a fantastic distraction.

That was it. What would Amy do in this situation? Thinking about it, Amy would probably charge the reception and leave this bitch hogtied behind her desk. Since I didn't really fancy that and was running out of time, I opted for a compromise.

'Excuse me, could I please use your bathroom?' I asked as politely as humanly possible. I bent my knees towards each other and bent down slightly, a pained expression on my face. Everyone knew that meant you needed a wee, right?

'Bathroom?' She kept her eyes trained on her computer monitor.

'Toilet?' I said, crouching more.

'I'm sorry,' she said. 'My English is not good.'

Her English was fucking flawless. Now I knew she was just being an objectionable twat.

'I need a wee,' I shouted across the desk. 'I'm going to wet myself.'

'Oh, *si*,' she smiled up at me before shaking her head. 'No, *mi dispiace*. No, I am sorry, no toilet.'

'But I'm pregnant.' I pushed out my stomach and attempted to look sad. Not nearly as sad as I would look if I really were pregnant but I thought I did a pretty good job. 'Baby?'

'Oh, *bambino*!' Suddenly, she looked delighted. '*Si, si, si*, this way.'

I rubbed my nonexistent baby and bumped her right up to the top of my list, following her across the reception, through a dark wooden door next to lift and waited while she worked away on three different locks.

What did she do when she was desperate? I wondered. Maybe she was never desperate. Maybe she was the only human on earth that didn't suffer a casual need to pee when she was outside that transformed into an uncontrollable, desperate urge as soon as she had her keys in her hand. Or maybe that was just me.

She waved at the loo like she was offering me the crown jewels before reaching out to press her hand against my barren, echoing womb and sighed happily.

'Is soon?' she asked. 'Baby is soon.'

I replied with a smile, keeping my mouth shut.

I'd got this far; blowing my cover by calling her a bitch wasn't going to help.

Safely inside the bathroom and surrounded by yet more black-and-white photographs of naked women, I turned sideways, checking my bump in the mirror on the back of the door. God help her if she thought this looked like a full-term pregnancy, I thought, patting my jeans, I didn't even have a food baby. Clearly, if your stomach was not concave in this building, you must be eight months along.

I waited a few minutes, sitting on the edge of the sink, my pulse sounding loudly in my ears. I knew this was a terrible idea but I had to get in and talk to Warren. I had to know why he was prepared to shaft his alleged friend Al on behalf of a boy he had spanked in front of an entire Parisian frow. Nick might be comfortable with moral ambiguity when it benefited his career but I wasn't prepared to let Al walk out at his party tonight and tell everyone his fashion line had failed before it had begun and not know why.

'I'll go in ten,' I told my reflection, pleased with my Burglar Bill-style black-and-white striped T-shirt, wrapping my hair into a bun and flexing into a couple of low squats in preparation. Badly. 'Nine. Nine and a half; nine and a third.'

'Oh, just go.' My reflection had about as much patience with me as my rubber duck. 'It's either going to work or it isn't.'

Mirror Tess was right. Sucking up a big deep

breath, I puffed out my chest, pulled in my belly and gave myself a nod.

'Don't be a chicken,' I mouthed at myself. 'Be brave.'

This was it. I bent down to my hands and knees and opened the bathroom door as quietly as I could and crawled along the floor, into the lift. At least the disinterested receptionist wasn't looking for me. What kind of pregnant woman crawled out of a toilet on her hands and knees and snuck into a lift? This kind. The kind that wasn't pregnant but was in fact a super genius; a super genius, who managed to get herself into a lift, only to find out that it was operated by a key card. Bollocks. The doors I had so cunningly opened, slid shut on me but the lift didn't go anywhere. I tried pressing all the buttons but nothing. Curled up in a ball, my arms wrapped around my knees, I pressed myself into the corner of the lift, waiting for something to happen. So much for my grand plan; so much for helping Al; so much for sticking it to Nick. So much for – oh, hang on a minute! I was moving.

The journey wasn't long, only to the third floor, but it was long enough for me to get to my feet and almost compose myself, although I did sort of need the toilet now. I really should have gone while I had the chance. The doors of the lift cracked open to show a red room I hadn't seen before but given the artwork on the walls, I would have known it belonged to Warren even if he hadn't stepped into the lift and bumped right into me.

353

'Bess,' he blustered, his hands held out to steady himself and accidentally on purpose grabbing right for my boobs. 'Do we have a meeting?'

'No.'

He was not removing his hands nearly quickly enough.

'Then apologies, but I am on my way to the airport,' he said, hands still holding up my rack. 'I have a car waiting.'

I glanced down at the weekend bag in the crook of his arm and the passport tucked into the top pocket of his leopard-print blazer.

'You're leaving? I stepped out of the lift, pushing him forward with my ample sweater puppies. It was amazing how well a man could be manipulated with boobs. Mine were entirely covered by my crew-neck T-shirt and still, I could have made him walk into traffic. 'But it's the party tonight.'

'Ah, yes,' he said, looking over my shoulder as the lift doors closed. 'Perhaps you haven't had a chance to catch up with Mr Bennett. I'm no long working on the project.'

'I heard, actually,' I said, channelling every hard-arsed woman I had ever seen on telly. I was Lady Mary and Peggy Mitchell and every character Helen Mirren had ever played, all rolled into one. 'But I didn't really understand why.'

'Creative differences,' he dismissed. 'These things happen.'

'Nothing to do with Artie, then?'

I was trying very hard to hold my nerve but it

had suddenly occurred to me what a very silly thing I was doing. No one knew where I was, no one knew what I was doing and I didn't really know anything about Edward Warren or Artie Bennett. What if he decided to kill me, skin me and wear me around the house like a snuggie?

'Nothing at all,' he replied, far too quickly.

I was a tall woman but Edward Warren was an even taller man. My righteous indignation and hugely inflated self-esteem had given me a few extra inches when the lift doors had first opened but now I was starting to waver.

'Al's really upset.' I decided to take a different tack and appeal to his heart. Failing all else, I could always pull up my shirt and then throw his passport out of the window. 'He doesn't understand why you can't work with him any more.'

'And I can only tell you what I told him,' he said, sidestepping me and pushing the call button for the lift. The power of my boobs had definitely worn off. 'I don't have the time and the designs aren't up to standard. Having thought about it, AJB isn't a project I feel I can contribute to.'

He looked away, at the ceiling, at the floor, out of the windows. He was looking at anything but me, boobs included. He was lying.

'That's really sad,' I said. 'I bet Jane would be really disappointed.'

He shrugged inside his black silk bomber jacket, unmoved. I was about four seconds away from switching to the boob offensive when another idea

355

struck me. Warren's walls might be covered in pictures of naked women but there was one even stronger influence in his decorating, one thing he loved even more than tits. Himself.

'And such a shame for, well, everyone. Those samples I saw were so beautiful. They might have been the most amazing dresses I'd ever seen,' I said, with a sigh, pulling my shoulders back, just in case. 'And I know Al has tons of journos coming. He was so excited to be working with one of his best friends on this, actually said there was no way it could happen without you. Really, I think everyone knew that you were the most important part of all of this. I mean, you're the one who really makes it happen, aren't you?'

'The pattern cutter is always forgotten,' he sniffed, flicking his luxuriant black hair away from his face. 'Artie is right; Albert Bennett is always the story. Al always will be the story.'

Bingo.

'Artie?' I crossed my arms across my chest. No more boobs for you, Edward Warren. 'He said that?'

'It's never a good idea to interfere with family, Bess,' Warren said, brushing an eyebrow into place. Not the first time I'd heard that piece of advice today. Not the first time he'd called me Bess, either. 'If there is one man on this earth more determined than Albert Bennett, it's Artie Bennett. How that man came from such wonderful people I will never know but I'm not going to sabotage my own career for the sake of a man I haven't seen in years.'

'Surely working on Al's collection is good for your career?' I argued, desperate to get to the bottom of this. 'It's going to be huge.'

'It's never going to happen.' Warren finally caved, dropping his bag on the floor and ignoring the lift as it chimed its arrival and opened its doors.

I stayed where I was as he strode back towards his desk, my hand hovering over the lift call button in case he was going to grab a weapon and I needed a quick getaway. I really didn't want to be a skin suit, even if the stitching was certain to be beautiful.

'And why's that?' I asked.

'Artie isn't going to let it happen,' he replied. 'He's blackballed Al with more or less every factory I've spoken with and he's done the same with every leasing agent in Milan, probably London, Paris and New York, I shouldn't wonder. And all Al knows is that his son has his knickers in a twist about stocking his line in Bennett's. It's depressing.'

'He knows you've bailed on him,' I added. 'I'm really sorry if I'm being stupid but what's in it for you? You don't sound that happy about shitting on your friend. Thankfully.'

Warren picked up a long, silver letter opener on his desk.

Oh fuuuck.

'I've been a pattern cutter for a long time,' he said, fingering the dull blade. Everything was starting to look a little bit Bond villain – and not in a good way. 'And I have wanted to produce my

357

own line for even longer but no one was interested. Once you're in your box, you stay in your box. Unless you have Al's money and name and prestige, of course.'

'You could start again,' I said, finger on the button. 'People can do that.'

'And people can fail,' he replied. 'I am the best pattern cutter in Italy, maybe in the world. You don't walk away from that. The fashion industry isn't the friendliest place, they don't look kindly on failure. If I had brought out my line and it didn't work, no one would have taken pity on me. Don't you remember Slimane's first collection for Saint Laurent?'

I pretended to think hard for a moment.

'Can't say I do.'

'Carnage,' he replied. 'Absolute critical carnage. Thank God it sold, or he would have been designing tea towels for M&S by the end of the year.'

'Everyone seems to be supporting Al,' I said, really wishing he would put that letter opener down. Didn't he have something less lethal he could play with? Basket full of puppies maybe? 'What's the difference between him and you?'

'A dead wife and an endearing beard go a long way with a lot of people,' Warren said, banging the letter opener down. 'Sorry, that was uncalled for.'

'Bit harsh,' I agreed, wondering how true it was. I did like that beard and even though I'd never met her, I did have a huge, wailing girl crush on Jane.

'Artie offered to help me and stock a capsule collection in Bennett's.' Warren sat down and smoothed his hair over his bald patch. 'So I made a business decision. It was nothing to do with Al.'

I was starting to wonder whether Nick was right about more than I cared to believe. I had thought that advertising was a cut-throat industry but I'd spent seven years cocooned inside one company, getting on with my job and just trying to do the best that I could, while the rest of the world was out there, shitting on each other from as great a height as possible. It was a bit depressing when you thought about it.

'He's going to be really hurt when he finds out,' I said, not sure where else to go. I'd appealed to his heart, I'd appealed to his ego and my ego knew that I'd never be able to appeal to his peen. If the receptionist hadn't made it clear enough, the photos on the walls did. Nothing over a size two got this man going. He wasn't even looking at my boobs any more. 'Didn't you ever think about asking Al to help you get your designs out?'

'Have you not been working in fashion photography for very long, dear?' Warren stood up and rounded his desk, picking up his weekend bag with a new resolve on his face. 'There are no favours in the fashion world. No one asks anyone for help.'

'Al asked you,' I said. 'And you were really quick

to help him out. You don't think he would do the same?'

He paused and looked like he was considering my question.

'I don't know,' he admitted. 'But it doesn't really matter now, does it?'

'I wish it did,' I said, stepping aside as he pushed the button for the lift. 'You won't change your mind? Talk to Al? See what he can do?'

'He can't do anything,' Warren replied as the lift doors opened. 'For me or himself. I suggest you take your photos and go home, Bess. Al's days are done.'

I hoisted my handbag onto my shoulder and watched as the doors closed behind him, relieved I was still alive but devastated that I hadn't really helped at all.

'Still,' I said to myself, calling the lift back up to my floor and half looking forward to the look on the receptionist's face when I walked out, 'I didn't end up as a skin suit so we can call this a win.'

CHAPTER 18

I didn't know what to do with myself.

I'd lost my pitch to Warren and returned home empty-handed. It was so much easier when you were pitching to a toilet paper company; there were fewer lives to ruin at the end of the day. Not that things didn't get brutal in the world of bog roll, let me tell you.

One good thing about spending almost every weekend in the office, whether it was because I was hiding from my flatmate or working too hard, was the alone time. I was used to spending a lot of time with nothing but my own thoughts and those thoughts had invariably been about Charlie. For the last week, I'd struggled to get more than a few moments to myself. All I wanted, as I sloped back through the gates of the palazzo, was to lock myself in my office with a KFC meal and sulk about an unrequited crush. It had been a simpler time. Without an office to go to, I wandered through the grounds, kicking a few stones that happened to be in my way, and headed straight to my secret garden. Only today, there was nothing secret about it.

Three gardeners in matching green dungarees looked up at me as I pushed open the door. The one who had decided the dungarees made more of a fashion statement without a T-shirt underneath wiped the sweat away from his forehead and gave me a decidedly lascivious grin.

'Oh, I'm sorry,' I said, backing out quickly. 'You're working.'

They all shouted after me but I didn't understand what they were saying and I wasn't interested in hanging around and playing charades to work it out. I was ignorant and I was tired. In just a few hours, Al was expecting me to trot into his party, all gussied up in a posh frock, no doubt, and take pictures of his fabulous bash with a smile on my face. I was going to need all the energy I could muster for that; I didn't have any to waste on the pervy gardeners. There was only one other place I could think of in the whole palazzo where I could be alone, where I could think. Pulling my handbag up high on my good shoulder, I steeled myself and set off inside, looking for sanctuary.

Even though Al had given me express permission to shoot in Jane's studio, I still felt like I was intruding as I turned the key in the lock and let myself inside. The room was huge but felt so much smaller than the bedrooms and salons that made up the rest of the house. The studio used to be the loft and had much lower ceilings than I was used to now. I stooped, even though I didn't really

362

need to, wondering how tall Jane had been. She looked so statuesque in all the photos I'd seen but she could have been wearing heels. Another person that felt so familiar when really, I knew nothing about her.

I watched a ruffle of dust flutter around in the light by the window, disturbed by the open door; and held my breath until it settled against the silence. It was clear that this room had been looked after; it was a little dusty but it was perfectly clean, and everything had been kept just so. I could easily imagine that no one had stepped foot in here since Jane had died.

The dresses Amy and I had shot were still on the dummies, all beautiful, heavy fabric and tiny, barely visible stitches. I could almost hear my grandmother's voice telling me they didn't make dresses like this any more. And now they never would, I thought sadly. How could Warren be such a coward? How could he live with himself?

Jane's work table was right by the window, perfectly positioned to make the most of the light. Pulling out the chair, I sat down, feeling sad and defeated and not just on Al's behalf, but also about everything. Amy wasn't going to get her dream job, Al wasn't going to get his fashion line and I wasn't going to get my happily ever after. I wasn't the girl for Charlie; I'd changed too much to go back to that. And Nick wasn't the man for me. How many times had I gone home and laughed at my friends when they told me how the arsehole

363

they were dating wasn't really an arsehole, he was just misunderstood. And now I was one of them.

There were a lot of things I could live with – smelly feet, bad taste in movies – but I couldn't pretend to be OK with a complete lack of moral compass. Sometimes, when you kissed a frog all you were doing was kissing a frog.

I aimlessly rolled a pencil back and forth along the desk, resting my temple in my hand and scanning Jane's magazines, her notebooks. Everything about the palazzo was beautifully put together, all crisp white walls and elegant gilt edging, perfectly appointed furniture accented by the most exquisite antiques; it screamed good taste. But this room was different. I hadn't noticed it when we were shooting – I was too busy shouting at Amy to lift up the reflector and trying to do a good job of the photographs – but this room, beautiful though it was, seemed to be a million miles away from the rest of the house. The walls were painted a warm creamy colour and the curtains at the window were light voile, designed to let the light through all day and night, whether it was from the sun or the moon, and the furniture looked worn and loved.

I pulled out what I thought was a leatherbound notebook from the bookshelf built into the side of the desk. Al had pulled out some sketches for us to look at and I hadn't investigated beyond them but suddenly I was curious about the big brown leather books stacked seven or eight to a shelf.

Opening it carefully, I was hit by the smell of old paper. It wasn't a notebook, it was a photo album, Jane's own photo album.

Looking around, I wondered, just for a moment, whether or not I should be looking at them. Surely Al knew they were in here? And he knew what a nosy cow I was; surely he must have had an inkling that I would have to take a peek? But then, if I'd learned anything over the last few days, it's that Al was far too trusting, I thought, flipping gently through the pages. And however unnatural it felt, that was something I was going to have to learn to let go of. Nick was right, I was too naïve.

The photographs were wonderful. I'd heard Al's version of his love story, I'd been in his houses, I'd seen Jane's clothes and I'd even talked to their friends but this was something else. It was as though she was telling me *her* side. The pictures started out in black and white, small and square and matte, with pencilled-in dates and descriptions by the side. The first album I had pulled showed me her life before Al, before she had been Mrs Bennett. Instead of glamorous parties, I saw her childhood, smiling mother, happy father, everyone much more erect that they really needed to be. Jane really had been very beautiful. As a teenager, she was all big eyes and long hair, carefully styled in ways that my hair would never have accepted.

As she got older, she only got better looking and

she documented everything. I wondered why Al had never told me what a keen photographer she had been as I pored over the pages. It seemed like she never left the house without a camera. There were weddings and birthdays and christenings and family holidays to the seaside, to visit family in Ireland – Jane had been a master of the selfie long before Instagram was even thought of. And then, halfway through the second album, her mother had disappeared from the pictures and her father couldn't seem to raise a smile. After a while, another man started to appear but it wasn't Al. I remembered him telling me how Jane had been engaged to another man when he met her and this had to be him.

At first, she looked happy in their pictures, holding his hand, resting her head on his shoulder, even though he looked incredibly suspicious of the camera. Jane's dad was in nearly every shot of the two of them and it almost seemed as though Jane's dad was crashing their good times. Her first fiancé was definitely a lot older than she was; there was a story there, for sure. And then it happened. The older man disappeared and Al arrived and with him, the light returned to Jane's eyes. I smiled as she smiled, staring up at Al with complete adoration and in turn, he couldn't keep his hands off her. There weren't that many pictures before I came to their wedding but once the rings were on their fingers, the fun really began. I couldn't name a country that they hadn't visited;

every page had photos stuck in from a different continent. No wonder they hadn't had time to launch a clothing line. It was hard to get any work done when you were riding an elephant through India.

Eventually, near the end of the fifth photo album, Jane started showing off a baby bump. Maternity wear was so much cooler in the sixties, I thought, eyeing her pedal pushers and swing tops with a touch of envy. And there he was. In the baby blue, leatherbound album, I was introduced to Arthur Albert John Bennett, six pounds and four ounces and the apple of his mother's eye. There was no shortage of photos of Artie, a babe in arms in New York City, toddling around Hawaii, scooting around the palazzo gardens on his tricycle. But there was a shortage of photos of Artie with his dad. Almost all of them were of Jane and her baby boy or Artie, standing proudly by himself.

I stared at one of the few family shots I found, all three Bennetts standing in front of the house in Hawaii. Clearly it had once been bright with the lurid colours of the seventies but now it was faded and Jane's flower-print maxi dress was almost pastel pink. Al had arms draped around his wife's neck and Jane was clutching Artie to her as though someone might try to take him away.

I pulled my phone out of my bag and dialled a number I usually avoided, still staring at the photo.

'Hello?'

'Hello, Brian, it's only me,' I said, sniffling into the microphone. 'Is my mum there?'

'She's watching *Pointless*,' he said in hushed, reverential tones. 'I don't know if you want to bother her.'

'Who is it?' I heard my mum shout from the living room.

'It's Tess,' Brian shouted back, deafening me for the next three hours.

'What does she want?' she yelled again.

'Can you please tell her I need two minutes,' I asked before there was any more bellowing. 'I'll be quick.'

'She wants two minutes,' Brian shouted. I really should have seen that coming. 'Come and get the phone.'

There was some muffled chuntering and complaining but eventually, my mum picked up the phone with a loud sigh.

'What's wrong?' she asked. 'I'm watching *Pointless*.'

'I know, I'm sorry,' I said. 'I wanted to call and say sorry for storming out the other week. I was out of order. I wanted to apologize properly.'

'Right,' she said stiffly. 'Are you all right?'

'Yes.' I rubbed my prickling nose and closed up Jane's photo album. 'Just fancied saying hello to my mum.'

'Well, I'm the only one you're getting,' she replied. 'You're sure nothing's wrong?'

'Everything is fine.' I smiled into the phone, not sure what I had expected her to say. We weren't the kind of mother and daughter that had long, pointless conversations. Especially during *Pointless*. 'You and Brian are all right? Liz? Mel?'

'Everyone's fine,' she said, clearly annoyed. 'Where are you? You're not still in Milan are you? Where's Charlie?'

'You get back to your game show,' I said, satisfied that everything was as OK as it needed to be. 'I'm fine, Charlie's fine, and I'll call you next week. Maybe I could come up next weekend, have that Sunday dinner?'

'Fine, I'll talk to you later.' Her attention was already back on the TV.

I hung up and rested my head on the desk, staring at the family portrait of the Bennetts and wondered who had taken the photo. Was it Kekipi? Kekipi's dad? I had so many questions – if only Jane was here to answer them, to make things right between Artie and Al. It looked like she was the only one who knew how.

'I feel really weird,' I muttered, following Amy out of our suite and down the hallway. 'We shouldn't be all dressed up for a party, I should be talking to Al.'

'You can't say anything now,' Amy said, fiddling with the front of her slashed-down-to-there midnight blue Naheem Khan gown. It was a little bit Seventies, a little bit sexy and entirely inappropriate. She looked amazing. 'Let him have this party, talk to him tomorrow.'

'I still don't know what I'm going to say.' I pulled at the cap sleeve of my own dress, a deep pink silk, off-the-shoulder, full-skirted affair, picked out by Kekipi. 'Thanks for the cocktails; by the way, your son is totally sabotaging your business.'

'At least you look nice,' Amy said as she straightened out the train of my frock. 'I still think the yellow sparkly ballgown was more fun but Kekipi insisted on this one.'

'I can't imagine why.' I attempted to flip the skirt out behind me – and succeeded in nothing more impressive than sending myself flying sideways into a wall. 'Although was a train really necessary? We're going to be so overdressed.'

'We are not overdressed. It's going to be dressy,' she assured me with a smile while I righted myself. 'And anyway, you need to look amazing. Make Nick hate himself.'

I frowned. 'Nick wouldn't hate himself if he lost a winning lottery ticket.'

'Which he has,' she said, stroking a strand of my hair into place. 'And don't forget it when he walks in looking all James Bond in his tux.'

'I won't,' I lied. I was dreading seeing him. 'I just wish I'd been able to get hold of Al. He isn't answering his phone; Kekipi isn't answering his phone, and I called Charlie and left a message for him to call me back yesterday and he hasn't. I'm starting to take it personally.'

'Left Charlie a message saying what exactly?' she asked as I rounded the first staircase, incredibly carefully. 'Tell me you didn't confess all about tall, dark and dickish to his voicemail?'

'Of course I didn't.' One step, two steps, three steps, pause. 'I'm not that stupid.'

'Yeah, you are, but whatever.' Amy trotted down the stairs like she was wearing trainers instead of four-inch borrowed Gucci sandals. 'He hasn't called you back?'

'No.' I shook my head. Downstairs, I could hear music swelling over muted conversation. How many people were down there already? 'I only called to make sure he'd got everything for the pitch. I didn't say anything.'

'It feels like we've been here forever,' Amy said, tossing her head and helping me around another corner. 'I know I was a bit mental yesterday but I've been thinking about everything and I'm really excited. For both of us. Thank you for bringing me out with you.'

'Are you kidding? What would I have done without you?'

'I don't know, took some photos, shagged a super stud, told him you loved him and then busted into some random bloke's office?' She gave me such a proud look. 'Oh wait, you did that anyway.'

'You're a fantastic influence,' I told her.

We took the last few stairs at a slightly faster speed, arriving in the lobby at the same time as two incredibly well-dressed older gentlemen, both of whom were seemingly very interested in Amy's almost visible navel.

'Fuck Al's shops,' she whispered. 'I'm going to marry a rich old man. Are they famous, do you think?'

'They've got a definite Berlusconi vibe to them, haven't they?' I held my camera tightly in my right hand, the left still clutching the banister. 'Not your usual type, though.'

'I don't know, I assume they have a penis,' Amy reasoned. 'After you?'

'You're such a gent,' I said, tottering after Silvio one and two.

I hated admitting when I was wrong but in this instance, I was the first to admit it: Amy was right. We were not overdressed for the party.

The last couple of days had been so strange. I'd been so worked up over everything – Charlie, Nick, getting Al's photos right, getting the Perito's pitch right and then all the Artie drama, not to mention the thought of spending another night walking around in an evening gown and too-high heels – I really hadn't given an awful lot of thought to the actual event. Al had called it a party. To me, a party was a few drinks, crisps and dips and perhaps a specially put together iPod playlist. When I saw the dress Kekipi had picked out for me, all fitted bodice and too many skirts, I just assumed he was playing dressing-up again, with me and Amy as his living dolls. I'd thought it would be nothing more than a few of Al's fanciest fashion friends, hanging out in the dining room, maybe the odd celeb that Amy would be able to point out to me and my camera, and way too much booze.

Well. How wrong could you be? Two of Al's invisible staff, all fancied up in their light grey suits and coordinating black ties, directed us towards a pair of double doors to the left of the staircase that I hadn't really paid attention to before and opened them with an understated flourish.

'Fuck me,' Amy breathed. 'Where did all this come from?'

'Just something I pulled out my ass.' Kekipi swept through the doors behind us, snaking his arms around our waists and drawing us into the centre of the ballroom. 'You like?'

We were in an actual, honest-to-God ballroom. It wasn't until I was standing in the middle of it that I realized I'd only I'd ever seen them on TV before and most of those were animated. Beauty and the Beast, eat your heart out; this place makes your ballroom look like a shed. I was struggling to work out the geography of exactly where we were in the palazzo, but the ceilings were at least twice as high as those in our suite and two huge chandeliers hung from the ceiling, glowing beautifully. At the far end of the room, there was what looked like half an orchestra sitting patiently in their all black outfits, holding their instruments and waiting for the nod. At the other, a small stage was set up with a microphone stand. On either side of the room were two long bars busy with bartenders shaking up cocktails or pouring champagne, and everywhere I looked, there were dozens and dozens of people in the most ridiculously beautiful clothes I had ever seen. I didn't even have a drink yet and I was already terrified of spilling it on them.

And hanging from the ceiling, on each side of the room, were my photographs.

'Kekipi, it's amazing,' I told him, my trigger finger itching on my camera. 'The photos—'

'*Your* photos,' he corrected. 'They were my inspiration. The centrepiece of the event.'

'I don't know what to say.' I tried to swallow down the thickness in my throat, I was not going to cry all this mascara off, mostly because I didn't want to have to go back upstairs in my heels to fix it, but also because I was so, so proud. 'Thank you for picking the dress for me. It's so pretty.'

'It's a masterpiece, just like you,' he said, cinching in my waist. 'You're so tiny.'

'The three words every woman wants to hear,' I replied, smiling. 'Especially after I had to pretend to be pregnant this morning and no one questioned it.'

'Am I missing something?' Kekipi asked, glancing at Amy. 'Will my next event be a baby shower? Please tell me we won't do the wedding until after you've lost the weight – it's vulgar.'

'You are missing something, but not that,' I said, struggling to concentrate on my friends when the constant swish of silk and tulle was calling to me. 'Is Al here yet? Is Artie here?'

'They're both here somewhere.' He gestured off into the crowds before stopping a waiter passing out champagne. 'Artie had some bizarre change of heart and decided to invite half of Milan at the last minute. I'm sure he's surrounded by all of his cronies somewhere. I would imagine near the food.'

I held out my hand to accept the champagne but was struck with a sudden flash of sobriety. 'Better not,' I said, pulling away. 'I'm sorry, I've got to talk to Al.'

'You can't do it here,' Amy begged, a glass of champagne in each hand. 'It's too awful.'

'But why else would Artie be here if it wasn't to cause trouble?' I asked while Kekipi's attention flipped between us like he was watching an especially dramatic game of table tennis. 'I'm not Nick, I can't stand around and let him make a fool out of Al in front of all those people.'

'I think you ladies need to tell me everything right now,' Kekipi said, drawing us off to the side of his masterpiece. 'What are you talking about?'

'All this trouble Al has been having getting the clothing line off the ground,' I said, pressing a hand into my waist and wishing I had eaten before I let Amy fasten me into my frock. The inner workings of it were more architecturally impressive than the Eiffel Tower. It was tight. 'It's Artie. He bribed Warren to pull out by offering him space for his own collection in Bennett's,' I explained. 'And he got the factory to cancel and God knows what he did to the estate agents, but that's why Al can't get the retail space he wants. It's all Artie. And maybe Domenico. But mostly Artie.'

'Domenico?' Kekipi's eyes widened and then narrowed sharply. 'He's in on it?'

'I saw him coming out of Artie's room,' I shrugged. 'When he was on the phone with China.'

'That *fucker*. And that little shit!' Kekipi turned his attention to the assembled masses, scanning for his nemeses. 'He's always been a self-obsessed turd but this is a new low. Kind of. Did I ever tell you about the time he tried to close Bennett's down by phoning in a bomb threat when Princess Diana was visiting in the eighties? No? Remind me after I've slapped him silly, it's a good one.'

The three of us scoured the room but it was very hard to pick out a tall, attractive grey-haired man in a suit amongst dozens of tall, attractive grey-haired men in suits. No matter how hard I willed it, I could not see his handlebar moustache anywhere.

'I've been so distracted,' Kekipi muttered, pulling out his mobile phone and dialling Al. 'This is all my fault. It's a shame when ambition is over-powered by psychosis. Jane and Al should have drowned him at birth.'

'Maybe they didn't realize at birth?' I suggested. 'Maybe he didn't turn mental until he was a little bit older?'

'Please,' he sniffed. 'I'm certain they shaved the horns off when they cut the umbilical cord. He is the devil. He's a rich, only child who was coddled his entire life and now his mother isn't here to hold his hand, he has to do things for himself and he doesn't like it. It isn't Al's fault that Artie never achieved anything, it's Artie's fault. If he put half as much effort into creating something as he does into destroying things, he'd be president of the USA by now.'

The colour drained from his face as his phone went straight to voicemail. 'Jesus, strike that, I don't want anyone giving him ideas.'

'Where is Al?' Amy asked, picking up and dropping her skirt in a huff. 'Why is he so hard to find at his own party?'

'I'm going to see if I can see him from up there.' I pointed to a winding staircase in the corner that led to a deserted mezzanine level above the ballroom. 'Might be a bit easier.'

'I'll look in his room,' Kekipi said, waving his phone at us. 'Amy, you stay here, eyes open. Call if you see either of them but don't do anything. I'm so pissed off, I could spit.' He gave the pair of us a look. 'What? Obviously I'm not going to.'

'Don't be mad at yourself,' I said. I knew how protective he was of Al and they'd been together for so long. 'You couldn't have known and I don't think Al would have believed it even if we had been able to tell him. You've been so busy organizing this amazing event, you can't be everywhere at once.'

'It's my job to take care of Al. He's not my boss, he's family – and he's my best friend,' he said with a sad smile. 'I took my eye off the ball because I'm an old fool. But don't worry, I'll take care of it. Is it wrong to spank a forty-eight-year-old man?'

'In what way?' Amy asked.

'Good point,' he replied, straightening the sleeve of my dress with a tight smile. 'Look at us, we're practically *Charlie's Angels*, only better.'

'I'd be much happier fighting crime in flats,' I mumbled to myself, tottering off towards the narrow spiral staircase that led to the mezzanine. 'The only person I'm likely to kill in these is me.'

The party was incredible. Up on the mezzanine, I was really able to appreciate the effort that had gone into it. From the music and the lighting to the guests and my bigger-than-life-sized photographs of Jane's dresses, the movement of the crowd below making them dance against the walls. Everything was so beautiful, so out of the realm of my experience, that I almost forgot my mission for a moment. This night was too pretty, too perfect, for someone like Artie to come along and destroy it. No matter how many times Kekipi said he was a spoiled brat acting out, I still couldn't understand.

My littlest sister was a spoiled brat. When she cut the hair off my Barbie doll because it was my birthday and she couldn't understand why I was getting presents and she wasn't, that was acting out. There had to be a middle ground to parenting; clearly Jane hadn't got it right by smothering her son until he turned into a lazy, evil genius but I really didn't think my mum's reaction to Liz scalping my birthday present was on the money either. Liz got sent to her room for doing it and I got sent to my room for 'overreacting'. I was all grown up now but I was almost certain that if someone destroyed my birthday present at my birthday party on my birthday, I would still push them over and then throw cake at them.

'Not one for the crowds?'

I was so busy snapping away at the beautiful ballroom and searching for Artie, I didn't even notice Nick sneaking up behind me.

'I'm looking for Al,' I said without flinching. 'Or Artie. And I'm not talking to you.'

'Who said I wanted to talk?' he asked, walking his fingers from the nape of my neck, all the way down my bare back until he found the edge of my dress. Oh good, he had slipped right back into slimy bastard mode. That was so much easier to reject.

'Don't even,' I said, shaking him off. 'I'm busy. Why don't you knob off and work on your story while I try to help my friend?

I turned to face him, steeling myself for the vision of beauty that would bypass my brain and divert all blood flow directly to my ladyparts but instead, I saw a tired version of the Adonis I had left in bed this morning. A middle-aged man with grey skin and bags under his eyes. Even in his tux, he looked like shit. It was brilliant.

'Well, I mean . . .' He dropped the cheesy grin and stuck his hands in his pockets, eyes firmly stuck to a spot just left of the top of my head. 'Isn't there anything I can do to help?'

I let my camera hang around my neck and attempted a pissy flounce of my skirt. It looked a bit like I was having a fit but still, he could tell I was annoyed with him.

'Help Al or help yourself?' I asked. 'I'm sorry to be so naïve but you realize I don't understand.'

'I was tired this morning,' he said, doing his own grumpy flounce. 'And I was a dickhead – is that what you want me to say?'

'I already know that.' I grabbed my hair and twisted it into a loose ponytail for something to do with my hands that wasn't touching or punching. 'What I want you to say is that you were wrong.'

'I was wrong.' He turned and rested his forearms against the banister. 'I thought about it all after you left, and you were right.'

'Oh . . .' I wasn't expecting him to belly up so quickly. I didn't know quite what to say.

'I'm not going to pretend that I can't be selfish sometimes,' Nick said, stretching out his back, eyes still trained on the crowd below. 'I haven't had to worry about anyone but myself for a really long time and I know this isn't going to make me more popular with you, but the Al and Artie thing? It had the potential to be a really big story. I took this job to see you again, not because I wanted to tell Artie's story. But then this came up and I realized how big it could be. Did I think about you? No, and I didn't think about Al either. I thought about selling it to *Vanity Fair* or *Vogue* and that was about it.'

'Heart-warming,' I replied. 'Such a nice story.'

'I'm a selfish shit.' He shrugged and looked over at me. 'That's not going to change overnight. But it doesn't mean I don't care about you and it doesn't mean I don't realize that I should have thought about how you would feel getting into all of this.'

I stopped twisting my hair for fear of an impending frizzbomb. Curly girls had so much to deal with – we couldn't even calm our nerves without fucking up our hair.

'If you had, would you have done anything differently?' I asked, holding on to the banister behind me, Nick's hand inches away from mine.

'Honestly?' He looked at me with open, honest eyes. 'Probably not.'

'Well, don't I feel special,' I whispered.

'I know I never said this was going to be simple,' Nick covered my hand with his and I let him, 'but if it happened again, I would do things differently. What happens next is up to you.'

'What happens next is we find Al,' I said, wishing I were a shallow piece of shit who could forget her friends' problems and pretend what he'd offered was enough. Stupid morals. 'It's up to you if you want to help.'

'I know where he is.' He pulled my hand away from the banister and wound his fingers around mine. 'I just talked to him and I told him everything. Like I said, you were right, I do owe Al. He's a decent man and there aren't many of them around.'

'What?' I blinked slowly. 'Why didn't you say so?'

He scrunched his shoulders right up to his ears and let them drop. 'I had to make things right with you first, didn't I?'

I looked over my shoulder at the party below and let Nick lead me back down the staircase and out of the ballroom. Everyone looked like they were having such a wonderful time. I really hoped things stayed that way.

My secret garden really wasn't much of a secret at all. Nick pushed the door open to reveal Al sitting at the tiny wrought-iron table with a glass of whisky and one of the old photo albums from Jane's studio. He was wearing his tux but the bow tie hung loose around his neck and the top two buttons of his shirt were undone. He stared at a page of the album, smiling and running a finger over the photograph. In that moment, I didn't want to be there. I wanted to pull on Nick's hand and take him away before Al saw us. This was too sad. I knew what was in that album, knew that he was looking at pictures of him and Jane. He had already had his heart broken when he lost the love of his life; how was he supposed to handle his own son acting like such a wanker as well? It was too much. Unfortunately, it was also too late.

'Ah, Mr Miller, you're back.' He looked up from

his memories and scratched his beard. I bloody loved that beard. 'And you brought Tess. What time is it? Am I dreadfully late?'

'It's just getting started,' I said, breaking off from Nick's hand and stepping forward to take the empty seat next to Al. 'You've got plenty of time.'

Nick hovered in the doorway for a moment and I wasn't entirely sure whether or not he was going to cut and run entirely but eventually, he stepped into the garden and closed the door behind him.

'I was just looking at these pictures from our last party here . . .' He pushed the album towards me and tapped the photo in the top right corner. 'The Eighties were kind to no one except for my Jane. Everyone else looks ridiculous.'

He was right, the photo was almost entirely taken over by shoulder pads and lamé and enormous hair, but there in the corner was Jane, her beautiful blonde hair shining against her classic black sheath and Al standing beside her, sporting some very impressive lapels. On the other side of Jane was a very grumpy-looking teenager in a smaller version of the same suit Al wore.

'Nice suit,' I said, closing my eyes and taking a calming breath. 'So, I went to talk to Edward Warren earlier.'

'Oh, I know you did,' Al said with a laugh. 'I wish I'd been there to see it. Sounds like it was a riot.'

'You *know*?' I opened my eyes and sat back in my chair, looking up at Nick. He shrugged his shoulders, protesting his innocence.

'Edward told me.' Al rested his hand on the family portrait. 'Actually. he told me someone called Bess had been to see him but it didn't take long for me to work out that it was you. Called me on his way to the airport and once we'd had a chat, he decided to postpone his trip. Should be here any moment, actually. He's never been one to miss out on a party.'

'Did he tell you what he told me?' I asked, twisting in my seat to look at Nick. He looked as nonplussed as I did. 'About Artie?'

'Oh yes, dear,' he nodded. 'And Nick filled in the rest of the gaps for me. I think Edward was quite surprised how much your intervention affected him; he seemed terribly shocked to be throwing himself on his sword for me.'

'You already knew?' I felt Nick's hand on my shoulder as I struggled to know what to say next. 'Are you OK?'

'I wouldn't say I'm OK.' Al picked up his whisky and sipped it, his face thoughtful. 'But I'm not as surprised as I would like to be.'

Nick raked a hand through his hair, squatting down at the side of my chair. 'Is there anything we can do?'

'If either of you have a time machine handy, I wouldn't mind popping back to the sixties and having another go at raising a decent human being.' Al drained the rest of his glass in one slug. 'But if that's not on the cards, I would suggest you both go back inside and have a very lovely evening.

Does the ballroom look wonderful? Kekipi always does such a fantastic job with these things.'

'It's gorgeous,' I said as Al began doing up his shirt buttons. 'Kekipi feels terrible, though. *We* feel terrible about all of this.'

'Why would anyone feel terrible?' he asked, moving on to fasten his bow tie. 'For better or worse, Artie is my son. I'll deal with it. Did Kekipi tell you about the time he tried to overthrow Anna Wintour and take over *Vogue* in the nineties?'

'No,' I said, slightly concerned that Al had gone mad. 'He started telling me a story about Princess Diana and a bomb threat, though.'

'Ah, yes.' Al laughed out loud. It felt out of place with the quiet of the garden. 'Such an ambitious boy, could have done anything; but he never wanted to put in the work to earn the things he wanted. Entirely mine and his mother's fault; little to be done about it now.'

'What are you going to do?' I stood up and let Nick take my hand again. Al beamed at the affectionate gesture between the two of us and clapped Nick on the back.

'I'm very glad that this is working out.' He nodded at the two of us and then adjusted his tie until it was perfect. 'I knew right away. Sometimes, you do just know.'

'Then you're better at this than I am,' I replied, glancing at Nick and then back at Al. 'We're a bit rubbish.'

'Oh, all the best people are,' Al said, waving us

out of the garden with both hands. 'That's part of the fun. If you don't fight, you can't make up and where's the fun in that? Nothing like a good argument to clear the air, it keeps you both on your toes. But you two are good for each other, I think.'

Nick didn't say anything, just smiled and squeezed my hand. Shaking my head at myself, I squeezed back.

'Nothing worth having was ever won easily,' Al summarized as he closed the door to the garden behind us. 'A lesson my son is about to find out for himself.'

'This is going to be brilliant,' Nick whispered as we sped up to chase Al back into the palazzo. Seventysomething or not, he had quite a sprint on. 'Make sure that camera is ready.'

'I don't think these are the photos I'm meant to be taking,' I said, wishing I already knew what as going to happen next. 'Are they going to fight to the death?'

'If they were guinea pigs, Al would kill and eat his young,' he said, hurrying me along as fast as my shoes would carry me.

I gave him the most disgusted look I could muster. 'Have you been hanging out with Amy or something?' I asked. 'Eww.'

I couldn't share Nick's thirst for blood. No matter how determined Al seemed to be, this had to be painful for him. It was definitely making me reconsider ever having children of my own. I would be damned if I was going to sacrifice my vagina for a tiny demon that would only grow up to try to destroy my life's work. I'd googled an episiotomy after reading it in one of my mum's book years ago and that shit was no laughing matter.

When we all arrived back at the ballroom, it was even busier than when we left.

'*Ciao*, Chiara!' Al was immediately caught up in a human tumble of air kisses and elaborate noncontact hugs. 'And Stefano, so glad you could make it.'

'Tess, over there . . .' Nick nudged my attention over to the corner of the room where Artie and his handlebar moustache were busying themselves at the bar with a woman in a dark blue dress. And not just any woman.

'Oh bloody hell, he's talking to Amy.' I pressed my right hand to my temples, trying to shove a burgeoning headache right back to wherever it came from.

'Had we better go and save her?' Nick asked, casually throwing around the term 'we' and expecting me not to notice. I did a tiny, silent squee and nodded although I was certain it was far more likely that Artie would be the one that needed saving from her before the night was out.

'Amy!' I descended on my friend with multiple cheek kisses, ignoring her confused expression and acting as though we always greeted each other this way as opposed to punching each other and shouting 'All right, slag!' across a crowded room.

'We've been looking for you everywhere. And Artie, so good to see you again.'

'Ah, Vanessa,' he took my hand in his and kissed it, his eyes twinkling up at me. 'Or did we decide on Tess in the end? I forget.'

'Shouldn't worry about it,' I said, digging my fingernails into my palms. Now I thought about it, killing him with a shoe would actually tie everything up nicely. 'It's so lovely to see you.'

'Couldn't miss the big party, could I?' He looked so sickeningly pleased with himself. 'And here's my favourite journalist. Good to see you, too.'

'My favourite monkey,' Nick smiled through gritted teeth. 'I was chatting with the organ grinder. Have you seen your father this evening?'

There were few things I loved more than being in the middle of an alpha male-off and since I was sleeping with the man who was winning this one, it was even more fun than usual. Amy gave me a quizzical look but I just smiled happily.

'It's fine,' I mouthed. 'It's all OK.'

'Your lovely friend, Amy, was just telling me how she's never been to New York,' Artie explained as Nick took two glasses of champagne from a passing waiter and handed one to me. This time I took it happily. I had a feeling I was going to need more than one before the evening was over. 'I told her she must visit.'

'And you promised to be my tour guide,' Amy reminded him with a light giggle that I knew must

388

have been like razor blades in her throat. 'Have either of you seen Kekipi on your travels?' she asked.

'No.' I gave the room a once-over but he was nowhere to be seen. 'Al's here, though. He's really looking forward to everything.'

'He is?' Amy's big blue eyes seemed to understand my overactive eyebrows and unnecessary emphasis. Nick and Artie looked a little bit lost but that wasn't their fault, they hadn't been reading between my lines for the better part of the last three decades. Hopefully Nick would catch up eventually. Hopefully I'd never see Artie again as long as I lived.

'I see someone I must speak to . . .' Artie excused himself with a shallow bow. 'It was lovely to make your acquaintance, Amy. And a delight to catch up with yourselves.'

'We are charmed,' Nick said, his voice ruffled as Artie walked away. 'I never fucking liked him.'

'But you were perfectly happy to let him shaft his dad for your story,' Amy said in a quiet voice, adding a short sharp punch to his gut to make her point. 'I knew I was right to give you that slap when I met you.'

Nick winced, not expecting the blow. 'Thanks,' he said. 'But it was totally uncalled for. Next time I deserve it, remember you're one-up, OK?'

'Not here, not now,' I warned the pair of them, all of my attention on Al. 'Where is Kekipi?'

'Over there.'

Amy pointed across the room where my favourite

middle-aged Hawaiian estate-managing gay man was engaged in a furious argument with my least favourite middle-aged Italian estate-managing sneaky bastard, Domenico.

Amy was not the only person to spot the disagreement. Everyone in the room had stopped what they were doing and turned to watch. Skirts swished and crystal clinked but no one was saying a word. No one except Kekipi and Domenico. They were saying all of the words. Most of them were in Italian but there were a few in the universal language of swearing and I was more or less fluent in that.

'What are they saying?' I looked to my multilingual lover for answers but he looked as nonplussed as the rest of us. 'Why don't they teach Italian in schools?'

'Because they didn't anticipate you needing to translate an argument at a millionaire fashion magnate's Italian palazzo at the age of twenty-eight?' Amy suggested. 'Or because you were shit at languages anyway and they wouldn't have let you take it even if they offered it?'

'This is insane.' Nick looked to the floor to cover a grin. 'You're not going to believe this.'

'I'm not going to believe what?' I whined, turning to look up at him. This was so unfair; everyone at the party knew what was going on but me. I was not built to withstand such agony. 'Tell me.'

'I don't think you need to speak Italian to get what's going on right now,' he said, grinning from ear to ear.

He was right. There was another international language that I understood perfectly and that was the language of sticking your tongue down someone else's throat. In the middle of Kekipi's impressive rant, Domenico, looking so sad and desperate, grabbed hold of the other man and laid one on him, right there in the middle of the party.

'I did *not* see that coming,' I said as Kekipi turned into a ragdoll in Domenico's arms and the smooch continued. 'What is happening?'

'My Italian isn't brilliant,' Nick said with an edge of false modesty. 'But from what I can gather, Kekipi was accusing Domenico of trying to shaft Al, Domenico was defending himself and then Kekipi said something like "how could you do this to me? I'm so stupid, you're such a liar, yada yada yada" and then Domenico said that he would never lie to him and that he loved him and then, well, you saw what happened next.'

'I am freaking out right now,' Amy took the half-empty glass of champagne out of my hand and necked it. 'Big time.'

'I mean, they look happy enough,' I said, unable to tear my eyes away. 'They look really happy.'

'They look like they need to get a room,' Nick replied. 'I'm an open-minded man but really, this is a fancy party.'

'Because two men kissing is worse than two men screaming at each other over the hors d'oeuvres?' Amy asked sweetly. 'Kekipi is hot, Domenico is hot, I say let them go for it.'

'Domenico wasn't in on it?' I was still keen to get to the bottom of what exactly was going on. 'I'm confused.'

'He said not,' Nick confirmed. 'And given the look on Artie's face, I'd say he's not happy about this.'

The empty stage at the end of the ballroom was bathed in a pale golden glow from the chandelier above, casting a long shadow from the microphone stand. Artie was glowering beside it, prowling up and down in front of the stage in his jet-black tux like a really pissed-off panther. Only, his elaborate facial hair made him look a little bit more like an angry goat wearing a nice jacket – considerably less intimidating. I watched, every nerve on end as Al broke away from his army of well-wishers and headed for the stage, clapping his son on the back as he hopped up the steps with the easy grace of a man half his age. I really had to find a way to take up surfing if I wanted to be so spry in my seventies. Or at least find a way to retire to Hawaii; I imagined that helped too.

'This seems like as good a time as any to say a few words,' Al said into the microphone as a spotlight appeared from nowhere to light him up. The almost silent crowd broke into a flurry of murmurs, reluctantly turning away from the new couple, who were still going at it, and giving their attention to their host. 'I would like to start by saying thank you to my very good friends Kekipi and Domenico for putting this bash together so beautifully.'

Everyone clapped politely. Amy whooped and gave a very supportive fist-pump.

'As you all know, it's a long time since I've been to Milan but I couldn't think of a better place to start my new venture,' he continued. 'I have been involved in the fashion world for a long time, longer than a I care to remember, really, but I've never been one to stand still for too long and so I'm very happy to announce the realization of a long-held dream of mine and my dear wife, Jane. Next season will mark the debut of AJB, our own collection.'

The room bubbled into life with more clapping and considerably more murmuring. The only person who looked less than delighted about the news was Artie. I took Nick and Amy's hands and pulled them through to the front of the crowd before taking my place at the side of the stage and prepping my camera. Through my lens, I could see the touch of sadness behind Al's smile. Sadness for the loss of his wife or for whatever was about to happen with his son, I wasn't sure.

'I couldn't be more excited to confirm whatever rumours have been running amok,' Al went on, waving to someone in the shadows at the side of the stage. 'AJB will be a collaboration between Bennett inspiration and the unparalleled creativity of Edward Warren, without whom, none of this would be at all possible.'

Warren mounted the stage in one huge step, his scarlet velvet dinner jacket looking a whole lot more confident than the man himself. He embraced Al awkwardly and then waved to the crowd.

It was hard to sneak around unnoticed in a ballgown but I managed to get myself onto the side of the stage without too much rustling to take a few photos of the rapturous crowd. The only person who didn't look happy was Artie. He flicked his blazing eyes from Al to Warren and back again, his beautifully manicured hands balling into tight, angry fists.

'Just leave,' I whispered, clicking a couple of pictures of him to send in to the Oxford English Dictionary just in case they ever needed a visual definition of 'fucking furious'. 'Just go away.'

But clearly that wasn't going to happen.

'And where will you be selling these clothes?' Artie shouted out from the foot of the stage. 'And where will you be manufacturing them'

'As much as I love giving a speech, I don't think anyone wants to listen to me rattle on with my business plan,' Al said, smooth as anything. 'Thank you, everyone.'

I watched Kekipi and Domenico sidle around the stage, until they were a few feet away from Artie. I was an aunt to three children and, admittedly, I didn't get to see them that often but I knew a child on the verge of a tantrum when I saw it. Artie's face was bright red and he was shaking with barely restrained rage. Either he was teething or he was about to lose his shit.

'No!' he shouted. 'You don't have a retail location and you don't have a manufacturer.'

'Arthur, do you really think this is the right time to have this conversation?' Al leaned away from the microphone to admonish his son, keeping his calm exterior in place. But that didn't seem to help. In fact, it seemed to make things worse.

'Don't patronize me!' Artie said, spitting as he spoke. 'You walked away from all of it when my mum died and left me to deal with everything on my own and now you want to start again and expect everyone to help you but I won't. Why can't you just retire?'

Every single one of Al's guests looked mortified. Well, everyone except for Nick; he looked delighted and already had his iPhone out, recording the entire exchange. Baby steps, I told myself, baby steps. I shuffled backwards away from the stage and over to my friends. Whatever Nick thought, I did not feel like capturing these moments with my camera. I wouldn't sully the lens with Artie's sulky mug.

'Artie, we're not having this conversation right now.' Al hopped down off the stage and took his son by the arm. He lowered his voice, in an attempt to keep the conversation from the ears of the by now gagging-for-the-dirt crowd. 'What you tried to do was underhanded and ungentlemanly and a disgrace to the Bennett name.'

'I wish I *wasn't* a Bennett,' Artie replied, shaking off his father like an angry teenager. 'I wish I was anyone else.'

'If he says "I wish I'd never been born", I'm going to die,' Amy whispered into my ear. 'And then I'm going to come back to life and kill him.'

Al took hold of his son's arm once more. 'Son, let's go outside.'

But Artie didn't want to go outside. Artie wanted to stay and play and he did not want to share his toys. And so he bleated out a very interesting, very loud impression of a dying sea lion and shoved his father as hard as he could.

'Oh no he didn't.'

I heard Kekipi before I saw him but Al's white knight was fast on his feet and grabbed hold of his oldest friend before he could even stumble. The assembled crowd took a group step backwards and their murmuring rose to a muttering, punctuated by an ensemble gasp.

In his defence, Artie had the decency to look horrified by his own actions, his hands pressed against his face, but there wasn't much he could do before Kekipi gave a battle cry Lady Gaga would have been proud of and launched himself at the moustache. Before I could blink, arms and hands were flying everywhere, Kekipi slapping at Artie and Artie trying to push the other man away.

'I changed your diapers!' Keipi shouted. 'I helped you with your homework!'

'No you didn't! You're only five years older than me,' Artie yelped back. 'And your answers were always wrong!'

Blinded by the absurdity of what was happening,

I froze as Artie's arm struck out sideways, slapping me right across the face. Stunned, I fell to my knees, more from shock than genuine injury, but it was enough to spur Nick and Amy into joining the fray. Amy first, obviously. When I looked up from my pool of tulle, all I cold see were arms and legs and very red faces. A hand reached down to pull me to my feet and drag me away from the melee. I took it happily, closing my eyes and letting whoever it was pull me to safety.

'Are you OK?' Al asked. 'I'm so dreadfully sorry.'

'Don't be, I'm fine,' I said, my voice wavering with slightly rubbish girl tears. Someone hit me. All right, it was an accident but still. 'I'm so sorry this happened tonight.'

'You know what they say,' he replied, the corners of his mouth turning up into a bitter smile. 'The only thing worse than people talking about you is people not talking about you. This just means we're going to have to come out with a bloody good debut collection.'

'I don't doubt it,' I said, turning back to see the scrap fizzle out. Domenico and the two grey-haired men Amy and I had followed into the ballroom pulled the various parties off each other.

'Are you OK?' Nick untangled himself from the snarl of arms and legs and appeared at my side, cupping my face in his hands and inspecting the damage. 'I think you're going to have a black eye.'

'Then I'll look badass,' I replied, gazing up at

him through the squinty eye that was beginning to close up of its own accord. 'I'm fine.'

He planted a very careful kiss on my forehead as Domenico restrained Kekipi and one of the Italian men attempted to hold Amy back without touching her anywhere inappropriate. Given her dress, it wasn't an easy job; he was a real gentleman.

Artie stood alone in the centre of the circle that had widened around him, one side of his moustache drooping sadly. Panting heavily, he pressed his hands up to his face, trying to repair the damage before looking around at his audience and seeing nothing but an ocean of Not Impressed. With one last wail, he dived into the crowd which parted like Moses' waves, and stormed out of the ballroom.

Everyone watched him go before turning all eyes onto the Greek tragedy at the front of the stage. Domenico holding Kekipi, Al and Amy and their Italian friend leaning against the stage, and then there was me, swollen and weepy, swooning in Nick's arms.

Every single pair of eyes in the ballroom was on us. I looked back out at them, hoping Al was right. Was all publicity good publicity? I wasn't so sure. It definitely didn't do Ikea any favours when the papers wouldn't stop going on about their horse meatballs. And phone hacking? Still not that popular. I didn't like being the centre of attention at the best of times and I liked it even less when the people eyeballing me were taller than me, thinner than me, richer than me and able to gossip about me in a language I didn't understand.

Still, there was one thing worse than being judged by people you didn't know. Staring out at all those tall, thin, rich, foreign strangers and seeing one person staring back who you knew very well indeed.

And in this case, that person was Charlie.

CHAPTER 19

Seemingly having lost the power of speech as well as the use of my legs, I stayed exactly where I was, waving my arms, opening and closing my mouth and staring at Charlie with all the grace of a dying goldfish.

'Christ on a bike!'

As usual, Amy nailed the situation fairly succinctly.

Once the smell of blood was out of the water, Al's guests made a silent, collective decision to raise their volume back up to 'excitable chatter'. From nowhere, the orchestra began to play again and the waiters were suddenly everywhere, a bottle of champagne in each hand. Clever waiters.

But Charlie was still stood in the doorway and while he didn't look angry as such, given that the girl he had just declared his love to was securely in the arms of another man, he certainly looked confused.

'Tess?' Amy nudged me with her hip. 'Have you had a stroke or something?'

'What would that feel like,' I asked, eyes still fixed firmly on the doorway. 'Because I might be having one right now.'

'Shit, is it getting worse?' Nick moved in front of me, his nose touching my nose. 'Can you see? Can you taste pennies?'

'No, I'm fine.' I pushed him away as gently as possible, needing to put at least a couple of feet between us. I couldn't taste pennies but I was definitely about to taste vom. What was he doing here? Why wasn't he moving? 'I have to go and—'

'What?' Nick remained completely oblivious while Amy kept guard, practically bouncing up and down on the spot. 'I think you've got a concussion, I'm taking you to bed.'

I looked at Nick's face, making an effort to memorize everything about it, every last detail. Not just his eyes that looked so blue in this light or his full lips and firm jaw but everything. I logged his dark blond eyebrows with a couple of unruly grey strays that I knew he would pluck later and pretend that he hadn't. The way he had more lines around his left eye than his right because he slept on that side. The very faint tan line on his cheeks where he'd caught the sun while wearing his sunglasses and the tiny, almost invisible spot of stubble that he had missed when he was shaving before the party.

When people talked about a horrible feeling, they usually described it in the pit of their stomach. This one was everywhere. My toes ached with it and my fingertips tingled as though anything I touched would explode. Worst of all, my insides felt completely empty. Whatever was going to happen, it was as though someone had hollowed me out in preparation. Whether it was to protect me or make room for what was coming, I didn't know. With Nick's face completely committed to memory, I moved away from him, turning towards Charlie.

'I was going to say surprise, but bugger me!' Charlie smiled brightly at Amy and me as he walked over but I could see there were questions on his face. 'You don't half know how to upstage a romantic gesture.'

'It's you!' Amy prised herself out of her new Italian friend's arms and launched herself on Charlie, smothering his face in kisses. 'You're here! I'm so happy. Tess hurt her head and has to go to her room right away but why don't we have a drink and wow, you look amazing and tell me all about your flight, I can't believe you came, you're the best!'

'Get off, you mental.' He batted her away like an overenthusiastic puppy. 'What do you mean, Tess hurt her head. Are you all right? What happened? Really, what happened? I walked in and I thought you were sacrificing a goat or something.'

'A lot of drama over nothing,' I said, fussing his hands away from my face. This was so awful I was starting to understand how people found the strength to fall on their own swords. 'Why don't you get a drink with Amy? I have to sort some stuff out here . . .' I waved my camera at him for effect. 'I'll be over in two minutes.'

'Aren't you going to introduce me?' Nick asked, placing a hand on my bare shoulder.

'No?' I only meant to think it but somehow, the word snuck out my mouth.

'Then I'll do the honours.' He took Charlie's hand in his and shook it to within an inch of its life. 'Nick Miller, good to meet you.'

'Charlie Wilder,' Charlie replied, looking at me as he spoke.

Even though Charlie was a good half a foot taller than Nick, he was at such a clear disadvantage he might as well have crawled in on his hands and knees.

'Charlie, is it?'

If Nick knew who he was, he wasn't giving anything away. He kept on pumping Charlie's hand as though it might come off if he shook it hard enough.

'Sorry I'm a bit underdressed.' Charlie's voice bounced as he spoke, his hand still stuck in Nick's handshake vice. 'I didn't know I was crashing the royal wedding. Tess, what happened to your eye?'

'Accidental slapping,' I said, as Nick finally let go of Charlie's hand although his grip on my shoulder remained very firm. 'Do you want to go and get changed? Amy could take you to get changed.'

'I don't think there's a lot of point.' He looked down at his jeans, shoes and shirt. 'I haven't got a penguin suit in my bag anyway.'

'Well, this party is black tie only,' Amy announced, stretching up to make the most of all of her five feet and nothing inches to grab his shoulders and try to drive him out of the room. 'So you'll have to wait outside until we're done.'

'How do you know Tess and Amy?' Nick asked loudly, stopping Amy in her wonderful tracks.

'How did you know we'd be here?' Amy interrupted Charlie's answer. 'Not that we aren't both very happy to see you.' She glued herself to his arm again and smiled brightly at Nick. 'I'm so happy to see him. I so love this lunk.'

'Since when do you love me? Are you on drugs?' Charlie peered down at Amy, a foot and a half below him. 'Don't you remember what happened at that party with the meow-meow?'

'I thought it was a joke,' Amy retaliated, kicking him in the shin. 'What sort of name for drugs is meow-meow? And it's not funny, I could have died.'

'So you're Charlie?' Nick said. 'Charlie Charlie?'

'You haven't told us how you found us,' Amy wailed, jumping in front of Nick. 'How did you know where we were?'

'Your friend Paige said you were staying here when she dropped off the pitch stuff,' Charlie explained, still trying to free himself of a limpet-like Amy. 'It all looks amazing, by the way. I thought I'd surprise you.'

'But you hate flying,' I said quietly, wondering whether or not Artie might like to pop back and knock me completely unconscious. Nick's hold on my shoulder was getting tighter by the second and I was a bit scared he was actually trying to do the Vulcan death grip. 'How did you get here?'

'Flew in from Portugal, took a train and then a taxi, all with the help of my friend Jack Daniels and a big dose of man-the-fuck-up,' Charlie gave me the same self-deprecating lopsided grin he'd been throwing my way for ten long years. 'And I don't even get a hug?'

'This is your friend, Charlie?' Nick said to me, everything falling into place for him, the floor falling away from under my feet. 'The one who shagged your flatmate? And then you?'

'I might have had one too many whiskies on the plane, but that's a bit out of order,' Charlie said awkwardly as my eyes widened so far I worried they might fall out. 'I'm not being funny, mate, but should I know you? Are you the gay fella that runs the show?'

'Nick Miller,' Nick replied. 'I'm a journalist. I met Tess in Hawaii.'

'Oh man, I'm so jealous.' Charlie ran a hand through his shaggy, copper hair, just like he always did when he was uncomfortable. 'Tess said it was amazing.'

'Did she?' Nick asked, looking at me. 'And what else did she tell you about Hawaii?'

I could feel each individual fingertip pressing into my collarbone and it was really, really starting to hurt. But what could I say? How could I get them apart? I'd done a good thing today – why was the universe paying me back by being such a complete and utter fuck-knuckle?

'Not much, to be honest.' Charlie's smile began to falter. 'We didn't get that much time to talk before she left for Milan. Tess, is everything all right?'

He might not be the most perceptive man in the world but he knew when something wasn't right and between my deer-in-headlights saucer eyes, Amy's refusal to let go of his right arm and Nick's impressive passive-aggressive questioning, Charlie would have had to be hit over the head with seventeen saucepans on his way here not to realize something was going on.

'Yeah, Tess.' Nick's voice was sour. 'Is everything all right?'

'Shots!' Amy shouted. 'We all need a shot! Charlie, why don't you come with me to the bar.'

'Tess . . .' Charlie's eyes flickered over to Nick and his jaw set into something far away from the smile he had shown up with. 'Who is this?'

'It's Nick,' I said weakly, waving at him like he was a prize on a bad game show.

'Is something going on?' he asked. 'With you two?'

'Is something going on with you two?' Nick asked Charlie.

'Oh God,' I whispered at my shoes, desperately trying to come up with a way out of this situation. Did that 'no place like home' thing really work? Even if it did, I didn't actually have a home, so there was no point trying that one.

406

'What's going on?' Charlie ripped his arm away from Amy but stopped a couple of feet short of me. Nick didn't budge an inch. 'Is this why you were weird when you got back to London?'

'What's that supposed to mean?' I asked. My fight or flight decision had apparently been made. 'Just because I didn't fall at your feet the second I got off the plane doesn't mean I was being weird. It meant I had a lot to think about.'

'I'm not saying you didn't but you've got to admit it was a bit weird.' Charlie was getting annoyed. I recognized it and I didn't like it. 'One minute you're all over me, the next you're kicking me out, then you're all over me again and then you run off to Milan. I think that counts as weird, doesn't it?'

'You told me to go to Milan,' I reminded him. 'You gave me the bloody camera. You said, go to Milan, have a nice time.'

'I didn't mean have *this* nice a time.' He pointed at Nick. 'What exactly has been going on?'

'Charlie, you need to calm down, we're in somebody else's house,' Amy said. 'Don't be rude.'

But if ever there was a case of trying to shut the gate after the horse had bolted, this was it. We were the third and final act in a comedy of errors and the crowd couldn't get enough: first the love story of Kekipi and Domenico; then the tragedy of Artie and Al; and now us, the play within a play.

'Can we talk about this upstairs?' I asked Charlie.

'Him or me?' Nick asked. 'Or should Amy fill me in on whatever parts you clearly didn't think I needed to know? Save you some time?'

'Nick, please don't!' I tried to cover his hand with mine but it was gone. My shoulder went cold as he let me go and I looked down to see four white fingerprints, like petals, turning ruby red as the blood rushed back into my skin.

'OK, it's OK . . .' I pushed my hair out of my face, thinking as fast as I could. 'Charlie, I told you I needed time to think. I told you we would talk when I got back from Milan. Nick, we can talk about this later. There are some things we haven't got round to talking about yet but they're things I didn't think were important.'

'You didn't think I was important?' Charlie asked. 'You're moving in with me!'

'I never told you I would move in with you,' I said, trying not to shout. 'I said I needed time to think about it.'

'And you don't think that's something you might have mentioned?' Nick asked. 'That between leaving Hawaii and arriving in Milan, you moved in with another man?'

'I didn't move in with him!' I was no longer trying not to shout. 'Is no one actually *listening* to me?'

'She didn't move in with him,' Amy said, coming to my defence. 'He asked her to but she didn't. And when he told her he loved her, she didn't say it back. She gave him a double thumbs up. She's totally in the clear.'

I stared at Amy and my jaw dropped.

'What?' she asked. 'I'm trying to help?'

'I've got to get out of here.' Charlie raked his hair back again and shook his head at no one. 'I'm not doing this.'

'Charlie, wait!' I threw my arms up but my feet didn't make a move to follow him. Instead I watched him stalk back through the crowd and out of the door. 'Amy?'

'On it.'

She took off her heels and pelted across the floor, weaving through the partygoers and chasing after our friend.

'Nick,' I turned around to face my love but instead, someone else had taken his place, someone cold and hard and entirely strange to me. 'Nick, it's not what you think,' I said. 'He did ask me to move in with him and he did tell me he loved me but I told him I needed time to think about everything. That's all that happened.'

'But you didn't say you wouldn't move in with him, did you?' he asked. 'You didn't tell him about me.'

'At that point, I didn't think there was anything to tell.' I reached for his hand, his arm, anything, but he pulled away entirely. 'I'd been calling you and leaving messages and you weren't replying to anything. I didn't think I was ever going to see you again.'

'Handy to have a replacement waiting for you, isn't it?' he asked, his face folding into a sneer that was incredibly unflattering and utterly heartbreaking. 'We should both feel so special.'

'I love you.' I tasted the tears that were steadily streaming from my swollen eye as I spoke, pressing my desperate hands to my chest but my camera was in the way. 'And I know it's crazy and un-expected but I do love you. But I thought you were gone and he was there. I'm not proud of myself but I thought if it wasn't going to happen with you, maybe it could work with him.'

He looked away sharply, his eyes turning grey as the light changed.

'But it can't,' I told him. 'I know that now and that's why I didn't tell you. I'm sorry.'

'All of this just proves me right,' he muttered, not really to me, not really to anyone. 'All of it.'

'Nick, I love you!' I tried to make every word, every syllable matter. To pack simple words I said a thousand times a day full of more meaning than there was in the world, but it felt used and cheap. There wasn't a word good enough for him, powerful enough to make him listen.

So I punched him in the stomach as hard as I could.

'Ow!' He turned his eyes back to me, clutching his gut. 'That's supposed to convince me you love me?'

'Yes! That's how much I love you. I love you so much I want to punch you in the stomach!' I yelled, really quite pleased with myself. 'I want to kick you in the shins and knock you out with how much I love you. I love your feet and your bones and your hair and your stupid motorbike and your stupid roll-ups that you don't even really want to smoke anyway.'

I paused to see if he would stay. He did.

'I love how you always roll up the sleeves of your shirt. I love that you are so passionate about what you do. I love when you make rubbish jokes that no one laughs at but you. I love that you like spicy food because I like spicy food too. I love how warm you are all time and that you don't pull away in the night even though my feet are always really cold. I love the fact that you make me feel like I'm not broken, that maybe I'm just missing a part and you're that part so with you I can be fixed. I don't know what your favourite film is or what the first record you ever bought was but I do know you and that's why I love you.'

I stepped out of my high heels and pressed my hands against his chest.

'I'll find all the other stuff out along the way,' I said. 'But I know all the important things already.'

'Oh, for the love of God, kiss her!' Kekipi shouted from nowhere. I had completely forgotten anyone else was in the room. 'If you don't, I will.'

Nick leaned down and touched his lips to mine, one hand holding my waist, the other carefully cupping my injured face. Somewhere a million miles away, I could hear glasses clinking together and distant *bravos* but they really didn't matter.

'Fuck it, I love you too,' Nick said as he broke

away. 'But just so we're clear, my jokes are never terrible.'

'I'll learn to live with them.' I let him wipe away a smudgy black tear, avoiding my newly throbbing black eye. 'I should go and talk to Charlie.'

'What?' Nick looked confused. 'He's gone. You're not going after him?'

'I've got to,' I said, looking to Kekipi for support that I clearly was not getting. 'I wasn't fair to him and I need to explain. He's been one of my best friends forever, I feel shitty.'

'I don't understand why you have to go running after him,' he replied, clearly having decided to be stubborn about this. 'Call him tomorrow, it'll be fine.'

'Would you answer the phone to me?' I asked. 'After all that?'

'Seriously, Tess, don't go,' he said, an edge of warning in his voice. 'I don't want you to.'

'Nick, I've got to,' I said, adamant. I knew in my gut I wouldn't be able to settle until I'd sorted things out. I wasn't someone who could live with ambiguity or bad feeling, especially when someone was so important to me and especially when it was all my fault. 'I'll be back in an hour.'

'Why are you going after him, though?' he asked. 'I really don't get it. What do you think you can say that will make him forgive you?'

'I don't know . . .' I attempted to explain as clearly and concisely as possible but I had already used up an awful lot of words for one day and my poor brain was very tired. 'But he's my friend. I have to make things right. This is no different to how it would be if it were Amy.'

'Except you never shagged Amy,' he argued. 'Unless you did but you didn't think I needed to know about that, either.'

'I've never had sex with Amy, no matter what my mum's next-door neighbour might tell you in the future,' I replied. 'And you need to get over this dick-swinging contest right now because I'm going to apologize to him and then I'm coming back here and then you're not getting rid of me ever again.'

'It's not a dick-swinging contest,' he blustered, hands on his hips in an impressively masculine little teapot stance. 'Not that there would be a contest anyway, but, whatever. I'm telling you, I don't want you to go.'

'And I'm telling you, I'm going,' I said, picking my shoes up from the floor and throwing him the frowning of a lifetime. 'I'll be back in an hour.'

I headed for the door, Kekipi close behind me.

'Are you sure you want to go?' he asked, taking my camera from me as I scrambled along the floor in my too long skirt. 'He does not look happy.'

'He is being an arsehole.' We dived into the first black SUV waiting outside the palazzo, Kekipi taking the keys from the driver and presumably explaining in very short Italian that he would drive. 'I told him I loved him – what more does he want?'

'He's a man,' Kekipi said. 'What he doesn't want

is you running out on him for another man. Can you see how he might take that the wrong way?'

'But everything I said?' I replied, checking my eye in the visor mirror. Nothing said sexy like a swollen-shut eye. 'It'll be OK.'

'I refer you to my last answer,' he said, gunning the engine. 'He's a man. It might not be.'

I pawed through my little black clutch bag, checked my phone and found a text from Amy, telling me Charlie had got a taxi to the train station. Typical Charlie. He would spend five hundred quid on computer games without blinking but spend a hundred euros on a taxi to the airport when he could get the train for twenty? Not a snowball's chance in hell.

'All I have to do is find the train that's going to the airport and stop him,' I reasoned, tapping my hands on my lap as we drove, ignoring that fact that we were going well over the speed limit of any country, whatever it might be in Italy. 'Can't be that hard, can it?'

'The station is biggish,' Kekipi said, pinching his face together. 'But I have faith in you.'

'You said it was biggish.'

I leaned out of the car window, craning my neck to look at the train station as Kekipi pulled up out front.

'It's fucking enormous,' I pointed out, my stomach dropping through the floor. 'It's the biggest train station in the world. Bloody hell!'

414

'It's not the biggest train station in the world,' Kekipi sniffed. 'I bet it's not even in the top three. I'll google it.'

'Word of advice,' I said, hitching up my skirts and leaping out of the SUV. 'Don't be afraid to exaggerate. Hyperbole would have been appropriate here.'

'Don't take your temper out on me.' He was busy staring at his phone, safely behind the steering wheel. 'I'll wait here. Call me if you need me.'

'It's going to take me half an hour to get inside,' I chuntered, trying a hybrid skip and jog in bare feet along the pavement.

I wasn't exaggerating. The train station was truly enormous. The massive winged horses hanging over the entrance made me feel like a flea and suddenly my hopes of conveniently running into Charlie at the ticket booth were dying by the second. Broken phone in sweaty hand, I darted inside, dodging people in their suits and ties, looking for their trains home, and dialled Amy. Maybe she had already found him. Maybe she had him tied to a chair in McDonald's and they were just waiting for me with a McFlurry. Mmm . . . McFlurry.

'It's me,' I shouted when she picked up. 'Where are you?'

'Underneath the departures board near the café.' I could barely hear for chiming bing bongs and loudspeaker announcements. 'He's raging, Tess. I followed his taxi but I lost him as soon as he got out. How massive is this place? It's amazing.'

415

'It's an architectural bloody wonder,' I shouted down the line. 'I'm coming to find you. You don't know what train he's on?'

'There are two going to the airport in the next ten minutes, platform three and platform fourteen,' she replied. 'I don't know which he's on. Got to be one of them though.'

I searched for the nearest platforms, stalking through the crowds, phone in one hand and as much of my dress as I could handle in the other. 'I'm nearest number three, can you go to fourteen?'

'And tell him what?' she asked. 'It might be better to let him go, let him simmer down a bit.'

'No, I need to explain,' I said, picking up speed as I raced towards the platform. 'He's got to let me explain.'

'I'll call you if I find him first,' she replied, hanging up.

I knew she was right. There was nothing I could say to Charlie right now that would make him feel better about flying across Europe to surprise me, only to be turned away for another man. What I was doing was selfish – I wanted to make myself feel better as much as I wanted to mend fences with him but it couldn't hurt to try, could it? If he saw that I had come after him, searched for him just to say sorry, wouldn't that make things better in the long run? I had spent a lifetime turning the other cheek and perhaps it didn't make me a very nice person, but when someone screwed me over it did tend to take the edge off things to know they at least felt shitty about it. I was only human.

Platform three was a million miles further away from the main concourse than by rights it should have been and by the time I reached the actual train, huffing and puffing, I was running out of time. I scrambled along the outside of the carriages, jumping up every few seats to get a better look inside. Charlie liked to sit in a window seat so he could watch the world go by, and because he got really anxious about travelling. And if he were by the window he would be the first to spot any erupting volcanoes or incoming zombie hordes. Charlie was quite certain about the inevitability of zombies. Charlie had watched far too much *Walking Dead*.

Finally, in the very last carriage, three seats from the front of the train, there he was. It was only when I stopped running that I felt something sharp in the bottom of my foot. But whatever it was, it would wait. Deep down, I hadn't really expected to find him. I had half-hoped that Amy might and that she would be able to talk some sense into him before I had to give it a shot. He sat staring blankly at the empty seat in front of him, lifeless and defeated. A wave of something hot and horrible washed over me. I realized that I wanted Amy to find him because I didn't really want to see him. I only wanted to be able to say I had tried.

But there he was, my needle in a haystack. I

tapped on the window, as gently as I could and pressed my palm against the glass. If Charlie was surprised to see me, he didn't show it and if he was happy to see me, it was even less obvious. I'd seen this look on him before but whenever he was upset in the past, I'd found him heartbroken and I left him happy. I was the one who cheered him up. This time, it was all my fault that he was unhappy.

'Charlie?' I said, not really loud enough for him to hear but he could see me.

He raised an eyebrow, waiting for the rest and I chewed on my bottom lip, waiting for divine inspiration to strike. Of all the words in the English language, which ones would make him forgive me and be my best friend again? He turned to look at me for a second, his brown eyes and coppery hair a mirror of mine, but where I looked sad and desperate, Charlie looked finished. He sniffed and wiped his face with the back of his hand, looking down on me from his high up train seat. And then, just as the train sounded its horn to announce that it was on its way, he pulled down the blind at his window. He was gone before he was even gone.

I stood on the platform in my absurdly beautiful pink dress, hair everywhere and make-up far from where I had originally applied it, as Charlie's train pulled out of the station.

'Did you find him?' An out-of-breath Amy staggered up beside me, bracing her hands against her knees while I watched the train vanish into the distance. 'Was he on there?'

'Yeah,' I said, tucking her left boob back inside her dress. 'He was.'

'What did he say?'

'Nothing.'

'At least you tried,' she said, sliding her hand into mine. 'At least that counts for something.'

'Yeah,' I said, not really agreeing with her. I looked down at the floor and saw a trail of blood behind us. 'Amy, are you bleeding?'

'No,' she said, turning up the soles of her feet. 'Are you?'

'Apparently so,' I said, paling at the sight of a half-inch gash on the bottom of my left foot. 'Ow!'

'Let's get you back to the car.' Amy pulled me down the platform while I limped along beside her. 'It'll be all right.'

I wasn't sure if she was talking about Charlie or my foot but as the next train arrived and travellers spilled off the train, making a wide circle around the two incredibly overdressed, sad-looking girls, I really hoped she was right.

CHAPTER 20

'Who wants the good news and who wants the bad news?' Kekipi asked as I flung open the door to the passenger side. 'Because I've got both.'

'Can we just have the good news?' Amy asked, climbing into the back seat on all fours. 'Because that didn't go very well and I think Tess needs cheering up.'

'Good news, we're only about twenty minutes away from Linate airport,' he announced, starting the car and tearing off down the street. 'I should have said, the good news doesn't make a lot of sense without the bad news?'

'Linate? Where's that?' I was so tired and so mad at myself, I really didn't care any more. 'I thought the airport was in Malpensa?'

'There are two,' he replied. 'Charlie has gone to Malpensa. Mr Miller has gone to Linate.'

'Why is Nick at the airport?' It was too much for my poor brain. 'What is happening?'

'Domenico called to say Mr Miller took a cab to the airport about half an hour ago,' he explained.

'He left a letter for you but Dom thought you'd want to know.'

'Again?' I smacked the back of my head against the headrest in the SUV and closed my eyes. This couldn't really be happening. 'He's taking off without talking to me, again?'

'I didn't think he seemed that mad,' Amy offered. 'And they say women are fickle.'

'It would have been better if he had been mad,' I said. 'I know what he's thinking when he's shouting at me. It's when he goes all quiet I've got problems. I never know what's going on in his head.'

'Calm down and fix your make-up,' he ordered, turning up the volume on the car stereo. I was rarely in the mood for Rihanna anyway but this was definitely not the right time. 'Leave everything to Kekipi. I have a plan.'

'This is the plan?' I asked, standing in the check-in hall of Linate airport. 'To get here?'

'I didn't think he could have checked in already,' Kekipi wailed. 'I was sure we'd be able to grab him on the way through.'

Even with his jacket over my dress, we were still quite the sight. Amy had a blanket from the car wrapped around her shoulders and aside from my messed-up make-up and enormous hair, I was also hobbling around with half a roll of duct tape wrapped around my foot in lieu of a plaster and it wasn't doing its job very well.

421

'Did Domenico say where he was going?' I asked. Kekipi shook his head.

The departures board had flights going out all over the world. London, LA, New York. Hadn't he said something about Hong Kong the last time I saw him? Nick could be headed anywhere.

'Maybe it's in the letter?' I suggested. 'Can he open it and see? Please?'

'Do you think maybe this time we should just let him go?' Amy asked as I pulled out my phone and dialled Nick's mobile for the fifteenth time. 'Chasing after Charlie didn't go terribly well.'

'No,' I replied, phone pressed right up to my ear. 'If Nick goes, he won't come back and I'll never hear from him again, I just know it. I've got to talk to him,'

'Then we'll find him,' she promised, kissing me on the cheek before sprinting over to the customer services desk. 'I promise.'

Not many people arrived at the airport wearing evening dress and a black eye and so I wasn't terribly surprised to be attracting quite a lot of attention. Travellers in their comfy jeans and leggings gave me a wide berth, as I tracked a bloody path back and forth under the departure boards, waiting for Nick to answer. He could be in the loo and not looking at his phone, it could have been switched off by the security scanner. There were a million reasons why he wasn't answering, but I refused to accept the most obvious one: that he just didn't want to talk to me.

'He's going to New York,' Kekipi shouted even though he was quite clearly close enough to just tell me. 'He said he's going to New York. When's the next flight?'

'In an hour,' I said, looking at the boards. 'Could he be on that one? Is there time to stop him?'

'Let's find out,' he nodded over at the American Airlines desk. 'Let me do the talking, I'm nicer than you.'

'You are not,' I huffed, hobbling behind him but not fast enough to stop him.

'Hi.' Kekipi put on his most charming smile for the desk attendant.

The desk attendant looked up, looked back down and rolled her eyes.

'I'm hoping you can help. Our friend is travelling to New York and we very much need to speak to him before he leaves.' Kekipi moved on to batting his lush eyelashes at the tired-looking woman behind the desk but nothing was working. 'It's practically a matter of life and death. Could you tell us whether or not he's on your flight?'

'I'm not at liberty to give out passenger inform-ation,' Debbie (according to the name tag on her jacket) replied in a flat American accent. 'Is that all?'

'You couldn't just put a quick call in and tell the lovely people on the gate that we need a word with him?' he asked. 'It is real important.'

'If you go to customer services, they'll put out a passenger announcement,' she said, eyes down the whole time. An ascending chime echoed over the loudspeaker at that exact moment.

'Could passenger Nick Miller, passenger Nick Miller, travelling to New York City please come to the nearest customer service desk, thank you.'

'It would be something like that,' Debbie said before returning to the very important business of not giving a shit. 'They're located by the front door.'

Debbie needed either a big cup of coffee or an attitude adjustment and I knew which I was happiest to give her.

'That was our announcement,' I slapped the desk to get her attention, barrelling Kekipi out of the way. 'I have to talk to that man. If I buy a ticket for the same flight, will you tell me if he's on it?'

'No,' Debbie replied. 'But if you buy a ticket for the flight, you would be able to see whether or not he's on it, wouldn't you?'

'Give me your credit card.' I held my hands out to Kekipi. 'I'll pay you back.'

'Have you gone crazy?' he asked. 'Where's *your* credit card?'

'I haven't got any money because we spent it all on clothes,' I shouted as Amy came bounding back from the customer service desk. 'Give me your credit card.'

'How much is a ticket to New York?' he asked our new friend, Debbie. 'For this flight.'

'We've got a couple of seats left . . .' She scanned the screen, suddenly a lot more interested at the prospect of making a sale. 'The cheapest will be just over four thousand euros. Will that be credit or debit?'

'Oh, this is brilliant!' Amy hopped from one foot to the other, clapping her hands. 'Can I come too? Is there another seat?'

'Let me check,' Debbie said.

'No one is getting any seat on any plane,' Kekipi yelled. 'Can you freaking tell us whether or not Nick freaking Miller is on that freaking flight?'

Debbie pulled herself upright and narrowed her eyes slowly.

'No.'

'No, he's not on the plane or no, you won't tell us?' I asked, clutching at Amy's hands.

'I'm afraid I'm not at liberty to give out passenger information,' she said again, more deliberately. 'Please step away from the desk before I have to call security.'

'I'm going to knock her out,' I whispered as Amy and Kekipi dragged me away. 'I'm actually going to knock her out.'

'No, you're not,' Kekipi replied firmly. 'Because I'm going to do it first.'

'She's not going to help us,' Amy shouted over the two of us, trying to play peacemaker and doing quite a good job. 'Why don't we go and see if he's still in security. He might not have gone through yet.'

'You're a genius,' I said, limping as fast as my lameness would carry me towards the escalators. 'Thanks, Debbie.'

'You're welcome,' Debbie called after us, determined to push her luck.

Luckily for her, I was too distracted by our new plan. Amy was a genius. For the first time in anyone's life, I sent up silent praise for the epic queue for airline security that greeted us at the bottom of the escalator.

'Shit, Tess, is that him?' Amy spun me around and pointed towards the front of the queue. A man about Nick's height, about Nick's weight was stepping up to the full body scanner as we watched.

'It could be . . .' I squinted, wishing he would turn to face me.

'Nick!' Amy didn't wait for verification. Instead she tore up to the front of the line and started shouting at the top of her voice. 'Nick! Nick! It's Amy! Turn around you arsehole!'

'Amy, wait!'

My foot was officially about to fall off. I half-ran, half-hopped all the way along the security line, the train of my bright pink dress billowing out behind me as I staggered along, apologizing to everyone as I passed.

'We're not pushing in,' I promised as I went. 'Just looking for someone. Hope you're all going somewhere nice.'

'Is she bleeding?' I heard someone ask. 'Is that blood?'

'Nick Miller!'

The force of Amy's voice bent her right over and the force of her bending right over meant that her

426

boob popped out of her dress again. Everyone in line for the scanners gasped, mothers covered their children's eyes and wives covered their husbands'. The single men in the queue seemed perfectly happy.

'Nick!' I caught up to Amy just as the man in the scanner turned around. His eyes met mine across the snaking lines of people and I felt every part of my body tense up.

It wasn't him.

'Not Nick.' Amy dropped her hands to her hips, defeated, before looking down to see her errant boob. 'Wardrobe malfunction,' she muttered, trying to tuck it away. 'Now I understand how this happens to celebs so often. I will never retweet another nip slip as long as I live.'

But Italian security guards at Linate airport weren't feeing nearly as magnanimous about accidental nudity as Amy. Two of them broke ranks from the front of the line, enormous guns slung across their chests the same way I might wear a satchel and scooped her and her boobs up in their arms, loudly decreeing something in Italian.

'Tess?' Amy yelped, her toes scraping along the floor. 'Help?'

'I'll go with her.' Kekipi touched my shoulder as he ran after my friend. 'I'll call a lawyer.'

'A lawyer?' I was feeling terribly faint all of a sudden. 'She needs a lawyer?'

He nodded before following them around a corner and disappearing.

So much for New Tess who didn't just sit around passively waiting for things to happen to her. At least Old Tess had never got her best friend arrested in an Italian airport. I held on to the closest thing I could find to keep me upright – sadly a particularly smelly bin – my phone with its seven per cent of battery tucked down the front of my dress, and gave up. For a moment, it was peaceful. I sank to the floor. My foot ached and my eye throbbed but in that moment, I felt light and free. I wasn't looking for anyone, fighting for anything, I wasn't racing against the clock. All I was doing was giving up – and it felt great.

That lasted for about four seconds.

'Excuse me.' A not-nearly-as-tall-as-me security guard looked down at me on the floor, his gun held at a jaunty angle in his hands – and pointing right at me. 'You must move now.'

'And go where?' I asked, throwing my arms up and letting them drop into the piles of tulle and lace around me before pointing at the bloody footprints behind me. 'I'm bleeding.'

'You must move now,' he repeated, gesturing to nowhere with the pointy end of his gun. I imagined that usually had a pretty impressive effect on people but I was just too exhausted to care. 'Now, please.'

Groaning loudly, I rolled onto my knees and pulled myself up with the assistance of the wall and my good friend, the smelly bin.

'Happy?' I asked as the guard started to walk away. 'I'm going.'

Only I didn't know where I was going to. Kekipi had the car keys, I didn't have any money and I didn't know the phone number for the palazzo. I was buggered.

I could go back and bother Debbie again, I thought, pulling a stray strand of hair out of my mouth. Or at least ask her to charge my iPhone long enough for me to call Al. Not that Debbie struck me as an iPhone owner. No one with access to the Weather Kitty app could be that bitter and miserable, but it was worth a try.

I was stumbling back along the security line, crying a little bit, feeling sorry for myself a lot, and enjoying everyone's disapproving looks when I saw him. Nick was on the other side of the scanners, staring up at the departure boards and checking his watch. I felt like someone had lit a fire underneath me. There he was, it was definitely him, one hundred per cent absolutely Nick Miller. Right. There was no way I had driven to the airport, shouted at Debbie, shown half of Linate Amy's boobs and watched my best friend get arrested for him to swan off to New York without getting an earful first.

I knew the security guards weren't going to let me through. I knew I didn't have a ticket or a passport or anything to barter with, financially or physically. If I had to pick one person out of everyone in the airport that I was prepared to let break all international travel laws, it would not be the mad giant in the fucked-up evening gown,

429

hobbling on one leg and sporting a black eye. But I had to do something.

Breathing in, I turned on my heel, the good one, and started back towards the front of the line, to where I could see Nick looking at his phone, presumably counting how many times I had called him and ignoring them all. It wasn't easy to be inconspicuous in bright pink and I knew all the guards were watching me as I sidled right up to the edge of the barriers and took out my phone. The red empty battery flashed up on the broken screen as I pulled it out of my boobs but that was OK, I didn't need to make any calls. It turned out an iPhone 5 made a really impressive projectile, whether it was fully charged or not. I hurled the phone as far as I could towards Nick – admittedly, not all that far but it served its purpose. The entire security area was in uproar and now I had everyone's attention.

'Nick!' I shouted at the top of my voice as two uniformed men and one uniformed woman sprinted towards me. 'Nick! Turn around, you shit.'

But if he did turn around, if he did see me, I didn't know about it. The last thing I remembered was seeing a tiny but incredibly fierce woman with a slick black ponytail charging at my midriff. After that, there was a bang and a shriek that might have been mine and then nothing but darkness.

CHAPTER 21

'*Signore.*'

It felt like forever until someone appeared outside our cell but really it couldn't have been more than a few of hours. Time dragged when you weren't having fun. I had no idea how, but Amy had fallen asleep almost as soon as she arrived while I sat on the floor, curled up in a small, tragic ball, watching planes fly by through our tiny scrap of a window. Every time one took off, I wondered whether Nick or Charlie was on board, eating peanuts and drinking whisky. They both like whisky and neither of them liked me very much so perhaps they would get on well enough after all.

'Oh my God, look at the two of you!' Kekipi appeared in front of the cell door, looking altogether the worse for wear. 'I'm getting you out of here. Is she asleep?'

'Don't ask me how.' I rose carefully, avoiding putting weight on my bad foot, and nudged Amy awake.

'Give me half an hour,' she muttered, rolling face first into the wall. 'You can shower first.'

'Get up!' I was in no mood for it. 'You're in prison. Kekipi has come to get us out.'

'Oh.' She turned over onto her back and blinked up at me. 'Fair enough then.'

The people in the airport police station weren't nearly as friendly as the people back in the one in Shoreditch. It could have been the language barrier or it could have been the fact that I'd been arrested for hurling a missile through an airport security area instead of having been mistakenly brought in for breaking out of my own house but who could say?

I didn't ask Kekipi what kind of deal he had struck or spell he had cast to get us out, I only nodded, smiled, signed everything that was handed to me and kept my head down. Twenty minutes later, we were in the back of the car, motoring back towards Milan.

'No word from either of them?' Kekipi asked. I looked in the rear-view mirror to see Amy snuggled up under a blanket, fast asleep and snoring.

'Wouldn't know,' I reminded him. 'I threw my phone across an airport and I haven't seen it since. Bit stupid.'

'You weren't thinking straight.' He patted my knee and handed me a bottle of water from his cup holder. 'You were in love.'

'I'm starting to think I had the right idea before any of this,' I said, resting my face against my seatbelt and staring out of the windows – there were so many stars in the sky, it seemed impossible. 'Keep your head down, get on with things, don't get in trouble, leave men alone. I was doing OK.'

'Do you wish you'd never met him?' he asked me. 'Mr Miller?'

I smiled and shook my head, hating myself for it. 'I can't even imagine how that would feel but I don't think it would really be better.'

'It's not over,' Kekipi promised, patting my leg. 'His pride is hurt. He's letting off steam.'

'On another continent,' I added. 'Again.'

Kekipi gave a distracted sigh, his eyes on the empty road ahead of us. 'Then perhaps it's not you who should be feeling bad. Maybe he isn't the one for you after all?'

'I wish I agreed with you,' I said, holding the cold water bottle against my sore eye. 'He is stubborn and proud and arrogant and he thinks he knows best about everything. And I love the shit out of him.'

'I hate when that happens.' He gave me a sideways glance. 'I'm right there with you.'

'Yeah, about that . . .' I pulled my hair over to one side and twisted it together. 'Do you want to tell me what's going on with you and I-hate-him-so-much-Domenico?'

A smile I recognized plastered itself all over his face, even when he tried to smother it. 'I don't know, I honestly don't,' he said. 'We were working on the party and he was making me so mad, then one afternoon he made me so mad the only thing I could do was kiss him. It doesn't make any sense, I know.'

'Makes sense to me,' I said, my eyes trained on the mountains outside the window. 'What's going to happen when you go back to Hawaii?'

'If you can tell me what's going to happen *tomorrow* I'll give you a prize,' he said. 'It's so long since I've had anyone in my life, I'm way past confused. Any suggestions?'

'I'm not even going to pretend to try and answer that,' I said. 'I'm really not.'

As much as I wanted to get back to the palazzo, take a shower and then get right back on with my mission to fuck up my life as much as humanly possible, my manky foot and complete physical exhaustion put a real crimp in my plans.

'I've got a doctor who will come and take a look at it in a few hours,' Domenico announced once Kekipi had carried me into the house and handed me over to two younger, stronger men who had the pleasure of making a human Stannah stairlift to get me all the way up to my room. 'It may need stitches.'

I wrinkled my nose and tried not to look too pathetic. I didn't want stitches. I wanted a time machine to go back twenty-four hours and have another crack at a day that didn't end in my arrest.

'Thank you,' I said, keeping my fantasies to myself. 'And I'm really sorry for telling Kekipi that you knew what was going on with Artie. I shouldn't have assumed.'

434

'Not at all,' he said, passing me a much-needed cup of tea. 'And now it is all well, I think.'

'I'm glad things are OK.' I tried not to smile. Mostly because it really hurt my face. 'He's basically one of the two best men I know and I don't think you're going to be making a move on Al, are you?'

'I don't think so.' He gave me the smile I couldn't quite muster. 'For the longest time, we argue all the time and then, from nowhere, this is happening. But who knows what happens next? Is a mystery.'

'Yes it is,' I replied, sipping the precious, precious tea. 'But I do get the arguing thing. Apparently that's my type too.'

'You haven't been able to reach Mr Miller?' he asked. 'I could place a call if you like?'

'He'll be on the plane, I think.' I shook my head. Now I'd stopped, I was too tired to even think what I would say to him. Maybe a nice eighteen-hour nap would clear my head. 'Maybe we can try tomorrow?'

'Tomorrow,' Domenico agreed. 'Kekipi says you are to get some rest, even if I have to restrain you to the bed.'

'Not necessary,' I said, putting the cup back on my nightstand. 'Thank you, Domenico.'

When he closed my door, I could already see a pale wash of light coming underneath my curtains. Almost dawn and I was only just going to bed; it was a long time since that had happened. I only wished it was for better reasons. Curling up around my duvet, I told myself to stop thinking about everything and to let myself sleep but the more I fought everything the harder it was to even close my eyes. Eventually, I rolled over, face first into the pillows, and gave in.

The tears only took seconds to come but instead of the huge, roaring sobs I'd been expecting, I felt quiet and still and just as though I was letting go. I cried about Charlie and Nick leaving; I cried for the children in the airport who had been traumatized by my best friend's breasts; and I cried for myself. Self-pity never got anyone anywhere but in that bed, high as a kite on painkillers, it felt entirely justified. I didn't have anywhere to live, my foot hurt, I had a black eye and I had been to prison. Again. And then, at the end of it all, I cried because I was alone. I'd chased what I wanted and ended up with nothing. That seemed like as good a reason for tears as any.

'I hoped you would be in here,' I said, hobbling into the little walled garden at the back of the palazzo to find Al in his favourite board shorts and Grateful Dead T-shirt, sitting with a pot of coffee and a sunny smile on his face.

'And I'm very glad you found me,' he replied, standing up and holding out the second iron chair. 'How's the foot?'

'They didn't cut it off so it could be worse,' I said, waving my bandaged hoof in the air as I sat down. 'But they did give me this crutch which I think will double nicely as a weapon.'

'Always handy to have.' He poured me a cup of coffee from the pot and pushed the milk and sugar across the table. 'Dare I ask about the other business?'

'You mean my friend showing up to declare his love for me and then me declaring my love for Nick and then both of them leaving me on my tod?' I asked. He nodded. 'No, nothing to report.'

'I can say lots of reassuring things, if it would help,' he said, stroking his beard and heaping a heavy teaspoon of brown sugar into his own coffee cup. 'However, I imagine you've heard all of them by now. I've never really had to handle anyone else's crises but my own, you see, so I'm not terribly original.'

'It might be the painkillers the doctor gave me,' I said, 'but I think it's going to be OK. I mean, it's got to sort itself out one way or another, hasn't it?'

'It has,' Al agreed, raising his cup to mine and clinking out a toast. 'You might be the most level-headed woman with a black eye I have ever had the pleasure of speaking to.'

'I'll take that as a compliment,' I replied.

Far too close to the coffee pot for my liking was Al's iPad and on the screen were several options for the AJB logo. They were all fantastic. 'Is everything really back on track with the collection?'

'It seems as though it is,' he said, holding up the

screen for me to take a closer look. 'Edward has almost all the samples finished already and we've got things moving with the factory again. And believe it or not, the party was something of a success. A lot of people have been in touch about stocking the line when the time comes.'

'That's brilliant.' I sipped my coffee and turned my face up to the sun, basking in the mid-afternoon glow. Today wasn't nearly as hot as it had been, and hiding in the shade of Jane's olive trees, the weather felt just about perfect. I really was enjoying those painkillers. 'Dare I ask if you've spoken to Artie?'

'I haven't.' Al didn't look especially moved by this, as if it wasn't particularly unexpected. 'He's already back in New York and I'm very happy to let him work out his tantrum over there for now. He needs time to simmer down and see the bigger picture, then we'll talk.'

'Really?' I asked. 'That's the best thing to do?'

Apparently everyone had got this memo except for me.

'In my experience, when a woman runs away, nine times out of ten, you can't go after her fast enough,' he said, 'preferably with a gift and a grovelling apology. When a man leaves, it's because he needs to lick his wounds for a while. If he's worth having, he'll come back.'

I pinched my eyebrows together and thought about it. 'So, we should just sit here and do nothing? About any of them?'

'You should get on with your life,' Al advised. 'Countless people asked me about your photographs at the party. You're going to be a very busy woman, Tess Brookes. That talent of yours can't be ignored because of a bruised heart.'

I blew on my coffee, not wanting to add burned lips to my litany of injuries. 'Bruised? Not broken?'

'Definitely not broken,' he said, eyes sparkling in the sun. 'Even if it feels like it might be, I don't think this one is terminal. You have to give him time.'

'I'm going back to London on Monday,' I said, turning my ponytail into a tight bun. 'I've got to make sure everything's all right with the pitch I was working on for Charlie.'

'Then you've decided on the advertising?' He looked genuinely surprised and more than a little upset. 'There's nothing I can do to change your mind?'

'No, I haven't decided,' I said, letting go of the ponytail, my hair spiralling down my back. 'But I can't let him down again, I have to do this for him. If I can get him the contract, we can work the rest out from there.'

'Then we'll get you a return ticket,' he told me, swigging down his red-hot espresso as though it was iced water. 'And you'll come back to us as soon as you're ready.'

'You're so nice to me.' I shook my head and turned my attention to my toes. 'I really feel like I don't deserve it.'

'Don't let yourself be under any illusion that

you're not worth it,' he reprimanded. 'I know you still don't really believe me but you're a bloody good photographer and I need someone I can trust, and you need a job. That seems like a fair trade to me. Now, which one of these logos do you like the best?'

I held my hand over my eyes to keep out the sun, listening to Al's opinions on the six almost identical logos on the screen, and smiled. It was like Amy always said, when life gave you lemons, the best thing to do was cut those lemons up, knock life down and rub them in its eyes, screaming, 'Have that, you bastard!' As philosophies went, I'd heard worse.

Someone at Gatwick airport must have got my memo about how sad I was to be leaving Italy because the second we touched down, the clouds broke over London and glorious sunshine lit up Monday morning in the old smoke. I had spent all day Sunday editing the photos I'd taken so far, trying not to refresh my email every seven seconds looking for something from Nick and listening in on Al and Amy's grand plans for their retail scouting tours around the world.

Any part of me that had questioned Amy's abilities was wiped clean away by the end of the day. She was drawing out floorplans, explaining what fixtures and fittings they would need, working up staffing plans and, quite frankly, being amazing. I hadn't given my friend enough credit; she was perfect for this job and I felt terrible for having doubted her. The only thing Amy really needed was the self-confidence to see it through and for someone to take her seriously. That might be hard if you were a Topshop HR woman and all you saw were neon thigh-highs, a cropped unicorn T-shirt and a CV with more holes in it than your average sieve, but I should have known better.

And now all I needed was for Charlie to decide he was speaking to me just long enough to get through the Perito's pitch without kicking me square in the uterus and then everything would be fine and dandy.

I had a loaner phone from Domenico and I'd called Charlie from the airport, leaving him a message to let him know I was coming, but he hadn't replied. I chose to believe he was quietly pleased rather than silently furious and, after flying through airport security, I arrived at the Perito's offices just in time. I pulled out a mirror in the lift, making sure the concealer I'd borrowed from Amy was still covering my black eye well enough that I wouldn't scare anyone.

'Right . . .' I took a deep breath in and closed my eyes. 'Be brave, don't be a chicken.'

The lift stopped on the seventeenth floor and I smiled at the receptionist as I hobbled out, so certain that I had got this right. Even if Charlie hated my guts, I knew how much he loved his job; he couldn't stay angry with me if we won the account.

'Hi, I'm here for the Perito's pitch,' I told the receptionist. I could hear muffled voices inside and felt the adrenaline coursing through my veins. 'Tess Brookes?'

'They've gone in already.' She looked down at her sign-in book and back up at me. 'Someone must have signed you in already.'

The adrenaline started to turn into panic. Charlie had started without me?

'It's just through there . . .' She pointed at the big wooden door with a chicken stuck to it. 'They only just went in; the last lot were out early and I think they want to get it over with.'

'Always bodes well,' I said, straightening my white silk shirt and patting down my printed trousers. 'Thanks.'

I peered through the tiny square of glass in the conference room door to see Charlie at the front of the room, standing in front of a big screen showing my PowerPoint presentation. Huh. I pressed my ear to the wood for a moment, trying to listen in.

'We've looked over the work you sent over and we're impressed,' someone was telling him. 'You've really got a hold on our demographic.'

'We were looking for something that would strike a chord with the younger, reluctant male cook,' Charlie said, an easy smile on his face. 'And we wanted something simple and visual that had a lot of impact.'

He couldn't have looked further away from the

man I'd seen on the train. He was calm, confident and in complete control of the room – without me by his side. This was an epic mistake, he didn't need me here, I realized. And what's more, he didn't want me here.

'And how would you see the roll-out?' Another person asked. 'Talk us through the media plan.'

The window door might have been small but it wasn't small enough. Before I could slope back into the lift and take myself to the nearest Häagen-Dazs' stockist, Charlie's eyes locked onto mine. I was busted.

He stared at me. I looked back at him. His mouth hung open for a moment before setting itself tightly.

'Charlie, the media plan?' the voice asked again.

'So sorry, I'm late!' I wasn't quite sure what possessed me but without thinking, I pushed the door open and walked straight up to the front of the room. 'There was an accident. My taxi was in an accident. Big one. Anyway, the plan would be to launch the shorts online at first, get a viral buzz going, encouraging people to share the videos, and then launch on TV, followed by print.'

I gave them all a smile so huge I was worried I was about to swallow my own ears.

'Right.' A bald man whose shirt was at least three sizes too big for him stared at me with as much confusion as Charlie. 'And who are you?'

'Tess?' I looked at Charlie, looked back at the men and then realized someone else was in the room.

Someone else was sitting on Charlie's side of the table. A blonde female, someone I had not expected to run into in my wildest dreams.

'Isn't that Tess?' another not-so-bald man asked.

'Tess?' The more times I heard my own name out loud, the less it sounded like my name in the first place.

Paige stood up and laughed with forced hilarity. 'This is our assistant, Vanessa,' she explained, pointing at me. 'She brought me some notes I left in the office. Isn't that's right, Ness?'

Speechless, I nodded and dug deep in my handbag looking for something to give to Paige. Charlie stared daggers into my back as I slipped past him and, without warning, the pain in the bottom of my foot suddenly began to scream again.

'Ness? The notes?' Paige's perfectly made-up scarlet lips pouted at me as I produced a napkin from the plane that I had doodled all over on the flight.

'Here they are,' I said, staring at the two men on the other side of the table. 'These are the up-to-date numbers.'

'That's great.' She took the napkin and quickly shoved it underneath her notepad. 'We'll meet you outside, yeah?'

'Yes.' I tottered backwards out of the room, crashing through the doors and throwing myself into an uncomfortable black leather armchair. I took off my shoe and rubbed the sore spot on the sole of my foot, wondering how many times I would have to drive the heel into my temple before I actually died.

I waited for fifteen minutes before Very Bald and Quite Bald exited the meeting room, casting doubtful glances at me on their way out. As soon as they were safely in the lift and on their way, I forced myself out of my chair and sloped back inside.

'What are you doing here?' Charlie did not look especially pleased to see me.

'I came for the pitch,' I said, pointing at Paige. At my friend, Paige. 'What are *you* doing here?'

'Charlie needed someone to stand in for you at the pitch,' she said carefully, with the look of someone who really didn't know what was going on. 'It was your idea.'

'Was it?' I asked. 'I thought we all agreed that pretending to be someone we're not was a bad idea in general?'

'I was trying to help you,' she said, holding her hands out defensively. 'I took the pitch materials over to Charlie, like you asked, and he said he was coming out to see you Friday and then he called me last night to see if I could stand in for you because you couldn't make it back from Milan in time. I texted you and you didn't reply. I assumed you were otherwise engaged.'

'Are you serious?' I wasn't sure which of them I was talking to.

'What are you doing here?' Charlie said again. 'Shouldn't you be in Italy with your boyfriend?'

'Oh!' Paige's eyes widened. 'In Milan? He saw?'

445

I nodded and pressed my lips together tightly, confused and annoyed and guilty and weirdly hungry.

'I came for the pitch, like I said I would,' I told him, as he started packing up his things. 'And Paige, I didn't get your text because I broke my phone throwing it at an Italian airport security wanker. Long story.'

'Why bother?' Charlie shoved his notebooks and pens deep into the beautiful leather man-bag I had bought him two Christmases ago, two bright red spots blossoming on his cheeks. 'Surely you don't think we're still going to work together on this?'

'I don't know.' I folded my arms across myself. 'I came because it's important to you. We both worked hard on it and I didn't want to see it fall apart.'

'Yeah, it looked like you were working hard,' he said, jabbing at the air between us with a pen. Paige began to shuffle slowly towards the door. 'You let me think you were nipping off to Italy to do your little art project and all the time, you were shagging somebody else.'

'I was not all the time shagging someone else,' I replied, not quite sure how to defend myself. 'Yes, I met Nick in Hawaii but I came home and I didn't think I'd ever see him again, and then he showed up in Milan. But I didn't plan it and didn't want to talk to you about it on the phone, so—'

There. The truth. That was a novel concept.

Charlie slung his back across his shoulder. 'Oh, fuck off.'

Albeit not a popular one.

'If it helps,' Paige piped up from the doorway, 'it's the truth. I was in Hawaii with them. But she really thought he wasn't interested when she got with you.'

'Thanks, Paige,' I said, rubbing my hand across my forehead. It was like having a blonde Amy. 'Very helpful.'

'No, yeah, that's great, I'm really happy to be the back-up,' he said, sticking his hands in his pockets. 'Has he dumped you again? Is that why you're really back?'

'That's not why I'm back,' I said.

'So he *has* dumped you again,' Charlie said, throwing an empty laugh in for good measure. 'Clever bloke. Too good-looking for you anyway.'

I wasn't used to Charlie being cruel. Angry, yes, upset on occasion and, very rarely, downright dickish but this was awful. Finally something I didn't know about Charlie: when he truly was hurt, he could be vicious.

'I came to help,' I said, recalling Al's advice and wishing I'd taken it sooner. He was still raw; it was my fault and I needed to back away and give him some space. 'But you didn't need me.'

'No, I don't need you,' he said, throwing his satchel around onto his back. 'In fact, I've got all your shit in my flat. You can go and get it and clear it out if you want, otherwise I'll put it back on the street where I found it.'

447

'How have you got my stuff?' Had I missed something? 'Why was it on the street?'

'I have it because Vanessa called me to say she was giving it away to tramps if I didn't come and get it,' he explained. 'And like a twat, I went. She tried it on again, actually. I didn't bother but maybe I should have. She knows her way around a bed, that girl. Better than some people.'

I couldn't move. If he'd slapped me round the face, it couldn't have hurt more.

'Let's get you out of here.' Paige reached over and grabbed my arm, and pulled me out of the boardroom, leaving Charlie standing staring at me, holding tightly to his man-bag.

Given how much had gone on in the week since I'd last seen her, it didn't take a terribly long time to catch Paige up on my adventures. Typically, she asked for a lot of detail on the outfits Kekipi and I had bought and just exactly how much discount he was good for on the streets of Milan but for the most part, she stayed schtum and drank her wine while I talked.

'I took today off so I could help Charlie out,' she said, topping off her drink and settling back in the sun. We had found a pub round the corner from the office that had the tiniest balcony in the world but since it was half eleven on a Monday, there wasn't a lot of competition for our table. 'I haven't heard anything about the Artie–Al drama. The girls on the fashion desk will be all over it, I'm sure.'

'I feel so bad for him.' I gingerly pressed a finger against my bruised cheekbone, half wanting to take the make-up off for extra sympathy from the attractive waiter and half never wanting anything with a penis to so much as look at me ever again. 'Imagine your kid being such a shit.'

'Rich people are beyond help,' she replied. 'Rich people and apparently everyone you have ever had sex with, ever.'

'I do not have a good track record,' I agreed, chucking back a handful of peanuts. 'I'm thinking about retiring my vag and becoming a nun. Can they drink? Because if they can drink, it might not be so bad.'

'I'm googling it,' she said, flipping down the screen of her fancy phone as she spoke. 'What are you going do now?'

'Drink this.' I pointed at the very full glass of wine in front of me and then began pulling the pins out my bun. 'Call my agent. Find somewhere to sleep that isn't the street. Take it from there?'

'You're welcome to my sofa.' Paige held up her phone in triumph. 'And the good news is, nuns can drink. So, there's an option for you.'

'And I really do like Italy,' I said, mulling it over. 'And black and white have always been good colours for me.'

She rested her elbows on the table and leaned her chin into her hands. 'What are you going to do about Charlie?'

I picked away at the label of the wine bottle,

449

hoping to find some secret wisdom underneath, but there was only more wine. Not that wine wasn't an answer. 'I could call him and say "Sorry, the person I thought was just a distraction turned out to be the person I love and the person I thought I loved turned out to be a distraction? And in case it's not clear, you're the distraction." Who wouldn't love to hear that?'

'I've heard worse,' she said, lining up all the tiny hairgrips that I was scattering on the table. 'What about Nick? You going to tell him that?'

'I did twenty-eight years of never telling anyone anything.' I pulled out the last half dozen grips and shook my hair loose. It felt good. 'And in the last three weeks, I've told everyone everything. I'm going to try for some middle ground. I told him where I'm at, I can't force him to be in the same place.'

'You're so clever,' she said with a frown. 'Why aren't I as clever as you?'

'I sound clever right now,' I agreed, rubbing my fingertips into my scalp. 'But that's because someone else told me to do that. Really, I want to bury myself under fifteen blankets and eat my way through an entire Chinese takeaway menu, screaming "why doesn't he love me?" after every bite. This is what's called a brave face.'

'You're very good at it.' Paige tucked her long blonde hair behind her ear and looked over the balcony at bright and shiny London. 'We should definitely get a Chinese tonight though.'

'I suppose I have to get on with it, don't I?' I said, running through the heartbreak handbook in my mind. 'Move on with my life, get over Nick, make some decisions?'

'Sounds shit,' she replied. 'Let's get smashed instead.'

Her phone, full of pictures of nuns, sparkled into life and a picture of an incredibly stern-looking woman replaced Julie Andrews and Mother Theresa.

'Fuck, it's work.' She stood up, taking her phone with her. 'I've got to take this. Back in a minute. Don't drink all the wine. Actually do, you deserve it. I'll bring more.'

She ducked inside, leaving me to watch a double-decker bus weaving its way through a tiny side street, under a bridge and back out again. I loved double-decker buses. When Amy and I were little, there was nothing more exciting than racing up the stairs to sit in the front seat to drive it – if someone was already in our seat, then God help them. And when I said little, this went on pretty much until we graduated. Now, whenever I took the bus, I made a point of not sitting there. I wasn't sure if it was because I didn't want to fall foul of a next generation Amy or because I was worried that it wouldn't be the same, that I was too old for it now. Probably a bit of both.

The bus rode right past me and I saw a woman sitting in the front seat, reading a book. She wasn't even looking out of the window. What a waste, I thought, next time I sit in the front seat again, I'll have my eyes open. And that was when I realized. I didn't want to get over Nick. I didn't want to move on with my life.

I pulled out my borrowed phone and my notebook, and dialled the first number scribbled on the inside cover.

'What?'

'Veronica?'

'Yes. What?'

'It's Tess,' I said, looking out for another double-decker bus. 'Tess Brookes.'

'You little shit!' she boomed on the other end of the line. 'I've been calling you for days and you haven't answered. What the fucking fuck is going on?'

'Loads actually.' I didn't think she needed the entire story, not on the phone anyway. Why deprive myself of the five years she would take off my life with her chain smoking when I saw her in person? 'Did you get the pictures I sent over yesterday?'

'Yes,' she said. 'Did you get any of my fucking messages? The deal is, I call you, you fucking well answer.'

'Did you like the pictures?' I asked.

'Of course I liked the pictures,' she replied. 'They're good shots and they're making us both a shit-ton of money. You better not have called me to say you're jacking this all in to sell me a pissing chicken because I will have you fucking killed.'

'The chicken thing didn't work out as well as it could have,' I admitted, spotting a new bus in the distance, headed my way. 'I've been thinking, I want to go back to Milan. Finish up the project with Al.'

'Halle-fucking-lujah,' she barked, breaking in the middle of her swearing to suck on her cigarette. 'Amazing. You're not a completely useless twat after all, are you?'

'Not completely useless,' I agreed. 'I'm trying.'

'You were trying my fucking patience,' she replied. 'Now get your arse back to Italy so I can get an invoice in. I'm not doing this for fun, you know.'

'No, I know,' I said, excited. 'I'm going to do a really good job, trust me.'

'Of course you fucking are, why wouldn't you?' Veronica asked. 'When are you going? Just so I know where in the world you're fucking hiding, otherwise I'm going to inject one of them tracker chips in you like I've got in the dog.'

I sat back in my seat and smiled. 'You've got a dog?'

'When are you going?' she shouted.

'Tonight,' I replied, unfastening the top two buttons of my shirt. 'This afternoon. I'll be back in Milan tonight.'

'Whoop-de-fucking-doo!' Veronica cheered. 'No more fucking mention of chickens?'

'No more,' I promised. 'Unless you want me to take a photo of a chicken.'

'Right fucking answer.' I could have sworn I heard her smiling. 'And yes. Two dogs. Yorkies. Little bastards, the pair of them.'

And then she hung up.

'You all right?' I asked Paige as she stomped back out onto the terrace, as hard as her kitten heels would allow. 'Not good news?'

'Someone's fucked up a spread.' She picked up her glass of wine and took a huge swig. 'I'm going to have to go in. Honestly, I can't even take one day off without some jobsworth cocking everything up.'

'Never mind, you'll get the holiday back, yeah?' I asked, finishing off my own glass and embracing the sudden tipsiness that went straight to my head. 'You can use it to come and visit me in Milan.'

'You're going back?' Paige squealed in a way that only very girly girls can get away with and gave me a big, skinny hug. 'When?'

'Now, I suppose,' I said, brushing my hair back and watching as the next double-decker bus rushed past us, two teenage girls in the front seat with their feet up on the rails, laughing in each other's faces. 'Am I mental?'

'Yes,' she said very seriously. 'But it's pretty cool. And I don't really want you crying on my settee for three weeks either.'

'That's fair,' I accepted. 'I am a bit gutted about the Chinese though. Have they got Chinese takeaway in Milan?'

'I'm googling it,' she replied. 'If they haven't, you're not going.'

Flying back and forth to Italy in a day probably wasn't a big deal for a lot of people, I thought, as I took my seat in one of easyJet's finest, but I couldn't have been more excited. Running away to Hawaii had been impulsive and silly, and borrowing someone else's identity was downright stupid, but this wasn't running away, this was making a choice. This time, I was running towards something amazing, something exciting. I didn't want to wake up one day as bitter as Edward Warren and so scared to try something new that I'd rather shaft my best friend than take a chance. And I didn't expect it to be easy; I knew this was something I was going to have to work for and I was so up for the challenge.

And there was something else I was ready to fight for. As the plane rolled down the runway, preparing for take-off, I pulled a small square of paper out of my handbag and promised myself it was the last time I would read it. At least for the duration of the flight. It was the letter than Nick had given to Domenico before he left.

He had given it to me on Friday night, unfortunately right after he had given me something strong enough to knock out an elephant, so I hadn't been able to concentrate on it then, let alone commit it to memory. The morning after, I'd been too scared as to what it might say. Sunday, I felt the same and

455

all the way back to London, I could feel it burning a hole in my handbag, hiding between the pages of my passport. But it wasn't until I was on the Tube, on my way to Gatwick, that I felt brave enough to read it. It was only then that I realized there couldn't be anything in the note that was worse than what I was imagining anyway.

I unfolded Nick's letter, leaning in to the window, away from the man sitting next to me. Now my decision was made, I wasn't afraid to read it. I was going back to Milan, back to Al and Kekipi and Amy, back to my camera and all the things that I loved.

'Dear Tess.' I whispered the words as quietly as possible. Reading it was still too hard, I could hear his voice in my head and it was too much.

Dear Tess,
I told you I didn't know if I could do this and it turns out that I can't.

I've been thinking about it all week but I can't see another way. Even if you hadn't left, I still would have been on a plane to New York in the morning, you just made it easier for me.

I'd been fooling myself into thinking I could do it, because it's so fun and so easy being with you but there's nothing fun and easy about being with me. I care about you so much my bones ache. You, Tess, are spectacular and anyone would be lucky to have you in their corner but I can't do this right now and it's not fair. I wish I could but it just wouldn't work so I'm walking away before I make this any harder for either of us.

Take care of yourself.

All my love,

Nick

My fingers folded the letter back along its already well-worn lines and slid it back inside my passport. I'd gone through so many emotions since the first time I'd read it that I was almost numb. I was furious that he thought he could make these decisions for me, heartbroken that he didn't really want me, let down by the fact that he didn't even want to try, and so sad that he was so hurt. But Al was right. Chasing after him now would mean fighting then and making up and running around kissing, laughing at other people's dogs again, but, ultimately, the same thing would just keep happening over and over.

I'd never really thought about the difference between the things I wanted and the things that I needed. Right now, whether Nick's letter was entirely honest or not, he couldn't be what I needed, even if he was everything I wanted. He needed time, I needed time and, thankfully, that was one thing I had plenty of. But, as I watched London slip away behind me, I knew that I couldn't give up on him, even if maybe I should.

And if he thought I would read his note, smile, nod and get on with life as though he had never existed, he was as stupid as he was hot.

And that would make him so, so stupid.

London had never really struck me as a beautiful city. It was where I worked, it was my escape from the village and from my family, but up here, flying over it at sunset, I couldn't help but feel a little bit sad to be leaving. I wished I had my camera to capture the fading light, casting its shadows over all of her stories. The next time I was in London, I promised, smiling at my reflection in the tiny double window, the next time, I'd be ready.